Praise for *Thoreau at Devil's Perch*!

"A favorite literary figure shows an unexpected flair for detection in this historical mystery. Original and charming."

—Laura Joh Rowland, author of *The Incense Game*

"Well researched, captivating and compelling until the very end, *Thoreau at Devil's Perch* is both mystery and love story during a time that appeared deceptively simple. Through their diaries, the main characters, Adam and Julia, become to feel like old friends you want to revisit again and again. I've never been a fan of using historical figures in fiction— B. B. Oak has changed my mind. Well done!"

—Anna Loan-Wilsey, author of *Anything But Civil*

"B. B. Oak brings Thoreau's nineteenth-century world to vivid life in this intriguing puzzler that will keep you guessing to the terrifying end."

—Victoria Thompson, author of *Murder in Chelsea*

Books by B. B. Oak

THOREAU AT DEVIL'S PERCH

THOREAU ON WOLF HILL

Published by Kensington Publishing

THOREAU
ON
WOLF HILL

B. B. OAK

KENSINGTON BOOKS
www.kensingtonbooks.com

KENSINGTON BOOKS are published by

Kensington Publishing Corp.
119 West 40th Street
New York, NY 10018

All Kensington titles, imprints, and distributed lines are available at special quantity discounts for bulk purchases for sales promotion, premiums, fundraising, educational, or institutional use.

Special book excerpts or customized printings can also be created to fit specific needs. For details, write or phone the office of the Kensington Special Sales Manager: Attn. Special Sales Department. Kensington Publishing Corp., 119 West 40th Street, New York, NY 10018. Phone: 1-800-221-2647.

Kensington and the K logo Reg. U.S. Pat. & TM Off.

eISBN-13: 978-0-7582-9026-7
eISBN-10: 0-7582-9026-8
First Kensington Electronic Edition: November 2014

ISBN-13: 978-0-7582-9025-0
ISBN-10: 0-7582-9025-X
First Kensington Trade Paperback Printing: November 2014

10 9 8 7 6 5 4 3 2 1

Printed in the United States of America

As far back as I can remember I have unconsciously referred to the experiences of a previous state of existence.

—Henry David Thoreau

I have just read of a family in Vermont who, several of the members having died of consumption, just burned the lungs, heart and liver of the last deceased, in order to prevent any more from having it.

—Thoreau's journal

ADAM'S JOURNAL

Wednesday, December 1, 1847

I had already done a day's doctoring, downed a dram of whiskey, and gotten chilled to the bone before setting down to breakfast this morning. And just when I was about to dig into a stack of flat-jacks fresh off Gran's griddle, there was a knock on the back door.

"Pray you do not have to go out on another patient call!" Harriet said, giving me such a look of concern I thought she might burst into tears. Although Gran's ward is nigh reaching womanhood, she still has the volatile emotions of a child.

"Adam ain't goin' nowhere afore he gits some hot food and coffee down his gullet," Gran said.

She declared this with such conviction you would think she still had a say in my comings and goings. I suppose it is only natural for her to fall into old habits now that I have taken up residence in my boyhood home for a spell.

Of course I would have disregarded her command and left my breakfast uneaten if the need for me were urgent. Such is the life of a country doctor, a life I never intended to have when I left Tuttle Farm for Harvard. Obligations have over-ruled ambitions, however.

It turned out the caller was Henry Thoreau. "Well, ain't you the early bird," Gran said as she ushered him in.

But it is never too early for Henry. He feels it unwise to keep the head long on a level with the feet, as he puts it, and appears to thrive on little sleep and much exercise. He looked full of vigor as usual this morning, the hawky, ever-present look of vigilance upon his clean-shaven visage. His erect carriage and the quick grace of his movements always call to my mind an Indian brave, as does his strong, large nose. At thirty, he is my senior by five years, but he still has the boundless energy of a boy. Or a colt. His ruddy, unruly mane was dank with morning mist, and he was clutching his broad-brimmed felt hat to his chest.

"On sich a cold, damp morn as this, you would have been better off wearin' that hat than carryin' it," Gran told him.

"If I'd kept it on my head," he replied, "in what would I have collected these?" He proffered his hat to her.

Gran's eyes lit up when she looked into the deep crown. "Chestnuts!" she cried.

"I came upon them not too far from here," he said, "and reckoned you might appreciate them, Mrs. Tuttle."

"You reckoned right," she said. "Roasted, stewed, or preserved, there ain't nothin' I like more'n chestnuts." She transferred the glossy nuggets into a basket. "How did you manage to find such a bounteous treasure of 'em so late in the season?"

"I simply looked where I thought a squirrel might," he said with a shrug and went to stand by the fire. He seemed to take for granted his ability to find treasures invisible to others. Often when we hike together, he unearths an ancient arrowhead, yet no matter how hard I look for them, I have never come upon a single one.

"Set yourself down, and I'll hot up the coffee fer ye," Gran told him.

"Thank you kindly but no coffee for me," he said.

"You sure? 'Twon't be no trouble at all."

"Henry does not take coffee, nor tea, nor any other stimulant," I told Gran. "Not even fermented cider."

"Not even cider!" That did amaze her. "Why, most menfolk drink it like water."

"I believe water is the only drink for a wise man," Henry said.

Gran sniffed. "Suit yerself."

Henry gave me an amused look, then a more careful study from head to toe. "Well, my friend, I see you have been up and about very early yourself. And even though you had a bit of trouble with your horse or gig on your way to the Yates farm, you still got there in plenty of time to deliver Mrs. Yates of a fine baby boy."

We all three stared at him. I had related those very facts to Gran and Harriet when I staggered in not ten minutes before.

"Mr. Thoreau is clairvoyant!" Harriet said.

Henry laughed. "Not clairvoyant. Observant." He pointed to my feet. "There in the cleft of Adam's boot heel is a leaf from the climbing fern."

"So what about it?" Gran said.

"That rare species of fern can be found in Old Sow Swamp, which lies between here and the Yates farm," Henry said. "Hence I surmised that's where Adam picked it up on his boot when he got out of his gig. But what would compel him to alight in a swamp? Obviously something was in need of fixing before he could go on."

"And so it was," I confirmed. "I stopped there to straighten the bit that had gone askew in Napoleon's mouth."

"But how'd you git from knowin' where some fern grows to knowin' why Adam went out afore daybreak?" Gran asked Henry.

"Ratiocination," Henry replied.

Gran and Harriet looked at him blankly. I own that I did too.

"You need to explain your reasoning process to us, Henry," I said. "If you don't mind."

Of course I knew he wouldn't mind a jot. If there's one thing Henry enjoys, it's showing off his powers of observation and deduction. He sat down at the table and elucidated.

"I noted the climbing fern in Old Sow Swamp a few days ago. And then, as I cut through a pasture behind the Yates farmstead, I saw the lady of the house hanging out her wash. She had a hard time of it for she was very far advanced with child. Thus I deduced that Adam went out that way early this morning to assist with the birth."

"But how did you know Mrs. Yates was delivered of a *boy?*" Harriet said.

"Why, Adam's breath," Henry replied. He folded his arms across his chest and said no more, no doubt waiting to be urged to.

He did not have to wait long. "Out with it, Henry!" Gran said. "You got me hooked now like a catfish danglin' on a chunk of dough. What in tarnation has my grandson's breathing to do with the sex of Mrs. Yates's newborn?"

"I can smell whiskey on Adam's breath," Henry said, his large and bright eyes dancing with quiet merriment. "Mr. Yates is famous for being closefisted and a man who seldom imbibes. So it would be a rare occasion indeed when before dawn he would bring out his best liquor. He already has three daughters, so another would not so inspire him. Only a boy would do the trick. And I wager this was the first time Adam ever quaffed a spirituous libation so early in the day. That would also indicate to me that the birth was a long and perilous one. Still, if I know him he toasted the birth of the boy to please the proud father more than to indulge himself."

I could only nod. He had deduced all from what seemed no evidence at all.

"Well, I'll be jiggered," Gran said. "You are as smart as a steel trap, Henry. And as a reward for yer fancy bit of cogitat'n I am going to serve you up a heapin' pile of flat-jacks."

Henry, not one to turn down an offer of food, pulled his chair closer to the table, but as Gran was mixing fresh batter there came more pounding at the door. Before anyone had time to answer it, Ezekiel Wiley's youngest child, Orin, charged in. He was panting so hard he must have run full speed all three miles from his farm.

"Ma wants you to come right away, Dr. Walker," he gasped out.

"Has Joanna taken a turn for the worse?" I had been expecting this since I'd visited his sister's bedside yesterday.

"No, it's Hetty!"

"Hetty?" I did not understand. His other sister had died in September.

"Ma wants you to stop them from diggin' her up!"

"Good Lord, why dig her up?"

"Uncle Solomon claims she ain't really dead. He says she rises from the grave every night to suck the breath out of Joanna."

"He must be deranged!" I said.

"Else he comes straight from the devil," Gran said.

"No, no, he comes from Rhode Island," Orin said, "where such things are done. Uncle Solomon has dug up many a body there, being a practitioner."

"A practitioner of what?" Henry said. "The Black Arts?"

"He is a slayer of vampyres. And he aims to slay the night-stalking horror that Sister Hetty has become."

Harriet gasped. "Hetty a vampyre? That cannot be! She was my dearest friend, and there was no soul better. She suffered like a saint, never complaining as the Consumption devoured her." Harriet turned to me, tears brimming in her gentle eyes. "Did you not say she was a good, brave patient, Adam?"

I could only nod. That I could do nothing to save the lovely young woman weighs heavily upon my heart, especially since her sister Joanna is now dying from the selfsame disease.

"What exactly does this so-called vampyre slayer intend to do after he exhumes his niece's body?" Henry asked Orin.

"Cut out her heart and burn it whilst Joanna breathes in the smoke." The boy's face twisted in a grimace. "Then poor Joanna must eat the ashes."

"Not if I can help it," I said, grabbing my jacket off the peg. "Subjecting that young girl to such horror might well put an end to her. She is weak enough as it is."

Henry put on his battered hat. "I will go with you, Adam. Irrational heads are always hard of hearing, and two voices might better penetrate their ignorance."

"Orin, you stay here," Gran ordered the boy. "Else you might see things not fit fer young eyes." That seemed to make him all the more eager to go with us, but Gran grabbed his arm and held him back.

Out we went to the barn, and in a trice Napoleon was back between the buggy shafts. Off we raced, and the good horse did not slacken his pace until we reached the Wiley homestead. Mrs. Wiley stood in the door yard, wringing her hands.

"They have just gone up to fetch Joanna," she said with a sob.

Henry and I went inside and up the stairs to Joanna's bedroom. The rusty odor of the girl's retched-up blood filled the room, emanating from a basin on the floor. Her father was lifting her from the bed.

"Pray wait, Mr. Wiley," I said, as calmly as I could muster. We had no legal right to be on his property, much less tell him what to do with his child. Or the bodies in the family graveyard, for that matter.

Cradling his emaciated daughter in his arms, he looked at me, his eyes filled with misery. "Wait for what? For her to die?" His voice was hollow and hoarse. "Despite all your doctoring skills, that is all you could do for her sister, is it not, Dr. Walker? You could only wait by her bedside and hold her hand till she breathed her last ragged breath."

The truth of his words seared me. What good am I as a doctor when I know not how to save my patients? Until a cure for Consumption is discovered, all I can offer them is the consolation of my presence. And as a most virulent form of the disease swoops through the area, claiming victims in a matter of days rather than years, 'tis no wonder remedies, no matter how irrational, are tried.

"I understand your need to do something to save your daughter, Mr. Wiley," I said. "But if you proceed with this madness, you will only hasten Joanna's death."

"If you try to prevent us, you will hasten your own damn death," the man standing beside the distraught father said in a deep menacing voice. He was of imposing height and broad-shouldered, with a full, black beard and pale eyes of penetrating intensity. "So get out of the way. What must be done here *will* be done."

Henry stepped right up to him and, reaching up, laid a hand upon the man's shoulder. "Hark this, sir. Your threats cannot prevent us from interfering. We will not stand by and let you haul this sick girl out in the cold for no rational purpose."

The man glared down in disbelief that one of Henry's slight stature would dare stand straight as a pine tree against him. "Who the hell are you?"

"The voice of reason," Henry said.

"Is that so? Well, I will silence your voice quick enough if you do not step aside!" the man bellowed.

"Easy there, Solomon. You will affright Joanna," Mr. Wiley cautioned his brother.

Too late. Poor Joanna, feverish, eyes as panicked as a fawn's, clutching a red-stained cloth to her mouth, burst into tears and hid her face against her father's chest.

"You must put her back to bed as any good father would," I told Mr. Wiley.

"Don't listen to him, Ezekiel," his brother said.

But thank God he did. He returned Joanna to her bed, and I stroked her hand to calm her until her sunken eyes closed and her breathing steadied.

"Can it be done without her?" Mr. Wiley asked his brother in a low tone.

"If it has to be. But I cannot promise it will be as effective," he replied.

"Best you forego it then," Henry advised.

"This is not your business," Solomon told him. "So be gone with you, and let us get on with it."

"Are you ashamed to have witnesses?"

"Ashamed?" Solomon lifted his massive head most proudly. "I am not ashamed of my calling, nor have I anything to hide," he declared. "If you and the doctor want to bear witness to the death of a vampyre, come with us."

And so, leaving the child to sleep in peace, we four trudged out of the house. "Don't do it! Don't do it!" Mrs. Wiley wailed as she chased after us.

Solomon stopped and faced her down. "Go see to your living daughter, woman. The other is lost to you." She looked to her husband, but he only shook his head. With a shudder, she turned back to the house.

Onward we walked up the grassy knoll to the family burial plot. Solomon pulled a half-dozen cheroots tied with string from his dirty jacket pocket. He offered them to us, and after we refused he lit one and puffed at it hard. "It helps spare the nose from what's coming," he said.

I tried my best to reason with Ezekiel Wiley. "Let Hetty rest in peace. Do not listen to your brother's false notions and violate her corpse."

"If all that remains of my dear daughter now is a dried husk, we will return her to rest untouched," he replied in a shaky voice.

"But if there are signs of life upon her body, it will be proof she is a revenant and must be destroyed," Solomon said.

"Three months is not sufficient time for her body to have completely decomposed," I said. "During my years of medical training I have seen many stages of decaying flesh and know of what I speak."

"As I do!" Solomon firmly declared. "This is not the first nor the last time I will unearth a vampyre. And you shall soon see that Hetty has become one, doctor. Poor Joanna is being sucked dry of her life blood by her elder sister, who comes to her like the savage wolf to the helpless lamb."

"Superstitious balderdash!" I shouted back at him.

Henry remained more calm. "How came you to believe your younger daughter was being preyed upon by her dead sister, Mr. Wiley?" he asked most courteously.

"When I awoke her in the night because she was moaning most piteously, she said there was such a weight upon her chest she could not catch a breath."

"Hetty sitting upon her torso feeding!" Solomon interjected.

"The weight poor Joanna felt was the fluid trapped in her lungs, blocking her breathing," I told Mr. Wiley. "Pay no heed to your brother's reckless conjecture."

"But 'twas Joanna herself who said to me that she saw Hetty looming over her in the night, eyes black as a demon's and mouth dripping blood."

"When did she tell you this, Mr. Wiley?" Henry inquired. "When first you awoke her?"

"No, not then, but the next morning."

"After her Uncle Solomon had talked to her?"

"I don't recall." Mr. Wiley looked to his brother.

"What I recall," Solomon told him, "is poor little Joanna pleading with me to save her from Hetty. And that is what I intend to do."

Mr. Wiley shook his head and commenced to weep. "How can we desecrate Hetty's body? She was such a good daughter."

"That is why we must save her too!" his brother said. "If we kill this vile thing Hetty has become, her soul shall be set free to go to heaven."

Mr. Wiley regained his resolve. "Then we must do it for her sake as well as Joanna's."

We had reached the burying ground at the top of the knoll, and on the grass lay a wooden casket they had already hauled out of the grave. I heard a piercing cry and looked up to see a hawk gliding in a wide, sweeping circle overhead. I had to wonder at what the hawk saw. Four grim men and an unearthed casket were but a part of a wider view from such a height. Spread out below the bird lay the rolling hills of the township, and atop one of them stood the Green, where the steeple of the Meetinghouse pierced the sky and the white clapboard houses clustered peacefully about the rectangle of grass and trees. Beyond the Green the ribbon of the Assabet River curved away south, with mills and water meadows along its banks. Carriages and pedestrians moved along the roads stretching through the landscape, chimneys puffed out smoke, and perhaps the sharp-eyed hawk could make out a train sliding along the gleaming rails of the new Fitchburg line. From such a height our individual, impassioned efforts below must seem as significant to a bird as the scurrying of ants does to us. I could not help but muse that as this hawk must circle and scream, we each have our destinies to act out, no matter how meaningless to other eyes. Yet as Henry oft reminds me, it is what man thinks of himself that really determines his fate. So our destinies are of our own making.

"It is not too late to put back the casket and let Hetty rest in peace," Henry now told the two brothers.

Solomon picked up a crow bar, gave Henry a vicious look as if to strike him with it, then turned his attention to the task at hand. As he pried loose the lid, the nails holding it down shrieked, and when he yanked it off and revealed the corpse within, Mr. Wiley shrieked too.

"Her eyes!" he cried in horror.

They were wide open, pools of viscous liquid without iris or definition. Her skin had a faint blush of color, and her body was so bloated that it pressed against the fabric of her girlish white dress. Although the smell of rot permeated the damp air, indicating decomposition, there were no signs of decay. I have seen the condition many times in bodies brought in for dissection classes, some, shame to say, robbed from graves such as this and sold to Harvard Medical School.

"Observe how she has turned herself sideways," Solomon said. Indeed, Hetty's body, distorted by the gas within, had shifted in the coffin. "She lives, Ezekiel!"

Mr. Wiley gazed at the body, his countenance contorted with horror. "She lives upon the blood of her own sister," he sobbed and pointed at fluid that had been forced out by the internal pressure of decay through the gaping mouth. "Look how she is swelled up on Joanna's blood."

"No. What you see is caused by the gases within the corpse," I began to explain. "It is a most common occurrence and does not mean—"

My words were cut off by the thrust of an ax swung by Solomon into the dead girl's chest, landing with a most sickening, squelching thud and cleaving through clothes, flesh, and into the sternum. The corpse shook, the arms rising in rebound from the force of the blow, the legs near jolted straight up in a most alarming fashion before falling back down. A gush of blood and fluid assaulted us, but Solomon did not falter. He swung and struck down once more with a ferocious and precisely directed blow, cleaving through the sternum entirely. He wrenched wider the split in the raw white bone to expose the heart, took out a curved knife, and savagely hacked around the organ. Then, without the slightest hesitation, he reached into the chest cavity and pulled the heart out with a sucking wrench. It leaked a red gore that was comprised of decomposed blood trapped at death within the now limp heart chambers.

"You see!" Solomon said, holding it up. "The demon's heart drips with Joanna's blood from last night's feeding."

Ezekiel staggered back. "Kill it!" he cried. "End it!"

Solomon stepped to the coffin and sawed through the corpse's throat and neck vertebrae, grunting with the effort. The head shook in a most gruesome fashion as if protesting this further indignity. A handful of fair hair broke free of the scalp as he yanked upward. He bent again, wound his hand in the tresses, and pulled the head free of the neck. So disturbed, the eyes poured out their fluid, and more gore dripped around the projecting black tongue and ran down the chin.

Solomon turned the head around and shoved it backwards into the coffin but now at the feet of the corpse. "There!" He regarded his handiwork with grim satisfaction. "All that is left to do is burn the heart."

Henry and I nailed the lid back on the coffin and, with Mr. Wiley's help, lowered it into the ground. As we shoveled the dirt back, Solomon lit a fire and burned the heart on a flat stone. It took a good blaze to accomplish the task in the mist. I will never forget the hissing and bubbling and the odor of roasting flesh until the organ was finally reduced to ashes.

"Joanna has not breathed in the smoke," Solomon said, "but we can bring her the ashes to ingest."

"No." Ezekiel kicked the mound of ash into the grass. "This must be enough, brother. I can bear no more."

Solomon relented. Henry and I went back to the house to

assure Mrs. Wiley it was over and her daughter was safely back in the ground. We did not, of course, mention the defacement done to Hetty's body, and I pray the two Wiley men spare her the details.

Henry and I rode home mostly in silence, each in his own thoughts. Mine were grim as I considered the ignorance and savagery we had just witnessed. Henry's thoughts, however, had taken an uplifting turn.

"Let us hope Solomon Wiley will evolve into a more enlightened creature in some future life here on earth," he said.

"Perhaps his soul will regress instead of advance, and he will return as a slug," I replied.

"That too is possible, I suppose," Henry said. "Indeed, I sometimes wonder if my own soul has regressed by returning to earth in the body of a civilized white man."

I smiled. "You think your past life as a savage suited your soul better?"

"Yes. But let us not speak of it anymore."

That had been our agreement two summers ago, when we had found the skull of an Indian that had proved to us the truth of Reincarnation. And we had only spoken of it once since then, when I had asked Henry's permission to write about his regression in a scientific article regarding hypnosis. When I assured him that neither his name, nor the evidence we found, nor any reference whatsoever to rebirth would be revealed in the article, he had given me leave to do so.

For the rest of the way home we returned to our private musings. We both have a great appreciation for silence. No doubt that is one of the major reasons we became and remain friends.

This evening, however, alone in my room, I find silence oppressive. Ghastly memories of what I witnessed in the Wiley graveyard slither through my mind. I do not want them to be the last images I recall before I fall asleep, else they will haunt my dreams too. In order to prevent this I shall conjure up images from the happy past, when Julia and I were together. Such golden memories remain untarnished despite her betrayal of our love. They comfort me far more than her presence ever could. Indeed, I would find her actual presence unbearable now. Frailty, thy name is woman!

JULIA'S NOTEBOOK

Friday, 3 December

Although I had no expectation of seeing Adam today, I now await his arrival with great impatience. A good half hour has passed since Henry went to the tavern to fetch him. To stop myself from pacing, I have settled myself at the kitchen table to record the day's events. My hand is nearly illegible, I see, for I am trembling with anticipation. I must take control of my emotions before Adam comes through the door. Indeed, I must always control myself in his presence now that I am a married woman.

Shackled though I am by matrimonial bonds, at least I have liberated myself from my husband's daily oppression. What a sense of freedom swept over me when I disembarked from the ship this morning! So relieved was I to set foot on American ground that I almost knelt down right there on the pier to offer up a prayer of thanks. Good thing I did not give in to that impulse, else I would have been trampled by my fellow passengers as they rushed down the gangway and into the arms of waiting friends and family. I pushed through the cheery throng and made my way toward a free hackney cab I had spotted. Unfortunately, a gentleman more swift of foot than I got to it first. Further attempts to engage a hack proved just as fruitless.

A lone woman is as good as invisible in dear old Boston. So off I went by foot to the railway station. It would have been an easy enough walk if not for my heavy portmanteau and a strong, cold wind coming off the Charles River.

By the time I boarded the train to Concord I was chilled to the bone. Fortunately there was a blazing stove in the ladies' car, and I took a seat as near as I could to it. My time in the south of France has made me too sensitive to stern New England weather, and I could not stop shivering.

The lady occupying the seat next to mine looked up from her book. "You are not dressed warmly enough," she said.

She was quite correct on that score. But I had little inclination to relate to a stranger that I had fled the prison that was so unfortunately my home with little more than the clothes on my back and a valise stuffed with undergarments.

"Here, wrap this around your shoulders," she said, shrugging off her woolen shawl.

"But then *you* will be cold," I protested.

"I assure you I will not be. I am wearing *three* flannel petticoats," she confided to me sotto voce. "Truly, you will be doing me a great service by alleviating me of this heavy shawl. I find the hot air radiating from that charcoal stove most oppressive."

She did not look to me to be the least bit overheated or uncomfortable. Her rather melancholy face was as smooth and pale as milk, without a trace of a flush or a hint of exudation. There was, however, great depth and forcefulness in her gaze, and I found myself following her directive and wrapping her shawl around my shoulders.

"I thank you kindly, ma'am," I said.

"Why, you sound as if you are from these parts," she remarked. "I presumed from your attire that you were foreign."

"I own that my garments and bonnet are of French design, and I have spent a great deal of time living abroad, but I am as American as a body can be," I informed her. "I consider the town of Plumford my true home, for that is where my heart is, and I intend to settle there now."

"Then we shall be neighbors. I am Mrs. Lidian Emerson from Concord. And who might you be?"

"Mrs. Julia Pelletier." I almost choked on my surname.

"Do you have family in Plumford, Mrs. Pelletier?"

"Alas, not anymore. Nor friends either. I do have a friend in Concord, however. Do you perchance know Henry Thoreau?"

"Indeed I do!" Mrs. Emerson gave me a more intense appraisal. "He is a friend of yours, you say?"

"I still consider him as one although we have not communicated since I left Plumford the summer before last."

"Is Henry also friends with Mr. Pelletier?"

"No, he has never met my husband. You see, I married soon after I returned to France." I changed the subject. "How crowded this car is! Such a lot of ladies coming back from Boston. What brought them all there today, I wonder. Perchance a temperance gathering?"

"I venture it was something far less noble," Mrs. Emerson said dryly. "Shopping most likely. Note all the parcels they are carrying. The Yuletide season encourages spendthrift ways, I'm afraid. Even one as frugal as I can be tempted to spend more than I should on presents for my children."

"And did you succumb to that temptation today, Mrs. Emerson?"

"I had neither the time nor the energy for shopping. My purpose for going to Boston was to consult with a homeopathist concerning a disorder that has been causing me much discomfort."

"I am sorry to hear that." I did not make so bold as to inquire what her disorder was.

She went on to inform me anyway. "You see, I suffer from dyspepsia. For years I took dosages of calomel on doctor's orders, which weakened rather than helped me. And the only advice I received from the homeopathist today was to eat less. Food you do not take in, he said, cannot upset you."

I did not think that such good advice for she was as thin as a rail already. "Perhaps you should consult with my cousin, who also has a practice in Boston," I suggested. "Dr. Walker uses advanced yet gentle methods to cure his patients."

"Dr. Walker? Why, I believe I met him at Henry's cabin when the Anti-Slavery Society congregated there. A tall, somber young man, is he not?"

"I would not describe my cousin as somber," I replied. "Indeed, Adam has a genial disposition and a ready smile. He is quite tall, however, and young enough, I suppose, being well under thirty. So we are most likely speaking of the selfsame person."

"Yet I seem to recall Henry's mentioning that Dr. Walker practices in Plumford, not Boston."

"Well, there are two Dr. Walkers. Or were. It was Adam's and my grandfather, Silas Walker, who had a practice in Plumford. Doc Silas, as he was called by all the patients who loved him, died quite suddenly of heart failure a few months ago whilst making his rounds." My voice began to warble, and I blinked back tears. "According to my cousin's letter, Grandfather's faithful horse brought him home and waited patiently at the front gate until his body was discovered in the gig."

Mrs. Emerson expressed her condolences, and then, to give me the privacy I needed to get control of my emotions, she turned her attention back to her book. For the rest of the short trip I gazed over her neat bonnet and out the gritty window. The sky was gray and gloomy, and the passing scenery of stubbled cornfields, ravaged woodlots, and stagnant swampland appeared most bleak to me, so unlike my sun-gilded memories of this countryside. I glimpsed a body of water through the naked tree boughs, and my heart rose.

"There's Walden Pond!" I declared.

Mrs. Emerson looked up from her book. "So it is."

"And lo! Henry's cabin!" I said, catching sight of it through the pitch pines. "He is most likely within, writing away at his desk."

"He is no longer there," Mrs. Emerson informed me. "He left two months ago."

That surprised me for I'd been under the impression Henry had been most settled and content at Walden Pond. "Where does he live now?" I asked Mrs. Emerson.

"With me," she replied softly.

As I was trying to comprehend this bit of information, the locomotive whistle shrieked, the conductor called out Concord, and the cars jolted to a stop. Mrs. Emerson and I stood up, and I commenced to remove the shawl she had lent me.

"No, no, you must not take it off yet," she enjoined. "You will need it on your ride to Plumford. The stage coach is but an open wagon."

"You are very kind. I will be sure to send it back to you forthwith."

"Better yet, fetch it back in person. I would very much welcome a visit from you, Mrs. Pelletier."

"Then I shall come see you soon," I promised.

The other ladies in the car had lost no time rushing toward the exit door as we talked, and we had to wait for a long brigade of petticoats to pass before we could step into the aisle. Hence, we were the last passengers to debark from the car. I looked toward the open stage coach waiting by the depot and saw that all the bench seats were already occupied. The only places left for me would have been beside the driver, who at that moment was expectorating a stream of tobacco juice, or upon some obliging lady's lap. No such accommodations could be expected for my bulky portmanteau, however, and I hoped I could make arrangements to have it sent to Plumford after me.

Mrs. Emerson offered me her hand in parting. As I shook

it I saw an amazing transformation come over her countenance. Her pallid cheeks blossomed pink, her eyes lit up and sparkled, and she became quite youthful-looking although I had initially reckoned her to be over forty. She was looking not at me but over my shoulder. I turned around and saw none other than Henry Thoreau coming toward us. He did not see me, however. His attention was riveted upon Mrs. Emerson.

"What brings you here, Henry?" she asked him, sounding quite flummoxed.

"What else but you?" he replied in that brusque way of his. "I was concerned that you would be fatigued by city bustle and borrowed a carryall to drive you home."

"Where are the children?"

"They are in it, awaiting you with much anticipation." He gave her one of his rare, sweet smiles. "You were sorely missed whilst you were away."

She laughed like a girl. "Such nonsense! I was gone but half a day. And the walk home is short enough. It is fortuitous that you have use of a carriage, however. You can drive a friend of yours to Plumford." She gestured toward me.

Henry had not so much as given me a glance until then, but when he reluctantly turned toward me his countenance expressed surprised recognition. "Julia Bell!"

"Julia Pelletier now," I said.

"Ah, yes. So I heard." Alas, there was no warmth in his large, intelligent gray eyes as he regarded me. "Well, if you need a ride to Plumford come along with us, Mrs. Pelletier." With that he took my bag from me and walked briskly away.

As we followed in his wake, Mrs. Emerson gave me a wry look, apparently amused by his abruptness. I myself was rather hurt by it. Although I knew Henry to be restrained in expressing his regard for his female friends, I had expected a friendly hand shake at least from the man who had once saved my very life.

When we reached the carryall Mrs. Emerson's children expressed much glee at her arrival, and as kisses were strewn about, Henry stood back and watched with a wistful expression. I know little of children, and my estimation of their ages may be off, but I venture the eldest, a girl, was no more than eight, the next oldest, another girl, was a few years younger, and the little boy was very young indeed. I had a great deal on my mind when introduced to them, so I do not recall their names, but I think each began with *E.* The carriage had plenty of room for my bag and me, and off we went, first heading toward the Emerson house. On the way the children prattled about a surprise awaiting their mama that Henry had made. Something to do with her gloves and a drawer built under a chair. Henry gently observed that it was no longer a surprise now, and the children, realizing this, looked very contrite. He laughed and told them never mind. A short time later he pulled up to the house, a fine white clapboard edifice with columned entrances, three chimneys, and a multitude of long windows. Mrs. Emerson invited me in for tea, but I declined, wishing to get myself settled in Plumford before nightfall.

After helping mother and children out of the carriage, Henry suggested I take Mrs. Emerson's place beside him, and we proceeded up the Lowell Road toward Plumford. We were like strangers together, and the silence between us stretched on for so long that I feared we would reach our destination, less than four miles away, without a single word exchanged.

"I am very happy to see you again, Henry," I finally said.

"You do not look very happy at all, Mrs. Pelletier."

"Do not keep calling me that."

"Why should it displease you to be called by your married name?"

"It is your cool formality that displeases me, old friend. You used to call me Julia. Married or not, I am still the same person, am I not?"

"Are you?"

"No, I suppose I am not. But you seem to be just the same, Henry. Leastways, you still have the same irksome habit of responding to a question with another question."

"Do I?" Catching himself, he gave out a short laugh. "I shall add that to my list of faults."

"A very short list, I am sure," I said.

"Long enough. I own that I am too ingenious at times. And that I play with words a bit too much. And I suppose my fondness for paradoxes can be somewhat annoying."

He supposed correctly, but what I found even more annoying at the moment was his avoidance of the subject most near and dear to my heart. "You have not mentioned Adam," I said. "Have you seen him of late?"

"Just a few days ago, in fact."

"How is he faring?"

"Well enough considering how little rest he gets. His patients command all of his time."

"Yes, I suppose Boston patients can be very demanding."

"I refer to his patients in Plumford, Mrs. Pelletier. The town has been rife with the Consumption of late, and it was left without a doctor when your grandfather died. The Selectmen implored Adam to take over Doc Silas's practice, and he felt it his duty to do so."

"What? He lives in Plumford now?"

"He resides at his Grandmother Tuttle's farm and practices out of your Grandfather Walker's office."

My heart started pounding. "Then we shall be down the hall from each other when I take up residence in the house. Do you think Adam will find my proximity disagreeable, Henry?"

"Why do you ask *me?*"

"Because you and he are friends. Has Adam not spoken of me to you?"

"There are some things which a man never speaks of, which are much finer kept silent about."

"He never mentions me at all?"

"Over a year ago Adam told me that you had wed. I have not heard him utter your name since."

"I am glad."

"You do not sound very glad, Mrs. Pelletier."

"Must you keep disputing me, Henry?"

"I am merely relaying my own observations."

"Well, perhaps I did not express myself accurately. Of course it does not gladden me to know that Adam has forgotten me so completely that my name never passes his lips. But neither does it sadden me, for it was my intention to put myself well out of his life."

"Then why have you put yourself back in it?" Henry inquired.

"I had no choice but to come back to Plumford. How was I to know Adam would be here now? Since I parted with him, we have communicated only twice. I wrote to inform him of my marriage, but he did not bother to respond. The one and only time he wrote to me was to inform me of our grandfather's passing. His letter was kind enough in tone until he abruptly closed it with the suggestion that I communicate directly with Grandfather's lawyer henceforth."

"Even so, don't you think he would have appreciated notice of your impending arrival?"

"I left France in such great haste that the letter would not have arrived here before I did. I would have sent it to the wrong address anyway. I thought Adam was residing in Boston. Anyway, I am here now, and there is nothing to be done about it. I have nowhere else to go."

Henry draped his arm around my shoulders in such a stiff, awkward manner that it rather felt like being hugged by a tree limb. Even so, I found the solidity of it comforting. "I sense you are deeply troubled, Julia," he said after a moment or two. "You have aged considerably since last I set eyes on you."

No woman welcomes such an observation as that, to be sure, but Henry's tone was exceedingly kind and he had at last addressed me by my first name, so I took no offence. "In truth I feel older than Methuselah," I admitted, "though I am only four and twenty."

"Not so young for a woman," Henry said with characteristic bluntness. But he gave my shoulder a comforting squeeze, and I was warmed by this gesture even after he took his arm away to guide the horse.

In a few minutes we came into Plumford. The Green was empty of people on this blustery afternoon, and the bare-branched elms and oaks populating it looked like foreboding sentinels. Henry pulled up in front of Grandfather's house— well, my house now—and it too looked rather foreboding with all the front windows shuttered. But I took comfort in noting how soundly the house sat upon its stone foundation and how upright the massive fieldstone chimney rose from its pitched slate roof. Built well before the War for Independence, this was a dwelling that had stood the test of time, sheltering three generations of my Walker ancestors. And now it would shelter me.

We are home! I recalled my mother saying as the stage coach stopped at the front gate sixteen years ago. Our home was in Boston with my father so I did not understand what she meant. I thought we had come to Plumford for a summer visit. Little did I know at eight years old that Mother had come back home to die. Indeed, I was as chirpy as a cricket when I alighted from the stage and heard the bell high atop the Meet- inghouse tower begin to peal, as if to welcome us. The Green was verdant, shady, and bustling, the fine homes and shops sur- rounding it all freshly painted and spruce.

As pleasing as my first sight of Plumford was, more pleasing still was my first sight of Cousin Adam. His eyes were as blue as the summer sky, and the summer sun had browned his freckled face and painted golden streaks in his auburn hair. He could not have been more than nine, yet he had seemed as confident as an adult when he took hold of my hand and swept me off to have our first adventure together. Despite my fear of heights I did not protest as he led me up the Meetinghouse bell tower. I had already made up my mind to be his doughty mate for the rest of my days. Although the bell had stopped ringing, it was still vibrating when we stepped onto the tower balcony. From so high up we could view all of Plumford and its environs of purple-hued hills and emerald dales, dark green forest and rich brown farmland, glittering disks of ponds and a long silver ribbon of river. Adam pointed to the Tuttle farmhouse halfway up a nearby hill, where he lived with his maternal grandparents. I could get there in a jiffy, he explained, by taking the north road out of town, a path by the river, and a shortcut through the woods. For the next three years, until I was snatched away from my countryside Elysium, one of us traversed this route to meet the other almost every day.

Recalling all this in a bright, happy flash, I jumped down from Henry's carryall and headed toward the small, one-story building connected to the house, hoping Adam was within. Oh, how I longed to see him! Much to my disappointment, a note was pinned to the locked office door.

If in need of Dr. Walker's services, he can be found at the Sun.

The house was also locked up, but I found the back door key in its old hiding place beneath the well roof. After Henry deposited my portmanteau in the hallway, I asked him to go over to the Sun and inform Adam of my arrival. I could not very well do so myself. Although the town tavern is but a short stroll down the road, it is considered well beyond the bounds of a woman's sphere.

Expecting Henry to return with Adam straightaway, I did not go off to buy food to stock the bare pantry. Instead, I went down the passageway that connected the kitchen to the office and took a look around. The small coal stove was still warm to the touch, and I surmised Adam had not left too long ago. I found it mighty singular that he would go off to the tavern during office hours and wondered how much he had changed since I'd last seen him. Grandfather's office had changed but little. Most of the furnishings were the same, from the consultation desk and chair in the center of the room to the sick-bay cot in the alcove. The Staffordshire jar filled with leeches no longer sat atop the medicine cabinet, however. Nor were Doc Silas's blistering cups and bloodletting lancets displayed on the shelf above it. Adam had replaced them with pots of medicinal plants and containers of dried herbs, accoutrements of a far more pleasant nature. Not so pleasant, however, was the new addition of a skeleton hanging from a hook in the corner, which gave me quite a start. There was also a new examination table by the window, long and narrow, adorned with leather straps. Placed upon it was a vessel labeled ETHER. I dared not touch it. But I did caress a knitted scarf hanging on the wall peg, assuming it was Adam's. When I held it to my face I was sure I smelled his pleasing essence upon it.

Back in the kitchen, I rummaged around the cupboards and found a nigh empty canister of tea and a tin containing two biscuits. Inept as I am at the simplest of household tasks, it took me a great deal of effort to fire up the stove and get the sink pump working, but I eventually succeeded in doing both. I filled a kettle with water, and, as it heated, I set about opening shutters to let in the waning afternoon light.

When I went into Grandfather's study, I found him regarding me from the shadows, as lifelike as you please. I smiled back at his nearly finished portrait, still perched on the easel as I had left it fifteen months ago. In my haste to flee Plumford, I'd also left behind an assortment of art materials. Alas, the tubes and bladders of paint have all dried up, and I shall have to order a fresh supply. But I shall be able to start sketching immediately on the pristine drawing pad I discovered behind the desk, using a collection of Thoreau pencils I found in the drawer. How dear they have always been to me, these pencils! And how dear is the man who makes them! No matter how coolly he first greeted me today, Henry still remains a warm friend in my thoughts.

But where is he? Why has he not yet returned with Adam? Nightfall is fast approaching. Rather than squander more time with my scrawlings, I'd best go out to the back woodpile for logs and haul them to my girlhood bedchamber. If I do not start a fire in the hearth pretty soon, my bed will be mighty cold indeed tonight. I must remember to heat up a brick to cuddle.

ADAM'S JOURNAL

Friday, December 3

Joanna Wiley was buried in the family graveyard this afternoon. She managed to survive only a day after her Uncle Solomon attempted to "cure" her by the horrific mutilation of her sister's corpse. As I watched her rough coffin being lowered, I fervently hoped such ignorance was being buried along with the poor, innocent child.

I learned otherwise when I joined the men who had attended the burial service for a drink at the Sun Tavern. There is customarily good cheer radiating throughout the taproom, but today gloomy talk of vampirism floated in the soft light of the whale oil lamps and the haze of pipe and cigar smoke. Even our sanguine taverner Ruggles, who is usually the most levelheaded of men, participated.

"Why, I had a guest at the inn just last week," he said, "who knew of a man who claimed to have seen a vampyre rise from the fresh grave of a Connecticut clock maker, change into a bat, and flit toward the dead man's home. And that very night the clock maker's wife died!"

More farfetched accounts of vampyres followed, all of them hearsay. Then our very own Constable Beers hoisted his bulk off his bar stool and stepped forward to relate an incident he himself had experienced.

"I was no more than seventeen when this happened, but I shall never forget it," he told us. "I awakened in the night to find a beautiful young woman perched upon my chest." That got every man's attention right off. "But this unexpected visitor to my bedchamber was not the angel she appeared to be," Beers continued. "Instead, she turned out to be a blood-drinking demon! I had to fight her off with all my might to prevent her from draining the life out of me, a battle that went on until sunrise, when at last the she-devil fled my bed, never to return."

"Never?" Ruggles winked and poured Beers another mug of ale. "Well, I too had nighttime visitations from a female phantom as a youth. More than once, mind you. And I freely admit I did not fight her off. Indeed, I most often let her have her way with me. You see, I came to realize 'twas not my precious blood this mischievous sprite wanted to drain me of but merely my manly fluid, of which I had a seemingly limitless supply in my salad days."

When the guffaws that followed subsided, an elderly cooper who used to pitch horseshoes on the Green with Doc Silas spoke up. "Best not to laugh off the notion of vampyres, gentlemen. Witiku might take umbrage and rise from the grave to prey on us again."

A young mechanic who worked at the carding mill laughed derisively. "Folks stopped believing in Witiku years ago, old timer."

"Even so, a whippersnapper such as yourself has heard of him," the cooper replied. "That proves he is not forgotten."

"Well, I never heard of this Witiku," Ruggles said.

"Then I take it you are not originally from these parts," said the cooper.

Ruggles shook his great shiny globe of a head. "No, I hail

from Down East in Maine, where we have more than enough Indian legends. But pray recount this Plumford one to me." He propped his elbows on his bar and gave the old man his full attention. Indeed, we all did, although most of us had heard the tale oft times before.

"Witiku roamed hereabouts in centuries past, wreaking havoc wheresoever he did go," the cooper narrated with relish. "He was a most savage vampyre, for he did not just suck the blood but sometimes ate the flesh of white men. We were called the Long Pigs by the Nipmucs, and Witiku was of that tribe. He could make himself into a creature with a wolf's head atop a man's body when he fed upon humans, and a mortal wolf pack would travel in his wake to devour his leavings. Their den was on the rise we now call Wolf Hill, and they were greatly feared. For they were Witiku's pack of familiars."

"You are getting your legends mixed up, old timer," the mechanic said. "The wolves that had a den atop that hill never ate humans. Just lambs and calves and such. But they were fierce all right. Tore out the necks of the cows. At night the pack would circle a farmer's house and howl, striking fear into all within. And women and children were advised to stay away from the hill even in broad daylight. Finally the farmers and townsmen got good and sick of the pack and organized a hunt. Fifty men circled round the foot of the hill, and up they went, making a ruckus so as to trap the wolves all on top, where they shot and piked the lot of 'em. Nailed their heads to the Meetinghouse wall and left the bodies to rot by the den. And that was the end of it."

"Was it?" the cooper said. "What about the wolf that got away? It was said to have been as big as an ox, yet no bullet could hit it. It just up and vanished."

"You saying that was Witiku?" the mechanic sneered.

The cooper shrugged. "That's the way I heard tell it."

"And was that the last seen of this Indian vampyre?" Ruggles asked, ready to put an end to the tale and start pouring drinks again.

The old man was not so ready. "Can it ever be said that the last has been seen of such a creature as that? Some believe he is just resting for a time, most likely in the Nipmuc burying ground near Farmer Herd's far pasture."

"Then let's dig him up!" Solomon Wiley strode to the front of the taproom, looking even more dour than usual in his mourning clothes. Although he'd been sitting quietly in a corner with his bereaved brother, I'd expected he would eventually take the floor. Was he not, after all, the self-styled vampyre authority? "These very hands"—he raised his mighty mitts—"have destroyed one after another fiendish vampyre. I have the gift for it. Indeed, I was a mere boy when I found my first bloodsucker. He'd been plaguing our village for months, yet no one dared seek him out. No one but *me!* I rode backwards on a white horse into the graveyard at night, all alone, and where the horse stopped I knew was the place where the beast was lurking. I convinced the villagers of this, and the grave was dug up. But none could do what had to be done next. Only I, a boy of twelve, had the mettle to take an ax to the vile creature the dead man had become. And he was a man I had known well when alive—my own stepfather!"

Solomon went on to describe, in grisly detail, other experiences with the Living Dead, which I knew were but decaying corpses. Intending to challenge his claims with medical facts when he was done mesmerizing his gullible audience, I gave him the same rapt attention and did not mark Henry Thoreau come into the Sun. Hence I was most surprised when he took a seat at my table.

"What is afoot?" I immediately asked him, knowing that he would not seek me out in a tavern unless he had something significant to communicate to me.

And so he did. He reported that he had just delivered my

cousin Julia to our grandfather's house, where she now awaited me. I remained silent, trying to digest this stunning news. My stomach roiled.

"Adam, did you hear me?" Henry said.

I nodded and drained my glass of cider. "Is her husband with her?"

"She is alone," he said.

"He will eventually join her, I suppose."

"She made no mention of it."

"That does not mean he will not."

"That you will have to ask her yourself. As I said, she awaits you at the house."

I did not move.

"I could accompany you there," Henry said, "or be on my way and allow you to greet Julia alone. Which would you prefer?"

"I would prefer that she never came back here."

Henry's countenance remained impassive, but his deep-set eyes regarded me with sympathy. "Well, she has, my friend. And now you must deal with it."

"In a while." I directed my attention back to Solomon Wiley holding forth. He, in turn, directed his attention upon us.

"There sit the two men who dared interfere with my last slaying," he pronounced, jutting his finger our way. "If they had not talked my brother out of taking Joanna outside to breathe in the smoke of her revenant sister's burning heart and then eat the ashes, she would be with us still."

Both Henry and I rose from our seats to meet his challenge head on. "You spew dangerous lies that go against the laws of nature," I shouted loud enough for all to hear.

"And against all goodness of spirit," Henry added. "What purpose do you serve with all this fear-mongering?"

"My purpose is noble," Solomon shouted back. "I know what must be done to stop all this dying." He turned from us and back to his eager audience. "Doctors cannot help you. You have seen this for yourselves as more and more of your friends and family die despite Dr. Walker's ministrations. Only I can stop the undead from feeding amongst your loved ones at night. That is why Divine Providence has brought me to Plumford. Any here who ask my help will receive it."

"I presume your so-called help carries a fee," Henry said.

Solomon bridled. "I do not do this for money! There are far easier ways to earn a livelihood than as a vampyre slayer."

"Yet you still choose to earn yours as one." Henry made no effort to hide his disdain. "Hence, you expect remuneration, do you not?"

"I would gladly perform my service for free but alas, I am not a rich man. I must have something to live on."

"Just as your fictitious vampyres must have blood to live on?"

Solomon gave Henry a hateful look, and for a moment I thought he might strike my friend. I instinctively fisted my hands, ready to retaliate if he did. But Solomon must have decided it would be more profitable to play to his audience than to take us on.

"My work requires a strong will and a hard stomach and is most dangerous," he continued, addressing the men at the bar. "Few care to attempt it, and some have disappeared in the act of performing it, for a vampyre can be the most deadly of foes. If one is preying upon your family members, fifty dollars is all I ask to destroy it. That is a small price to pay to save a loved one from the grave, is it not?"

"No man could disagree with such a sentiment as that," Ruggles said.

"Nor is it unlawful to kill those already dead," Constable Beers pointed out and offered to buy the Great Vampyre Slayer a drink. The offer was readily accepted by Solomon, but before his grog could be poured the tavern door was thrown open by a youth with a pair of rabbits slung over his shoulder and a fowling piece in his hand.

"I come to fetch the constable," he called out. "His missus told me he could be found here."

Beers reluctantly left the bar and went over to the boy by the door. After listening a moment Beers motioned for Henry and me to join him outside.

"Young Tim here," Beers told us as we stood under the swinging tavern sign, "was hunting instead of being at school as he should have been and found a dead man on Wolf Hill."

"He *looked* mighty dead," the boy said.

"Were his eyes open?" I asked him.

"He was lying on his stomach. I couldn't see his eyes, and I didn't want to get close up to him. He did not budge when I shouted."

"He could be unconscious," I said. "If so, we may still be able to help him. Let us make haste."

Without further delay off we all went in Beers's wagon, which was standing in front of the tavern as usual. The boy directed us less than a mile down the highway and then, on foot, about forty yards up Wolf Hill and into the woods. The body lay by the narrow path cutting through the woods, one both Henry and I often took as a shortcut between Concord and Plumford. It was so steep and narrow that most pedestrians kept to the highway although doing so made the journey between the two towns a quarter hour longer. The well-traveled public road below was visible through the bare trees, but the path was not visible from the road.

It had rained heavily in the early morning, and the man was lying facedown on a sodden bed of leaf litter, moss, and loam. I turned him over, and his blue eyes, cloudy in death, stared up at the sky. I immediately knew how he had died.

"His jugular vein has been ripped open, causing him to bleed to death," I declared. "We need a Coroner's Jury convened here right away."

"I'll go tell Mr. Daggett to round one up," Beers said. And off he hurried to his wagon, the boy following close at his heels.

Henry bent down to examine the body with me. "I know this man!" he said. "His name is Chauncey Bidwell from Concord."

"If he was a friend of yours, I am sorry," I said.

"He was a student of mine at the Concord Academy about eight years ago, but we were never friends. In truth, I liked him very little," Henry said. "I did like his father very much, however. Mr. Bidwell was a gunsmith of great skill, acknowledged as a master craftsman. He died about a year ago, and now Mrs. Bidwell and her daughters must endure yet another loss." Henry gently brushed leaves and dirt from the corpse's face and closed the eyes. "Pray they are spared the sight of Chauncey's horrible neck wound. They admired his good looks almost as much as he himself did."

The dead man had even features, curled blond hair, and a luxuriant mustache. He was wearing a fine black overcoat with a thick astrakhan fur collar, and his silk hat lay close by his head. I unbuttoned his coat, looking for additional wounds. I saw no blood on his velvet frock coat, gold brocade vest, or tight, checkered trousers. Even his white satin shirt and carefully knotted silk cravat were spotless. The moist ground he had lain facedown upon must have soaked up all the blood pouring out of his open vein.

"How long do you estimate he has been dead?" Henry asked me.

I felt his limbs, still stiff with rigor mortis. "No more than eighteen hours. Of course the cold ground and low temperature make such an estimation little better than a guess."

"If the body had been out here more than a single night, the crows and foxes would have gnawed at it," Henry said.

"Perhaps small animals did nibble around the throat wound a bit," I said. "Look how the flesh has been wrenched away. A knife would not leave such a wide gash."

"I do not think the weapon used was a knife," Henry said. "I surmise a hooked blade of some kind was sunk into the throat and then yanked from it, disgorging tissue. To accomplish this, the murderer had to be facing Bidwell. But Bidwell did not fall backward after being struck. He must have turned from his attacker and tried to get away before he collapsed facedown. Yet the attacker did not strike at him again."

"One strike was all it took to kill him," I said.

"If murder was the intention, why not a few more vicious slashes to be sure the job was done?"

"The intention could have been robbery, not murder."

"Possibly," Henry said, but when he searched the victim's jacket and vest pockets he found a small brass key, a beautifully carved ivory comb, and a handsome calf-skin wallet containing bank notes and coins.

"So the killer wasn't after Bidwell's money," I said.

"Nor his fancy hair comb," Henry said wryly. He replaced the articles, checked Bidwell's overcoat pockets, and found another brass key. It was bigger and more ornate, with a fleur-de-lis at the base, attached to a black, twisted silk cord. He put it back and sniffed the clothing beneath the heavy coat. "I discern a sweetish scent," he said.

I too sniffed, but picked up nothing. I was not surprised. Henry's sense of smell is far more acute than most people's. Indeed, I have heard it remarked that no hound can scent better than Henry David Thoreau. "Does it smell like perfume?" I asked him.

"Perhaps," he said. "The scent is unfamiliar to me, but I know nothing about perfume. I venture a dandy like Bidwell would apply it upon his person, however."

"Was Bidwell coming from or going to Concord when he was murdered, I wonder."

"What does the ground tell us?" Henry moved around the body looking for tracks. "He must have been killed before the rain storm, for I discern no trace of footprints."

He sifted through the undergrowth bordering the path and found nothing. He directed his attention to the trees, and something about a birch caught his attention. He stepped closer to it and called me over to regard some slashes on the bark. There were about twenty of them at shoulder height, no more than six inches long but quite deep.

"They look like the markings a bear's claws would leave," I said.

"Unfortunately, bears in these parts were hunted out decades ago, along with the wolves," Henry said. "Farmers have no tolerance for wild creatures. No, these gouges were made by an implement fashioned by man. Could it have been the same one that felled Bidwell?"

"Yes, the wound to his neck seems to be the result of the same slashing motion. But what sort of weapon or tool would it have been? And why strike it against a tree trunk?"

"Perhaps to vent crazed anger or mad impatience whilst waiting here to confront Bidwell."

I regarded the horrible slash to the young man's throat. "Crazed and mad indeed."

We heard a wagon approaching. I looked down toward the road to see it was Beers returning. He had left the boy back in Plumford and had brought with him Coroner Fred Daggett and one of the men Daggett had chosen to be a juror. It was Solomon Wiley. As soon as Daggett came up the hill I took him aside to protest.

"Is it not your duty as coroner to select suitable jurors?" I said.

That put his nose out of joint right off. "And so I have."

"Solomon Wiley is not a Plumford resident," I said. "He does not even reside in the Commonwealth of Massachusetts."

"According to him, he has removed from Rhode Island and now lives here with his brother," Daggett replied frostily. "Thus he qualifies as a juror."

"He is not *mentally* qualified," I said. "He claims he is a vampyre slayer."

"And many in town believe him," Daggett said.

I was shocked to hear it. "Do you?"

"Mr. Wiley seems of sound enough mind to me," Daggett said. "It was hard enough to gather up six men to form a jury this quickly without being too damn particular."

The other five jurors arrived, two in a chaise, one in a buckboard, one in a sulky, and one on horseback. Except for Solomon, they were a sensible and sober enough bunch, and Mr. Jackson, the sawyer, also conveniently served as town undertaker and casket maker. His son Hyram had come with him, but he stayed a good distance away whilst the rest of us gathered round the body.

Henry identified Bidwell, and I gave my opinion regarding cause of death. We pointed to the slash marks in the tree and suggested that the weapon that had made them could have been the same one used on Bidwell's neck. The jury quickly voted in agreement with my opinion that the man had been murdered.

"I shall inform Justice Phyfe of our verdict, and he will institute an investigation," Coroner Daggett said.

Solomon Wiley spoke up. "There is no need to investigate further. I can tell you right off who murdered this man. A vampyre did it."

"That is ridiculous!" I protested and looked to Daggett. I

could tell from his dismayed expression that he had come to the realization that Solomon should not have taken part in the inquest. But apparently Daggett was still all haired up that I had questioned his judgment, for it was me he reprimanded.

"No one interrupted you when you were giving your point of view, doctor," he said. "Now we will hear Mr. Wiley out."

And so we did.

"There are revenants who feed on their living kin, but they are not the only such fiends," Solomon began, modulating his voice to sound almost reasonable. "There exist some far worse. These roam the earth for eternity and suck blood and kill and make more of their own kind at their whim. You see here the victim of one such." He explained all this to us with the self-assurance of a seer.

"This man is talking humbug, and he is making a sham of your inquest," Henry told Daggett.

The coroner was finally ready to agree. "Thank you for your opinion, Mr. Wiley," he said. "And now we will conclude—"

"*Fact,* not opinion!" Solomon interrupted. "All the evidence is right before your eyes. The slashes on that tree yonder—made by a vampyre's talons. The gash in the corpse's neck—made by a vampyre's fangs. The poor man was then sucked dry!"

"As I have already explained, he bled to death from his wound," I said.

"Then where is the blood?"

"It seeped into the ground," Henry said.

"Wrong! It went into the vampyre's maw. 'Tis blood from the living that keeps the dead alive."

In the gathering gloom I observed the whites of the jurymen's wide eyes as they looked around them. "Ain't it time we left here?" one of them suggested.

"Yes, let us depart," Daggett said.

Solomon held up his fist, forefinger extended. "I have only
one more thing to say. Indeed, one word." He paused dramatically until all eyes were again upon him. Then he raised his
voice to a boom. "Witiku!"

"You think it was *him* that done this?" a juror said, sounding betwixt doubt and belief.

"None other!" Solomon said. "All this revenant activity
hereabouts has roused Witiku from his long sleep, and he is on
the warpath once again. But do not fear. If anyone can put a
stop to him, I can."

"What drivel," Henry said, struggling, I could see, to keep
his voice calm. "This charlatan hears a hoary tale in the tavern
and now twists it to his own advantage."

"I shall pass on your opinions concerning how this man
died to Justice Phyfe," Daggett told Wiley with cool formality.
"And I now officially close this inquest." It was clear he
wanted nothing more to do with it.

Undertaker Jackson called to his son, but Hyram did not
move. Jackson went over to him, and they talked in low tones
for some time as jurors gave worried glances westward at the
setting sun. Finally, Jackson grabbed his son's arm and hauled
him up to the body.

"Hyram claims he feels too feeble to lift dead weight
today," Jackson told us. "But I reckon he is just too lazy."

I stepped forward to take a look at the young man. He is an
ungainly lad for sure, with lanky limbs and bad skin, but he did
not appear ill to me, merely frightened by talk of vampyres.
"Pay no attention to Mr. Wiley's wild speculation," I counseled
him. "That unfortunate young man was killed by one as
human as you or I."

That did not seem to much comfort Hyram. When his father told him to pick up the corpse's feet, he shook his small,
bullet-shaped head most vehemently. But after Jackson gave
him a forceful whack on the back he complied, taking an

ankle in each hand. Jackson placed his hands under the dead man's arms. They raised him up and began to walk down to the buckboard, Hyram going backwards as he had the lesser load, when all of a sudden Hyram let out a scream. He dropped the legs, tripped as he backed away, and fell down hard on his posterior. His father, still holding up his end of the body, looked down at his son in puzzlement.

"What the devil's got into you, Hyram?"

"His eyes come open, and he looked straight at me, Pa!"

"It happens sometimes, son," Jackson said in a gentler tone. "A corpse's eyes just fly open. Now get up and let's get on with it."

Hyram continued to sit on the ground, trembling.

Jackson looked mortified by his son's behavior. "Hyram ain't used to handling the dead yet," he told us.

Hyram looked up at his father, his homely face contorted with fear. "He *spoke* to me, Pa!"

"God save us! The corpse lives!" Solomon pronounced. "He is a vampyre in the making."

As the rest of the men shrank back from the body, Henry stepped forward and took up the feet. "Let us get this deceased fellow into your wagon before that madman defames him further, Mr. Jackson."

"My son is not a madman!"

"I was referring to Solomon Wiley."

"Mad, am I?" Wiley bellowed. "Did they call Isaiah mad? Did they call Jeremiah mad?"

That Solomon had the audacity to compare himself with prophets from the Old Testament did not surprise me. What did surprise me is how he could hold the rapt attention of my fellow townsmen.

"What did the dead fiend say to you, boy?" Solomon demanded, looming over Hyram.

The boy gazed up at him and opened his mouth. But no words came forth, only a sob.

"Go home, son. You ain't no use to me here," Jackson said, and with that Hyram leapt up and ran off.

After Henry helped Jackson carry the corpse to the wagon, he offered to go along and help him unload it, but Jackson said one of the saw mill workers would give him a hand at the ice house. Henry also offered to inform the Bidwell family of Chauncey's death, and Beers, ever eager to evade unpleasant duties, gave him leave to do so.

Everybody took off fast as lightning after that. Daggett, it appeared, wanted nothing more to do with Solomon and squeezed himself into the chaise for a ride back to town. Beers offered to take Henry and me back, but we didn't much care to ride with Solomon either and decided to travel by foot instead.

We walked along the highway in silence as dusk descended, both lost in our own thoughts. Mine centered on Julia as each step took me closer and closer to town and to her. I could not quite believe she was really there at the Walker house, waiting for me, after all these months apart. Whilst she was in France I was at least spared the sight of what I most desired and could never have. That she has ruined all our chances of a life together makes me almost hate her. To feel such animosity toward someone I have loved for most of my life makes me sick at heart, but I cannot help it. I try to remember Julia and myself as we were during our halcyon childhood years, loving each other ardently but without carnal desire. How happy we were in each other's carefree company. And how happy I had been to see her again twelve years later, my childhood chum now a woman more lovely than I had ever imagined her becoming. At first sight she truly had taken my breath away. And all my manly powers of will. It would not be fair to say she seduced me. I know that. Yet she *did*—by her every small gesture and smile and look. I never wanted a woman more. And then she made sure, by marrying another, that my desire for her could never be satisfied.

"Adam, might you pick up your pace?" Henry said, breaking our silence. "I have yet to drive back to Concord and bring my sad tidings to Mrs. Bidwell and her daughters."

I immediately lengthened my stride. "That is not an easy duty you have taken on, Henry."

"Better for them to hear it from me than from that fat-headed lubbard of a constable. What chance think you Beers has of finding Chauncey Bidwell's killer?"

"Near to none," I replied. "Rounding up errant schoolboys or stray farm animals seems to be the extent of his abilities. To be fair, that is all Plumford taxpayers expect of him."

"And all we should expect of him, too," Henry said. "We have had disappointing dealings with Constable Beers before."

"Even so, we cannot take the law into our own hands again, Henry."

"Why not, if it proves necessary to do so?"

I might well have expected such a response from Henry, for I have learned during our association over the last year and a half that he follows no laws but his own. (And he has also looked the other way when I did what I felt to be right rather than lawful.)

"Since there are no other men in the Bidwell family to take on the responsibility, I will make arrangements with the Concord undertaker to fetch Chauncey's body home," Henry said, and we agreed to meet at the ice house the next morning.

Reaching town, we made our way across the Green and toward the Walker house. The white clapboards looked luminous against the purple-tinged twilight sky, and a room upstairs glowed with golden candlelight. 'Twas Julia's bedchamber, and I could not help but recall our last childhood adventure together, when I hooted like an owl beneath her window to signal her and she climbed out her window and down the trellis. Taking her hand, off I had run into the night with her, my fleet-footed, fearless friend.

Henry bid me Good Night and climbed up on the carryall he had driven from Concord. He gazed down at me with what looked to be pity. He glanced up at the lighted window. And then, without a word, he drove away.

I stood outside the gate and saw Julia approach her upstairs chamber window and look out at me. She raised her hand in greeting, but a rush of emotion against her made me turn and walk to the barn. I unstabled Napoleon, backed him between the traces, and urged him off, away from town. Neither his steady pace nor my breathing in draughts of the cold night air could soothe my unsettled spirit as I drove to Tuttle Farm.

My day ends far more troubled than even it began.

JULIA'S NOTEBOOK

Saturday, 4 December

Oh, how my tears did flow as I watched Adam drive away last evening! Apparently he did not think it worth his trouble to stop by and welcome me back. Went to bed desolate. Awoke ravenous.

I dressed with more haste than care and set out across the Green to Daggett's Market. When I entered the store the familiar scents of molasses and coffee greeted me, along with the strong smell of burning tobacco coming from the short-stemmed pipes of the men gathered round the stove. They all stopped talking to regard me, but none uttered a word of greeting. Elijah Phyfe tipped his glossy beaver hat to me, however. Even such a slight salutation as that was more than I expected from him. He has never much cared for me. Nor I for him! I have not forgotten how he would rap his ferule on my knuckles for no good reason I could discern when he was the Plumford schoolmaster. He has certainly come up in the world since those days—or at least come up in the town. If a man's wealth is measured by how many people owe him money, Grandfather used to say, then Elijah Phyfe is the richest man in Plumford, for he has privately lent money to many farmers and invested in a good many town enterprises. How pompous

and well-fixed he looked compared to the store loiterers surrounding him as he lounged in the seat of honor, the only
chair with rockers.

Mr. Daggett left his place at Phyfe's elbow and slid behind
the counter to assist me. He offered his condolences for the
loss of my grandfather and in the very next breath his services
as my property agent.

"Why would I need a property agent, Mr. Daggett?"

"You plan to sell your grandfather's house, do you not?"

That he knew I had inherited the house did not surprise
me. Grandfather's will is of public record, and Mr. Daggett,
along with being the town postmaster and coroner, is the town
clerk. Moreover, he is the self-appointed town crier, and all
who wish to know what he does need only congregate at his
store.

"My only plan at the moment," I informed him over the
rumble of my empty stomach, "is to stock my larder."

I handed him my list, and, whilst he went about collecting
the items on it, another woman came through the door. The
chatter around the stove stopped once again as the lollygaggers
regarded her.

"Ain't you fellows ever seen a beautiful lady before?" she
quipped in a bold, high-sounding voice, staring right back at
them. Then she heeded me. "Well, I reckon they have at that.
For you are a beauty to be sure, dearie."

I paid the compliment no mind. Not only was I quite certain I looked wan and worn from travel and hunger and weeping, but my clothes were in need of a good brushup and
looked shabby and drab indeed compared to this stranger's
striking costume. Some might have called her apparel ostenta-
tious, but the artist in me much appreciated such a vivid show
of finery and flair. Her knee-length coat was of indigo velvet, and
beneath it was a many-tiered taffeta skirt of deep, shimmering
red. Her veiled bonnet was sea green, and from it sprang forth a

frothy white plume. Her hands were tucked into a luxurious ermine muff that I could not help but covet.

Mrs. Daggett popped out of the counting room, looking most eager to assist this apparently affluent customer. "What may I show you, ma'am?" she said, and without waiting for an answer, opened up the display case on the counter. "A string of jet beads perhaps?"

The stranger shook her head, making her bonnet plume quiver. "It is a string of garlic I am in need of."

Mrs. Daggett's sharp features drooped. "Did you say garlic, ma'am?"

"Yes. To ward off that Indian vampyre who just rose up from the dead!"

Mr. Daggett stopped measuring out the pound of coffee beans I'd requested and looked toward Justice Phyfe.

"The chambermaid at the inn called him the Plumford Night Stalker," the woman continued, "and I fear he will be coming for me next, alone as I am in the world!"

Justice Phyfe unfolded his long body from the rocker and came over. "Dear lady, please allow me to assuage your fears," he said in a mellifluous tone, raising his hat to her. "I am Plumford's Chief Magistrate and First Selectman, Elijah Phyfe."

"How do you do, sir? I am Mrs. Swann with two *n*'s." The lady extracted her lace-gloved hand from her muff and offered it to him. "And there is nothing a friendless, defenseless woman such as myself could want more than to have my fears assuaged by an important town official such as you."

Justice Phyfe gave her hand a gentle shake and held on to it. "The rumors concerning a vampyre in our midst have no basis in fact, I assure you, Mrs. Swann."

"Was not a man just murdered in the nearby woods?"

"Unfortunately that part is true."

"And was his body sucked dry of blood?"

"According to the doctor who examined the body—"

"Would that have been Dr. Walker?" I interjected.

Justice Phyfe, who does not like to be interrupted, gave me a brief, dismissive nod and went back to mollifying the exotic Mrs. Swann. "As I was saying, the doctor concluded that the victim's great loss of blood was due to a deep cut to his neck. And that wound was inflicted by a mortal man, most likely a wandering tramp, and certainly not a vampyre. Is that not what you and your jury concluded, Coroner Daggett?"

The storekeeper stepped forward. "That's right. Pay no mind to the tattle of a silly chambermaid, ma'am."

"Did she just make it up to scare the living daylights out of me then?"

"She merely repeated the rantings of fools and fear mongers," Phyfe said. He patted Mrs. Swann's hand. "There is no vampyre roaming about Plumford. Trust me, dear lady."

"Indeed I do, kind sir." She tilted her face to coquettishly peek at him around the brim of her bonnet. "You have such a commanding bearing that I trust you implicitly."

His chest puffed up so much I thought the gold buttons on his embroidered waistcoat might pop. "My wife used to say much the same."

"Used to? Does she say it no more?"

"Alas, *she* is no more, Mrs. Swann. My dear wife went to her final reward five years ago."

"My dear husband is also departed," Mrs. Swann said.

"Ah, then we share the same sorrow."

To be quite frank, neither of them looked the least bit sorrowful as they regarded each other.

"Do you still want that garlic, ma'am?" Mrs. Daggett said.

"No. This good gentleman has convinced me I do not need it."

"I never heard tell garlic kept away vampyres anyways," Mrs. Daggett said.

"Well, a gypsy once told me it did."

"In Europe that superstition is quite prevalent," said I.

"In Rhode Island too, according to one Solomon Wiley," one of the loafers by the stove called out.

"Now there is a man who knows whereof he speaks, for he has had personal dealings with revenants and such," another stove-hugger put in. His companions bobbed their heads in accord.

"I would take Mr. Wiley's claims *cum grano salis,*" Justice Phyfe said. He paused to let us appreciate his ease with Latin, as oft he had when he was schoolmaster. "We cannot let some newcomer from the smallest state in the Union lead us by our noses into the Valley of Fear. Do you not agree, Mr. Daggett?"

"Indeed," the storekeeper said. Never once had I heard him disagree with Phyfe. "But others at the inquest found Wiley most persuasive."

"He had no business being there as a juror." Justice Phyfe glared at Daggett. "In fact, he has no business in my town at all."

"He declares slaying vampyres to be his business," Daggett's wife said. "And at fifty dollars a kill, it could well be a mighty lucrative one here in Plumford."

"Those who turn fear into profit are despicable," Phyfe said loftily. Such fine sentiments, however, do not keep him from threatening those with overdue loans with lawsuits and even imprisonment. I was tempted to remind him of this, but held my tongue.

Mrs. Daggett did not hold hers. "Nothing wrong with making a profit by supplying folks with what they want," she asserted, and with that she turned away from us, opened the trapdoor, and descended into the cellar.

"I overheard other talk at the inn," Mrs. Swann said to Justice Phyfe. "Talk that disturbed my sensibilities even more than the vampyre rumor."

"And what was that, dear lady?"

"I hesitate to voice it."

"Pray do," he urged her.

"I heard there is to be a *slave* auction here at the store this morning."

Justice Phyfe's regal countenance grew florid. "We do not traffic in slaves in the Commonwealth of Massachusetts, madam."

"Then what meant the chambermaid when she told me a boy called Jack Rabbit will be auctioned off?"

"She was referring to a vendue auction, an entirely different procedure. The town will pay the winning bidder to feed, clothe, and board the boy, who is an orphan. He is called Jackrabbit in jest, because of his . . ." Phyfe lightly patted his upper lip and left off further explanation.

"What is his real name?" Mrs. Swann inquired.

Phyfe looked toward the storekeeper. "Robinson, is it not?"

Mr. Daggett nodded. "Noah is his Christian name."

"And he has no kin?" Mrs. Swann said.

"Other than his deceased parents, none that we know of," Phyfe said. "Jackrabbit himself claims to know of none, and we have nothing further to go on. The Robinsons came to Plumford about a year ago, rented a cottage a few miles from town, and kept to themselves. Their boy was left without money or property and hence became the responsibility of the town's Overseers of the Poor. That would be myself and the other two Selectmen."

"If he is your responsibility, you should take turns keeping him in your own fine homes," I opined.

Justice Phyfe shook his head and sighed. "As I recall, you were always coming up with preposterous ideas as a girl, Julia. The vendue system is how we deal with our poor hereabouts. It is a time-honored tradition that has proven to be efficient and economically sound."

"But is it humane?" I said. "To be put on the block and bid upon must be most humiliating, especially for a child."

Phyfe waved away my objection. "Jackrabbit will just have to endure it again."

"Again? You mean he has been through such an ordeal before?"

"Only once," replied Phyfe in a weary tone. "A farmer by the name of Shrove took Jackrabbit on six months ago, but can no longer keep him. So today we must bound the boy out again to the lowest bidder."

"The *lowest* bidder?"

"Yes, of course, Julia. The bidder who offers to accept the least amount of money from the town to keep the boy shall get him. The vendue is really an auction in reverse. Low bid wins."

"And poor boy loses," I muttered.

Justice Phyfe did not acknowledge my comment and turned his attention to Mrs. Swann. "Your tender heart need not be troubled about this auction, madam. I would never let a child go to an unsuitable caretaker."

"Once again you have alleviated my apprehensions," she told him.

A glowering, disheveled man came through the door and, looking neither right nor left, marched over to the stove and settled into the chair with rockers. His pants were so filthy with charcoal dust that I doubted Phyfe would ever place his own elegantly clothed backcheeks in that seat again.

"What a horrid-looking creature!" Mrs. Swann said, pressing a palm to her generous bosom. "Is he going to be put up for auction today along with the boy?"

"No, just the boy," Daggett said. "That man is a bidder, not a pauper, ma'am. He is the master collier at the charcoal pit, and he's always in need of laborers to replace the ones who get injured. Don't know where it would be worse to end up—hell's fiery pit or Abner Skene's charcoal pit."

This greatly alarmed me. "A child should end up in neither place!"

"Skene only bids on able-bodied men," Daggett said. "A feeble boy like Jackrabbit would hold no interest for him."

"Then what is he doing here?"

Daggett shrugged. "He must have misconstrued the auction notice I posted."

Two men in beaver hats not quite as high as Justice Phyfe's entered the store. Betwixt them was a thin, small boy. He kept his head down, and all I could see was the soiled crown of his ragged, wide-brimmed felt hat. Phyfe left Mrs. Swann's side and went to greet the two men. Daggett informed us they were the other town Selectmen, and the boy with them was none other than Jackrabbit. The boy shuffled off as they talked and went behind the stove, where he hunkered down on the floor, head buried in his arms.

I felt compelled to go to him. I put my hand on his shoulder to comfort him, but he did not acknowledge my touch. Nor did he look up at me when I voiced his Christian name, Noah. But as soon as Phyfe called out Jackrabbit, he scrambled to his feet and went over to him. Phyfe hauled him up on the counter like a bag of potatoes, where he sat in a slump, head down, and poorly shod feet dangling.

"We will begin the auction forthwith," Justice Phyfe announced, watch in hand.

"Maybe we should wait for more bidders," Daggett said.

"No. It is well past the time posted, and I am sure no more will come. Let us get on with it." Phyfe returned his watch to his waistcoat pocket and proceeded to do just that. "What hear I bid for the care and housing and feeding of this boy Noah Robinson, born . . ." Phyfe glanced at Daggett.

The storekeeper leafed through a ledger on the counter. "December 25, 1835."

"What an unwelcome Christmas present he must have been," one of the stove lollygaggers commented.

"Five dollars a week!" another called out. "I would not take on the creature for less payment than that."

"Why, that is ten times more than we struck him off for last time," Phyfe said. "Either make a serious bid or risk a fine. Now who here will accept fifty cents per week for supporting this boy?" No one spoke up. "Come now, gentlemen, that is a most generous sum to get from the town. Just look at the lad. He will not eat much at all."

"That's right. More food will drop out of his mouth than get in it," another loafer remarked. The others laughed.

I looked at Mrs. Swann in puzzlement for I could not understand what was so amusing.

"I'll take sixty cents to keep him," a gruff voice called out. It belonged to the master collier Skene.

I expected Phyfe to ignore him. Instead he started to bargain with him. "Will you not accept fifty-five cents, Mr. Skene?"

"I will not! A puny lad like that will likely fall into the pit and get incinerated to a crisp afore he earns me back a copper of his keep."

"Very well then. If yours is the only bid, Mr. Skene, I shall have to let you have him for the payment of—"

"Justice Phyfe, you cannot place Noah with this man!" I interrupted. "You told us you would not let a child go to an unsuitable bidder."

"Did you not hear his age stated, Julia? This boy will be twelve come Christmas, and that is no longer a child." Phyfe turned away from me. "Noah Robinson has been bid of by Abner Skene at sixty cents a week. I will strike him off to Mr. Skene unless I hear a lower bid."

Phyfe slammed his fist on the counter once, then twice, and then I cried out, "A penny! I will take on this boy and give him good care for a penny!"

"A penny a week?" Phyfe asked me, amazed.

"A penny a year!" I shouted back at him.

Phyfe stared at me a long moment. I thought he was going to deem my offer invalid because it came from a mere woman, but he did not. Instead, a sly smile lifted up his lips, and he nodded to Daggett. "Write up the purchase paper and have her sign it," he said.

I went over to the boy. Seated as he was on the high counter, his head was level with mine. "Noah," I said softly, "you are coming to live with me. Will that suit you, dear?" He lifted his head and looked me full in the face.

I just about fainted away. Indeed, I might well have if Mrs. Swann had not grabbed my upper arm and propped me up until I collected myself. I prayed the boy did not perceive my shock, but he was no doubt used to such a reaction at the first sight of him. His mouth was severely distorted into a snarl, with the upper lip split into two twisted sections that tugged upward into his left nostril. The resulting gap revealed his gum and teeth, and the effect was most disturbing. I now understood his nickname. He was called Jackrabbit because he was a harelip.

When I signed the purchase paper, assuring the town that I would pay all damages if I reneged on the deal struck, my hand was shaking. But I did not for a moment regret that I had taken on the boy.

Mrs. Daggett, who had emerged from the cellar, sadly shook her head at me, and then directed her attention to arranging in a basket the garlic bulbs she'd brought up from below. As her husband was packing my provisions she murmured something about adding some sweets for the boy free of charge. He did add a bag of candy ginger, but I believe he charged me for it. No matter. I paid for my purchases, hoisted up the wooden box that contained them, and directed Noah to follow me out of the store. We passed by Mrs. Daggett just as she'd completed writing something upon a pasteboard. She propped the board against the basket of garlic on the counter. Revenant Repellents, One for a Dime, Twelve for a Dollar.

Outside the store Noah grabbed at the box I was carrying and made sounds I did not understand. But I perceived that he wished to carry the box for me, and I handed it over to him.

"Pray halt!" a voice called behind us, and I turned to see Mrs. Swann bustling forth. She took my hand and shook it hard. "You are a most admirable lady," she declared.

I had to laugh. "You say that only because you do not know me."

"But I would like to know you," she said. "Indeed, I would like to work for you."

"*Work* for me?" I eyed her fancy clothes and luxurious muff.

"I am not what I appear to be," she said. "That is, my fine apparel belies my present situation. You take me to be a lady of means, and so I was before my husband died. I knew nothing about Mr. Swann's business, and his nefarious partner managed to steal away all that was due me. Now I am almost destitute and must find a way to support myself. Other women in my situation might crumble, but I am made of sturdier stuff, as I suspect you too are, dearie." She gave me a hearty pat on the back. "I am not afraid of hard work, and if you hire me on as your housekeeper you will not be sorry. I can provide you with sterling references."

Already concerned as to how I could care for Noah and at the same time manage to earn a living as a portraitist, I made yet another spontaneous decision and engaged Mrs. Swann right there and then. She tried to take the box of food from Noah, he would not let go of it, and a tussle ensued. Mrs. Swann's determination to win out rather surprised me, but I suppose she was just trying to demonstrate her own eagerness to be helpful. I suggested they carry the box between them, and so it was resolved. As the three of us marched across the Green we received many a curious glance. I reckon we made an odd enough trio, but the good people of Plumford will just have to get used to us.

When we arrived at the house I left Mrs. Swann and Noah in the kitchen to unpack the provisions and went down the hall, hoping to find Adam in the office. So I did. He was grinding medicine in a porcelain mortar, his back to me, and I noted how his auburn hair, always in need of a trimming, brushed his collar and curled around his ears just as it had when I'd last run my fingers through it. I called out his name, and he slowly put down his pestle and turned to look at me.

Oh! To gaze upon that face again! But it was not the amiable face I had so often conjured up over the past months. There was no humor or affection in his countenance now, only fatigue and distrust. My heart squeezed tight, and I froze at the threshold, waiting for him to make the first move. But he remained rigid as a statue, his wide mouth compressed and his blue eyes cold as ice. And thus we greeted each other after all this time apart—two ossified beings staring across a chasm of regret.

"Hello, cousin dear," I finally said. I extended my arms out to him, but awkwardly dropped them to my sides when he made no move toward me.

"Your visit to Plumford is ill-timed, Julia," he said. "We are in the midst of a Consumption epidemic."

"So Henry told me."

"You should not linger here."

"I have nowhere else to go."

"Go back to France!"

"I am sorry if you find my presence here so objectionable, Adam, but rest assured I will keep well out of your way. And I shall direct Mrs. Swann and Noah to stay away from your office too."

"Who might they be?"

I recounted what had occurred at Daggett's store. "And right after I assumed responsibility for the boy, Mrs. Swann kindly offered to help me keep house," I concluded.

"So you have taken in two complete strangers," Adam said.

"You disapprove?"

"I was simply making an observation. You may do whatever you wish. I have no interest in the matter. It's your house now."

His dismissive tone pained me, and I struck back. "Do you feel aggrieved that Grandfather left it to me instead of you?"

"Why should I? It is fitting and right that you have inherited the house of your Walker ancestors."

"But they are your ancestors too, Adam."

He looked away. "I told Doc Silas I did not want him to leave his house to me."

"Ah, now I understand why he left it to his female grandchild instead. What I do not understand is why you didn't want it."

My question seemed to vex him. "I will have enough property to worry about when I inherit Tuttle Farm someday. I harbor no resentment concerning your inheritance, I assure you."

"Then why are you acting so unfriendly toward me, Adam?"

"How do you expect me to act? You *left* me!"

"And it broke my heart to do so."

"Well, you have a very resilient heart, Mrs. Pelletier, for it mended with amazing speed. You married within a month of our parting."

"But not for love."

"For money then?"

I could not deny it so I said nothing.

"I suppose I should prefer money rather than love to be your reason, although I never realized you were so mercenary." Adam regarded me grimly. "When will your husband be joining you here?"

"He will never be joining me."

Adam's expression softened. "Are you so soon a widow?"

Happy thought! No, I strike that off. I wish no one dead, not even Jacques Pelletier. "My husband was alive and well when I left him. And I do not think a separation from me will much affect his health."

"But you will return to him eventually," Adam said.

"That is *not* my intention."

"Intentions can change. Facts do not," Adam said. "And the fact remains that you are a married woman, Julia. As soon as I can make other arrangements, I will remove myself from this office."

"But why?"

"I do not wish to be in such close proximity to you."

"You make me feel so unwelcome, Adam! We are blood relations, after all. For the sake of our dear grandfather's memory, pray do not forsake his office just because I have taken up residence in his house. Here is where your patients expect to find you, and here is where you should remain. Such a needless relocation would be a wasteful expenditure of your time and energy, and you look exhausted enough as it is."

He rubbed the back of his neck as he considered my reasoning. "You are right about one thing. I should not let my personal feelings interfere with my duties as a doctor. People desire constancy during times like this. The rampant spread of Consumption is alarming enough, and now I fear terror-filled rumors may start spreading along with the disease."

"Indeed they already have," I said. "They were saying at Daggett's store that a young man's life was sucked out of him by a vampyre. But surely most people in Plumford are too sensible to believe such a thing."

"These are dark times, Julia. So many have died of late. And when people lose those most dear to them, they are apt to believe almost anything to explain their loss, even dead relatives returning as predatory bloodsuckers. And now, with this young man's violent death, the idea of a vampyre striking down random, healthy people may take hold and bring about a panic."

"The real culprit must be found out as soon as possible then."

"Uncovering a murderer is no easy matter, Julia."

"We have done it before—Henry, you, and I!"

Adam's expression became most severe. "You must have no part of this horror. Promise me you will stay out of it."

"Only if you promise me you will stay in Doc Silas's office."

"Very well. I am out on patient calls most of the time anyway, so we will have little contact with each other."

"Do you truly find my company so unbearable, Adam?"

"Yes," he said softly and turned back to his work with mortar and pestle.

I left him without another word. Yet so much remains unspoken between us! And always shall remain so. Never again can we indulge in the familiarity and intimacy we once shared. It would only lead us down the path of temptation once again. Even so, I cannot prevent the waves of yearning that sweep over me whenever I think of Adam, much less see him in the flesh.

All this afternoon I busied myself making ready bedchambers for Noah and Mrs. Swann. I have given the boy the room next to mine, and Mrs. Swann the master chamber across the hall. Upon entering it, I felt Grandfather's presence envelop me. How vividly I could picture him in the four-poster bed, looking about with the bright impatience of a squirrel. Good thing I'd come from New York to tend to him or I am sure he would have hobbled around on his broken leg before it healed properly. I had kept him entertained by reading aloud bizarre tales authored by a young writer named Poe. And by singing to him. How Grandfather did laugh at my pathetic attempts to carry a tune! I did not mind for I allow that I am absurdly tone deaf. As was he. Adam too. Must be a Walker trait.

I recalled too the quiet pleasure of sitting by Grandfather's bed and sketching his likeness in preparation for the oil painting I did of him. As much as he had welcomed my presence, he did not much like being the object of such attention, another trait he shared with Adam. They shared few facial features, however. Grandfather claimed Adam inherited his good looks from his father. Although Owen Walker had been lost at sea shortly after Adam was born, Grandfather had told me a day never went by that he did not mourn the loss of his only son.

Grandfather had shared much that was in his heart with me when I came back to Plumford to nurse him. No matter that we'd been apart for a decade whilst I resided in Europe. The warm relationship I'd had with him as a child had been easily resumed. As was my warm relationship with Adam, but that warmth soon turned to heat. How difficult it must have been for Grandfather to watch us falling in love that summer. I shall never forget how forlorn he looked when he explained to me why being Walker cousins prevented Adam and me from ever marrying.

Such were the memories that tugged at my heart as I cleared the wardrobe and the many drawers of Grandfather's bonnet-top highboy for Mrs. Swann's use. I do not know what luxuries she is used to, but surely she will be comfortable in the master chamber, with its large fireplace and soft bed. Why, she will even have her own hip bath.

ADAM'S JOURNAL

Saturday, December 4

Julia and I spoke this morning. I cannot remember half of what was said, but I remember every expression upon her mobile countenance, every intonation of her compelling contralto voice. Her face is thinner. She now arranges her hair so severely that nary a wayward curl can escape, and this loss of freedom seems to have diminished the burnished gold sheen of it. Her complexion too has lost its golden glow. And her wide-set eyes, which I used to find so endlessly fascinating as they changed from gold to green, have dulled into a settled shade of light brown. Even so, I still desire her to the depths of my soul. I had hoped this would no longer be true if ever again I saw her. But to my continued damnation it is. Cursed be a man who is in love with a married woman.

Mood bleak, I left the office immediately thereafter to meet Henry and the Concord undertaker, Mr. Mudge, at the ice house. Jackson came out of his saw mill to unlock the door for us, and the moment we went inside a shiver ran up my spine. This was not a reaction to the freezing temperature but to the sight of Chauncey Bidwell's body lying on the stone floor. Fresh blood smeared Bidwell's face and pooled in his open mouth.

Undertaker Mudge frowned at Undertaker Jackson. "You might have cleaned him up a bit."

"So help me God, I did!" Jackson protested. "There was no blood upon his face when I laid him out over there yesterday." He waved a hand that had but three fingers toward a couple of ice blocks. The layer of sawdust that covered them bore the indentation made by Bidwell's body. "I have seen much in my day, Mr. Mudge. As a sawyer I have seen body parts lost in the whirring blades. As an undertaker I have seen heads stove in by kicking hooves. But I never did see a dead man *move* before."

"He did not move himself," Henry said in a voice far calmer than one I could have mustered.

"I made sure to lock the door when I left him. And I have the only key."

"Well, somebody managed to break in here somehow," I said. "Better go alert the constable, Mr. Jackson. If he's not at his shoe shop he will most likely be at the Sun."

Off Jackson went, leaving us with Mr. Mudge.

"This does not set well with me," he muttered. "It does not set well at all. I have a mind to drive away right now without the body."

"That body, Mr. Mudge, was only yesterday a vital young man," Henry said. "Chauncey Bidwell had a mother and sisters who loved him, and when I informed them of his death last evening, I assured them that he would be brought back to Concord this morning. How will you explain to them your empty wagon?"

"I will tell them that I did not wish to get mixed up in whatever skullduggery is taking place here."

"You will tell them nothing of the sort," Henry said sternly. "They need not know his body was defiled like this."

"Well, *you* can talk to them then. Tell them whatever you please. It is none of my affair." Mudge turned to go.

Henry forestalled him by taking a firm grip of his shoulder. "Consider this, Mr. Mudge. If you leave the body behind, it will raise questions in Concord. Do you wish to make the Bidwell ladies suffer even more by instigating dark rumors concerning Chauncey's death?"

Mudge looked at the corpse and back at Henry. "I knew his father. Not well, but well enough to respect him. The Bidwell hallmark upon the guns he crafted assured their quality, and it would be a shame if rumors concerning his son tarnished his fine name."

"Then you must not abandon this body. We will take it home for proper burial as soon as I sort all this out," Henry said. "And I shall do so in short order, I assure you."

I was relieved when Mudge agreed to stay, but wondered how Henry would be able to keep his promise to him. Things seemed a long way from being sorted out.

Less than ten minutes later Jackson returned with Beers. Unfortunately, he was also accompanied by two tavern denizens, the old cooper and the young carding mill mechanic. Henry and I blocked the ice house door before any could enter.

"This is not a Barnum sideshow, gentlemen," I said. "Only Constable Beers has business here."

"A curious business indeed," the cooper said, stretching his scrawny neck to try and see over my shoulder.

"Is something amiss with the corpse in there?" the mechanic asked. He tried to nudge Henry aside to get a better look, but met with an immovable force.

"Good Day to you both," I said, and firmly shut the door in their faces as soon as Henry pulled the constable inside.

Taking in Bidwell's blood-filled mouth, Beers's own mouth dropped open. For one so fat he has an extremely delicate stomach, and I feared he would vomit. Mercifully, he managed to contain his breakfast and whatever he'd imbibed at the Sun. He swallowed hard and asked, "Whose blood did he drink?"

"The corpse did not drink any person's blood," Henry told him firmly.

Beers nodded as if he understood. "It was demon blood he drank then. The vampyre fed him."

"No!" Henry said. "Can't you comprehend that this is a fraud, constable? All you see here is a stratagem intended to trick you into thinking a vampyre was at work or that the dead man has become one himself."

"Well, which is it?" Beers demanded, only listening to half of what Henry said. "Did a vampyre come into the ice house to feed blood to Bidwell? Or did Bidwell go out and feed on someone else?"

Henry shook his head. "You ask the wrong questions, constable. The only two you should consider in this investigation are these: Was Bidwell's murderer responsible for this bloody piece of mischief to distract you from solving the crime? Or did someone else have reason to stage such a scene? The solution to this mystery revolves around the principle of cui bono."

Beers looked confounded. "Kwee what?"

"A Latin phrase that means to whom does this benefit," Henry explained, ever the teacher. "Who would have something to gain by this vile act?"

"Obviously, a vampyre would," Beers replied.

"The vampyre is the scapegoat!" Henry shouted, losing his limited patience. "The perpetrator is using belief in such creatures to his own advantage."

"Tell me, Mr. Thoreau. Have you ever dealt with a vampyre?" Beers said.

"Of course not. They do not exist."

"You say that only because you have never seen one," Beers said.

"Have you?"

Steeling himself, Beers looked back at Bidwell's body. "I may be seeing one right now."

Henry turned away from Beers, his tolerance for the constable's obstinate obtuseness at an end. He examined the wide loading doors, barred from the inside by a ten-foot-long plank resting on iron brackets. "How else might an intruder get in the ice house?" he asked Jackson.

The sawyer shrugged. "One way or another, I suppose. I ain't too concerned about securing the place. These blocks of ice have been setting in here since last winter, and I never lost a wink of sleep worrying about them. They each weigh a hundred-fifty pounds and are not so easy to steal."

"Then why did you lock the side door?" Henry said.

"I always lock it when I got a body stored in here for burial. Seems the proper thing to do."

Henry looked up at three windows close under the eaves. "Too small and too high for entry," he concluded.

"Not for a bat," Beers said.

Ignoring his remark, Henry left us to walk around the spacious interior, examining the wall boards.

"You'll find no openings between the boards," Jackson called to him in the frosty air. "I make sure to keep this building tight and well insulated to hold in the cold. At a penny a pound, I do not want my inventory to melt away on me."

Henry pointed up at a pair of unbarred bay doors cut into the upper part of a wall. "Where is the ladder to reach those doors, Mr. Jackson?"

"There is none," Jackson said. "Only that chute." He gestured toward a long wooden trough that lay on the floor close to the wall.

"Was the chute set up last night?" Henry said.

"No, it's been there since we used it last winter. We slide blocks of ice down it after they've been lifted up the outside chute to those doors. When the blocks start to pile up we take the inside chute down because it takes up space we need for storage."

"Do you keep that outside chute in position all year?"

"No reason to take that one down."

"So a man could climb up it and push open those doors from the outside to get in here," Henry said.

"Jumping down from up there would most likely result in a broken limb," I said.

"The taller the man, the less risk," Henry said. "I estimate the height from floor to door to be twenty feet. A man six-feet tall could first hang from the door ledge by his hands, giving him an additional two feet of arm length, and then he would only have to drop down twelve feet or so."

"But then how would he leave?" I said. "All the exit doors on this level remain locked or bolted."

"He would leave the same way he came in, of course," Henry said.

"It is one thing to drop down from an entry twenty feet up," I said. "And quite another to go back up to it without a ladder."

"Vampyres employ magic to overcome gravity," Beers said.

"And men employ more practical means," Henry said. "Note the smears of mud ascending the wall. Those are boot marks, I wager. The perpetrator hauled himself up with a rope." Henry carefully examined the floor beneath the bay doors. "Yet for all his athletic maneuvers he did not spill a drop of blood. What sort of vessel did he bring it in, I wonder."

"A corked jar?" I suggested.

"More a risk of breaking that than his own leg," Henry said. "Let us take a look outside."

We all went out and around the building to the mill pond side to regard the narrow chute that slanted up from the water's edge to the bay doors. We were unfortunately joined by the cooper and the mechanic, who had been lingering outside in wait of us.

"When this pond freezes over I employ a crew of fifty men

to cut blocks of ice out of it and then haul 'em up the chute," Jackson boasted.

"Fifty men!" Mudge sounded impressed. "There must be good money to be made in ice."

"More now than ever," Jackson said, "what with the railroad to transport it to Boston so quick. From there some of my ice gets carried by ship all the way to India. I've been told the English who rule there want it to cool their whiskey."

"You don't say?" Mudge regarded Jackson with new respect. "And you own the saw mill too?"

"I do. Get wood for the caskets and sawdust for ice insulation from my mill."

"You sure got it all figured out, Mr. Jackson," Mudge said. "Do you have sons to carry on after you?"

"Only one. Hyram is a hard worker, and he will take over the saw mill and ice business just fine. He sure ain't got what it takes to be an undertaker, though."

Mudge sighed. "Not many do, my friend."

"And to think what little respect we get for it." Jackson sighed too. "Anyways, that corpse in the ice house scared the bejesus out of my son when first he saw it."

"Such an awful neck wound is not easy to behold," Mudge said. "Thoreau told me about it on the way here so I was at least prepared."

"A singular character, that Thoreau feller," Jackson said. "Full of energy and purpose, he is. He knows what he's about."

"Or thinks he does," Beers said.

We all looked toward Henry, who was climbing up the outside chute. When he got up to the top he examined the bay doors most thoroughly, then scrambled back down, nimble as a quadruped. He handed Beers some bits of rope.

"I collected them by the post up top," he said. "What does that tell you, constable?"

Beers took on the attitude of a recalcitrant schoolboy. "Not much."

"Well, it tells me that our perpetrator tied a length of rope around the post, and used it to go down to the ice house floor and come up again," Henry said. "His malicious hoax done, he cut off the rope with a knife rather than take the time to untie it."

"All that deducing from a few shreds of hemp?" Beers rolled his eyes at his drinking cronies who were hovering in the background.

If Henry noticed he gave no sign of it. "Let us search the area for further evidence, Mr. Beers," he said.

Beers reluctantly followed in his wake like a sluggish whale as Henry thrashed about in the bushes along the pond edge. "Aha! I have found the vessel that held the blood, constable," he said, lifting up a headless rat by the tail.

Beers shrank back in disgust. "It looks to me that you have found a very dead rodent."

"One and the same. I know now why no blood was spilt," Henry said. "The rat was brought into the ice house alive, and its head was cut off over the corpse. The flow of blood that resulted filled the corpse's mouth. The perpetrator then pocketed the rat and its severed head, climbed up the rope, went through the doors and down the outside chute. Before going on his way he threw the rat's body where I found it, along with its head."

"But you did not find the head," Beers said, as if this discounted Henry's logical hypothesis.

"I am sure some animal has consumed it by now," Henry said.

Beers gave a noncommittal grunt and started walking off in the direction of his cronies. I waylaid him and asked if we might have a private moment. He reluctantly agreed, and we wandered out of earshot of the others.

"There should be no doubt about it in your mind, Constable Beers," I said in a low voice. "A mortal man is responsible for defacing Bidwell's corpse. Henry has proven that conclusively. And a mortal man slayed Bidwell, as I proved conclusively during my inquest testimony yesterday."

"Did you now? Well, I reckon you think yourself smarter than the rest of us since you got that medical degree, Adam Walker. But I remember you when you were no higher than my belt buckle and didn't know your left shoe from your right."

I could not help but smile for he was correct on that score. "The only point I am trying to make," I said, "is that a vampyre had nothing to do with any of this."

"I have heard as much evidence that one did as didn't," Beers insisted.

"From whom? Solomon Wiley?"

"He is far more familiar with the ways of vampyres than you."

"He is an ignorant fabricator with motives of his own, Mr. Beers. Think upon this. Wiley fits the description of the perpetrator that Henry hypothesized. He is tall, for one thing. And he would benefit if vampyre fear spread through Plumford. Tell no one about the condition in which we found poor Bidwell's body. That is just what Wiley wants!"

"I will do what I see fit," Beers pronounced. Raising his double chins in irate dignity, he waddled off. As he lumbered up the hill toward the Green, he was joined by the cooper and the mechanic. My guess is they were headed back to the Sun Tavern, where Beers would offer up this latest report of the Plumford Night Stalker in exchange for a free drink or two.

The two undertakers, Henry, and I returned to the ice house. The big bottom doors were swung open, and Henry helped Mudge bring in the casket. Before the body was lowered into it Mudge assured Henry that he would make it look presentable for the Bidwell ladies. We all four of us carried the casket outside and slid it onto the back of the hearse wagon, and off Henry and Mudge went to Concord.

"Glad to see the last of that troublesome corpse," Jackson said.

I confess that I was too. We parted and went about our business.

JULIA'S NOTEBOOK

Monday, 6 December

When I came down to breakfast this morning I found a basket of warm muffins on the kitchen table. I thanked Mrs. Swann for rising so early to bake them, but she insisted that it was no trouble at all on her part.

"Has Noah breakfasted yet?" I asked her.

"I have not seen hide nor hair of him," she replied. "My guess is that the lazy boy has not gotten himself out of bed yet."

"Oh, but he has," I said. "I heard him rustle about his room at the crack of dawn and then tramp downstairs."

"Well, who knows where he ran off to then."

"The schoolhouse, I trust."

"Most doubtful," Mrs. Swann said. "That boy cares nothing for learning."

"What he does not care for is being taunted by other children," I conjectured. "I propose we tutor him at home, Mrs. Swann."

"What a waste of our good time that would be! Surely you have observed how slow-witted the boy is."

"Slow of speech but not wits," I countered. "Noah's eyes shine with intelligence whenever he looks at me. Which is rarely, I admit. He is very shy, and who can blame him? We are strangers to him still, and most strangers, I suspect, have not treated him well. We have to win his trust, Mrs. Swann. And in order to do that, we must make sure to be affectionate."

"Indeed!" she agreed and kissed me heartily on the cheek.

I laughed in surprise. "Affectionate toward the boy is what I meant."

"It is in my nature to be affectionate toward *everyone,*" she said.

I was most happy to hear it. Between Mrs. Swann and me Noah will be sure to receive the loving-kindness he deserves and must sorely miss since his parents' passing.

Having nothing to wear but the clothes I'd fled France in, I went up to the attic after breakfast and searched through chests and trunks for possible attire. What a treasure I discovered: a handsome hooded cape of brown wool that belonged to my grandmother. It is sure to keep me warm all winter. Alas, all the other clothes I found were too outmoded to wear in public unless I aspired to be the town laughingstock. That would not have troubled me the least in the past, but now I must be taken seriously as an artist if I hope to make a living by it.

So off I went to Daggett's store to purchase some yard goods with my limited funds. Mrs. Daggett informed me that the town tailor, Micah Lyttle, had recently wed a most capable mantua maker, and I took my bolts of cloth to his shop right next door. His wife was eager to take me on as a customer, assuring me she would sew up what I needed right away. Her name is Kitty, and an apt one it is for she is as adorable as a kitten, with soft ginger hair and a tiny pink nose. She and Micah seem a most compatible pair, both small and lean and nimble-fingered, with bright eyes and eager smiles. Happy, happy. The shop is also their home, sparsely furnished but airy and bright, with plump patchwork cushions all about and colorful, unmatched curtains on the windows, obviously stitched up from left-over fabric snippets. I found the effect of the many hues and textures charming. When I complimented Kitty on her artistic flair I was not surprised to learn she had sewn costumes for the stage before her marriage, first in London and then in Boston. I commissioned her to make me two simple gowns of wool challis, a painting apron of cotton duck, and three muslin blouses. (Would have preferred silk, but budget does not allow for it.) She took me into the bedchamber to measure me in privacy, leaving Micah to his work in the parlor. I could hear him whistling a jolly tune as he cut out a garment, and the caged canary in the bedchamber chirped away as if to accompany him.

"What a cheerful work environment you have," I remarked.

"Oh, yes, Micah and I are very happy here!" Kitty said and then looked slightly abashed. "I do not mean to boast of our happiness when so many have suffered during this horrible Consumption epidemic. We pray every evening that it shall soon pass."

"And the fear of vampyres with it," I said. "Have you ever heard such superstition?"

"Indeed I have," Kitty said. "In the English village I come from, stories concerning the walking dead have been passed down since medieval times. They are referred to as revenants, however, not vampyres. When a revenant returns from the dead to feed on family and neighbors, the only way to stop it is to cut out its heart."

I sighed. "Always the heart."

"Well, that is where the spirit resides, is it not?" Kitty said.

"Surely you do not give credence to these stories of revenants or vampyres or whatever you want to call them, Kitty."

"No. But I do believe the very essence of our humanity is centered here." She placed her little hand over her own heart.

I smiled back at her. "As I do."

Witnessing the happiness Mr. and Mrs. Lyttle shared had

lifted my spirits, and I hummed the tune Micah had been whistling as I made my way home. My spirits rose even higher when I found Adam seated at the kitchen table playing checkers with Noah.

"He is trouncing me!" Adam said, and Noah laughed with glee. His speech may be garbled, but his laugh is as clear as a silver bell.

I refrained from asking Noah why he was not attending school. We shall sort that out later. Meanwhile, his time could not be better spent than in Adam's company. I had never seen Noah look so happy. Yet when Adam made mention that he would be going to Concord this afternoon to pick up medical supplies at the train depot and invited Noah to ride there with him, the boy refused.

"Have you something better to do?" Adam said.

Noah shook his head.

"Do you dislike Napoleon?" Adam said.

Noah shook his head again.

"Ah, then it is my company you find objectionable," Adam teased.

Noah shook his head most vehemently, close to tears that Adam would think so.

"The boy is shy," I said. "He does not care to have strangers stare at him."

Noah nodded.

"But I will safeguard you," Adam assured him. "No one at the station will make you feel uncomfortable in any way."

Noah gave him a disbelieving look.

"The more you get out, the more used to people you will become," Adam said.

"No!" Noah cried most emphatically and ran out of the room.

"I did not mean to upset him so," Adam told me. He looked almost as stricken as Noah. "I was trying to be kind."

"You *are* kind," I assured him (even though he had not been so to me of late).

"I have yet to learn how best to treat the boy," he said.

"If Noah does not wish to go out in public, I suppose you should leave him be."

"Leave him to go through life as a hermit?"

"Perhaps that is the only way he feels he can survive."

Adam got up from the table with a most determined look upon his visage. "If I can find a way to correct his deformity, I will."

"I have been hoping you might help him."

"I can promise nothing, Julia." With that, he started to head for his office.

"Would you mind taking me along to Concord instead of Noah?" I called after him. He turned to me, and the look on his face told me he minded very much. I did not let that dissuade me. "I would like to return a shawl Mrs. Emerson kindly lent me and perhaps have a short visit with her."

"Very well. Let us set off at two," he replied.

It is now eleven. I am counting the minutes. I own that I look forward to the short ride alone with him far more than I should.

ADAM'S JOURNAL

Monday, December 6

D rove to Concord this afternoon with Julia. She wanted to visit Lidian Emerson, and I could hardly refuse her request for a ride. Henry was standing in front of the Emerson house when we arrived, fixing the sagging fence gate. He was wearing a black armband on his jacket, and I guessed he had attended Chauncey Bidwell's burial earlier. Before I could inquire about it, Mr. Mudge pulled up in his empty hearse wagon.

"More trouble concerning the Bidwell body," he proclaimed without preamble.

"What happened?" Henry said. "When I left the cemetery less than an hour ago, I thought both his body and any trouble concerning it had been put to rest."

"So I thought too," Mudge said. "But after the mourners left and the gravediggers finished filling in the grave, a stranger approached the Bidwell ladies and me as we were arranging wreaths upon the mound. He asserted most severely that Chauncey's body would *never* be at rest unless certain measures were taken."

"Solomon Wiley," Henry said.

"That's who he said he was, all right. He told Mrs. Bidwell that her son had been killed by a vampyre and would become one himself unless his body were dug up and decapitated. He offered to perform this grisly ritual for a hundred dollars, a cheap enough price to pay, as he put it, to save her son's soul. In response to this outrageous claim, one of the daughters took up a shovel left behind by a gravedigger and struck Wiley upon the chest with it. He did not so much as blink. He merely repeated his offer, adding that if Mrs. Bidwell did not accept it she would forever regret it. So would all the townspeople her vampyre son attacked, he added. Leaving us with that dire warning, he marched out of the cemetery. I drove the poor, distraught ladies home and could think of nothing more I could do but come tell you, Henry. My duties as an undertaker ended when young Bidwell was buried. You can take up the matter from here if you are so inclined to. I am not." And with that Mr. Mudge drove away.

Henry turned to me. "Will you accompany me to the Bidwell home, Adam? As the medical examiner who officially pronounced Chauncey dead, your presence will do much to reassure the ladies."

Leaving Julia to visit with Mrs. Emerson, off we went to the Bidwells' house in the hub of Concord. A gaunt young woman opened the door to us. Her sad, red-rimmed eyes brightened considerably at the sight of Henry.

"Mr. Mudge told us what just happened at the cemetery, Varina," he said. "We have come to be of help." He introduced me, and when I took her hand I noted how ice-cold and bone-thin it was.

Varina ushered us into the chilly parlor, where another youngish woman sat by the empty hearth doing some sort of handiwork. An elderly woman reclined on the sofa and with great effort sat up to greet us. Henry introduced me to Mrs. Bidwell and her other daughter, Zenobia. Their hands, too, when I took them, felt cold and skeletal.

"Pray be seated," Mrs. Bidwell said and motioned us toward two straight-backed chairs across from her. "Varina dear, pray go prepare a nice pot of tea for our guests."

"We have no tea, Mother."

Mrs. Bidwell acted surprised to hear it. "Why, we must have just run out of it!"

"Don't drink tea anyway," Henry said.

No other refreshments were offered, nor was it suggested that a fire be lit. Varina took a chair beside her sister's and picked up handiwork of her own. They were both some years past the customary age to wed and not nearly as comely as their dead brother had been handsome. Of course, tears and grief do not put a lady's face at its best. And I am sure their heavy black mourning gowns made them look even paler and plainer than they were. I observed that the handcraft they were both doing was not how ladies usually kept their dainty hands busy. In fact, plaiting strips of imported palm leaf into hats was work farm girls did to earn money. Harriet had taken it up for a time, but Gran did not like to see her doing such piece work. She thought it akin to factory work and beneath her ward's station. Harriet herself concluded that the meager payment of twenty cents a hat was not worth her effort. Apparently the Bidwell sisters were not of the same opinion. During the conversation that ensued they never stopped plaiting, and I detected abrasions upon their forefingers and thumbs from the narrow lengths of stiff, split leaves.

"Henry and Dr. Walker have heard about the horrible man who accosted us at Chauncey's grave, Mother," Varina said.

"We know him," I said. "Solomon Wiley has caused much distress in Plumford with his wild talk of vampyres."

"Do people there believe such talk?" Mrs. Bidwell said.

"My town is in the midst of a Consumption epidemic that has brought forth notions that would be considered insane during normal times," I said. "Vampyres are being blamed for many recent deaths."

Mrs. Bidwell clutched her hands to her breast. "Including our dear Chauncey's death?"

"At the inquest I declared him to have been murdered by mortal hands," I replied, not answering her directly. "And that was the verdict of the Coroner's Jury."

"Yet some still allege he was murdered by a vampyre?" Mrs. Bidwell persisted.

"Solomon Wiley instigated that rumor," Henry said. "And now he is trying to extort money from you to put an end to it."

"Even if I had a hundred dollars I would not pay that vile man to disinter and defile our dear Chauncey!" she said.

"What if he does so anyway out of spite?" Varina said. "He might get enough people to believe his wild story. Vampyre fear is spreading throughout the region."

"Nothing is so much to be feared as fear," Henry said. "And the only way to combat fear is with the truth. When Chauncey's real murderer is discovered, it will put an end to this obscene rumor. Time is of the essence, and Dr. Walker and I shall begin an investigation immediately."

That was news to me, and I gave Henry an astonished look.

Mrs. Bidwell gave him one filled with gratitude. "My husband always claimed that you were a man to be counted upon, Henry." She turned to her daughters. "Remember how your father would oft advise our Chauncey to be self-reliant like Henry Thoreau?"

"Indeed!" Zenobia said. "And Chauncey would laugh and say he did not fancy living like an impoverished monk in a cabin no bigger than a hat."

"Really, Zenobia. Such banter is not worth repeating," Varina reprimanded.

Her sister bowed her head. "I meant no offence to you, Henry."

"I took none," he said. "As I recall, Chauncey made sport of everything and everyone."

"It was part of his charm," Mrs. Bidwell said. "He could never have lived alone as you did on Walden Pond, Henry. He was far too fond of society."

"And luxury," Varina added a bit wryly.

"It was our pleasure to provide him with whatever little indulgences we could afford," Mrs. Bidwell said. "He was our joy, our pride, and the light of our lives."

"I recall Mr. Bidwell's telling me that he hoped his only son would take over his business one day," Henry said.

Mrs. Bidwell sighed. "Chauncey had no inclination to learn the craft of gunsmithing from his father. He felt he was destined for a profession rather than a trade."

"My brother had too fine a mind to spend his time working with his hands," Zenobia said, her own hands never ceasing the work of braiding palm leaves.

"He aspired to be a lawyer," Varina said. "He was apprenticing at the Boston law firm of Curtis, Hayden, and Lardner and, according to Chauncey, all three partners thought he had a brilliant legal mind."

"We need not tell Mr. Thoreau how brilliant our Chauncey was," Mrs. Bidwell said. "He knows from having taught him as a boy."

"He must have been your favorite student," Zenobia said to Henry. She did not seem to notice his lack of a response and went on talking. "Oh, what a lovely boy he was! All those golden curls."

"And what a handsome young man he became," her sister said. "Young ladies found him irresistible."

"Did he have a special sweetheart?" I asked.

"No girl could be special enough for our Chauncey," Zenobia said.

"Our hope was that he would marry well," Mrs. Bidwell

said. "Chauncey hoped so too. When he attended balls and tea drinkings and such in Boston, he made sure to put forth his best appearance."

"He had such beautiful shirts and frock coats!" Zenobia said, unconsciously touching a roughened fingertip to the frayed collar of her dress. "Only the best tailors in Boston would do for Chauncey."

"Was he in debt?" Henry said.

"Well, what young man just starting out isn't?" Mrs. Bidwell said. "We did our best to help him out."

"Help him out of trouble, you mean?"

"No! My son was not the sort to get into trouble. He did not drink spirits or gamble or indulge in *any* bad habits, but living in the city is expensive, especially if one aspires to associate with those in the higher echelons, which Chauncey did."

"It wasn't that he was a snob," Zenobia quickly added. "He was just ambitious."

"Ambitious young men sometimes have enemies," I said.

"Not Chauncey!" Mrs. Bidwell said. "To know him was to love him."

"Yet somebody murdered him," Henry said.

"It must have been a stranger," Mrs. Bidwell insisted. "A cutthroat thief who waylaid him on that dark path." Tears began to flow down her haggard cheeks. "What was he doing there, I wonder?"

"I was hoping you could tell us," Henry said. "Whom did Chauncey know in Plumford?"

"Wasn't there a girl from there he rather liked?" Varina asked Zenobia.

"From Plumford? No, I thought the one he met at the Grange dance last summer resided in Bedford. Or was it Maynard? Well, wherever it was, he lost interest in her months ago. Leastways, he never mentioned her to us again."

"He thought he had all the time in the world to find a

mate and settle down," Varina said and started weeping along with her mother. As did her sister.

I am used to seeing women weep. What doctor is not? But Henry could not bear it. He stood up abruptly, and I thought he was making ready to leave, but instead he asked Mrs. Bidwell if we might examine Chauncey's room, in hopes of finding some clews that would further our investigation. She assented and directed us upstairs to the first room on the left.

Its contents were unremarkable but for the splendor of the dead man's clothes and shoes, which the sisters had alluded to. Henry took no interest in them and directed his attention to several legal texts on the desk. The pages had not yet been cut, much less the spines cracked. We continued to search about, looking for nothing in particular. And finding nothing of particular interest, either, until Henry discovered a large-bored fowling piece deep in a closet.

"Crafted by his father," he said, examining the stock. "Why would Chauncey want to hide it?" He raised the gun to his shoulder. "Something is amiss here. The balance is too far forward."

He lowered the gun, peered down into the barrels, then turned the muzzle downward and tapped it on the floor. A red silk purse fell out of one of the barrels. Henry untied it and upended it over the desk. Ten pea-sized dark brown balls slid out.

"Amber beads?" Henry guessed.

"I think not," I said, picking up a ball and rolling the small, malleable mass betwixt my forefinger and thumb. I gave it a sniff. "I believe this to be opium. We were shown the drug in all forms at medical school. I doubt any legitimate apothecary would sell opium in such a concentrated form as this, however. These pills were not produced for medicinal purposes but to be smoked in a pipe for recreation. The habit is highly addictive."

Henry carefully returned the pills to the silk purse and tucked the purse into his jacket pocket. He saw my frown and smiled. "You think me a thief and drug smuggler, Adam? Well, so I am. I must remove this opium to prevent Mrs. Bidwell from chancing upon it. Did she not just tell us that her beloved son had no bad habits? Why disabuse the poor lady of that belief?"

"Those pills may be worth a goodly sum," I said.

"Then I reckon we should try to sell them and give the money we receive for them to Mrs. Bidwell. Looks to me she could use it. With the loss of her husband's income, the dear lady seems very hard up indeed. The parlor has not a decoration or bauble in sight, and I know how fond ladies are of such things, so I wager she has been selling off whatever she can to make ends meet. Worse yet, a glance out the window showed me that the woodshed is already empty, and it is but the first week of December."

"Yet Chauncey had money enough to purchase opium for himself," I said.

"For himself? Or was he peddling it to others at a profit?" Henry said. "That could be why he was murdered. We must find out more about his life in Boston."

We returned to the parlor, and Varina composed herself to see us out. As she led us down the hall I glanced into an adjoining room, where I saw piles of split palm leaves and high stacks of completed woven hats. It was small wonder the fingers of the two sisters were so raw. They were literally working them to the bone.

Before we departed Henry asked Varina if the two keys, the ivory comb, and the wallet that he had found upon Chauncey's person had been returned to them. She assured him that they had.

"Is either of the keys to your house?" he asked her.

"No. We assumed the larger key was to the front door of the house where he boarded in Boston, and the smaller one was to his room."

"May I have them?" Henry said. "It may prove useful to inspect his living quarters there."

Varina went back inside to fetch the keys and gave them to Henry, along with Chauncey's boardinghouse address on Oxford Street.

"One last question, if you please, Varina," Henry said. "Who was it whacked Solomon Wiley with a shovel at the cemetery?"

"It was I!" she declared, chin up, shoulders back. "And I have no regrets about it."

"Nor should you," Henry said and gave her a brief but hearty hug in parting.

Drove back to the Emerson house, gulped down a glass of Mrs. Emerson's god-awful beer, departed with Julia, and stopped at the station to pick up my delivery of medications. By then it was late afternoon.

"Will we make it home before sunset?" Julia said, gazing up at the darkening sky as we trotted toward Plumford.

"Are you such a silly goose as to fear coming upon the Plumford Night Stalker?" I teased.

She turned to me, and her lovely oval face, so pale beneath the hood of her dark cape, seemed to be floating in space like a vision from my dreams. But the poke in the arm she gave me proved she was real enough. "Silly goose indeed! Was I not your fearless chum when we were children?"

"Fearless enough, I suppose, for a female."

"For a female?" She poked me again. "My sex did not limit my bravery. And you regarded me as your equal in those days." She sighed. "Sometimes I wish we had never met again as adults, Adam. We would most likely both be much happier now."

"No, Julia. We would be much happier now if you hadn't left me," I could not help but point out.

"How can you say that? Think of the consequences, cousin."

I was sorely tempted to tell her the truth then. But what good would it have done either of us? So I said no more, and the soft clop of Napoleon's hooves filled the silence until the piercing sound of children screaming pricked our ears.

"That does not sound like children at play," Julia said.

Agreeing, I nudged Napoleon to go faster toward the Gray farm just ahead. We pulled into the farmyard to find the three shrieking Gray children grouped around their wailing mother, who was kneeling by their supine father. Grabbed my bag, leapt out of the gig, and ran to them. Saw immediately that Mr. Gray had sunk his broad ax into his thigh. He was bleeding so profusely that I feared the blade had struck through the femoral artery. Thank God this was not the case or he would have died from exsanguination in a matter of moments. He was lying beside the log he had nigh squared up. He must have struck a knot or lost control just enough for the ax to glance up and penetrate his thigh. The strapping young fellow was hardly conscious. His pant leg was soaked through with blood from cuff to crotch.

I threw off my frock coat and vest, took off my belt, and wrapped it about the leg above the wound. "Keep a taut hold on it whilst I draw out the ax blade," I told Mrs. Gray, and in that moment her eyes rolled back and she fainted. "Julia!" I called out, not realizing she was already right there, having run after me. She knelt down and took hold of the belt.

I pulled the broad ax blade out of Gray's thigh, using a great deal of force but as much care as I could. It came out slick and clean, but was accompanied by a rush of blood. I yanked off my shirt and pressed it against the wound to staunch the flow. Julia stepped out of her petticoat and commenced tearing it into strips. We wrapped them tightly around my shirt to keep it in place over the injury.

"I need to operate on him," I told Julia. "Are you strong enough to help me carry him to the house?"

"Of course I am," she said, and lost no time picking up his feet.

"Keep him steady," I said, as I took up his torso. We staggered up to the farmhouse, the oldest child, a girl about ten, following behind with my bag. Thankfully, she had stopped screaming. The other two children stayed by their prostrate mother, patting her hands and face.

A fire burned in the kitchen hearth. We heaved Gray onto the big table in front of it. "Is there any whiskey in the house?" I asked the girl.

She gave me a most disapproving look and pointed to a jug on a high shelf. Julia had to stand on a chair to reach it. She found a pan to soak my instruments in the whiskey, and I doused Gray's wound with it too, after removing the makeshift bandages and slitting away his pant leg. Although the ax head had fortunately missed the main femoral artery, the descending branch of that artery was sliced open and pumping out a copious amount of blood.

"Bring me honey if you have it," I told the girl. Again she scowled at me, but went and fetched a pot of honey.

"If we are going to save him," I said to Julia, "we must work quickly."

"Tell me how to help you and I will do it," she said, taking off her cloak and rolling up her sleeves. Her calmness did not surprise me. We had worked together to save a life once before, and she had proven to be a woman who was not afraid of blood.

Turned Gray on his left side to better get at the wound and instructed Julia to thread a fine needle with a length of silk from my bag. She then held the wound open for me, and blood pulsed out in a thin spray onto her cheek. Took a serrated forceps and clamped it down on the artery above the slice, then slowly and with care stitched the tissue walls of the slippery artery back together. Removed the forceps, and blood began to flow through the artery again instead of pulsing out. By this time Gray had lost consciousness completely, and for this I was glad, for the next step would be most unpleasant. Told the girl to heat up a poker and then leave the kitchen. Held the white-hot poker to the wound area to cauterize the exposed tissue. The sound of hissing flesh and the smell of burning blood rolled up around Julia and me. 'Twas a frightening stink. Threw the poker aside and splashed whiskey with a generous hand over all of my work.

Gray came back to consciousness and began to moan and shift. Told him in a loud voice that I was fixing him and he must lie still. Julia brought the whiskey to his lips and poured in a good mouthful, meanwhile murmuring soothing words. Her female voice quieted him more, I think, than the whiskey.

Sewed up the gaping wound with catgut and my thickest curved needle as Julia held the sliced flesh together with both hands. Tied off and knotted every other stitch to give the repair more chance of holding. Worked from groin toward knee and left an inch open at the lowest point of the wound for pus and fluid to drain.

The sewing took but a few minutes, twenty stitches in all. Triple folded a piece of cotton petticoat, soaked it with honey, placed it atop the sewn gash, and kept it in place by winding more petticoat fabric, ripped into strips, around Gray's leg.

"Thank you for the use of your unmentionables," I told Julia.

"Do not mention it." She smiled at me. Gray's blood had crusted around her mouth and nose, and I had a fleeting fancy that she looked like a beautiful, irresistible vampyre that I would gladly allow to suck me dry. Glanced away from her and spotted Gray's wife standing in the doorway.

"Is he dead?" she asked in a quivering voice.

"Just drunk," I replied. "Your husband will survive, Mrs. Gray. As severe as the ax cut was, his nerves and ligaments as well as major arteries and veins remain intact."

She rushed forward and bestowed a tender kiss upon her

husband's sleeping face. Fortunately, the kitchen also serves as the Grays' sleeping chamber, and it was easy enough to settle the injured man in his bed. Mrs. Gray asked what I charged for my services. Told her we could discuss that later. The Grays do not seem to have a penny to spare, and if I had quoted my standard Boston rate for such a surgery, she might have fainted on me again. She insisted on giving me Mr. Gray's best Sunday shirt to wear home, for my own was blood-soaked, and as far as I'm concerned that is payment enough.

We set off in the dark, and Julia leaned into me for warmth, placing her head on my shoulder. I did not object.

"How good you must feel right now, Adam," she said in a low voice.

"Oh, I own it feels good to have you pressing against me," I replied rather gruffly.

"You mistake my meaning, cousin," she said, but did not pull away. "I was referring to the sense of satisfaction you must feel after saving a life."

"A successful surgery does give me great satisfaction," I allowed. "Of late, I have felt myself useless as a doctor."

"Useless? What would Plumford do without you during this epidemic?"

"All I can offer most of my patients is comfort, along with laudanum to ease their pain, Julia. Old-fashioned methods such as bleeding only weaken consumptives more, and the latest medications may be just as harmful. Doctors have been dosing patients with medicines containing prussic acid or creosote, for instance. Even boa constrictor excreta!"

"Surely you are jesting about the boa constrictor."

"I wish I were. And it is a very expensive treatment indeed. Another treatment I have heard of is less exotic and far cheaper. A doctor in Vermont has been rubbing *lard* into the bodies of his Consumption patients. Why? He has observed that butchers seem immune to the disease."

"Now I have heard everything," she said.

"Not quite." Although frank discussions concerning medical procedures are not considered fit for the shell-like ears of delicate females, I have never hesitated to talk about such procedures with Julia. And I did not hesitate now. "Hark this, Julia. A highly lauded doctor in New Haven uses coal gas to ease congested breathing in consumptives. He pumps this vile gas into the rectums of his unfortunate patients, claiming it works its way into the lungs to good effect."

"Well, I am not a learned doctor, of course," Julia said, "but I always thought vile gas was meant to exit the rectum, not enter it."

Vulgar humor such as that had much delighted us as children, and I confess it still did, for we laughed all the rest of the way to Plumford. Our only excuse was that we were both exhausted. I left Julia off at the house and continued alone to Tuttle Farm, greatly missing her company. How easily we still work together, talk together, laugh together. Yet what does any of that matter when we cannot *be* together as man and wife? That is entirely Julia's fault, and I cannot find it in my heart to forgive her. Doubt I ever will.

JULIA'S NOTEBOOK

Monday eve, 6 December

A young farmer would have surely bled to death this after-noon if Adam had not come along in time to sew up his slashed artery. I assisted him as best I could. After the operation the farmer's wife brought us a basin of warm water to wash off the blood, and I am ashamed to admit I forgot all about the poor, injured man then asleep in his bed as I stole glances at Adam. He was bare chested, having used his shirt as a compress for the wound, and I could not help but admire how well-muscled and broad-shouldered he has become since last I saw his naked torso when he was a lanky lad of twelve. If the farmer's wife and three children had not been right there in the kitchen observing our every move, I might well have pressed my cheek against his nakedness. Better yet, my lips. Wanton woman! Has my experience as Jacques Pelletier's wife corrupted me entirely? Did I not vow a life of chastity upon leaving him? My base human nature is wayward indeed.

If only I could be as pure-spirited as dear Lidian Emerson. How ethereal and innocent of heart she does seem. And yet . . . there is something simmering beneath her cool, serene surface. Perhaps I am not the best judge of people, having been fooled far too often by men, but I do think I know something about my own sex. And what I know about Lidian is that she is far deeper and more complicated than she lets on.

When I visited her today I caught her in the midst of brewing beer. "I raise the hops and celandine myself," she told me. "And Henry kindly collects the pyrola in the woods for me."

I apologized for intruding, but Lidian insisted that I had come at a perfect time for she had just put aside a pot of wort to cool. She whipped off her apron and ushered me into her parlor. It is a neat, handsome room, the walls covered in cream-colored paper with a crimson border, the floor overlaid with a red and yellow carpet, and the windows curtained with buff cambric. The bookcase and tables are of rosewood, and the chairs and sofa are upholstered in red moreen. A print of Correggio's *Madonna* hangs on the wall, handsomely framed. Lidian flitted about the room, minutely adjusting the position of various ornaments. After she had repositioned a vase to the very center of the card table and nudged two candlesticks directly over the pilasters of the fireplace mantel, she finally sank down beside me on the sofa.

"Much better!" she said in a relieved tone. "Lisette dusted in here this morning, and she always puts things back wrong. I cannot seem to make her comprehend that any decorative object becomes mere litter when it stands an inch or two out of position. I suppose most people would not even notice, but I have a carpenter's eye and cannot bear to see anything even a hairsbreadth off. I venture you share this sensibility, Mrs. Pelletier. Henry told me you were an artist. Your desire for visual harmony must be most acute."

"I desire it on the canvas but not necessarily in my surroundings," I said. "Painting is a messy business, Mrs. Emerson, and I fear you would find the disorder in my workplace quite shocking."

She laughed. "Oh, I am not so easily shocked as all that. I think I would much enjoy visiting your artist's studio."

"It would be presumptuous of me to call the place where I have recently set up my easel a studio," I said. "It served as my late grandfather's study, and I have not had the heart to move out all his clutter. Instead, I have simply added to it. But you are most welcome to visit me in Plumford any time."

As Mrs. Emerson was thanking me for the invitation, her little boy, called Eddy, scampered into the room. After him, the aforementioned Lisette clomped in, a heavy-set, elderly woman rather than the lively little maiden I had imagined from her name. Lisette added another log to the fire and inquired if we wanted tea.

"Or perhaps you'd prefer a glass of the currant wine I made this fall?" Mrs. Emerson asked me.

"I would indeed!" I said, surprised and delighted by the offer.

Lisette returned shortly with a tray holding three small crystal glasses of wine, and for a moment I thought one was for the boy, who could not have been more than three. But no, it was for Lisette herself. She plucked it up, plopped herself into a chair with a groan, and complained that her bunions were acting up.

"Oh, dear, not again. Poor Lisette," Mrs. Emerson said with the most sympathetic of smiles. "I was going to impose upon you to bring us some crackers, but I will go fetch them myself." And up she sprang, lithe as a girl, to do just that.

Lisette quaffed her wine in one gulp and then silently regarded me. "Are you related to Mrs. Emerson?" I inquired, attempting a bit of conversation.

Lisette gave me a puzzled look. "No. Why think us kin?"

"Well, Mrs. Emerson treats you so kindly."

"Oh, that she does. But she treats *everyone* kindly, don't she? 'Specially young Mr. Thoreau. He ain't her kin neither. What he is to her I cannot say. He works the property 'longside my husband Antoine, but he ain't hired help like us. We sleep out yonder in the barn, but young Thoreau sleeps right here in the house with the missus. I do not mean to say he sleeps in her room." She leaned toward me and lowered her voice. "Leastways, I have found no sign so far that he shares her bed."

I glared at her. "Yet you dare insinuate it."

"I'd as soon cut out my tongue as say a word against the wife of Mr. Emerson," she replied huffily. "Such a fine gentleman! He employed us right afore he set sail for Europe and asked us to take good care of his lady and children. I reckon he asked the same of young Thoreau."

At that point Mrs. Emerson returned to the room and must have overheard Lisette's last remark. "Who asked what of Mr. Thoreau?" she inquired in a sharper tone than usual.

"Your husband, ma'am," Lisette replied meekly. "To look after his dear family."

Without commenting, Mrs. Emerson turned to me and proffered a platter of crackers. I took one, but Lisette did not. And Eddy shook his head most vehemently when his mamma waved the platter in front of him. Since children are always greedy for treats that surprised me—until I bit into my cracker. Dry as sand and just as tasty.

"I made them myself from buckwheat flour," Mrs. Emerson told me proudly. "I should be most happy to give you the recipe."

"I am not much of a cook," I demurred.

"Neither was I until I married. Indeed, for the first thirty-three years of my life I rarely entered a kitchen. But now I could get around one blindfolded. Is that not so, Lisette?"

"Yes, ma'am. When you are in the kitchen, you might as well be blind."

Mrs. Emerson continued without missing a beat. "Henry sowed our back property with buckwheat last spring, and it yielded a fine crop. Hence I use buckwheat flour for most everything, from muffins to johnnycakes. Even puddings! I consider it most healthful for the children." Eddy scrunched up his face, and Mrs. Emerson laughed. "The children say my pudding tastes like the roof of a house, but how, pray, would they know what a house roof tastes like?" She ruffled her son's silky hair.

I took a sip of wine to help wash down the cracker. It might as well have been vinegar. No doubt that was why Lisette had downed hers like medicine. I promptly drained my own tiny glass, much relieved to be done with it.

Mrs. Emerson observed me with her benevolent smile. "I fear the currants this year were a trifle tart. Do you find the wine so?"

"Not at all," I said, making a great effort to keep my mouth from puckering.

"Would you like another glass? I'll fetch the decanter."

"No, no, one glass is sufficient. I am sure it shall keep me warm all the way back to Plumford."

"You be from *Plumford?*" Lisette's eyes widened. "Why, that is where the vampyre stalks!"

"There are no such things as vampyres, Lisette," Mrs. Emerson said gently.

"There are and always have been!"

"Have you ever seen one?"

"No, but few have. Vampyres shun the sun and only come alive during the night."

"Then I may well be a vampyre myself," Mrs. Emerson told her. "I too shun the sun. You have often seen me close the shutters against the glare of it through the windows, have you not, Lisette?" The old woman nodded. "Indeed, I am greatly relieved at sunset and feel my best at midnight," Mrs. Emerson continued. "I am also inordinately pale. You yourself have remarked upon it, Lisette. And have you not noticed my fangs?" Mrs. Emerson smiled without showing her teeth.

Lisette did not smile back. "As sure as I am that you are not a vampyre, ma'am, I am sure one roams in Plumford. I'd not set foot in that town any sooner than I'd set foot in hell. That young man from Concord should have stayed away too. 'Course he was on the road to hell anyways, along with that Plumford gal he took carnal pleasure with. She lured him there sure as she was the vampyre's helper."

"Lisette, enough foolish talk," Mrs. Emerson said.

"Foolish is it? Well, I seen the two of 'em carrying on with my own eyes last summer at the Grange dance. I was hired to serve the wine, so I well know how much the Plumford miss imbibed afore that fop Bidwell dragged her off to a dark corner to canoodle. I do not care to speak ill of the dead, but he was not to be trusted with foolish young ladies. Even got one in the family way, I hear tell, and—"

"I do not countenance gossip," Mrs. Emerson interrupted. "Best you go about your household business if you have nothing of more consequence to say." Apparently Lisette did not, for off she did go most speedily, despite her sore bunions.

"You are very tolerant of her," I remarked.

Mrs. Emerson sighed. "Lisette comes from up Canada and is not accustomed to our discreet ways. Pay her prattle no mind. I for certain do not."

"Gossipers can be treacherous," I said most emphatically. "Especially if they talk about those who employ them." I gave Mrs. Emerson a steady look and waited for her to pick up on this hint.

She did not. "I wish my two girls were here to enjoy your company, Mrs. Pelletier," she said. "They go to the Alcotts' house every afternoon to be tutored by the eldest daughter, Anna. They had their own governess until Miss Foord left our household in September, as did my excellent housekeeper, Mrs. Goodwin. I would be quite alone and without help dur-

ing my husband's long absence if not for Henry. And Lisette
and Antoine of course. But they are strangers to me and reside
in rooms above the barn."

"So Lisette mentioned to me. And more."

"More?"

"She made a point of telling me that Henry sleeps here in
the house." There! I waited for Mrs. Emerson's reaction.

Raising her long chin, she returned my look with unwa-
vering eyes. "Yes, Henry has the room at the top of the stairs,
and there he shall remain for as long as he chooses. Since I
have never paid any mind to gossip about others, I see no reason to mind gossip about me, either. I trust my friends will also
disregard it."

That made me like her even more. "May I be considered
your friend?" I said.

"Done!" She took up my hand and pressed it between her
cool palms to settle the matter.

Thenceforth we addressed each other by our Christian names
and chatted most amiably until Adam and Henry returned. Lidian
persuaded Adam to have a glass of her home-brewed beer before
we departed, and from his expression I surmise it tasted as bitter as
her wine.

Less than ten minutes into our journey back to Plumford
we came upon the badly injured farmer. Hence, I had no opportunity to question Adam about what transpired during his
visit with the Bidwell ladies. Perhaps I can find out more from
him tomorrow. It *seems* we are on better terms now.

ADAM'S JOURNAL

Tuesday, December 7

Henry and I took the milk train to Boston this morning and went directly to Bidwell's Oxford Street boarding-house. We let ourselves in when our knocks on the front door went unheard due to the deafening clamor emanating from the dining room. We found there a dozen or so young men seated at a long table, and although they appeared from their attire to be aspiring professionals of one type or another, I must say they were behaving more like pigs at a trough. The strong-armed serving girl could barely keep up with their demand for *more* of everything. As quick as heaping platters of corn bread, grits, boiled eggs, fried potatoes, sausage, bacon, pork steak, codfish, and salmon were brought out from the kitchen and laid upon the table, hands reached out to grab and push other hands aside. But the men were cheerful enough as they jostled each other, all the time chewing and talking at breakneck speed.

This spirited mayhem was presided over by a stout, beady-eyed woman of middle age standing at the head of the table. She wore a formidable frown under her frilled cap and brandished a long wooden serving spoon that she looked ready to crack upon the knuckles of any who overstepped whatever loose rules of dining etiquette there were. She gave us an appraising glance and then walked over to where we stood at the door.

"I am Mrs. Barker, proprietor. If you young gentlemen are in want of breakfast, you will have to wait for a seat and make do with whatever is left over after my boarders get through stuffing themselves. I will charge you accordingly, of course. If you are in want of a room, I have one available. It is rather small for two, but again, I will charge you accordingly."

"What we are in want of, Mrs. Barker," Henry said, "is information regarding a boarder of yours, namely Chauncey Bidwell."

Her tiny eyes narrowed. "You do not look like coppers to me."

"Nor are we," I said. "My name is Walker, and I am a doctor. This is Mr. Thoreau and he is a . . ." My mind searched for a way to introduce him. Teacher? Surveyor? Carpenter? Pencil-maker? I was about to settle on writer, albeit an unpublished one, but Henry finished my sentence for me.

"A friend of the Bidwell family," he said.

"And has Chauncey's family sent you to pay his back rent?" When Henry shook his head, she folded her arms and looked even crosser. "He owes me for a month's room and board, and since I ain't seen hide nor hair of the rascal for the last week, I reckon he has run off and left me high and dry. Indeed, it was *his* room I was offering you."

"He did not run off on you," Henry told her. "But neither will he be coming back."

"You speak in riddles," she said.

He ushered her away from the boisterous dining room and out into the hallway, where he told her the circumstances of Bidwell's demise.

"Poor scalawag," she said and looked sincerely sorrowful. "What is his family's address?"

"Do you wish to send them a letter of condolence?" I asked.

Her face hardened again. "I wish to send them a bill!"

"Pray do not trouble them," Henry said. "They are in deep mourning and have no money to spare."

"Then I shall sell whatever Chauncey left behind in his room."

"Let us see what there is to buy," I said.

She led us up to the third floor and stopped before Bidwell's locked door. Henry tried the smaller key Bidwell's sister had given us. It fit the lock. He showed Mrs. Barker the larger key, but she did not recognize it.

There was not space enough in Chauncey's small room for the three of us, so Mrs. Barker lingered in the hall, her small, bright eyes watching our every move as we searched. Beneath the bed we found a pair of well-made, polished shoes and a box containing three spotless white collars and two cravats of high quality. A very fine woolen frock coat hung on a peg, along with a red satin waistcoat and a pair of striped trousers.

We continued to search the room. In the desk drawer all we found were playbills and ticket stubs from the Howard Theater. We proceeded to turn over the bed, upend desk and chair, and peer into every crack and cranny. Mrs. Barker did not try to stop us. In fact, she encouraged us to look well and good, supposing we were hunting for treasure. But when we came up empty-handed she was not the least bit surprised.

"He was such a spendthrift, that Chauncey. Went out every night."

"Did he have visitors?" Henry asked.

"If it's women you mean, they are not allowed upstairs. This is a respectable house. He had no male visitors, either."

"Was he friends with any of the other boarders?"

She shook her head. "He considered himself superior to them. And he was in a way. He was clean and polite and well-spoken. You could tell he'd been raised up proper. And he was

such a handsome young man! He always looked quite the dapper spark." A film of tears softened her eyes as she recalled this.
She blinked, and her eyes beaded up again. "How much will
you give me for his clothes?"

I pulled out my wallet and gave her all the bills I had.

"That does not cover what he owed me."

"Keep the clothes then, along with the money," Henry said.
"We have no use for them, and neither do the Bidwell ladies."

After leaving the boardinghouse we went straight to the
offices of Curtis, Hayden, and Lardner on Tremont Street. Informed the young man at the desk in the foyer that we wished
to speak to a senior partner regarding Chauncey Bidwell. He
looked at us with some curiosity and seemed on the point of
speaking to us, but then went off to announce us. We then cooled
our heels for nigh an hour until we were shown into Mr. George
Hayden's office. Without rising, Mr. Hayden gave me a fleeting
glance, and then peered over his pince-nez spectacles at Henry,
apparently put off by his country clothes and stout, unpolished
boots. Henry, in his turn, stared back at Hayden with his usual
aplomb.

"I have little time to give you concerning Chauncey Bidwell," Hayden told us, clearly annoyed that we should presume
to have asked for something so precious. "Now tell me why
you are here and be quick about it."

Henry did just that. "We are here to learn as much as we can
about Bidwell in the hope of finding out who murdered him."

"Chauncey has been murdered?" Hayden's pale eyes widened
behind his spectacles. "My God!" As astonished as he was with
this news, in the next moment he seemed resigned to it. "I feared
he would come to no good end after he left here."

"He gave up his apprenticeship with your firm?" I said.

"We gave *him* up," Hayden replied. "Young Bidwell was let
go months ago."

"Really?" I glanced at Henry, but he did not seem much surprised.

"His family had such high hopes for him," he said to Hayden.

"As we did." Hayden's countenance became more benign. "Chauncey was a most impressive young man, intelligent, articulate, and in possession of considerable social graces. But his eagerness to pursue the law was not sustained beyond a few months, and he fast showed more attention to the fit of his britches than to the form of a case brief. So full was he of empty airs and excuses for unfinished work that we decided there was no room left in him for improvement. It fell upon me to dismiss him. And Chauncey did not seem to be much affected when I did so. He gave me a deep bow in parting, to mock or respect me, who knows? And then he sailed out of this office as if he had not a care in the world."

Hayden asked for details as to how Chauncey was murdered and seemed truly distressed that his demise had been so violent. He slipped off his spectacles and pressed a fingertip to his dampened eyes. But after a moment's silence he told us he had no further information to impart and made it clear he was done with us by taking out his pocket watch and giving it, not us, his full attention.

We next made our way the short distance to Scollay Square and the Howard Theater. As we approached, Henry asked if I'd ever attended a performance there.

"Often when I was a student in Cambridge," I said. "And you?"

"Never," Henry said. "I was far too poor to pay for entertainment when I attended Harvard, and I hardly desire to do so now. My life itself is my amusement and never ceases to be novel."

"How fortunate for you to find such enjoyment in your own company," I said wryly.

"Yes, I am fortunate indeed," he replied with a straight face but a twinkle in his eye. "I am not averse to the simple sounds made by an Italian music box, however. Or the voices of my friends singing, of course."

When we reached the theater Henry took in the Gothic façade. "Mighty elaborate exterior to house such a flimsy enterprise," he remarked.

A notice upon the locked entrance door informed us it would be open at seven in the evening for admission to see Junius Brutus Booth in a performance of *Hamlet*. "Shakespeare can hardly be called flimsy," I said.

Henry made no reply. His attention was taken by a group of boisterous young men and women who had walked past us and turned down an alley at the side of the building. He set off after them, motioning me to come along. When we saw them enter the theater by a stage door, we followed. A boy of about ten was stationed at the entrance, and he raised his wooden sword to block our way.

"Halt or I shall slay you," he declaimed as if reciting lines on the boards.

"And who may you be, young man, to threaten us so boldly?" Henry inquired with great seriousness.

"Why, I am John Wilkes Booth, son of Junius Brutus Booth." He lowered his sword and took a bow. "Someday I shall be even more famous than my father, and you will not have to ask such a stupid question."

"And for what will you be famous?" Henry said.

"Acting, of course." Up went his sword again, pointed at Henry's throat. "And slaying varlets who offend me."

"Why, we mean no offence," Henry said. "We are here on an important mission and would like to enlist the aid of a brave soldier such as yourself."

The boy immediately picked up on this plot change in his invented play. "At your service, sir!" he said and gave a smart salute. "Tell me whom you would like me to assassinate, and I will go do it forthwith."

"Do not be so eager to draw blood, pretend or not, lad," Henry told him. "Our mission is to find a murderer, not engage one. Tell me, did you know a young man called Chauncey Bidwell?"

"By sight only," the boy replied. "We never exchanged so much as a word. Whom did he murder?"

"It was he who was murdered, I'm afraid," Henry said.

The boy did not so much as blink his dark, strange eyes. "Who would want to kill a mere nobody like him?"

"We don't know why Mr. Bidwell was murdered," I said gruffly, put off by the child's coldness. "We would like to talk to anyone who was acquainted with him here."

"Follow me," John Wilkes Booth commanded and marched off with great haughtiness. He was a most insufferable child, but follow him we did.

He led us across the stage floor, where men were removing a painted canvas scene of a forest glade and replacing it with one of a palace entrance. Above us hung a labyrinth of ropes and pulleys, and below us were the pit stalls where I had sat with my friends as a student, preferring them to the stuffy box seats, which we could ill afford anyway. The boy then took us round back of the stage and down a narrow hall. At the end of the hall was a large room with doors flung open. Inside, twenty or so young women of exceptional pulchritude were chatting and laughing and staring at themselves in mirrors that lined the walls. I don't know about Henry, but I felt mildly intoxicated by such an abundance of uninhibited femininity. We men see so little of women when they are open and expressive instead of defending their social position and virtue or assessing a candidate for a suitable marriage. That is why Julia has always enchanted me. She never cared a whit for such things. It occurred to me she would have made a superb actress. For aught I know she might have been acting a part when she declared her everlasting love for me two years ago.

Young Booth ran into the room and was greeted with hugs and kisses by the actresses. Henry and I remained in the doorway, hesitant to intrude. But we were beckoned to enter by more than one fair damsel. Apparently they were used to male visitors encroaching upon their female sphere.

"Have you come to see our rehearsal?" one of the beauties inquired. "We'll be performing it for the public next week, but I suppose you want a teasing little preview such as this." She lifted the edge of her skirt just enough to show off a slender ankle. "Curtain up!" she cried. Then dropped the hem much too quickly. "And curtain down!" The girls all laughed.

"They have come to investigate the murder of Chauncey Bidwell!" the boy bellowed most dramatically over their titters.

His announcement was met with more mirth. But then, as the actresses regarded our serious visages, the laughter faded. "Is it true?" the bold teaser asked. "Chauncey is dead?"

Henry nodded and gave a succinct account of how and where death had come to Chauncey. Lest they thought us Boston police, he explained we came from Concord seeking justice on the mother's behalf for her murdered son. His simple and honest manner put them at ease, and they let loose a flood of sad recollections of the young man's handsome face and generosity. Not a single woman, however, could suggest any reason whatsoever for his murder. He had no enemies they knew of, or even jealous rivals. It seemed Chauncey was not taken very seriously by anyone.

Before we could inquire further the actresses were called to the stage for their rehearsal, and the precocious Booth boy followed after them. The only one who remained was a handsome woman of perhaps fifty who was seated at a table mixing tinted powders into a jar of paste. To my surprise Henry took a seat beside her and introduced himself. She told him her name was Mrs. Perry, and he inquired if she too was an actress.

"I used to tread the boards when I was younger," she said, obviously flattered that he thought she still did. "Now I stay behind the scenes painting faces and gluing on false hair and noses. Hardly as exciting."

"But still important," Henry said. "Do not the illusions you create backstage make it possible for actors to create them on-stage?"

"Well put!" she said. "I can indeed make an actor look young or old, beautiful or ugly, or any which way in-between with these tools of my trade." She waved her hand over her collection of shallow pots, saucers, jars, tins, and vials. "Or should I say the *tricks* of my trade? For I am as much a conjuror as a craftsman. See you this?" Mrs. Perry picked up a short, thick white stick and waved it before Henry's face. "It's called French chalk, and it can do wonders. I could lighten your sun-browned complexion with it, if you'd like." Henry quickly pulled back, and she laughed. "I don't suppose you have any use for my India ink or lampblack, either. Or my rose powder tinged with carmine." She pointed to a pot of crimson pigment.

Henry looked back at the table with renewed interest. "Carmine is a dye derived from the cochineal," he said.

"What, pray, is a cochineal?"

"A scale insect of the order Hemiptera, suborder Sternor-rhyncha."

"Are you telling me I have bugs crawling around in my rouge pot?"

It was Henry's turn to laugh. "Not at all. What you have in there is the carminic acid extracted from the female scale insect's body and eggs."

"Good Lord a'mercy!" she gasped.

"There is no cause for alarm," Henry told her. "I should

think the substance would be quite safe to apply upon the face."
He glanced at me. "What think you, doctor?"

Having far less knowledge of invertebrates than Henry, I
merely shrugged and said, "It is probably safer than applying
arsenic to the face at any rate."

"I use arsenic rarely but to great effect," Mrs. Perry said. "A
dusting of it gives the performer's visage an eerie glow. An even
better effect is to prepare the skin with an alkaline wash, fill in
any wrinkles and depressions with paste, and then enamel it
with lead paint. But enough about my methods. It is Chauncey
Bidwell you have come to learn about, is it not?"

Henry nodded. "Did you see a great deal of him backstage?"

"Oh, he was always hanging about here. 'Don't you have a
home, Chauncey?' I would ask him. 'My home is where my
pipe is,' he'd reply." She gave Henry an arch look. "I don't suppose you know what he meant by that."

"I venture he meant that his home was an opium den."

Mrs. Perry raised her painted eyebrows. "You are not as
green as you appear to be, young man. Have you smoked
opium yourself?"

"No, but I admit to smoking lily stems once."

"Lily stems!" She gave Henry's arm a playful slap. "Such a
devil you are!"

"Do you know where Bidwell went to indulge his opium
habit?"

Mrs. Perry leaned closer to Henry. "Well, I know he once
took several of the girls to a most disreputable place called
Chandoo Gate on Ann Street. They would probably not admit
to it if you asked them, though."

"Then I shall not," Henry said. "What else can you tell me
about Bidwell?"

"Nothing you didn't already hear from the girls. They'll
miss him, I suppose, but not for long. He'll be replaced by oth-

ers of his ilk soon enough. Chauncey might have thought himself special, but alas he was not."

"To his family he was," Henry said.

"Ah, yes. His poor mother." A head shake and a sigh were the extent of Mrs. Perry's commiseration. "Now if you'll pardon me, I must get back to my mixing, gentlemen. I am preparing face paint for an actor who is due here soon to fetch it. At present he is not engaged in a theater production, and to make ends meet he performs Shakespeare soliloquies at lyceums in the region. Such amazing range! He can play Hamlet one moment, and Ophelia the next. You will be recognized for the fine actor you are one day, Orlando, I tell him."

We left her to her commission and went out the way we had come in. As we were crossing the stage we saw the pretty actresses to one side of it, grouped around a most fortunate man of medium height and slender build. They were giggling and chattering away with him, and it appeared that Bidwell had been forgotten even sooner than predicted. Forgotten too was the Booth boy, sulking to the side of the cluster and looking most distressed about being ignored.

"Orlando!" he shouted. "Look at me! Look at me!" He jumped up and down a few times, did a somersault, and then stood on his hands.

The elegant man looked the boy's way for a moment, giving Henry and me a brief opportunity to see his classic profile, and then turned back to the young women. Ignored once again, John Wilkes Booth lost his balance and fell down in a heap.

Upon reaching the street Henry and I shared a bag of roasted chestnuts, all we could afford with what little money I had left. We then parted for a few hours, agreeing to meet again at the Boston Athenaeum. Whilst Henry consulted reference books there to learn what he could about vampyres, I betook myself to the Medical College to consult with my old professor Dr. Holmes, hoping to learn what I could about something equally obscure—how to correct a harelip.

Dr. Holmes greeted me most warmly and loaned me journals from Germany and France in which the latest surgical methods for such a procedure are discussed. He also encouraged me, once again, to accept a staff position at Massachusetts General Hospital and have full use of its modern operating theater.

Of course I feel honored by his proposal. As Ralph Waldo Emerson is to Henry Thoreau, Oliver Wendell Holmes is to me—an inspirational champion of the new age. I have always followed Dr. Holmes's credo to help rather than hinder the natural healing process of my patients, and I accept wholeheartedly his theory that the unhygienic methods of physicians can actually spread infection from patient to patient. I told him, however, that I could not see fit to leave Plumford at present, for I was the town's only doctor and Consumption was rampant.

Dr. Holmes related to me this anecdote in parting: A country physician, when asked to define the word Consumption, replied thus, "Con means that the condition is constant, sum means that some shall always have it, and shun means, shun treating the ailment if you can, for it cannot be cured." Perhaps "Uncle Oliver" was only trying to be humorous with a pun, as is his wont, or perhaps he was obliquely advising me to give up the thankless and insurmountable task I had taken on and return to my true avocation, surgery. But I cannot forsake my hometown just yet.

My visit with Dr. Holmes lasted longer than I had intended, and it was almost sundown by the time I reached the Athenaeum's new building at the foot of Beacon Street. Found Henry in the spacious reading room on the second floor and apologized for keeping him waiting. But he had not even noticed the passing of time, so enthralled was he by a discovery he had made in the library archives. I sat beside him at a table by the high window overlooking the Old Granary Burying Ground, and he showed me a dusty treatise written by a Benedictine monk that chronicled apparitions, spirits, vampyres, and revenants in all the countries of Europe through the ages. One such account was of a shepherd in Bohemia. Villagers believed he came back from the dead at night to prey on the living, so they dug up his corpse, impaled it on a stake, and left it to rot in the sun.

"How little progress we have made in the last five hundred years," Henry said. "That so many can *still* believe such foolishness makes me lose hope that our race will ever surmount superstition and fear."

As he spoke I gazed out the window. The setting sun was casting its last long golden bars across the somber graveyard below, and my eye was drawn to movement among the headstones. 'Twas the figure of a very tall man in top hat and cloak emerging from behind a crumbling old tomb. He suddenly looked up at the window, and when his glinting eyes met mine I felt a distinct chill. I quickly turned my head away as if struck.

"What is it?" Henry asked, regarding me with concern.

"Nothing. A twinge in my neck. But look down there at that fellow." I pointed toward the burying ground. "Is there not something odd about him?"

"What fellow?" Henry said, peering through the window and into the darkness. "I see no one."

"No matter. He is gone now."

But he was not gone! For in the next *instant* the man I had just observed a story below, or his exact double, was standing behind Henry, peering over his shoulder at the book on the table! Feeling his presence, Henry turned around to look at him.

"Do I know you, sir?" he asked.

"I do not think so," the stranger said, backing off. "But I recognize that ancient text before you."

"And I feel that I should recognize *you,*" Henry said. "There is something of the familiar about you. My name is Thoreau."

The stranger shook his head. "I know no one called Thoreau. I am Dr. Luther Lamb, and the porter told me I could find Dr. Walker in this room."

"And so you have." Steeling myself, I stood up to meet eyes with him. Had to tilt up my head to do so, for he was well over my own six feet. His eyes were deeply set in their sockets, and their darkness glinted like polished black hematite, but I could not say for certain that these were the selfsame eyes that had so alarmed me only moments ago. Rather, I should say for certain that they were *not,* for it would have been impossible for him to have made it from down in the burying ground to the upstairs reading room so quickly. It had merely been an ocular deception on my part.

"Dr. Walker, I am most pleased to meet you. In fact, I have come all the way from Augusta, Maine, to do so," the stranger said.

"But how could you have known you would find me here at the Athenaeum today?"

"Sheer luck!" Lamb did not bother with further explanation. "I took great interest in the dissertation you published in the *Massachusetts Medical Journal* concerning hypnotism, Dr. Walker. I think it brilliant."

I confess I took prideful pleasure in hearing this, especially after hearing nothing at all in regard to it from my Boston colleagues. But I did my best to maintain a modest demeanor. "Whatever brilliance can be found in that essay, Dr. Lamb, originated with the Englishman who invented the term *hypnotism,* not me. I have merely followed up on Dr. James Braid's methods and reported my results."

"Well, I should like to follow up on *your* methods, Dr. Walker. Might I consult with you this evening?"

I told him I had to return to Plumford, where I was currently practicing, and suggested he visit me there at his convenience. Dr. Lamb eagerly accepted my invitation, and when I began to explain how to get there he said there was no need to for he was familiar with the area. We parted without further ado, and Henry and I hurried off to the Causeway Street terminal to catch the last train to Concord.

"I am happy to leave the city behind," Henry said, settling in his seat. "Unfortunately, we will have to return soon enough if we hope to find more information concerning Bidwell. I do not look forward to venturing into the Black Sea district, but it seems we must."

"We have been there before, and it did us no harm," I said, recalling our last investigation together. "I suppose it will be an easy enough matter to find this Chandoo Gate on Ann Street. Do you think Bidwell's murderer was an opium peddler?"

"It seems unlikely. Why kill off a good customer?"

"Perhaps Bidwell owed him money. Opium is not cheap."

"More reason to keep him alive," Henry said. "One cannot get blood from a turnip, nor money from a dead man."

"His murder might have been meant to serve as an example to others who owed the killer money."

"If so, it would have been better to kill him in Boston rather than in some backwater like Plumford."

"Backwater it is, indeed," I agreed, recalling Dr. Holmes's offer to practice at Massachusetts General Hospital.

"Is it not odd that your great admirer Dr. Lamb not only knew of Plumford, but had even been there?" Henry said.

"Well, people do occasionally visit our little hamlet, after all. And as for Dr. Lamb's being my great admirer, he merely congratulated me on a journal article."

"He called it brilliant," Henry said. "No one has yet called *my* writing brilliant."

"I should like to read your latest endeavor when you complete it, Henry. What is it about?"

"Life," he said. "Life in the woods."

That did not sound particularly interesting to me, and I went back to a subject that was. "I wonder if Dr. Lamb will take the trouble to visit me in Plumford," I said.

"I would be careful in my dealings with him," Henry said. "Methinks the name Dr. Wolf would suit him far better."

I laughed. "Yes, he does have a rather hungry look about him, but that just could have been because he was wanting his supper. You told him he looked familiar to you, Henry. Do you recall meeting him before this evening?"

"I cannot recall the specific incident. I might have come across him on one of my trips to Maine. With his straight black hair and sharp cheekbones and nose, he reminds me of Indians I have met there."

"Perhaps he is merely related to one of them," I suggested.

"No. I am sure I have had personal dealings with Dr. Lamb." Henry leaned back in his seat. "The circumstance will come to me eventually." And with that he fell asleep.

I must have slept too for before I knew it the train had stopped at the Concord depot. I bid Henry Good Night and went to the stable where I had left Napoleon this morning. The ride back to Tuttle Farm in the dark was uneventful.

JULIA'S NOTEBOOK

Tuesday, 7 December

I have landed a commission! And my three charming subjects—the Misses Arabel, Beatrice, and Calista Phyfe—have
already commenced sitting for their portrait. How this came
about was by no means an accident. Indeed, my trap was well
laid. Firstly, I drew an exceedingly flattering sketch of Mrs.
Daggett and presented it to her as a gift. Just as I hoped, Mr.
Daggett exhibited it at the store for all his customers to admire. When two of the Phyfe sisters came in to purchase gew-
gaws, they were immediately captured by the sight of it and
hurried across the Green to ask me to please sketch them too.
"Will you step into my studio?" said the Artist to the Girls.
("Will you walk into my parlor?" said the Spider to the Fly.) I
rapidly sketched each of them gratis, but before they ran home
to show off their likenesses to their papa, I gently suggested
doing an oil portrait of them posed together. They mentioned
a third sister, and I exclaimed that I had always wanted to do a
portrait of the Three Graces.

I blush at my wheedling words as I recount them, but their
father is, after all, the richest man in town, and if I am to provide for a small boy and a large housekeeper, as well as for myself, I must earn some money. What little Grandfather left me

will not last for long, I fear. Mr. Daggett has ordered me art supplies on credit, and I must pay Kitty for her needlework as soon as she completes it. Noah is in need of shoes, and my one pair will soon wear out, not to mention my unmentionables. At least Mrs. Swann seems amply supplied with fine clothes. The trunk she had delivered here from Boston was enormous!

At any rate, no less than an hour after I'd sent the Phyfe sisters on their merry way, who should knock on the front door but Justice Phyfe. Mrs. Swann led him into the study, where I confess I was daydreaming rather than working. Fortunately, I did have a pencil in my hand and a sketchbook in my lap and made a show of putting them aside to spare the time to talk with him. He offered me fifty dollars to paint his three girls. I informed him in the most courteous manner I could muster that I would be paid triple that amount in Europe. He remonstrated most sharply that I was no longer in Europe. This I could not dispute, but still insisted on a hundred and fifty American dollars. Justice Phyfe declared that he found it unseemly to discuss money matters with a female and abruptly departed from my objectionable presence. But as he made his way to the door, Mrs. Swann waylaid him in the hall. She must have somehow persuaded him to reconsider, for the Phyfe sisters came for their first sitting today.

Such delicate, docile, innocent little maidens! With their tiny, regular features, smooth, petal-soft skin, and rosebud mouths, they remind me of flowers. Well, the youngest, Calista, is more a gangling dandelion weed than a flower. But the middle girl, curly-headed Beatrice, is most cultivated, reminding me of a frilly pink chrysanthemum. And the eldest—pale, elegant Arabel—seems as delicate and mollycoddled as a hothouse gardenia. Together the three are a veritable tussie-mussie of femininity, so why not portray them as such? I sat them down on the chaise longue together, and Mrs. Swann was most helpful in adjusting the position of their torsos and arms until

I was satisfied with the effect of entwined limbs and tilted heads, conveying the impression of a nosegay.

They happily prattled away as I made my preliminary graphite sketches. Actually, the two younger ones did all the talking whilst Arabel remained mute. She did not look at all happy and sat so rigidly that I kept directing her to relax, but that only made her tense up more. I assumed she was cold, for she had chosen to pose in a gown that bared her sloping shoulders, but when I suggested that she might be more comfortable with a shawl draped about her, she shook her head so hard that her chestnut ringlets trembled.

"Just tell me how I can make you more comfortable," I implored her. "Pray do not suffer in silence."

"Oh, let Arabel be," Beatrice said. "Suffering is what she does best. Especially of late. Goodness knows why, but she has refused to leave her bedchamber for days now. If not for this chance to have her portrait painted, she would be there still. Vanity overcame whatever was ailing her."

"If you are ill," I told Arabel, "we can postpone these sittings until you feel better."

She shrugged off my concern. Rather haughtily, I must say.

"I think Arabel was hiding in her chamber all week because she was scared," little Calista said.

"Of what?" I asked.

"Why, the Plumford Night Stalker, of course! When Arabel heard that a young man had been murdered on Wolf Hill, she fainted straight away. We had to revive her with smelling salts."

Beatrice rolled her eyes. "My elder sister is always fainting. She thinks it makes her more romantic and refined."

"At least this time Arabel had good reason to faint," Calista said. "I nearly did so myself when Papa told us where the body was discovered. We have often taken that very same path!"

"Our Aunt Gussie's cottage is but a half mile off it," Beatrice said. "It is nicely situated by a spring-fed pond at the foot of the hill."

"Well, I should not care to live in such an isolated spot as that," Calista said. "With only wolves for neighbors."

"There haven't been wolves on that hill for over a hundred years, you simpleton," Beatrice said, rolling her eyes again.

"But now there is a vampyre roaming about up there!" Calista countered. "I daresay that is far worse."

"You are such a muttonhead," Beatrice told her. "Did not Papa assure us there is no such thing as a vampyre?"

"Even so, I am thankful our dear auntie is safe in heaven now."

"Aunt Gussie passed away near a year ago," Beatrice informed me. "And her cottage has been empty since."

"Papa's cottage, actually," Calista said. "Aunt Gussie was his sister and had no property of her own."

"The poor dear was an old maid, you see," Beatrice said. "Upon my soul, I would rather be murdered by a vampyre than end up like her!"

I could not help but reprimand the girl. "That is a very foolish thing to say, Beatrice."

"Indeed!" Calista said. "You just said Papa assured us there is no such thing as a vampyre."

"That's not quite what I meant," I said. "It is foolish for a girl to say she would prefer to be murdered than unmarried."

"Well, these young ladies need not worry about ending up that way," Mrs. Swann put in. "They are far too pretty to remain maidens."

I turned around. "Oh, are you still here, Mrs. Swann?" I hoped my question would remind her she had household duties to attend to. Apparently she did not, however, for she made no move to withdraw.

"It is so sad," she continued, "when a young man, with so many pleasures ahead of him, dies so early in life."

"And so violently!" Calista said.

"I hear he was very handsome too," Beatrice said. "I wonder what evil, human or inhuman, was lurking in those woods that night to do such mortal harm to him."

"Stop!" Arabel cried, covering her ears with her pretty little hands. "You know I cannot bear to hear such gruesome talk." She began to sob.

Mrs. Swann rushed forward and pulled Arabel up and into her arms to give her a comforting hug. "No need to be affrighted, my dear," she said, pressing the girl against her. "Mrs. Swann is here to protect you from any big, bad vampyre."

The other two sisters rose from the chaise and joined in on the cuddle, melding to Mrs. Swann's supportive frame. "Such sweet little pussy cats," she declared, kissing the tops of their heads. "What say we have some tea and chocolate puffs, my pets?"

Perhaps I should have minded Mrs. Swann's interruption of my work, but how could I possibly object to chocolate puffs? Indeed, as my officious housekeeper herded her "pets" into the dining room, I followed close at their tapping heels. The table was most elegantly set with the Wedgwood jasperware usually displayed in the corner cupboard, and the pastries were displayed on a silver cake stand that had been in dire need of a polishing but now gleamed like starlight.

"How lovely, Mrs. Swann!" I said. "Thank you for going to all this trouble."

"No trouble at all, I assure you, my dear. Now sit down and I shall pour out the tea."

"I'll call Noah to join us. Is he in the kitchen?"

"I do not think these young ladies would appreciate his presence at table," Mrs. Swann stated most emphatically.

Ignoring her objection, I sang out Noah's name, but got no response.

"He must be off on one of his secretive walks," Mrs. Swann

said. "Do not concern yourself about the lad. I shall put aside some sweets for him, and he can eat them in private as he prefers to do."

It was true enough that the boy does not like eyes upon him as he eats, and I realized, had he been home, I would have caused him more embarrassment than pleasure by insisting that he join us.

There was a knock on the front entry door, and Mrs. Swann hurried off to answer it. A moment later she led Justice Phyfe into the dining room. He did not bother to wait for an invitation from me but took a seat at the head of the table. Mrs. Swann was quick to set a cup and saucer and plate of puffs in front of him.

"Why thank you, madam. You are the very essence of hospitality," he said.

"It is always a pleasure to wait upon a fine-looking man," she replied.

Phyfe's daughters giggled, and he tried to hide his blush by stroking his muttonchop whiskers. "You are quite the flatterer, Mrs. Swann," he said.

"I only speak the truth," she declared most fervently.

He bit into a puff and rolled his eyes in ecstasy. "What angel on earth could have baked such heavenly pastries as these?"

Mrs. Swann lowered her eyes most demurely. "I am no angel, sir."

"Pray tell me how you made such light and airy tidbits as these, Mrs. Swann, so I can duplicate them at home for our dear papa," Beatrice demanded. "Did you use chocolate or cocoa?"

"Chocolate," Mrs. Swann quickly replied.

"Really? But how did you keep it from oiling?"

Mrs. Swann did not reply so quickly this time. Instead, she raised her finger to her lips and shook her head.

Beatrice's plump little mouth turned down in a pout. "You do not care to share your culinary secrets with me?"

"I hardly know you, my dear."

Justice Phyfe smiled approval. "Mrs. Swann is teaching you a lesson in manners, Beatrice. You are presuming too much familiarity with her. Before she feels free to share any secrets, we must become more intimately acquainted with her." The look he gave Mrs. Swann across the table boded his intention to do just that.

He regarded me with less benevolence and proceeded to interrogate me about my training as a professional artist. His questions indicated that he doubted I had any. I took no offence for it is sadly true that art academies both here and in Europe do not accept women. I informed Phyfe, however, that I had been trained by one of the most respected American portraitists abroad, namely Ellery Bell, my own father. I went on to describe how I had served as his studio assistant in Paris for over ten years, stretching his canvases, mixing his paints, and taking instruction from him. I did not add that by the time I was twenty I had become so skilled that I was completing much of Papa's work for him, whilst he went off to pursue other passions. Nor did I mention that I learned far more from Papa than technique. Along with teaching me how to paint portraits, he had taught me how to drum up paying subjects.

Of course I appreciate the part Mrs. Swann played in obtaining my current commission. If not for her, I surely would have lost Phyfe's good will and patronage. It is clear that he is quite taken with her, but what is not clear to me is *why.* I should think Mrs. Swann's boldness would be off-putting to him for he is clearly of the opinion that women should govern their tongues and be submissive. And it cannot be that her great beauty blinds him to her brash temperament for in truth Mrs. Swann is a most homely woman. She has neither the del-

icacy of facial features nor the slight, willowy form men pro-
fess to admire in a female. Men! They demand us to be one
thing and then desire just the opposite. I reckon it is Mrs.
Swann's originality that attracts Justice Phyfe. Or could it simply be that he is a lonely widower on the prowl? If so, I need
not worry about Mrs. Swann's vulnerability. If there is any woman
who can defend herself against untoward advances, it is she.

After Phyfe and his daughters departed, I offered to help
with the washing up, but Mrs. Swann insisted upon doing it
herself.

"After all, that is my job now," she said.

"We have not even settled on your wages yet, Mrs. Swann.
What compensation do you require?"

"All I require is what you have already given me, a comfortable place to live and your pleasant company, my dear. Pay
me with kindness and affection, and we shall all be happy. Now
go back to your work whilst I see to mine." With that she
commenced clearing the table.

I returned to the studio to evaluate the sketches I had
made of the three Phyfe sisters. A short time later I heard a
crash in the kitchen and went to investigate. I found little
Noah standing on a stool in front of the soapstone sink, dish-
cloth in hand and tears in his eyes. On the floor around him
lay the pale blue fragments of my grandmother's cherished
Wedgwood teapot.

"Never mind," I told him. "That pot can be easily replaced." Some would say it is wrong to lie to a child, but in this
case I think not. He did look so upset over the mishap.

As we picked up the broken pieces together, I asked him
where Mrs. Swann was. His enunciation is so poor that I could
not understand the boy. Nor could I understand why Mrs.
Swann had let him wash the delicate china instead of doing it
herself. She was nowhere to be found on the first floor, but

when I went upstairs I saw that her bedchamber door was closed. About to rap upon it, I hesitated. Perhaps a violent headache had come upon her. I decided to let her rest. I shall let the matter of the teapot rest too. It is broken beyond repair, after all, and nothing can change that.

ADAM'S JOURNAL

Wednesday, December 8

U p at first light. Got a good fire started to warm the kitchen for Gran and Harriet and took off on patient calls before they awoke. Kept the gig top down to see the sunrise. Napoleon's breath burst out his mouth in heavy plumes of vapor as he pranced down the long lane to the road, his hooves crunching through the thin white ice coating the frozen puddles. He seems content enough to have me at the reins now, but he must miss Doc Silas. God knows I do, even though we hardly ever agreed on medical treatments. As devoted as I was to the old doc, I could never have shared a practice in Plumford with him. Better to have honed my skills in Boston. And Boston is still where my ambitions reside.

But not my heart. I looked back at the rambling homestead where I had been raised, set halfway up the side of the broad hill, smack-dab in the middle of a hundred and fifty acres of meadow, pasture, woodland, and orchard. The sun was just coming up behind the hill and cast golden light upon the old house and the string of attached barns and sheds that had been added over the decades as necessity dictated. *This is where I belong,* thought I; *this is where my true heritage lies.* Whoever my father might have been, I know for certain Tuttle blood runs through my veins. And Tuttle Farm is where I can always find peace and refreshment.

When we reached the road I gave Napoleon free rein, and we glided past the shorn hay and corn fields at a good pace. The Assabet danced between its frost-lipped banks as the gig rumbled over the bridges, and I began to sing over the rumble, as if all were well with the world.

But then I passed the Wiley homestead and was reminded that all was *not* well. Ezekiel and Solomon were out front, butchering a hog not a dozen yards from their well. Ezekiel knows better than to do this. I have told him that butchering so close to a well will pollute the water with animal seepage and make it unfit to drink. But no doubt his brother insisted upon doing it there anyway for the sake of convenience. Ezekiel nodded as I passed, and Solomon only glared. Close by their bloody labor Mrs. Wiley was making soft soap. She stood over a roaring fire ladling scoopfuls of potash into an enormous kettle in which thick slabs of fat sliced from the hog were being boiled down. She might well have been a wraith as she squinted through the thick smoke at me. Poor woman. Two daughters dead within six months of each other. And a brother-in-law from hell.

My first call was to the Gray farm. Mr. Gray's wound is draining well. No smell of infection or visual evidence of it. Charged Mrs. Gray to alert me immediately if there was. But as each day passes there is less likelihood that I will have to amputate. My next call was at the Yates's farm, where I found the babe I delivered last week in blushing health. Halleluiah!

Rode out to the Herd farm after that to see how their grandson Billy was faring. Farmer Herd informed me that my young patient had been moved to the barn so that he could breathe in the cows' health-inducing exhalations. Herd had learned of this advanced therapy from a train conductor whilst at the Concord depot loading his milk cans for Boston this morning. The conductor claims his very own father was cured of Consumption as a boy in Prussia when he was moved into the cow house. Did not know whether to laugh or weep when Herd told me this. Did neither, of course, and spent a good half hour trying to induce him to move Billy back to the house where humans rather than bovines could look after him. Doubt I would have managed to persuade him if his wife had not taken my side. She knows best how to talk sense into that stubborn codger. Indeed, he would be dead now if she had not convinced him to allow me to cut off his badly infected finger a while back. She had made sure to keep Billy warm under a pile of quilts during his barn visit, so I don't think any further harm came to him there. He is wasting away at a rapid rate, however, and I doubt he will survive the winter. Herd will no doubt blame me for interfering with his cow cure, just as Solomon Wiley blamed me for interfering with his vampyre ritual. Who else but the doctor is there to fault when galloping Consumption claims life after life?

Better that than faulting the patient, however. On Sunday I heard a visiting preacher claim from the pulpit that Consumption is a spiritual rather than a physical malady, brought on by the sufferer's lack of faith. I could not refrain from shouting "Hogwash!" loudly enough to be heard throughout the Meetinghouse. I shout the same when I hear medical men put the blame on their patients—he or she overindulged in food or drink, or didn't exercise enough, or danced too much, or rode in a cold carriage, or practiced solitary sex! Excuses abound, and none make sense to me. Neither does the latest scientific theory about the illness. Although I have seen tubercules upon the lungs of Consumption victims during autopsies, I cannot credit that these tubercules accumulated there because the heart of the deceased was too weak to pump cleansing blood through the lungs to wash them away. What *causes* these nodules? The disease seems to run in families. Is it hereditary? If so, I fear for Julia. There is a history of Consumption in the Walker family that goes back generations, and her own mother died of it.

Left Billy settled back in his room, cheeks flushed with fever but resting peacefully enough, poor, exhausted lad. He is so frail and thin his shoulder blades look like bird wings. Passed Tuttle Farm on my way to town and turned off for a quick cup of coffee. Gran was not in the house. Nor was she in the barn, dairy room, or chicken coop. Harriet was nowhere to be seen, and neither were any of the winter farmhands. Or even the dog. With a murderer possibly still at large in the area, I started getting mighty anxious. Finally went down to the root cellar and felt great relief to discover Gran there, working in the light of a tallow candle. She sat on a stool, brushing aside the layer of hay on the dirt floor to inspect her store of turnips, carrots, parsnips, radishes, and potatoes. Her hands are always moving. As a boy when I came in from the cold she would not just hold my hands to warm them but pat and clasp and caress them till the cold was gone. Now her keen, commonsensical mind and plain speech soothe my mind like her hands warmed me then.

"No one is about the farm," I said.

"Sent the men up to the east woodlot to cut trees."

"And where is Harriet?"

"Sent her to town to stay with friends until all this vampyre flummydiddle ends. I reckoned it was time for Harriet to leave when I asked her to kindly fetch me some turnips up from the cellar and she refused to do it. Never before has that dear girl refused me a favor, so I knew something was amiss. Sure enough, she was all of a biver concernin' the vampyre. She'd gotten it into her head that he might be sleeping down here during the day.

Why a vampyre might choose the Tuttle root cellar as his daytime lair she could not tell me, but her fear was real enough."

"I suppose girls are prone to such imaginings."

"Not just girls. Men too. My farmhands told me only an hour ago that they will be stopping their work well before sunset to avoid walking home in the dark."

"Because they fear this so-called Night Stalker?"

"And all his minions! They have heard talk that Witiku has risen from his grave and brought upon the Consumption plague to create a vampyre army."

"I cannot understand how Solomon Wiley has managed to get people to believe these wild fantasies."

"Well, I ain't one bit surprised," Gran said. "In a way it is a comfort to credit some evil as the cause for all the suffering going about. Evil can be stomped out."

"How? By digging up corpses and mutilating them? There is only one evil that needs to be stomped out, and that is ignorance."

"You are right, of course, Adam. But that don't mean folks will listen to you. They may even turn on you for tryin' to reason with them. You might well end up the lightning rod for all their pent-up anger and frustration. Better to let them take it out on the dead."

"No, I will not stand for that," I said. "Better to stand up to Solomon Wiley."

"That will not be so easy to do, my boy. He is building up a mighty big following," Gran said. "By latchin' onto that old Injun legend he is dredgin' up old fears." She gazed at the shadows the flickering candlelight cast upon the stone walls. "When I was a bit of a girl my grandfolks scared us with stories about Witiku. Threats of him stalkin' through the night lookin' fer white children to feed upon could make us nigh hysterical."

We fell quiet. I set myself down on a keg containing fermenting pear perry, and Gran busied herself for a time retying and rehanging strings of pole beans and peppers from the roof beams. "How goes it with you and Julia?" she finally asked. "Must be upsettin' to have her back in your life again."

"She may be back in Plumford," I said, "but I am determined not to let her back in my life. My heart is shut tight to her now."

"Because she went and married somebody else?"

"Need I a better reason than *that?* I thought she loved me as much as I loved her, Gran. Instead she forgot all about me less than a month after we parted."

Gran held her candle close to my face and must have seen the hurt in it, for her own face sagged in sorrowfulness. "How can you ever forgive me, Adam?"

"It is Julia I cannot forgive."

"Then you are blamin' the wrong person, my boy. I am the one at fault for not tellin' you who yer real father was."

"You need not keep tormenting yourself about it, Gran. In the end you did tell me."

"Too late! Julia had already sailed off."

"How were you to know she would act so rashly?"

"She would not have done so if she had knowed you two have no blood connection."

"I am sorely tempted to tell her so now."

"Don't do it, Adam. It would only cause her pain of mind."

"Good!"

Gran tutted. "I never heard you sound spiteful afore, Adam."

"You never heard me lie before, either."

"What lie have you told me then?"

"That my heart is shut to Julia. In truth, it is still an open wound."

Gran took my hand and rubbed it. "I wish to heavens she had never come back here."

We said nothing more about Julia. Best to stop writing about her, too. Better yet, I should stop thinking about her. That was hard enough to do when an ocean separated us. But now I am plagued by the alluring sight of her every damn day.

JULIA'S NOTEBOOK

Thursday, 9 December

I went to Daggett's store this forenoon to see if my order of art supplies had arrived from Winsor & Newton. Alas, no. But to compensate for this disappointment there was a post from Lidian Emerson communicating her intention to call on me with Henry tomorrow afternoon.

Heading back home across the Green, I noticed Harriet Quimby, Granny Tuttle's ward, coming toward me. When she noticed me too, she veered off in another direction, but not one to be snubbed so easily, I took chase after her.

"Good Day, Harriet!" I called out as I caught up with her. "How pleased I am to see you again." When she turned to face me I saw from her expression that the pleasure was not mutual. I looped arms with her anyway, and we fell into step. "You are well, I trust."

"I am very well, thank you," she replied with stiff politeness, but did not inquire as to my own health.

I ignored this rebuff. "And I pray Granny Tuttle is well, too."

"Mrs. Tuttle is not *your* granny," Harriet said huffily.

"But she is Adam's," I said. "And he is my cousin. Hence, she and I are related in a way."

"No, you are not," Harriet insisted. "That your mother's

brother was married to Mrs. Tuttle's daughter does not make you her kin."

"You are right about our family connection, or rather the lack of one, Harriet," I allowed, not wishing to renew our acquaintanceship with an argument. "But I have known Gran— that is, Mrs. Tuttle since I was eight years old, and always heard Adam call her Granny. So that is how I came to think of her. Not that she ever gave me leave to call her that. She is no more fond of me than you are." I laughed.

Harriet did not. But leastways she did not tug her arm free of mine. We strolled in silence for a while. "I knew you would not be able to stay away from Adam," she finally said.

"He is not the reason I came back."

To show her disbelief Harriet gave out a sniff, a practice she must have picked up from Granny Tuttle, having been her ward for ten years. "What I cannot conjecture is why you bothered to leave Plumford in the first place if your intention was to return."

"That was not my intention, I assure you."

"And I suppose it was not your intention to send Adam on a wild goose chase to Paris, either."

"Adam went to Paris?"

A frown creased Harriet's high, smooth forehead. "You didn't know?"

"No! This is the first I have heard of it."

"Then I fear I have spoken out of turn. In truth, I wish I had not spoken to you at all!"

She tried to disengage her arm from my grasp, but I would not let it go. "When did Adam go to Paris? Whom did he see there?"

Harriet remained as silent as a stone. I own that I was tempted to twist her arm a bit to encourage her to talk, but instead I released it and off she dashed away from me.

Off I dashed too—but not in pursuit of her. It was Granny Tuttle I needed to talk to. My pace was as rapid as my heartbeat as I headed up the road toward Tuttle Farm, and despite the chill in the air, I became so overheated I threw open my cloak. I fastened it up again quick enough when I took a shortcut through the woods, where high pines shoulder out all the sunlight, and thoughts of that poor Concord man's brutal murder crept into my mind. The wind howled through the trees most plangently, and for an instant I mistook a swooping crow for a black-caped vampyre.

I broke into a run, thankful there was no snow to impede my progress, and did not slow down until I came out of the woodland and onto a far pasture of Tuttle Farm. To get onto it I had to climb over a tossed stone fence that had been created many generations past by brawny Tuttle men. Adam, a Tuttle on his mother's side, is the last of them, and I recalled how, as a boy, he once claimed that he would have seven strapping sons of his own one day to help him work the land. How would he get these sons? I'd asked him in complete innocence. He would not explain the process to me.

Today, as I crossed the frost-browned pasture, I conjured up the memory of how it had looked on sweet summer mornings those many years ago, when Adam would drive his grandmother's cows there as a boy, and I would come from town to meet him. Sometimes we would lie on a verdant, dewy knoll amidst all the buttercups to stare up at an azure sky and interpret the shapes of clouds. More often we would go tramping over hill and dale, brook and bog. We were young freebooters without a care in the world, and we never considered the future. That was the realm of adults. But when adults threatened to separate us, after we had been inseparable for three idyllic years, we decided to take charge of our own destinies and run away. Such an easy solution could not be countenanced by those still in control of our lives, however. 'Twas Adam's grand-parents who hunted us down three days later, on a dusty high-way heading west.

"Git in the wagon, my boy," Grandpa Tuttle had com-manded Adam in that gentle but resolute tone of his.

Granny, not so gentle, had grabbed me by the arm and hauled me up to sit beside her. She had spoken nary a word to me all the thirty miles back to Plumford. Nor had she come to the dock to bid me farewell when my father and I left for Eu-rope the next week. She had allowed Adam to see me off, though. Much to my regret I had wept so hard that tears had blurred my last view of his freckled, twelve-year-old face. Never saw those dear freckles again. He'd outgrown them by the time I next laid eyes on him, a man of twenty-four.

As my thoughts brought me back to the past, my feet brought me closer and closer to the Tuttle homestead, and be-fore I knew it I was at the back door. As I waited for a response to my knock I spotted a shiny new horseshoe nailed upon the lintel. To repel vampyres? It did not seem likely that such a sensible soul as Granny Tuttle would give any credence to them. I looked about the empty farmyard. Not a creature was in sight, and the only evidence of life was the lowing sound of cows and oxen in the attached barn. Then I heard angry bark-ing, and a big, black dog came charging toward me.

At first I had no fear, supposing the dog to be the one Adam and I had found many years ago, lying in the road all torn up. "Patches!" I shouted, calling him by the name I'd dubbed him after Adam had stitched him up. "Don't you re-member me?"

The dog stopped in his tracks, but his growl was hardly a sign of fond recognition. Noting the absence of white hair in his muzzle, I realized this dog was far too young to be the one I'd helped nurse back to health as a girl. Baring his teeth, he stalked toward me, tail between his legs, and I lost no further time waiting for my knock to be answered. Lifting up the iron latch, I pushed myself inside and promptly closed the door behind me.

The vast kitchen was just as I remembered it. Herbs hung from the thick ceiling beams, the rough plastered walls were freshly whitewashed, and the wide-planked floor, painted with a mixture of milk and ocher clay, looked clean enough to eat off except for a patch of sand spread in front of the massive fieldstone fireplace to catch grease spatters. A big teakettle hanging from the long crane hissed over the banked fire in the hearth, and the aroma of bread baking in the beehive oven wafted through the warmed air. And there in front of the fire, beside her little spinning wheel, sat Mrs. Betsey Tuttle, also just as I remembered, in a blue-checked apron and red neck-kerchief, her snow-white hair tucked under a neat muslin cap. She silently stared at me.

"You don't look surprised to see me, ma'am," I said. Nor did she look very pleased.

"I heard you was back," she replied.

"Did you not hear me knocking on your door just now?"

"Nope. Could be I'm gettin' a little deaf." She pronounced it "deef."

"You might indeed be getting deaf if you did not hear your dog's crazed barking. He so frightened me that I took the liberty of letting myself in."

"Oh, I heard Blackie all right, but paid him no mind. Nor should you have. His bark is far worse than his bite."

"Hah! His fangs looked more fearsome than a vampyre's."

Granny gave one of her dismissive sniffs. "Are you so foolish as to believe in vampyres, Julia?"

"Don't you? I saw the horseshoe hanging above your door."

"Little Harriet nailed it there. All this blather about blood-sucking night stalkers has affrighted her. I reckoned she'd be better off in town fer the time bein' and sent her to stay with friends there."

"I met up with Harriet on the Green this morning. That is why I came to see you."

"Did you suppose I was hard up for company? Well, I ain't."

"I shall depart soon enough if you find my presence here so irksome, ma'am."

"Now don't get all brustled up, Julia. I reckon I can tolerate your presence well enough. And I am very sorry Blackie greeted you so rudely."

No apology for her own brusque greeting, however. And to think we had not seen each other for near two years. But no matter. I decided to attempt some polite chitchat before getting to my purpose for the visit. "At first I mistook Blackie for Patches," I said.

"Patches sired him. Up and died last winter."

"I am sorry to hear it."

"No need to be sorry fer Patches. He lived a long, happy life thanks to Adam's mendin'."

I nodded. "Adam had fine doctoring skills even as a boy."

"Can't mend his own heart though," Granny muttered.

"What was that?"

"Never you mind, Julia. Just make yerself to home and set with me a spell." She gave me a good looking-over as I slipped off my cloak and hung it on a peg by the door. "Ain't that yer Grandmother Walker's cloak?"

"I'm surprised you recognized it," I said, sitting down on the settle across from Granny.

"Why, I am as familiar with that particular garment as I am with the back of my own hand," she said. "The wool came from sheep I bred. And 'twas I who spun that wool into yahn, then dyed that yahn with apple root and wove it into fabric.

Must have been . . . let me calculate . . . a good fifty years ago. John Adams had just come into office. And yer grandmother had just been delivered of her first child."

"That must have been my mother's elder brother."

"That's right. 'Twas yer uncle Owen."

"Adam's father," I added.

Granny fell silent and gave me a long look. I wondered if she had forgotten her train of thought, but a moment later she got back on track. "Anyways, I warrant that cloak will last *another* fifty years," she continued. "That's how well we made garments back in them days. But I don't spin wool anymore. I am not so elastic as I once was, and my old legs can't take all that to-and-fro in front of a big walking wheel. Besides which, you can buy mill-made woolen cloth so cheap nowadays that it ain't worth the effort. But linen is another matter entirely." She dipped her fingers in a bowl of water and resumed her spinning. As her foot moved up and down on the treadle, she pulled strands down from a bundle of flax fibers tied to the distaff and fed them into the whirring wheel. "Store-bought ain't near as good as home-spun. The bed linen in little Harriet's dowry chest was all spun and woven by me. And of course I would not want Adam to wear mill linen against his body. I will make him a new shirt from the thread I am spinning now."

"What a good grandmother you are to him," I said, and thoroughly meant it.

But Granny Tuttle shook her head so vehemently her cap almost fell off. "No, I ain't. I wronged him greatly. You too."

"I don't understand. Do you mean that you have also wronged me or that I have also wronged Adam?"

"Both," she replied. She can be as maddening as the Sphinx.

"How can you claim I wronged Adam?" I demanded.

She took her foot off the treadle, and the wheel fell silent. "By runnin' off on him like you done."

"No! I did the right thing by leaving him. I have no regrets on that score. And when one day Adam holds a healthy babe he has sired in his arms, he will be thankful he did not marry me."

"I doubt that day will ever come, Julia. He has shown little interest in takin' a wife since he come back from France."

"This is what I came to talk to you about! Pray when did Adam go to France?"

"You don't know?'

"I only heard of it today from Harriet."

"Well, he set sail less than a week after you did, Julia, intendin' to fetch you back. But afore his feet touched dry ground, you had plighted yer troth to another. Yer father gave Adam the happy tidings. But I reckon he did not tell you of Adam's visit to his studio."

I shook my head, too stunned to speak.

"Ah well, I suppose your father felt it would have done you no good to know. I can see how miserable it is makin' you feel even now. Best to let go of things you can't do nothin' about, Julia. I tell Adam the same, but I hope you pay me more mind than he does."

"When he returned home without me, you must have been greatly relieved."

"No, I was greatly grieved."

"But I thought I was the last woman on God's earth you wanted your grandson to marry."

"True enough. I feared you would not make him a good mate."

"And I would *not* have! When Grandfather Walker told me our family history, I realized that I could never wed my first cousin."

"You should have ignored those stories from the past, Julia."

"Are they not true?"

Without replying, Granny commenced pumping the treadle again.

"Are they not true?" I asked again, raising my voice over the whir of the spinning wheel.

"Yes, they are true!" she shouted back at me. "You reckon Doc Silas would lie to you? Enough jabberin' about the past. Sich talk as that does no one any good."

She rose from her stool and picked up a wooden paddle. She was frowning so deeply she looked ready to hit me with it. But she turned her attention to the chimney oven, pulling open the arched wooden door and sticking the paddle deep inside it. She pulled out a golden loaf of bread and tossed it in a basket.

"That's fer you to take home," she told me. She went into her pantry and came back with a big round of her much lauded cheese. "This too." She wrapped it in a napkin and added it to the basket, along with a crock of applesauce and a hunk of gingerbread. "Fer that unfortunate orphan you took in," she said.

And then she sent me on my way.

Upon my return home I found Noah alone in the kitchen blacking the cookstove. "This is far too hard a job for you to take on," I told him. It must have sounded more like a reprimand than a commiseration, for he hung his head as if he'd been caught doing something wrong. "No, no, dear, I do not mean to chastise you," I quickly said. "But where is Mrs. Swann?"

I gathered, from his mumbled words, that she had retired to her bedchamber once again. So what else could I do but help the boy finish up? To ready myself for the dirty job, I cut a hole in an old sheet and pulled it over my head, wrapped a dishrag around my head, and put on a pair of Grandfather's old kid gloves. Noah found my getup as amusing as I found his laughter pleasing. Together we went at the stove with our brushes, rubbing on the blacklead paste and polishing it off, until every inch was shiny.

I then went at Noah with soap and water, scrubbing his smudged face and hands almost as hard as we'd scrubbed the stove. He did not find that half so amusing, but tolerated my ministrations well enough. I proposed that after the water in the stove boiler tank heated up again, he might avail himself of the wash tub in the kitchen alcove, where I myself had bathed as a child, but he did not seem inclined to take up my suggestion. Thinking him an exceptionally modest boy, I next proposed he use the zinc hip bath in my chamber, promising him complete privacy. I even offered to help him carry up the heavy cans of hot water for he is such a slight little lad. But he shrugged off my offer, and I let the matter go for the time being.

We rewarded ourselves for our hard work with a meal of Granny's delicious victuals, and then I adjourned to my studio to ready it for another session with the Phyfe sisters. Noah followed me there and, unbidden, got a roaring blaze going in the hearth. He does so love to poke at fires, but when I gave him a pencil and a sheet of paper he just as happily amused himself with drawing instead. Peeking over his shoulder, I saw that he had an innate talent and could not resist giving him a lesson. He is both eager and quick to learn. If only he could make himself better understood, people would not judge him so backward, but his deformity prevents him from enunciating words correctly.

I answered the door to the Phyfe sisters at two. When I led them into the studio, I was not surprised that Noah had vacated it. He only feels comfortable in my company or Adam's. But not in Mrs. Swann's company, I am sorry to say. Indeed, he reacts to her like a mistrustful cat with hackles raised whenever she makes overtures of friendship toward him.

My pretty young subjects, on the other hand, welcomed Mrs. Swann's friendly advances most readily when she joined us for their sitting. As she took it upon herself to tenderly arrange them in yesterday's pose, she seemed completely recovered from whatever malady it is that keeps her to her room for so many hours each day.

After the girls were posed, I took up my pencil with the

firm resolution to execute their portrait with the highest degree of art I am capable of producing. It matters not that Justice Phyfe considers me no better than any self-taught, itinerant country limner for hire; I shall keep my vision pure and my standards high. With this in mind as I sketched, I discarded my initial conception of portraying the Phyfe sisters as vacuous hothouse flowers. They are three individual souls, after all, and it is therefore my duty as an artist to try and capture each girl's essential nature.

Easier said than done, however, for they are a fidgety threesome indeed. Arabel is the worst, often excusing herself to stroll about the house to prevent her limbs from getting numb. The other two are constantly rearranging the folds in their skirts, the ribbons in their ringlets, and the multitude of decorative silk cords in various hues around their necks and wrists. They keep their fingers busy braiding these cords from long strands of thin ribbon they store in their reticules, and they are always swapping colors back and forth, except for Arabel, who works only in black.

Mrs. Swann, to her credit, managed to settle them down when she commenced reading to them in her deep, mellifluous voice. The story started off with a heroine named Fanny repairing to London with her guardian. Reckoning it to be a sentimental romance of little consequence, I stopped listening.

Instead, I gave my full attention to my subjects, concentrating first on Arabel. She appeared even less well than she had yesterday, her cheeks more sunken, her complexion more wan. Is she truly ailing? Or is she simply trying to look like the listless, fragile creatures depicted in fashion plates? Like many a foolish girl, Arabel probably doses herself with arsenic and belladonna to achieve this look, and she most likely eats chalk for good measure to keep her figure as sylphlike and willowy as those of the models in *Godey's Lady's Book*. Yet the aura of melancholy emanating from her eyes seemed genuine enough, and I began to regard her with more and more sympathy as I delineated her delicate features.

My pencil came to a sudden stop, however, when the words Mrs. Swann was reading aloud made their way into my consciousness: *"He revealed to me a member so large and of such prodigious stiffness that I knew my satisfaction was assured when we engaged in congress."*

"Mrs. Swann!" I cried out. "What in God's name are you reading to them?"

"Why, *The Memoirs of a Woman of Pleasure.*"

"Cease immediately! Chaste young ladies should not hear such things."

"Indeed they should, dear Julia, so that when the time comes for them to part with their maidenheads they will know what to expect. Most girls do not, and the shock of it takes away from the pleasure." Mrs. Swann smiled at the wide-eyed Phyfe sisters. "And I assure you, my pets, there is nothing more pleasurable than an orgasm."

"What's that?" Calista said.

"Never mind," I said.

But Beatrice seemed to think she could enlighten her little sister. "Don't you remember what Papa taught us, Callie? An organism is an individual form of life, be it animal or vegetable."

"I am still confused," Calista said. "Pray who is this large member of Congress?"

"I am not sure," Beatrice admitted. "But if he is so *stiff*, he is most likely a Whig."

I glared at Mrs. Swann. "There, you see! They are complete Innocents! They don't even know what you are talking about."

Arabel ran out of the room in tears, and Mrs. Swann's smile grew even wider. "That one does," she said.

I assumed Arabel had gone out to the Necessary, as she had

done a few times during yesterday's sitting, but when I glanced outside and saw her bonneted head bob past the front windows, I realized she was heading home. It seemed pointless to continue without her, so I dismissed her sisters, requesting that all three come back for another session tomorrow. After they left, I turned to Mrs. Swann, more puzzled than angry.

"Whatever possessed you to read to them from such a salacious book as that?" I said.

She shrugged. "It amused me."

Her glib reply infuriated me. "Your reckless amusement might well cost me dearly, Mrs. Swann. If the girls tell their father what they heard here today, they will never be allowed to return."

"Girls never discuss such things with their fathers."

"How can you be so sure? I need this commission in order to pay for food and coal and wood. Indeed, in order to pay for *your* services, Mrs. Swann, however much or little they are worth."

"From your tone I infer you do not think my services are worth much at all, Julia. But allow me to point out, my dear, that you have not paid me a penny for them."

"Only because you refuse payment!"

"Well, there you are," she said, throwing open her arms, palms up, in a theatrical manner. "So you have nothing to complain about, do you?"

I found arguing with Mrs. Swann most frustrating. "My complaint concerns your inappropriate frankness with the Phyfe girls about sexual matters."

"Permit me at least to be frank with *you,* dear Julia. After all, we are married ladies with experience in such matters. Let bigoted churchmen and canting hypocrites rail against the sin of carnal knowledge all they want to; we both know what delight there is in copulation, do we not?"

I remained silent.

"Have you never experienced such delight with your husband?" Mrs. Swann said.

Again, I said nothing.

Mrs. Swann sighed. "You were doubtless a bridal virgin, ignorant of all passionate desires."

I did not think it necessary to confess to her the passionate desire I had felt for my cousin before I married Jacques Pelletier. "A virgin, yes," I allowed.

"Then you most likely discovered on your wedding night that ignorance was *not* bliss."

Oh, how right she was on that score! "Never mind about me, Mrs. Swann. We were discussing the Phyfe girls."

"Well, why should they remain ignorant of fleshly pleasures? Indeed, I have taken it upon myself to educate as many young ladies as I can." She rose from her chair and came to stand close to me, redolent of bergamot and sandalwood. "I would be most happy to educate you too, dear Julia, on the various ways to pleasure the male member."

I turned away from her and back to my drawing. "I do not care to continue this conversation, Mrs. Swann."

"Very well. I was simply trying to explain to you why I took it upon myself to enlighten the little Phyfe fillies. But I shall never bring up the forbidden subject of sex with them again if that is what you prefer."

"I do. Now if you will allow me to go back to my work"—I began shading my drawing—"I shall let you get back to yours. You must have various duties to attend to."

"Such as what?" she inquired, sounding genuinely perplexed.

"Surely you know better than I, Mrs. Swann," I replied. "The management of my husband's chateau was already well established when I married him, and he wanted me to have nothing to do with it. Which was just as well, for the skills I learned during my girlhood were those of an artist's apprentice rather than a housekeeper. You, on the other hand, have had long experience maintaining a house, or so you claimed when first we met."

"I suppose I could go about rousting dust or something," she said vaguely. "Or leastways get that boy to make himself useful."

"Noah is not a servant here, Mrs. Swann. Pray do not treat him as such anymore."

"What makes you think I have?"

"I found him blacking the stove earlier today for one thing."

"Well, I never asked him to do so, I assure you. But let us not forget, my dear, softhearted one, that he would have been called upon to perform far harder and dirtier tasks if he'd been bound out to the charcoal pit."

"Thank God he was not. And he is *not* to be treated as a servant here," I repeated even more firmly.

"Very good, madam. Your wish is my command," Mrs. Swann said in a mock British accent and gave me a parody of a curtsy before she exited the room.

I could not help but smile. Despite her improprieties (or because of them), she does amuse me. I have never encountered a woman quite like Mrs. Swann before. Nor have I forgotten that I am beholden to her for the Phyfe commission. I only hope she has not lost it for me!

ADAM'S JOURNAL

Friday, December 10

As I was making my afternoon rounds today, Napoleon of a sudden began to favor his right foreleg. Climbed down and saw the horseshoe on that hoof had pulled loose and shifted so as to unbalance him. Fortunately, we were less than a mile from town. Pulled the shoe off and turned him around and walked beside him to the blacksmith shop. Left him there and went to my office for more bottles of laudanum to replenish the low supply in my bag. Try to be careful dosing my patients with such an addictive drug, but what else can I leave with consumptives to ease their pain and help them sleep?

It was most providential that I was at the office when I am normally away from it, for as I was opening the medicine cabinet I glanced out the back window and heeded a thin trail of smoke wafting out the open barn door. Ran into the barn and followed the smoke to where it rose heaviest. Found young Noah passed out behind the stacked bags of oats. He was lying not a yard from flames that were licking through hay and heading right toward his inert form. Snatched him up and got him out of there. He was limp and loose-limbed in my arms as if in deep slumber.

Laid him on the ground, made certain he was breathing and unharmed, and rushed back inside. Used an empty grain sack to beat down at flames that now flared high as my waist. Managed to whack them down to smoldering embers, then kicked away the hay. The smoke near overcame me, though. Fell to my hands and knees and crawled blindly away, butting my head hard against a post. Followed the glow of light through my eyelids to the barn door and out. Fell over beside Noah and blinked my eyes clear.

Checked the boy's breathing again and found it steady and slow. Went to the well and filled a bucket of water and washed his face of the black hay dust. His eyes blinked open. He clutched his hand at my coat, mumbled incomprehensible words at me, and then fell back silent again. Patted his cheek to reassure him.

After I thoroughly doused the burnt hay with water to be sure no rogue sparks remained, I carried Noah into my office, put him on the sick-bay cot, and covered him with a blanket. Stoked the stove and kept watch as he continued to sleep deeply. Heard Julia come through the back door and called to her. When she entered the office and saw Noah passed out on the cot, she went almost as white as he was. Told her how I'd found him in the barn and reassured her that he was not injured, just overcome by smoke inhalation.

"He would have suffocated or burned to death if not for you," she said.

"That I came along before he did so proves it was not his time to die," I said.

"What it proves to me is that you are a hero, Adam."

Could not help but feel like one under her admiring gaze. When I was a boy I would risk life and limb in foolish acts of bravery to get that shining look from her. I loved her then with all my heart, but it was a chaste, noble love. Only later, when we met again as adults, did base physical desire compli-

cate our once innocent relationship. And still does, I am sorry
to say. Whenever she is in my presence, no matter how much
she has hurt and disappointed me, I still *desire* her, damn it.

"Where is that housekeeper of yours?" I asked her rather
gruffly.

"I have no idea where Mrs. Swann is. She was in the
kitchen when I left for the tailor shop about an hour ago. I told
her I was expecting guests this afternoon and asked if she
would be so kind as to bake some of her special chocolate puffs
for them. She assured me she would do so, but as I passed
through the kitchen just now I saw no sign of them. Nor was
she herself there. Perhaps she had one of her unfortunate
headaches and is resting in her room."

"If so, I should think she would have noticed smoke coming from the barn," I said.

"The windows face the street. I gave her Grandfather's
bedchamber."

"Did you?"

"Why shouldn't I have?"

"Did I say you should not have, Julia?"

"Your countenance did."

I made an effort to readjust my expression. In truth, I did not
like the idea of Mrs. Swann, a complete stranger, living in the
Walker house, much less occupying the master chamber. But it is
Julia's house now, and if she sees fit to give her housekeeper the
bedchamber her grandparents had once occupied, that is her
business, not mine.

Noah awakened and sat up groggily. Julia and I urged him
to lie down again and continue to rest, but he pointed to the
skeleton hanging in the corner and shook his head.

"Noah does not seem to care for the macabre company
you keep, Adam," Julia said with a small smile. "He would rest
more easily in his own bed, don't you think?"

I carried Noah up to the room I had occupied two sum-mers ago whilst Doc Silas was recuperating from a broken leg. Many a sleepless night had I spent there, fighting down the temptation to go knocking on the door of the adjacent room, where Julia slept. That I never did is to my credit, I suppose. And to my everlasting regret.

We tucked Noah in his bed, and he fell back asleep imme-diately. Went out to the hall and rapped my knuckles sharply on the door of the master bedchamber. No reply came forth, so I opened the door and peeked within. Mrs. Swann was nowhere to be seen. Stepped inside to look about. Might well have invaded the woman's privacy further by opening a large trunk at the foot of the bed if not for the padlock on it. Might have looked in the wardrobe and drawers, too, if Julia had not been watching me from the doorway. The scent of lavender and bergamot hung in the air, and some of Mrs. Swann's lace-trimmed underthings were scattered about the room. I heard a carriage pull up in front of the house and looked out the window.

"Why, it's Henry and Lidian Emerson!" I said, turning back to Julia. "What a pleasant surprise to have them call."

"Pleasant to have them call, indeed," she said. "But not a surprise to me. They are the guests I told you I was expecting."

"You might have mentioned their names."

"You might have asked me their names."

"It is not my business to inquire whom you invite to your home, Julia. Or even whom you invite to *live* in it."

"Do stop harping on Mrs. Swann, Adam."

"I think I have shown great restraint."

"Restraint in expressing your disapproval?"

"Yes!" I admitted, for she had finally worn me down. "I think you acted most rashly when you took her in. But then you always do."

"Do what?"

"Act rashly, Julia. And because of it, you have wrecked our happiness."

"All my past actions were meant to *insure* your happiness, Adam."

"Foolish, foolish woman!" How in God's name did she think I could be happy without her as my wife?

"Foolish, am I? Perhaps so. I was a fool to think we could be friends again."

"I don't want to be your friend, Julia."

"You have made that most obvious, cousin, and—"

Our argument was interrupted by the sound of pounding on the front door, and we hurried downstairs. When we opened the door, Mrs. Emerson gave us a benevolent smile, but Henry looked rather annoyed, which led me to suppose he had been kept waiting on the doorstep far longer than he saw fit. He can be amazingly patient when observing nature, but social calls set his teeth on edge.

His expression immediately changed to one of alert interest as he regarded me. "How did it start?"

Since I had not even had a chance to open my mouth to greet him, his question took me aback. "How did what start, Henry?"

"The fire in the barn behind the house, of course." Henry brushed some charred straw off the sleeve of my frock coat and gave me a sniff. "From the lingering scent of smoke upon your person, I surmise it occurred less than an hour ago. And seeing that the barn is still standing, I would like to congratulate you for successfully putting it out. But you have not answered my question yet, Adam. How did it start?"

"I have not had a chance to investigate that yet."

Henry's eyes lit up. "Then let us do it together right now!"

We took leave of the ladies and made our way to the barn. When I pointed to where I had found Noah lying unconscious, Henry asked how old the boy was but said nothing more about him. He searched the barn's littered floor, found what was left of five locofoco friction matches, and held each up to examine.

"Four are burnt down to the end," he said. "That suggests they were lit for amusement, since it does not take but one lit match to start hay going. This last match is burnt to charcoal, however. It looks to be the one that dropped into the hay and started the fire."

"But was it dropped intentionally," I said, "or accidently?"

"That boy started the fire on purpose, or my name is not Mrs. Swann!"

Henry and I swung around to see Julia's housekeeper standing behind us. "We did not hear you come in," I said.

"I have little cat feet," she replied.

I introduced her to Henry. He nodded but did not extend his hand. Nor did she offer hers to him. Instead, she twirled a finger around one of the sausage curls that peeked out from beneath her frilly cap. Henry took a few steps back and observed her as he would any object of nature that caught his attention. (Although the bright yellow color of those curls was hardly natural.)

"Julia just told me how you saved both the boy and the barn from burning up," she said to me. "Bravo, doctor. I applaud your pluck."

That she actually clapped her hands together, as if I had put on a performance, irritated me. "Where have you been all this time, Mrs. Swann?"

"At Daggett's market. Chin-wagging the last hour or so away with Solomon Wiley. He has me near believing in vampyres, so convincing are his accounts of personal dealings with them. Vampyres have mortal minions, he told me, to do their evil bidding during daylight hours. Evil such as this."

"Such as what exactly, madam?" Henry said.

"Why, setting fire to a barn! If it were an accident, it might be called boyish mischief. That it was deliberate can only be called evil."

"Why are you so sure the boy set the fire deliberately?" Henry said.

"Because I have witnessed him doing so in the house."

"He has set things afire in the *house?*" I asked most anxiously.

"Yes, but nothing so bad as what he has done here!" She gestured toward the burnt hay. "He enjoys lighting bits of paper and cloth and such and then dropping them into the stove or the sink. No harm comes of it, so I have not mentioned it before now. Julia does not like to hear a word said against the boy, so I dare not tell her how much he frightens me."

"He frightens you when he burns bits of paper and cloth?" Henry asked in a disbelieving tone.

"Indeed he does. When he strikes a match and gazes into its sulfureted flare, he looks like a soul possessed. Why, Satan himself could not look more delighted. I wager you found spent matches here in the barn. He does so like to watch them burn in solitude. I have tried to put a stop to it, but he always manages to filch kitchen matches no matter where I hide them."

Several small bats were flitting fretfully overhead as Mrs. Swann spoke, and one unexpectedly dropped down and swept not a foot from her left ear. Much to my amazement, she did not budge an inch or even blink.

"You are a most unnatural woman," Henry told her.

She took umbrage, as any female would. "And what do you mean by that, sir?"

"Most women are terrified of bats."

"As I am!" She glanced over her right shoulder at the creatures flying high up near the beams. "I have been keeping an eye on them, and if they come any closer I shall immediately depart. Hideous, unnatural creatures!"

"Nothing unnatural or hideous about them," Henry said. "They are viviparous quadrupeds with furry bodies that suckle their young. Usually they are torpid in the winter, but the dangerous scent of fire has disturbed them. In the summer they come out at night and feed on small insects."

"They feed on humans, too!" Mrs. Swann said. "They draw blood from sleeping people, especially babies."

"Not true," Henry calmly refuted. "There is nothing I would welcome more in my bedchamber on a warm summer eve than a visit from a roving bat."

"More than a visit from a roving harlot?" Mrs. Swann inquired with a leer.

Henry turned away from her without replying. He does not care for bawdy remarks concerning sex or women, yet he will talk frankly about either in a respectful way.

A silence ensued, and Mrs. Swann concluded correctly that we did not wish to continue conversing with her. She wished us Good Day and went back to the house.

"I do not care for that woman," I said to Henry as soon as she left the barn.

"How long has she been Julia's housekeeper?" Henry said.

"Julia took her on the day after she came back to Plumford. So that would be seven days ago."

"What do you know of her?"

"Not much. There is something about Mrs. Swann that puts me off whenever she comes near, and I do my best to avoid her. I have heard men at the tavern remark that she is handsome, but I do not find her at all attractive."

"Nor do I," Henry said. "Yet I can understand why some might. She has a classical Greek profile, and such symmetry is appealing. Of course, her eyes are off-kilter."

"I did not notice. Is one higher than the other?"

"No. But the left one is blind."

"Are you sure?"

"Quite sure," Henry said. "She did not flinch when a bat swooped toward her left side. Yet she kept a wary eye on the bats to her right. Apparently she has been keeping a wary eye on Noah, too. She makes him sound like a little demon. Who is this boy, Adam?"

"Only a poor orphan Julia felt compelled to take in. You know how impulsive she can be."

"Our impulses reflect the true nature of our souls," Henry said.

"Be that as it may," I said, not caring to get into a transcendental discussion with him at the moment, "Julia has become rather fond of the boy. And so have I, for that matter."

"I would like to go talk to him now," Henry said.

"Let me tell you something about him first."

"No. Allow me to meet him without knowing any more so that I may form an unbiased opinion of him."

We went back to the house and found Julia and Mrs. Emerson in Doc Silas's study, which I reckon I should get used to calling Julia's studio. They did not think it a good idea to wake Noah, and I promised that we would not disturb him if we found him still asleep.

Noah was staring at the ceiling when I came into the room, looking as bored as any boy put to bed in the daytime might be expected to look. He seemed happy enough to see me, but when I asked him if he would like to meet a friend of mine who was waiting in the hall, he replied with a loud *"NO"* and pulled the blanket over his head. I was not surprised, for Noah is most wary of strangers.

An uncannily eerie and low cry began to emanate from the hall. Noah uncovered one ear to hear it better and then could not resist pulling off the blanket to take a look over his shoulder. I looked toward the doorway too, half expecting to see a bird fly into the room. Henry sauntered in, instead.

"What am I?" he asked the boy and made the sound again.

"A screech owl!" Noah managed to say distinctly enough.

"Correct," Henry said. "And what am I now?" He made a soft but sharp barking sound, and Noah guessed correctly that it was a fox rather than a dog. "You are a boy who pays attention to the natural world around him. I like that," Henry said, plunking himself down on the edge of the bed as if he were visiting an old chum.

Henry proceeded to regard Noah with such a long, penetrating gaze that I expected the boy to hide under the blanket again. But he did not. Indeed, he seemed to appreciate being looked upon with such uncritical intensity. Most people avert their eyes from Noah's face, but Henry studied him as he would any wondrous natural phenomenon. Also, there is something about Henry's demeanor that encourages trust, especially in children. Perhaps it is his natural simplicity and direct manner.

"Tell me, young fellow," he said after a moment. "Do you perchance have upon your person the magical arrowhead I lost?"

Noah frowned with puzzlement and shook his head.

Henry leaned toward the boy and touched behind his ear. "Then what is this?" he said, coming away with a quartz arrowhead in his fingers.

Eyes wide, Noah sat up, stared at the arrowhead, and felt behind his ear.

Henry laughed and ruffled the boy's sandy hair. "You didn't know it had hidden itself there, did you? I am sure you would have admitted to it if you knew, for you look to be an honest, truthful boy. Am I correct?"

Noah nodded his head.

"Good. Let us talk about the fire in the barn now," Henry said. "Do you know how it started, Noah?"

The boy responded with vigorous head shakes.

"A fire can start up quite unexpectedly," Henry continued in his reasonable, quiet tone. "I know of what I speak, for I once set fire to the woods. I did not *mean* to do it. I lit a small fire in a tree stump to cook some fish my friend and I had caught, but when sparks flew into the grass around the stump, a fire suddenly spread out of control, and three hundred acres of woodland went up in smoke. I admitted what I had done and took responsibility for it. If I had not, I would have felt far worse about it. It is always best to be honest and forthright." He paused and looked at Noah. Noah looked right back at him and said not a word. "Just tell us what happened in the barn," Henry urged softly.

The boy raised his boney shoulders to his ears.

"Why did you go there?" Henry said.

Noah mumbled a reply. Henry could not understand his enunciation and looked to me.

"Noah claims that he doesn't remember going into the barn today," I said and turned to the boy. "But if that is where I found you, that is indeed where you went, isn't it?"

Another shrug is all I got for an answer. The boy's eyes drooped, and he fell back upon the pillow.

"We will let you rest," Henry told him. "If you say you do not remember going to the barn, we must take you at your word." He stood and made to leave, then turned back to the boy. "Would you like me to give you the arrowhead I found behind your ear?"

Noah's eyes lit up, and he put out his hand to receive it.

Henry made a motion to give it over to him, but then pulled back. "I should tell you something about this particular arrowhead before you take it into your hand." He lowered his voice in a confidential manner. "It can sear the flesh of those who do not tell the truth. Do you still want it?"

Noah nodded most vigorously and kept his palm open.

When Henry dropped the arrowhead into it, the boy clutched it in his fist, murmured a thank you, and fell immediately asleep.

We left him to rest and came upon Mrs. Swann in the hallway. "I am on my way to my chamber to lie down," she said. "I have another of my cursed headaches."

"I will give you a dose of willow bark powder mixed with water," I offered. "I have found it to be a most effective natural medication."

"No thank you, doctor. I do not countenance taking medications of *any* sort," she said most sanctimoniously. And with that she went into her chamber and closed the door firmly behind her.

"She did not even inquire as to how Noah was faring," I said.

"She might have had no need to inquire," Henry said. "Who knows how long she has been standing in the hall on those little cat feet of hers, eavesdropping?"

We went down to join the ladies in the studio, where there was a fine fire crackling in the hearth. Julia was making a sketch of Lidian Emerson, who sat in an armchair across from her, looking prim and reserved in her heavy black silk dress and light white gauze cap. Henry and I recounted our brief conversation with Noah to them.

"It is most odd that the child can remember nothing," Mrs. Emerson said.

"Perhaps he doesn't *want* to," Henry said. "He could be resisting the memory from coming forth."

I nodded in agreement with his theory. "If I hypnotized him, the memory might well come to the surface."

"No, Adam," Julia said. "I cannot countenance such experimentation on a child."

"You were eager enough to have me experiment on you," I reminded her.

"And you would not do it but once!" She glared at me and then addressed Mrs. Emerson. "When last I was in Plumford, Adam hypnotized me, and I recounted to him a past life in ancient Rome. When I came out of hypnosis, I had no recollection of it, however. I was all for trying again, this time with Adam's instruction to remember, but he refused to repeat the procedure, no matter how much I beseeched him."

"I can well understand why you would want to remember," Mrs. Emerson said. "Henry treasures the memory of his own past life as an Indian."

I was most surprised that she knew of his regression, for Henry was most secretive about it. I gave him a questioning look, and he smiled back sheepishly.

"I tell Lidian everything that is important to me," he said. "She is my confidante."

Mrs. Emerson beamed her gentle smile at him. "As you are mine, Henry."

Julia and I exchanged a swift look, for we too had been the dearest of confidantes at one time. And now we could not converse for more than a minute without quarrelling.

"What do you know of the boy's past?" Henry asked Julia.

"Not much. As you must have heeded, Noah has difficulty speaking, and because of this he is quite reticent. But we have only known each other for little more than a week, and I am sure he will become more comfortable talking to me the better acquainted we become."

"Where did he reside before he came here?" Henry said.

"He'd been staying with a farm family named Shrove, but they could no longer keep him."

"Why?"

Julia shrugged. "Justice Phyfe gave me no reason."

"The Shroves have a small farm up the river," I said. "They barely subsist on it and have a good number of their own children to feed."

Henry nodded and asked no further questions about Noah. Instead, he went to stand over Julia's shoulder and watch her draw Mrs. Emerson.

I, in turn, regarded Mrs. Emerson in the flesh. Flesh there is little enough of on her frame, and her long, smooth face was tinged yellow, leading me to conclude she was slightly jaundiced. All the same, being long of limb and graceful in carriage, she is attractive enough. But she is no great beauty to be sure, and I could not help but wonder why Henry is so enthralled with this staid married woman a good decade older than he is. I joined him behind Julia to take a look at her work and understood better. Lidian Emerson's inherent beauty was clearly evident in the drawing, for with the quick strokes of her pencil Julia had somehow managed to depict her subject's nobility of character and gentleness of spirit. Fittingly enough, Julia was using a Thoreau pencil.

When Henry remarked upon this she said, "I prefer the drawing pencils your family manufactures to all others, Henry, and told you as much when first we met, if you recall."

"Indeed I do. And I further recall that I offered to give you a box of them."

"Alas, I told you I could not accept such an expensive gift from you. Much to my everlasting regret, I might add. But at the time I was rather miffed at you, for you had suggested that I should devote my talents to something *useful,* such as botanical depictions, rather than depictions of people."

"Well, I am not suggesting it now," Henry said as he continued to stare at the drawing of his dear friend. "And I will renew my offer to give you a box of pencils."

"Only if you allow me to pay for them. I appreciate how dear they are."

"Perhaps we can strike a deal," Henry said. He leaned toward her and murmured something in her ear.

Julia nodded, and when Henry and Mrs. Emerson made

ready to leave a short time later, Julia gave him the rolled up drawing she had sketched of Lidian.

Whilst she and Lidian were bidding each other adieu by the carriage, Henry and I quickly made arrangements to meet again late tomorrow evening. We did not want the ladies to overhear, of course, that we planned to go to an opium den.

ADAM'S JOURNAL

Saturday, December 11

Departed from Concord at ten p.m. last evening, and it took over two hours to drive to Boston. Napoleon kept up a pace of close to ten miles an hour, not bad for a horse his age. Even though a train would have gotten us there much faster, it was just as well none run at night, for Henry and I both prefer traveling in the open air under a starry sky rather than inside a stuffy, smoke-filled car. Left Napoleon and the gig in a horse car stable, and we walked up Tremont, past Faneuil Hall, and then onto Ann Street, which led us deep into the Black Sea district.

Assuming that the opium den we were heading for catered to gentlemen, I'd dressed for the occasion in my formal black tailcoat and white waistcoat and cravat. But Henry wore his usual attire of rough country sack coat, corduroy trousers, and heavy boots, all better suited to stalking through brambles than treading city streets. When I expressed my opinion that he might have made more of an effort to dress like a man about town, he waved a hand dismissively. "I say if you have any enterprise before you, try it in your old clothes. Besides, any others I have are no better."

Midnight along Ann Street proved to be most interesting. There are grogshops and bordellos aplenty servicing boisterous sailors fresh off ships, and right alongside them are dining establishments and saloons catering to college and business men. Along with the sounds of coarse laughter, boisterous singing, and vile cursing, the cold night air carried a current of electrifying energy fueled by manly desires of every ilk. Females caroused freely with the men, but of course not a decent woman was in sight.

We approached a hack driver and asked if he knew a place called Chandoo Gate. He pointed us to a brick building, its windows covered over with red paper that let through a faint glow from within. We had expected a guard to be posted outside the door, but there was none, so we went right in. A sweet, incense-like odor that was rich and earthy and at the same time conveyed a sense of ripe decay enveloped us.

"I recall there was a trace of just this scent on Chauncey's clothes when we found him in the woods," Henry said.

Before we could get past the foyer a giant Chinaman sprang out of a dark recess to block our way. He silently glared at us with one glinting eye. His other eye, I assumed, was missing, for the lid had been sewn shut with a ragged line of black stitches. Would have done a far better job of it myself. But I doubt a trained surgeon had made the sutures, much less removed the orb. Most likely it had been gouged out in a fight. Some thugs, I have heard, purposely grow their thumbnails long to facilitate the gory practice, and if that were the case, the Chinaman was lucky to have survived. The insertion of a foe's filthy finger deep into one's cranium could easily result in infection and painful death. Could not help but have trepidations that Henry and I might end up in a brutal fight ourselves given the way the giant regarded us with almost palpable menace. Our intrusion into this den of iniquity was obviously not welcomed.

"We have opium to sell," Henry pronounced loudly.

The giant gave no sign of understanding. He laid a mighty paw on Henry's shoulder, and I saw my friend brace himself for the expected heave-ho. I tensed, too, ready to come to his aid, although I had doubts that even the two of us together could stand up to such a muscled colossus of a man.

A bodiless voice rang out in the darkness, speaking a tongue that sounded Chinese, and the giant immediately stepped aside to allow Henry and me to pass through the foyer and enter a long hall with numbered doors on each side. A very small, elderly man, also of the Yellow Race, sat cross-legged on a red lacquered chair at the end of the hall. When he beckoned us to him, his extremely long, curved fingernails looked like lightning bolts shooting off his hand. Dressed in a black padded silk robe trimmed with gold and a black skull cap with an upturned fur brim, he conveyed an air of refinement and cultivation. A thin smile stretched his lips as he watched us approach.

"My name is Zang," he said, "and you have aroused my curiosity, gentlemen. Why do you carry coals to Newcastle?"

Henry smiled back and removed the silk purse from his pocket. "Have you no need for more coals, sir?" he said, tossing the purse into Zang's lap.

"I always have need for more," Zang replied, emptying the contents of the purse in the folds of his garment and then examining each of the ten opium beads closely. "The demand grows faster than the supply. But where did your coals come from?"

"Most likely from you," Henry replied. "Did you not sell them to a fellow named Chauncey Bidwell recently?"

Without replying, Zang regarded Henry for a long moment. "I read honesty in your face, young man, so I will assume you did not steal these opium pills from him."

"Would it matter to you if I had?"

"Not at all. But I do not want Mr. Bidwell coming here and causing trouble over it."

"I assure you he will not," Henry said. "Does he usually come here alone or with friends?"

"He comes with other men and sometimes women from the stage. I cannot say if any of them are his friends."

"Can you say if any are his enemies?"

"I prefer to say nothing at all about those who come here." Zang pulled a leather pouch from the voluminous sleeve of his robe and shook an array of coins onto the table beside him. "Take ten gold Liberty Eagles as payment for the ten *chandoo* you brought me," he instructed Henry.

Henry glanced at me and I shrugged. Each Liberty Eagle was worth ten dollars, but I had no idea how much ten opium pills, or *chandoo* as the elderly Chinaman called them, were worth. Even so, a hundred dollars was a handsome sum, and Henry decided to accept the deal on behalf of the Bidwell ladies. He plucked up the coins and slid them into the deep pocket of his jacket.

"And now, gentlemen, either adjourn to a smoking room or leave," Zang said. "I do not allow lingering in the hall."

"We will go to a room then," Henry said, surprising me. We had not discussed the possibility of actually smoking opium.

"First return to me four Liberty Eagles as payment for two *chandoo*," Zang said.

"But you are now charging me double for what I just sold you!" Henry said.

Zang sighed. "Such is the way of the world. I am not charging you any more than I charge my other customers."

"Twenty dollars a pill seems mighty steep. Why, I once built a sturdy home for myself for near that amount," Henry said.

"Most men who come here are rich enough to afford it."

"The way I see it, a man is rich in proportion to the number of things which he can afford to let alone," Henry said. "And that man is richest whose pleasures are the cheapest."

Zang smiled again, this time displaying gold teeth. "You sound like Confucius, young man. But even if you were the Great Teacher himself, I would still ask you to pay me forty dollars for two *chandoo*. Pay me or leave. You choose."

Henry reluctantly handed over four gold coins, and the man called out in Chinese again. Expecting the ungainly giant to reappear, I was most pleasantly surprised when a young, willowy Chinese woman in a blue satin robe came forward. She led us down the hall and into a small room furnished with two long couches draped with silken fabric. She then turned to Henry and commenced unbuttoning his jacket. He allowed her to do this without protest, and I wondered what next he would allow her to do. After relieving him of his jacket, she snatched up the silk fabric on the couch and held it out to Henry. I saw that it was a robe, and when he slipped into it he looked quite the Ming mandarin, with his sun-browned face and serious demeanor. Rather than go ahead and remove my own coat, I waited for the young beauty to help me out of it as she had helped Henry, thinking this the courteous thing to do (and, in truth, for the thrill of it), and then I too put on a robe. The silken texture felt most soothing.

Our hostess gestured for us to seat ourselves upon the two couches and left us. A moment later a Chinese boy in yellow pajamas came into the room, carrying a small wooden serving table laden with two extremely long bamboo pipes and an assortment of paraphernalia. He placed the table on the floor between our two couches and knelt before it.

"Shall I start preparing your pipes?" he asked in perfect English, striking a match and bringing it to a small brazier of polished metal.

Henry held up his hand. "We are not ready to imbibe. Please go. But leave the tray here."

"Very well, sir." The boy blew out the match and departed.

"Now what?" I asked Henry.

"Now we bide our time," he said. "Is this not the ideal hunting blind to await members of Chauncey Bidwell's species? A species, I might add, so profligate it seems doomed to extinction. But whilst members of it still come out to this watering hole under cover of night, let us try to snare one who will be more garrulous than the reticent Mr. Zang."

So we waited, listening to customers arrive and make their arrangements with Zang. Business was conducted in a surprisingly muted, polite, and orderly manner, but eventually we heard a loud, arrogant voice that snagged Henry's attention.

"Did you hear me, Zang? Set me up with a pipe. Chopchop!"

"Twenty dollars please, my good sir," the elderly Chinaman responded.

"Just add the amount to my account."

"You owe me too much already."

"How dare you speak to me that way, Zang? You know very well that I am good for the money."

"I know very well that you owe me too much already," Zang repeated patiently.

"Cock and bollocks!" the man roared back.

Henry sprang up from the couch. "The imbecile out there sounds just like Forest Orton. That was his favorite expression when I knew him at Harvard." He opened the door to take a stealthy look into the hall. "It's Orton all right," he told me. "You wait here whilst I lure him into our trap." Henry stepped out into the hall.

"May I extend hospitality to a former classmate and invite him to smoke a pipe at my expense?" I heard Henry say.

There was a pause followed by a burst of laughter that I thought carried a note of derision. "Is that you, Judge? I cannot believe it! I have not laid eyes on you since our days in Hollis Hall. You of all men an opium smoker? Why, this beggars all credulity! Yes, of course I shall accept your offer. I have lost every cent I had on me at the gambling houses, and beggars cannot be choosers, after all."

Henry returned to the room with a pudgy, dapper blade. I stood up to greet him, and he eyed me suspiciously.

"Harvard too," Henry said of me to Orton. "The class five years after ours."

"All right then," Orton said, and no further introduction was required. Comfortable with the situation, Orton shrugged off his cape and threw himself down on the couch I had vacated. Henry and I seated ourselves on the one across from him.

"Cock and bollocks!" Orton said again, staring at Henry. "To see you of all people here is a *thorough* shock. You were such a *thorough* teetotaler during college days." He winked at Henry after each play on his name, and then turned to me. "During our days at Harvard together, our friend here used to be as sober as a judge. Indeed, he was called Judge. My own set of chums also referred to him as Beau Brummell. In jest, of course. Henry was anything but a fashion plate. Despite the requirement that students wear black frock coats to lectures, Henry had the gall to wear one of green homespun!"

"It was the only frock coat I owned," Henry said in his calm, quiet voice. "In fact, I wear it still when the occasion demands. And I can still button it, too. I wager you cannot claim the same in regard to your own college coat."

Orton smiled and gave the bulge beneath his vest a fond pat. "Indeed, I cannot, but why should I care? I have a new coat tailored to my measurements whensoever I please."

"Then I also wager that your tailor is more lenient about extending you credit than your opium supplier is," Henry said.

Orton's smile stiffened. "Did you not invite me here to share your own supply?"

Henry gestured toward the serving table. "Help yourself. Or shall I call for the boy to do it for you?"

"No, no, he'll expect a gratuity. I can do it just as well myself."

Orton plucked up a needle-like copper skewer and jabbed it into one of the opium pills. "Light the brazier," he ordered Henry imperiously, and then held the pill over the flame to warm it. Once the heat had softened it sufficiently, he spread it around the tiny ceramic bowl of the pipe, all the time breathing heavily—in excited anticipation or because of an asthmatic condition, I know not. He then heated the filled bowl over the brazier until the opium began to turn to vapor. At that point he took the pipe to his lips, inhaled deeply, rolled his dull eyes, and closed them. After that he stopped breathing altogether, and as the seconds passed I became more and more concerned. I was just about to leap up from the couch and give him a hard slap on the back when he gave out a long exhale through his nostrils, sighed, and lay back against the cushions, smiling.

"Thy poppy throws around my head its lulling charities," he murmured.

"Bed, not head," Henry replied. He had observed this whole process with obvious distaste. "If you are going to quote Keats, at least do so correctly, Orton."

"Same stickler as you always were, Henry," Orton said lazily.

I picked up the used pipe he had thrown aside and examined it out of curiosity. "Now I understand why meconium, which is the ancient Greek word for opium, is also the medical term for a babe's first bowel movement," I told Henry. "Same viscous, sticky appearance."

He smiled. "Did you hear that, Orton?"

Apparently not. Orton's attention was completely taken by the remaining opium pill on the serving table. "I would not refuse another pipe," he said.

"Let us talk a little more first," Henry said. "Do you perchance know Chauncey Bidwell?"

"Oh, yes, he is a denizen of Chandoo Gate and likes to hobnob with his betters."

"You refer to yourself as his better?" Henry said.

"Well, after all, Bidwell is *not* a Harvard man. He is a highly entertaining fellow, though; I will give him that. Especially when he brings along those pretty actresses he knows. I was hoping he might do so tonight. But come to think of it, I have not seen Bidwell around of late. That little country wench of his must be keeping him amused."

"Is he courting a girl in Concord?" Henry said.

"Somewhere thereabouts. But courting would be putting too fine a point on it. He claims he stole her virtue and can do whatever he likes with her now, without so much as an if you please or thank you, ma'am."

"Did he name the girl?" Henry said, keeping his voice expressionless.

"Interested?" Orton said, leering at him.

Henry stared back at him with a stone face. "Did he name her?" he repeated evenly.

"Only as his Poppy Poppet. Not only did the wicked boy introduce her to fleshly delights, but he succeeded in binding her over to poppy smoke, all the better to make her his utter love slave."

As much as I have seen of life as a doctor, especially of late, I was still shocked to hear this. I looked at Henry. He too seemed shocked, but when he spoke, his voice was as calm as a pond.

"What more did Bidwell tell you concerning this young woman?" he asked Orton.

"Is that not enough to tell about any woman?"

"Did he describe her?"

"Well, he claimed she is beautiful, of course. And he related to me intimate details concerning her anatomy. But clothed I would not know her from Eve. He never mentioned the color of her eyes or hair or such as that. And neither did I care."

"Did he ever mention where they would meet for their liaisons?"

"Not precisely. He has alluded to a mossy little love nest where he can leave the pipe and they can have at each other like two minks in a burrow. He brags that he has her so bound to the drug that there is little need to talk of love at all anymore. Just poppy smoking and rutting. Some men have all the luck, do they not? You should ask Bidwell about Poppy Poppet yourself if you are so fascinated, Henry. He is always hard up for cash and may be willing to share her for a fee. If you get her drugged up enough, she may not even notice you have taken his place between her legs."

Henry stood up abruptly and loomed over Orton. "You think like a pig, speak like a pig, and even look like a pig. In short, you are a pig, sir."

I fully expected some sort of challenge from Orton, but he merely turned his eyes to the opium pill on the serving table again. "Have we not talked enough, Henry?"

"Indeed we have. We shall leave you to suck up more excrement."

We shrugged off our robes, threw on our coats, and went off into the cold night without a backward glance at the Chandoo Gate.

As we rode to Concord we pondered over what we had heard from Forest Orton's befouled lips concerning Bidwell and the maiden he'd seduced and habituated to opium.

"If Bidwell was as vile as that," I said, "there could be dozens of people who might want to kill him."

"But only one did," Henry said. "And let us hope the murderer had no connection to the unfortunate young woman. If he turns out to be her enraged father or brother or sweetheart, then the whole sordid story will become known to one and all. The Bidwell ladies will realize what a villain their beloved Chauncey really was. And the young woman in question will become an outcast in society."

"Perhaps it would be best to stop investigating his death," I suggested.

"No," Henry said. "We can never stop searching for the truth. But what we do with it when we find it is another matter."

And that is how we left it when I dropped him off in front of the Emerson house.

JULIA'S NOTEBOOK

Sunday, 12 December

Well, the Phyfe sisters returned today for another sitting so I can only assume they did not tell their father about Mrs. Swann's indecorous comments. I thought for sure that they had when they canceled the last sitting, but the reason turned out to be that Arabel had not been feeling well. At any rate, today's session went very well. And Mrs. Swann behaved most properly with the young ladies. I shall start working in oils tomorrow.

After the sitting, I wanted to stretch my legs, and my feet took me in the direction of the Shrove farm. What an uninviting place it is, located in an isolated area upriver with only the burnt-out remains of a cottage nearby. The lack of trees on the fallow fields surrounding the farmhouse is evidence that a valiant attempt had once been made to clear the land for tillage, but countless saplings have sprung up to replace their downed forebears, and even more than saplings, there are rocks everywhere to impede a plow's progress. The house itself looked more and more ramshackle the closer I got to it. I spied two men and three little boys standing on the sagging front porch, and as I drew nearer still I realized that one of the men was none other than Henry T.!

If Henry was as surprised to see me as I him, he did not show it when he introduced me to Mr. Shrove. The farmer looked to be as worn out as his threadbare overalls and shabby boots, yet when he smiled at me I saw that he could be little more than thirty. My prejudice against him for forsaking Noah prevented me from smiling back.

"So you are the kind lady who took in the unfortunate orphan," he said.

"Far better me than the collier at the charcoal pit," I replied rather sharply. "We were the only two who bid on the boy at the vendue auction."

"So I heard," Mr. Shrove said, looking as shamefaced as I thought he should. One of the children, little more than a babe, started wailing, and Mr. Shrove picked him up and pressed his lean, bristled cheek to the child's soft cheek. "There, there, my boy," he said softly, and I liked him a little better for that. At least he cared for his own.

"I came here to inquire if Mr. Shrove wanted his property surveyed," Henry said to me, "and he informed me that he'd just given up his lease on it. He and his family are heading west."

"We're leaving for Illinois tomorrow to join up with relatives," Mr. Shrove said, "then on to Oregon in a wagon train. Land is far cheaper out there, and the soil is much richer."

"Beets grow up to three feet around in Oregon," the tallest boy, who looked to be about seven, said.

"And turnips grow five feet around!" his brother topped him.

A weary-looking young woman stepped onto the porch. She was wrapped in a patched shawl, carrying yet another child in her arms, this one still of suckling age. "We have not kept back any possessions belonging to Noah, if that is what you have come for," she told me coldly. "We took him in with only the clothes on his back."

"My reason for calling was to learn more about Noah from

you," I said. "And I also thought you might care to know how he was faring."

"Well, tell me then," she said impatiently, moving the mewling babe from one hip to the other.

"He's doing well enough, but keeps to himself most of the time," I said. "And he will not go to school."

"As far as I know, Noah never went to school," Mrs. Shrove said. "But he knows how to read and cipher well enough. His father must have taught him. Mr. Robinson was a clever, city-bred man."

"What did he do for a living?" Henry said.

"He was a carpenter of sorts. Built sets for the Howard Theater in Boston," Mr. Shrove said.

"Or so he claimed anyway," Mrs. Shrove said. "For all the time he was our neighbor, I never saw him lift so much as a finger, much less a hammer. Who knows when last he worked? He left a lot of debts unpaid in Weymouth or Falmouth or wherever it was they lived before removing to Plumford."

"We know because a debt collector came by here last month looking for the Robinson family," Mr. Shrove said. "I pointed to Noah mucking out the barn and told him that was the only Robinson left."

"For a debt collector, he was such a personable, refined young man," Mrs. Shrove put in. "When he learned that both the boy's parents were dead and he could not collect a penny, he went over to Noah and gave *him* a penny. Was that not kind of him? But I reckon he considered the sight of such a peculiar deformity worth paying for."

"Ma made Jackrabbit give that penny over to her," the eldest boy said.

"Of course I did," she said. "We shared our home and food with him, so it was only right he shared whatever he came by with us. The town gave us a mere pittance for his upkeep."

"But he did make an effort to earn his keep," Mr. Shrove said.

"Oh, I have no complaints on that score," Mrs. Shrove allowed. "Noah could keep house better than most hired girls twice his age. He could even bake pastries. Not that he ever did so for us. We could ill afford to spend money on sugar and chocolate to make those fancy puffs he used to bake for his mother."

"He did all the cooking, washing, and cleaning for his mother," Mr. Shrove said. "That's why I bid for him at the vendue auction. I reckoned he would be as much help to my wife as he'd been to Mrs. Robinson."

"Not that I need as much help as a blind woman," Mrs. Shrove said irritably.

"Noah's mother was blind?" Henry said.

"From birth, she told us," Mrs. Shrove said. "That might well have been a blessing, for she could not perceive how repugnant her child was. Indeed, she lavished a great deal of affection upon him. I tried my best to be kind to Noah when he was with us, but I could not be affectionate. I could see very well what he looked like."

"Methinks Noah's blind mother truly saw him, whilst you merely looked at him," Henry said. "Who then is the one without vision?"

Mrs. Shrove frowned at him. "I do not understand."

"I did not expect you to."

"You need not speak to me in that superior manner," she told Henry. "I am a well-educated woman. Indeed, I attended Amherst Academy."

"That is where I met my wife," Mr. Shrove said. "I taught there."

Henry gazed out at the fallow fields. "I wager you did not teach agriculture."

"No, indeed," Mr. Shrove conceded.

But Mrs. Shrove became more affronted. "If you are imply-ing that my husband is not a good farmer, I assure you he did the best he could with this sorry piece of land. And we did the best we could for that sorry boy, too. Noah Robinson is no kin to us, yet we did our neighborly duty by taking him in after the fire."

My heart jumped. "What fire?"

"Why, the one his parents perished in, of course," Mrs. Shrove said. "You must have seen the charred ruins of their cottage on your way here from town. Mr. Robinson managed to save his son, but when he went back inside to find his wife, he died along with her."

"How did the fire start?" Henry asked.

"A faulty chimney, it is assumed," Mr. Shrove said. He glanced up at the crumbling chimney of his own domicile. "The place the Robinsons rented was in as bad a shape as this one."

"Have you been troubled by fires yourself?" Henry asked.

"Not in the chimney, thank God."

"But elsewhere?" Henry pressed gently.

"Well, some rags in the corner of the kitchen caught fire," Mrs. Shrove said. "A hot coal from the stove must have rolled into the pile."

"Was Noah living with you at the time?"

"He was the one who discovered the fire and stomped it out," Mr. Shrove said.

Mrs. Shrove eyed Henry suspiciously. "You ask a lot of questions."

"So I have been told."

"Well, we have little time for them. We must make ready for our journey." With that, she went back inside the house.

Mr. Shrove, although not so abrupt as his wife, also made it clear that he had better things to do than talk about Noah with us. So Henry and I bid him Good Day and went on our way.

As we crossed the rocky field together, heading for the road, neither of us mentioned Noah at first. Instead, I commented that the weather had turned much colder, and Henry predicted that the ponds would freeze solid by week's end. Finally, I asked him if his true reason for stopping by the Shroves had been to inquire about a possible surveying job.

"I would have accepted one readily enough, so there was no lie in such an inquiry," he replied. "I did have another reason, however, that I did not wish to reveal to the Shroves. Like you, I wanted to find out more about Noah."

"But I was not motivated by suspicions regarding him."

"Nor was I," Henry said. "Suspicion often proceeds from the apprehension of evil, and I do not think the boy evil. Yet I do think it would be unwise for you to ignore what you heard today, Julia. Noah has been associated with three recent fires."

"There is no proof that he started any of them."

"No concrete proof," Henry said, "but some circumstantial evidence is very strong, as when a boy is found alone in a burning barn beside four struck matches."

"I allow there is a possibility that he started the fire in my barn," I said. "But childish carelessness such as that does not make him an arsonist."

"You should also allow for the possibility that he might set fire to your house, either deliberately or carelessly," Henry said. "You have reason to be concerned for your safety as long as Noah stays under your roof, Julia."

"But what about *his* safety? If I do not keep Noah under the protection of my roof, he will become a ward of the town again and most likely end up working at the charcoal pit. That would put him in grave danger."

"So it would. 'Tis a dilemma for sure."

I waited for him to say more, but he did not. "Well, Henry, have you no opinion regarding the matter?"

"Yes, but the evidence that supports it is hardly irrefutable.

Hence, I hesitate to express it. Moreover, you do not need to hear my opinion to help you determine what course to pursue, Julia. All you need do is listen deeply to your own inborn intuition, and you will make the right decision."

By now we had reached the road, and I took Henry's hand before we went off in opposite directions. "You are a good friend to me and always have been," I said.

"Even though I do not give you advice?"

"Better yet, you give me wisdom," I said, and I would have kissed his cheek if I had not feared he would balk at such a physical demonstration of my regard.

Before we parted, he brought to my attention the bright-yellow sulfur lichens gilding a tumbled stone wall along the road. Such intense, glowing color! And to think I would have passed by without noticing this unexpected gift from Nature on such a cold, drab winter day. Thank you, dear Henry.

ADAM'S JOURNAL

Monday, December 13

Today began badly and ended badly, and I foresee only more misery to come. The Consumption spreads, and some say that a wrathful God is punishing Plumford. For what I cannot fathom. Our once peaceful little town of hard-working shop-keepers, craftsmen, and farmers is hardly Sodom or Gomorrah. It is almost easier to credit Solomon Wiley's explanation that vampyres led by the ancient Indian Witiku have taken over our community, fastening their fangs into victims to infect them. I myself believe something even more insidious and destructive has caused this venomous disease to consume so many of our population of late: contagion. Most of my medical colleagues reject this contagious theory as a superstition on par with vampyrism, convinced that the disease spontaneously begins from within. But I am of the opinion that Consumption enters the body from *without,* else why would we be having this epidemic? How the infection is transmitted from one to another I know not, however, and my inability to cure my suffering patients troubles me exceedingly.

Julia's proximity is also troubling. To have the woman you love close at hand is sublime, but to have the woman you love but *cannot have* close at hand is pure hell. Although I try to stay away from her as much as possible, I had no choice but to seek her out first thing this morning. Found her mixing paints in her studio.

"Julia, someone has been stealing laudanum from my office," I announced without preamble. "I have two bottles less than I can account for and cannot help but suspect Mrs. Swann."

"No, of course you cannot help it." Julia impatiently tossed aside her palette knife and wiped her hands on her apron. "You have been prejudiced against the woman from the moment I took her on as my housekeeper."

"She has full access to my office, does she not? I keep the front door locked when I'm away, but there is no lock on the inside door."

"I have instructed Mrs. Swann, along with Noah, to never enter your office."

"That does not mean they heed you."

"You are accusing Noah, too? Why not accuse me as well?"

"Don't be ridiculous, Julia. I consider you above reproach."

She threw up her hands. "All you *do* is reproach me!"

I ignored this baseless accusation, for although it is true that I blame her for my discontent, I believe I have shown great restraint in expressing my feelings to her.

"And as for Noah," she continued, "I do not think him a thief any more than I think him a fire starter."

"A thief, no," I agreed. "But who else could have started that fire in the barn?"

"Why don't you simply blame poor Mrs. Swann for it? As you do for everything else?"

It came back to me then—the absolute exasperation I have always felt arguing with Julia. As a girl she irritated me beyond measure with her convoluted reasoning, and my impulse at age twelve or so had been to end such arguments by throttling her. Instead, I would turn on my heel and walk away. And she would run after me and hook her arm in mine and look up at me with the sweetest smile on her little heart-shaped face and all would be well between us again. Oh, how easy it was in those days.

"Let us get back to the topic that brought me in here," I told her most patiently. "To wit, two missing bottles of laudanum."

"Are you sure you counted correctly?"

"Pray do not insult me by questioning my ciphering abilities, Julia."

"Could a patient of yours be the culprit?"

"I do not think it feasible that a patient could manage to steal a bottle of tincture of opium before my very eyes."

"Do you lock up your supply?"

"The medicine cabinet doesn't even have a lock. Doc Silas never had reason to distrust the inhabitants of his house."

"Nor do you, Adam." She turned from me and busied herself mixing paints again.

Impossible woman! Left her and went on my rounds.

When I returned in the late afternoon I discovered the laudanum thief. I simply walked into the office from the kitchen passageway, and there she was, about to stuff a bottle of the potent drug into her lace-trimmed drawers. So startled was she at my arrival that she dropped it instead, and it shattered on the floor, filling the office with the scent of the brandy into which I dissolve the opium powder.

"Miss Phyfe," I said. "What in God's name do you think you are doing?"

Arabel stood wordlessly before me, staring at me with eyes sunken in their sockets but morbidly bright. Her cheeks were hollow to an emaciated degree that went beyond fashionable thinness, and there was a hectic flush upon them. I might well have been looking at a painted death mask, for I saw the unmistakable signs of galloping Consumption infusing her every delicate feature.

"I think I understand," I said gently. "The laudanum relieves your pains. But it will only make you sicker if you take too much."

"My system has become accustomed to the drug," she said in a hoarse voice just above a whisper, holding her throat as if it pained her to talk. "I *need* it, doctor. And my need has reduced me to common thievery. Pray forgive me. Papa will repay you for the bottle I broke. And for the other bottle I confess I stole just yesterday."

"And the one you took two days ago," I reminded her. "If you are making a confession, it might as well be a full one."

"But I only stole *one* bottle," she insisted.

Did not press her. It mattered not to me if her father repaid me or not. In fact, I see no reason to mention this to him now that Arabel has come into my care. And much care she will need until the end.

Asked if she would allow me to examine her, and she complied only after I promised I would give her a dose of laudanum. Held her wrist. She had an accelerated pulse rate of one hundred and twenty. Took my stethoscope to her heart and heard its weak, hollow thump. Moved it to her chest and heard the gurgling, deadly congestion that clogged her lungs. Felt her legs, thin as sticks, yet swollen. Asked her about fatigue, joint pains, and night sweats. She nodded yes to each symptom. She broke into a coughing fit, and blood spouted from her mouth. Embarrassed, she covered her mouth with her palm. Gave her my handkerchief, and she continued to cough into that. When I examined it, I saw bits of lung tissue mixed with the blood and phlegm. Looked down her throat and saw ulcers.

Gave her some laudanum as a sedative, and she gulped it down with a gurgling moan. "More," she said.

"I cannot in good conscience give you more now."

"More!" she demanded as loudly and forcefully as she

could. But then she fell back on the examining table and lightly dozed.

Left her and went to the studio, where Julia and the other two Phyfe girls were patiently awaiting her return, along with Mrs. Swann, who was reading from the Bible to them, and Noah, busily sketching his own hand. Motioned Julia to step out in the hall and told her what had occurred.

"I was wrong to jump to conclusions and accuse Mrs. Swann," I concluded.

Julia waved away my apology. "Poor, dear Arabel. I will help you take her home."

We went back to the office to rouse Arabel, but she was gone! We looked out the window and could see her crossing the Green, clothed only in her pink silk frock, swaying from side to side, occasionally swigging from yet another stolen bottle of laudanum. Ran out and picked her up in my arms. She was no heavier than a bag of goose feathers. Paid onlookers no mind as I carried her to her fine home at the top of the Green. Put her to bed and had the housemaid go find her father, who was out on business. Meanwhile, Julia arrived with the other two sisters in tow. They were weeping profusely. Did not want them disturbing their sister and made them wait outside the bed chamber door. Julia, however, stayed with me, soothing Arabel with words and caresses. Julia has had much practice soothing ill people, starting as a child with her mother, whose own form of Consumption caused her to linger at Death's door for years. Whether it is a blessing or a curse, Arabel will be taken quickly. When Justice Phyfe returned to the house, I told him my diagnosis without mincing words. His response was that he would take Arabel to warmer, sunnier climes as soon as she got well enough to travel. Not sure he fully comprehended that his daughter is dying.

How the hell can anyone comprehend why our species is

cursed with such inexplicable illness? I admit that, despite all my learning and training, I cannot. As a doctor I pledged to keep the sick from harm and injustice, but I am powerless to do so against this damnable Consumption. As I was leaving the house I could hear Phyfe's other two daughters praying in the parlor. If there is a God, I wanted to shout at them, what *good* does He do? Julia must have seen the anger and frustration in my face, for she took me firmly by the arm and impelled me out the door. We walked home together slowly, as if we too were invalids. Yet when I looked into her lovely eyes, the energy of life coursed through me, and I wanted her so badly my knees near buckled. But we parted without so much as a hand shake, and on I went to Tuttle Farm.

JULIA'S NOTEBOOK

Tuesday, 14 December

Poor Arabel Phyfe. After examining her yesterday, Adam concluded she has galloping Consumption. 'Tis no wonder she craved laudanum. That she stole it from Adam's office will remain a secret between him and me. Although I do not know the girl well, having met her little over a week ago, I am most distraught that she has fallen victim to this dread illness. I sensed something amiss when I commenced sketching her, but I thought it more an illness of the spirit than of the body.

Kitty Lyttle came by this afternoon with the garments she'd sewn for me and managed, as always, to lift my spirits. I brought her up to my chamber for a final fitting and lit the fire Noah had built in the hearth, as he does for me every day. The room was soon cozy, and I began trying on my new clothes. Kitty has made up the two challis gowns, one of sage and the other of plum, in the latest fashion, with long, pointed bodices, narrow sloping shoulders, and tight sleeves.

"That color in particular suits you very well," Kitty said when I put on the sage gown.

"But the style hardly suits my work." I raised my arm to the height of a canvas set on an easel and felt most constrained.

"I should hope you will not paint in your gowns!" Kitty said. "It would not do to bespatter them. Try on the muslin blouses. You will find them far less constricting." She lowered her voice although we were quite alone. "You do not even need to wear a corset under them."

"What? Not wear a corset? Unthinkable!" I shrilled. "I'll have you know, missy, that an uncorseted woman is a bawdy woman. And the more tightly laced a lady's corset is, the more virtuous she be."

Kitty laughed. "That's exactly how my mother sounds, too."

"Actually, 'twas my Grandmother Walker I was mimicking," I said. "She used to threaten to put me in stays when I was but eight to settle me down. She thought me quite the hoyden, and no doubt I was. My mother was too ill to concern herself with my comings and goings, and I ran around wild and free with my cousin Adam."

"Adam Walker, the doctor?"

"The very same."

Kitty gave me a little smile and sideways glance. "Dr. Walker is quite handsome. I wager you were in love with him as a girl."

"I loved him beyond measure, but not in the sentimental way you imply, Kitty. We were *mates*. We shared a special bond, both having lost our mothers young. But our childhood friendship was abruptly ended when my father removed me from Plumford to live with him in Europe."

"So until a fortnight ago, you had not laid eyes on Dr. Walker since he was a boy?"

"Actually, this is not my first visit back to Plumford since Adam and I were children. The summer before last I returned here to nurse our grandfather, who had broken his leg. Adam had taken over his medical practice whilst his leg mended, and we . . . became reacquainted."

"Did you?" Kitty gave me an appraising look. "Were you married then?"

"No." I turned my back to her so she could unbutton my gown. "I married soon after I left here."

"Tell me about your husband," Kitty said as her nimble fingers worked free the buttons.

"What about him?"

She laughed. "Well, where is he now?"

"In France."

"And what is his business?"

"Pray stop asking me so many questions, Kitty!"

"I was just making conversation," she said. "But I beg your pardon for overstepping. I forgot that I was merely your hired seamstress and not your friend."

"Of course you are my friend!" I turned round and saw that her sweet kitten face was all puckered up. "And I beg *your* pardon for being so curt, dear Kitty. It is just that I do not care to talk about my husband. Why don't you tell me about yours, instead?"

"With pleasure!" she said, her countenance smoothing. And as I tried on the rest of the clothes she had sewn up for me, she went on and on about how loving and kind and adorable her spouse is. I have no reason to doubt her, for I have only witnessed the tailor's mutual adoration of her.

"But enough about my Micah," she said at last. She fell silent and looked about the chamber, taking in the yellowed lace bed canopy, the faded toile wallpaper, the limp dimity curtains, and the worn Aubusson carpet. "What a quaint room this is. Did you sleep here as a girl?"

"Yes, and it looks exactly the same now as it did then," I told her. "Indeed, nothing has been altered for over seventy-five years."

Kitty looked scandalized. "That is a mighty long time to make do with the same old décor! If you are ever inclined to change it, I will be happy to assist you, for I do so enjoy decorating."

"Let's do it then," I said. "This room really could do with a refreshing. It has harbored much sadness."

Kitty's ever-changing countenance became most sympathetic. "Were you very sad here as a girl?"

"Oh, I cried myself to sleep many a night after my mother died. But in the morning I would leap out of bed and run off to find Adam. We were exceedingly happy together. So there is no reason to feel sorry for me, Kitty. The sadness I referred to has to do with another."

"Will you tell me who?" Kitty perched on the edge of the bed and looked at me most expectantly.

"My great-great-aunt Eugenia. She bore a child in this room, and it died within hours," I said. "I only learned of this when I came back to nurse my grandfather. He thought the time had come to tell me of my Walker heritage. You see, Eugenia's baby was most horribly deformed, and she had only herself to blame for it. She had done the most irresponsible thing possible. Not only had she fallen in love with her first cousin, she had married him."

"Queen Victoria is married to her first cousin," Kitty said, sounding rather indignant that I should cast aspersions upon the English monarchy. "And in the last seven years the dear queen and her consort have produced five handsome children who seem perfectly healthy."

"I know nothing about royal blood lines, only mine," I said. "Walker unions of cousins in the past have resulted in babes with similar tragic birth defects. And there is no reason to think it will not happen again if Walker cousins would be so reckless as to mate."

Kitty's eyes widened in sudden understanding. "Such as you and Dr. Walker!"

"Yes. He deserves a wife who can give him a normal family."

Mrs. Swann entered the chamber at that moment without bothering to knock. "Oh, I did not know you had company, Julia," she said, glancing at Kitty. "I came in to dust." She brandished a rag.

As I introduced my newly industrious housekeeper to Kitty, I threw a shawl over my shoulders to cover myself. As comfortable as I had been to be with Kitty in just my shimmy and stays, I did not feel so in front of Mrs. Swann.

Kitty regarded Mrs. Swann most intently. "I do believe I know you," she said.

"Well, my dear, I do not know you."

"But surely we must have met before."

"I cannot fathom how. I have only recently come to Plumford."

"I too am a recent resident," Kitty said. "I come from England originally."

"Never been there," Mrs. Swann said.

"What about Boston? I sewed costumes at various theater companies there before I married."

"How interesting," Mrs. Swann said blandly. It was clear that she was not the least bit interested. "I'll come back later to dust," she told me.

"Do not let me interfere with your work, Mrs. Swann," Kitty said, springing off the bed. "I must be off anyway. Mr. Lyttle is attending a town meeting this evening, and I want to prepare an early supper before he departs. This shall be the first evening we are separated since we wed, and I fear I will be quite lonely. Here's a jolly idea! Why don't you both stop by for a visit?"

"I have promised Justice Phyfe that I will sit with his ill daughter whilst he presides over the meeting," I said.

"What is this meeting about?" Mrs. Swann said.

"Revenants!" Kitty said. "The townsmen are getting together to decide on how to deal with the growing fear of them. A vote shall be taken."

"So of course women are excluded," I put in, "since we cannot vote. That makes no sense to me."

"It does to me," Mrs. Swann said. "Is it not a man's world?"

"Indeed it is. But why should it be?"

"Now, now, Julia." Mrs. Swann patted my arm. "Let the menfolk do all the hard work of running things, and let us ladies reap all the benefits."

"But why should we have to rely on them for our benefits?"

"My dear, any female who looks like you should not have any trouble benefiting from men." Mrs. Swann gave me a wink. "And you, Mrs. Lyttle, are a delightful creature yourself. You must have that husband of yours eating out of your little paw."

Kitty smiled and blushed and gave Mrs. Swann another close look. "I am certain I have met you before. Sooner or later it will come to me where, for I never forget a face. Perhaps if you call on me this evening we can sort out where our paths might have crossed. I live just across the Green in the yellow house with blue shutters."

"I would very much like to call on you, Mrs. Lyttle, but I too am engaged this evening," Mrs. Swann said. "I have promised the dear boy who resides here that I will read to him out of *The Last of the Mohicans*. And I would be loath to disappoint him."

How delighted I was to hear that Mrs. Swann and Noah have at last become friends! And that reminds me. I must go hunt up a book to read to Arabel this evening when I visit.

Something lighthearted and romantic. *Emma* perhaps. Miss Austen may be out of fashion, but she delights all the same. I am sure there is a copy around here somewhere, for I recall Grandmother Walker reading it to Mother as she lay in her sickbed.

ADAM'S JOURNAL

Tuesday, December 14

Reason reigned in Plumford earlier this evening, but after the horror that shortly followed, I doubt it will continue to hold sway.

Our Selectmen had called a special meeting to decide what to do about the growing vampyre terror in our town, and both Henry and I attended to recount what we had witnessed at the Wiley farm. Our description of Solomon Wiley's callous, brutal treatment of his own niece's corpse brought gasps and groans from all the sane men present and did much to influence the vote that followed two hours later, after everyone had said his piece. How Wiley did glare at me when I testified against him, and how I did glare back at him. But I reckon he had as much a right to be there as any man. He was even allowed to speak in his own defense, which he did most effectively. His voice is deep and persuasive, and he can sway a crowd like a revivalist tent preacher. But 'tis common sense that usually wins out with us Yankees, and it did so at the meeting. After Justice Phyfe expressed how injurious to businesses of every sort it would be if Plumford got the reputation of being a vampyre-crazed town that condoned the barbaric desecration of the dead, a law was passed banning the disinterment of corpses. The penalty for breaking it shall be arrest, a heavy fine, and immediate expulsion. Wiley thundered out of the Meetinghouse and headed for the tavern. The rest of us departed with more decorum and less speed, lingering on the steps of the Meetinghouse to chat about less disturbing matters for a while, our confab centering on the going market price for milk and the possibility of a gunpowder factory's being built on the Assabet.

As Henry and I crossed the Green a few minutes later, the tailor Micah Lyttle came running toward us from his house. He too had attended the meeting but had not stayed as long to palaver.

"You must come help my wife, doctor!" he cried. We hurried back to his house and entered through the front door. "In there!" he said, pointing toward the kitchen.

The coppery scent of blood immediately hit my nostrils, and we found Mrs. Lyttle lying facedown on the floor by the back door. Henry picked up the lamp on the table and held it over her immobile figure. Blood pooled beneath her head and upper torso, spreading over the floor boards. I knelt and lowered my head close to hers. She was not breathing, and the eye visible to me was open and unblinking, the pupil dilated.

"Please save her," Mr. Lyttle implored, hovering in the shadows.

I stood and went to him. "I am sorry, but there is nothing I can do. She is already gone."

"Nooooo!" Mr. Lyttle wailed and covered his face with his hands.

Led him to the parlor and sat him down on the sofa, where I left him staring blindly ahead, too stunned to feel anything yet. Shock offers a brief reprieve from pain.

Returned to the kitchen, and Henry and I studied Mrs. Lyttle's procumbent body. One arm was folded beneath her torso and the other extended out and to the side, fingertips touching the whitewashed stucco wall, which was lightly daubed with blood. We carefully turned her over. Blood soaked her fair hair and the side of her face that had lain in the pool. The cause of death was clearly evident. Her jugular vein had been slashed. She was wearing only a velvet dressing gown, and the belt had come undone. Henry looked away as I covered her nakedness and retied the belt.

"That she fell facedown tells me that her throat was cut from behind," Henry said.

"Her heart kept pumping until she bled to death," I said. "Thankfully, that was in a matter of minutes. Three at the most."

"How long ago did she die?" he said.

Bent down and gently moved her head from side to side. "At the longest, three hours ago. Her eyes have not yet filmed over, and the muscles around her jaw have not begun to stiffen."

"Well, 'tis certain the husband didn't do it," Henry said.

I had never for a moment thought that Lyttle had! But I could not help but ask Henry how he could be so certain.

"We know Mr. Lyttle came home from the town meeting no more than ten minutes ago," Henry said. "Although that would have given him sufficient time to kill his wife, it is not enough time for the blood that poured out of her wound and formed a pool around her to have congealed around the edges the way it has. And if he had killed her *before* he went to the meeting, the blood would have dried up far more. It appears to be still moist, however."

I dipped my forefinger into the dark red puddle and rubbed it against my thumb. "It has thickened some," I said. "It would take about an hour for this amount of blood to coagulate to this consistency, I estimate."

Henry directed his attention to the back door. "The bolt has been slid back. It appears that Mrs. Lyttle willingly opened the door to her murderer."

"Then it must have been someone she knew," I said. "A lady wearing only her dressing gown would not likely open her door to a stranger."

"Nor to any man she knew other than her own husband," Henry said.

"Or her lover."

Henry gave me a sharp look, but said nothing.

"Well, I very much doubt a woman killed her," I said. "It would have taken a great deal of strength to hold her from behind with one hand and cut her throat with the other."

Henry directed his attention to blood streaks staining the wall in the area where Mrs. Lyttle's hand had been positioned before we turned her over. "That looks to be writing." He lowered the lamp to shine on the markings. *"R E V,"* he read out. "The poor woman spent her last bit of life force scrawling those characters with her own blood. They could be her killer's initials or the first letters of his name."

We went to the parlor to see if Mr. Lyttle could tell us what the letters stood for. He had not moved a muscle since I had left him there. I addressed him, but he did not turn toward my voice. He was in another realm, no doubt as far away from reality as his mind could take him.

Henry sat down beside him. "Mr. Lyttle," he said in a soothing voice, "you must help us find your wife's murderer."

Lyttle roused himself. "Kitty was *murdered?*"

"Her throat was cut, and she bled to death."

Lyttle began slapping at his own face. "Awake! Awake from this nightmare!" he bade himself. And then he slid back into an unreachable reverie.

There was a knocking on the front door, and I opened it to Constable Beers. He had not been at the town meeting, and from the fumes emanating from him, I surmised he had spent yet another evening at the tavern.

"Good Evening, doctor," he said, holding onto the porch railing to steady himself. "I trust you are here on a social rather than a patient call."

"Neither," I replied curtly. Beers was the last person I wished to see at the moment.

"Well, I am here on official business myself," he said. "I have been calling house to house round the Green to inquire about a stranger seen in the vicinity earlier this evening. Indeed, Widow Jasper went so far as to hunt me down at the Sun to report that this suspicious individual looked right into her kitchen window and ogled her. She is sure it was the Plumford Night Stalker."

"I am afraid there is something far worse than an old lady's imaginings that you must deal with tonight, constable," I reluctantly informed him. And with that I beckoned Beers in and led him to the kitchen.

"God save us!" he bellowed, shrinking back from the sight of Mrs. Lyttle's body. "Another throat clawed open!"

"The tool used to cut this poor lady's throat was not the same as the one that ripped open Bidwell's throat, as you can plainly see," Henry said in a reasonable tone.

But Constable Beers would not look at the body again. Instead, his eyes darted everywhere else around the small kitchen. "Are those devil symbols?" he said, pointing to the bottom of the wall. He has amazingly sharp eyes for a drunken dolt.

"They are simply letters of the alphabet. Mrs. Lyttle wrote them out in her own blood before she expired," Henry informed him.

Beers leaned toward them for a closer look. *"R E V,"* he said aloud, as slowly as a child reciting from his hornbook. He straightened abruptly. "Revenant! Her murderer was a revenant!"

And that was that. No matter that the inquest that followed was conducted without one mention of revenants, and the only conclusion reached was that Mrs. Lyttle had been murdered most heinously. The eyes of the jury members and the coroner kept skidding back to the letters on the wall. And even though Constable Beers held his tongue at the inquest, it is doubtful he will do so at the tavern.

Mr. Lyttle, meanwhile, speaks not at all. Beers brought him to stay the night at the Widow Jasper's house next door. To-morrow I shall endeavor to get more information from him.

JULIA'S NOTEBOOK

Wednesday, 15 December

K *itty Lyttle is dead*. Clever, cheerful, charming Kitty. Who could be so vile as to have murdered her? Half the town believes she was slain by the Plumford Night Stalker. And I confess that I half believe it myself after talking with the Widow Jasper today.

    'Twas last evening that I learned of Kitty's murder, whilst still at the Phyfe house. Justice Phyfe had just come home from the town meeting and was thanking me for watching over Arabel when Constable Beers pounded on the door to relate the horrific news. He declared that a revenant had done the deed. Justice Phyfe enjoined Beers to keep his foolish theories to himself, but since when has Beers ever done that?

    The two men walked me home and went on to inform Mr. Daggett that he must once again gather together a Coroner's Jury to convene over a body. I went inside and found my two housemates sound asleep in the parlor—Noah sprawled on the sofa and Mrs. Swann in Grandfather's rocker, *The Last of the Mohicans* lying facedown upon her lap. I was sorry to disturb their innocent peace, but awake them I did. After sending Noah up to his bed, I told Mrs. Swann what had happened to Kitty. She took me in her arms, and we wept together. I was most appreciative to have another woman's sympathetic company.

This afternoon Adam asked me to accompany him to Widow Jasper's house, where Micah Lyttle is staying until he recovers his wits. Adam hoped that, because of my friendship with Kitty, I might be able to get Micah to talk about last night's events. Mrs. Jasper led us into her parlor, informing us that Micah had spent the night seated in a straight-back chair, barely moving a muscle, never forming a word.

"Tried to spoon-feed him some porridge this morn," she said, "but he would not even open his mouth to take nourishment. So I am in doubt he will do so to talk to you."

I took off my bonnet and cape and pulled up a chair beside Micah. He did not acknowledge my presence, and I do not think he even recognized me. He was numb to the world around him, and I could think of no way to get through to him. I blathered some inanities about how Kitty was in a better place now and patted his arm. He gazed down at my hand, or rather at the cuff of my sleeve. It was decorated with an embroidered daisy, and he began stroking the raised stitching. 'Twas one of the blouses Kitty had so recently sewn up for me, and he must have recognized her work.

"She thought the garment too plain and charged me not a penny extra for the decorative embroidery," I told him.

"How like her," he said. "How very like her."

And then he commenced to cry with abandon, his face pressed against my shoulder. His tears were so copious they soaked through the muslin fabric of my blouse. Adam, seated across from me, looked on silently, patiently, compassionately. I remember how he had let me cry like this on *his* shoulder after my mother died fifteen years ago. Oh, what a friend he was to me then!

As suddenly as Micah had started weeping, he stopped. He straightened himself up, adjusted his rumpled cravat, and cleared his throat. "Whoever killed my Kitty must be made to pay for it," he said.

"Then tell us all you can to help make that happen," I urged him. "Did Kitty have any enemies?"

"Does an angel have enemies? Everyone she encountered loved her. Little children would run after her in the Boston Garden. Even the vain actors she sewed costumes for at the theater adored her."

"What theater was this?" Adam said.

"The Howard. I induced her to come away with me to Plumford, where I thought she would be happy and *safe*." He pressed his fists against his head. "How stupid I am! We should have gone back to Boston after that young man was found murdered on Wolf Hill!"

"Perhaps the murders are connected," Adam said.

"How could they be?" Micah asked hoarsely. "Did I not just tell you that my Kitty had no enemies?"

"Do the initials *R E V* mean anything to you?" Adam persisted.

Micah shook his head adamantly and then slumped in his chair. "I am so weary. All I long for is sleep. Yet I cannot sleep. Whenever I close my eyes I see Kitty lying on the floor in all that blood!"

"I will give you something to help you sleep," Adam said. "But allow me to ask you a few more questions first. Were the doors of your house locked when you left for the town meeting?"

"Yes. I am certain of it, for I checked the back door bolt three times to make sure it was in place before I departed. Kitty laughed at my concern. But in our entire married life I had never left her alone at night before. I locked the front door behind me and put the key in my pocket. I unlocked it upon my return."

"And when you went to the kitchen, did you unbolt the back door?"

He shook his head. "At first sight of Kitty I knew she was horribly injured and immediately ran out the front door to fetch you, doctor." His bloodshot eyes suddenly widened as he regarded Adam. "The back door was unbolted?"

"Yes. Was your wife expecting a caller?"

"She made no mention of it. The last thing my darling told me before I went off to the meeting was that she would be counting the minutes until I returned." Micah covered his anguished face with his hands and moaned. "How I wish I had died with her!"

Adam gave him a potion and led him upstairs to the chamber Mrs. Jasper had readied for him but could not induce him to use last night.

I found the old widow in her kitchen, knitting by the stove. "How is Mr. Lyttle faring?" she asked.

"Dr. Walker has put him to bed. You were kind to take him in, ma'am."

"Well, I could not let the poor soul spend the night in that charnel house, now could I? Constable Beers told me there was blood enough in the kitchen to drown in. But I reckon he exaggerated a mite."

"He does do that," I said. "Indeed, he has been telling everyone in town that you espied the Night Stalker last evening."

"And so I did. Saw him through that very window." She pointed with her knitting needle to the little window that faced her backyard. "His hair was black as the devil's boots, and his face was white as chalk. It had an eerie glow to it. And when he paused to jeer at me through the window, he showed off a pair of fangs! Fangs that could slice open a woman's throat in one fell swoop." She swiped the tip of her needle across her own throat to demonstrate. "Well, I froze right here in my chair, for I thought he'd come for *me!* But then he gave me a jaunty wave and went on his way. Soon as I collected myself I ran out to fetch the constable. But it was already too late to save poor little Mrs. Lyttle. And now I understand why the Night Stalker did not harm me. He had already satiated his blood lust on her." With a sigh and a shake of her head, Mrs. Jasper resumed her knitting.

I retold her tale to Adam after we left the house and were walking across the Green together. Knowing Mrs. Jasper to be a sensible person, he could not understand why she would come up with such an outlandish story.

"You think she fell asleep by the kitchen stove and dreamt it?" I said.

"That's very likely," Adam said. "Or perhaps she really did see the murderer. A man she did not recognize and hence found strange in appearance. A friend of Mrs. Lyttle who had come from Boston, for instance."

"A murderous *friend?*"

"Mrs. Lyttle was dressed in only a robe, with nothing beneath it, and in such a state of dishabille, who else would she open her door to but a friend? A very dear friend."

"Are you suggesting Kitty had a lover, Adam?"

"I cannot help but think it a possibility."

"What if she just threw open the door to get a breath of fresh air," I speculated, "and the demented killer, a complete stranger, was standing right outside by coincidence?"

"Improbable," Adam said.

"No more improbable than Kitty Lyttle's having a lover. You were not as well acquainted with her as I was, Adam."

"You knew her for less than two weeks."

"Enough time to know that she was deeply in love with her husband."

"Was she?" Adam looked up at the gloomy winter sky above the skeletal tree branches. "Did she love him as much as you once professed to love me, Julia?"

I stiffened. "That I cannot say."

"Can you say if she had as fickle a heart? She might have met another man—on a ship, let us say—and fallen in love with him in short order, forgetting all about how deeply in love she supposedly was with another."

"You are being cruel to me with your sarcasm, cousin. And crass to the memory of a murdered woman. It is beneath you."

"Well, there you are," he said. "At one time you could raise me up to heaven's heights, Julia. And now you can reduce me to behaving beneath my own lowly self. What a range of influence you have over me."

"Stop this," I commanded and came to a stop myself.

He followed suit. "You are right. I must stop badgering you. What is done is done."

"And you must stop feeling so injured about it. What does it matter that I married another? I could not marry *you!*"

"I did not marry another. I most likely never shall."

I wanted to scream at him, but we were on a path in a public common, so I lowered my voice instead. "You had better marry one day, you blockhead, else my sacrifice was all for naught. I want you to have a good, normal life, Adam. I want you to have children. I want you to have unrestrained sexual relations with your wife."

He glanced around. There was no one within hearing distance. "And is that what you have with your husband?"

The question was risible, but I did not feel much like laughing. "That is none of your concern."

"Indeed it is not." And with that he turned on his heel and went in the opposite direction, rather than back to his office.

I continued on my way. We had tried to be careful not to draw attention to ourselves, but evidently we still had, for I perceived people strolling the Green look toward Adam and then toward me as the distance between us widened.

ADAM'S JOURNAL

Wednesday, December 15

Henry came by Tuttle Farm early this evening, wanting to know if more information had surfaced concerning Mrs. Lyttle's murder. Told him that her husband had confirmed to me that he'd secured both the front and back doors last night. Also related Mrs. Jasper's description of the face peering through her window near the time of the murder. Neither of us believe she saw a supernatural creature, but we do believe she saw Kitty Lyttle's killer. That Mrs. Lyttle had worked at the same theater that Chauncey Bidwell had frequented seemed to me to be no more than a coincidence, but Henry thinks it would be worthwhile to go to the Howard again and talk to Mrs. Perry. Told him I would do my best to go with him, but it did not seem likely I could find the time for another trip to Boston next week.

Gran invited Henry to stay for supper and partake in the stew she had been simmering over the fire since morn. "Along with taters and turnips, there's a brace of rabbits in my pot."

"How'd they get themselves into such a stew?" Henry, ever the punster, asked.

Gran pointed to her trusty old flintlock hanging on the

oak-beam lintel. "That's how. I come from folk that like to return from a walk with supper swinging off the belt."

"I reckon we all come from such folk," Henry said, "but I have no doubt that it is a part of the destiny of the human race, in its gradual improvement, to leave off eating animals one day."

"What flummydiddle!" Gran took up her big wrought iron spoon, and I feared she was going to rap Henry's noggin with it. But she dipped it in the pot hanging off the crane instead and took a taste. "Mighty flavorsome if I do say so myself." She turned to Harriet, who was seated on the settle, pensively gazing into the fire. "Fetch me four bowls, my dear, so I can serve up suppah."

"Pray, no stew for me," Henry said. "I lost my appetite for flesh during my sojourn at Walden Pond."

"I shall not partake either," Harriet said. "When I conjure up images of dead little bunnies, it makes me want to weep."

Gran sighed. "Poor Harriet has been weepin' all day, but it ain't got a thing to do with my stew," she told Henry. "The poor girl is most upset over last night's killin'. She was stayin' in town when it happened and ran back here this morn, soon as she heard the Green has become the Night Stalker's latest huntin' ground."

"When I conjure up images," Harriet sobbed, "of that foul creature sinking his fangs into poor Mrs. Lyttle's—"

"Cease yer conjurin', my girl!" Gran bade her. "Else you might summon up the very thing you most fear."

Henry nodded. "What we create in our minds, we find in our lives, Harriet." He tilted his head. "Hark. Is that a carriage?"

I heard nothing, but Henry hears as with an ear trumpet. Got up from the table with some reluctance, for I was salivating for Gran's stew, and opened the back door. Sure enough, I did now hear the faint sound of horses' hooves and the jingling

of harness. Henry joined me, and we went round to the front
of the house to look down the lane. Two huge amber eyes
gleamed in the darkness as they came closer and closer. Of
course I knew them to be carriage lamps, and in the next
minute a phaeton with overlarge wheels came to a halt in front
of us, a pair of black stallions snorting and stamping. A tall figure jumped down from the high seat and landed lightly in
front of us. 'Twas Dr. Lamb, dressed for an evening in the city
rather than a country visit.

He removed his elegant top hat and swept it down to make
a short bow to me. "Thank you for inviting me to call on you,
Dr. Walker."

"I had expected you to call at the office," I replied with
more surprise than graciousness.

"But you are here and not there," he said as if to an imbecile. "Of course, if this is an inconvenient time for us to converse, I shall drive back to Boston directly." His tone was now
injured.

"Your timing is perfect," I said, regaining my manners. "We
were just about to partake in supper, and if you do not mind
simple fare served in a simple fashion, you are most welcome
to join us."

"As Leonardo da Vinci once claimed, simplicity is the ulti-
mate sophistication," Dr. Lamb replied.

"My friend here would claim the same," I said.

Dr. Lamb had paid Henry no heed until then. "Good Evening," he said curtly, and Henry nodded curtly in return. It
seemed they had taken an immediate dislike to each other at
the Athenaeum.

Gran came out, lantern in hand, to find out whom we
were jabbering with. I introduced her to Dr. Lamb. She lifted
up the lantern to get a good look at him, but the wind blew
out the candle.

"Will you kindly invite me into your home to dine?" he asked her.

Gran did not respond. Thinking Dr. Lamb's formal manner and dress had made her shy, I responded for her. "Gran is always eager to set another place at her table," I assured him, "and in the name of Tuttle hospitality, I too invite you to enter my family's humble homestead."

He bowed his acceptance, and we all proceeded inside. Once Gran was back in her kitchen, she became far more hospitable. She fetched a jug of applejack from the pantry and directed Harriet to get the gilt-edged glasses from the cabinet in the front parlor. When Harriet returned with them a short time later I observed that she had switched from her everyday apron to the lace-trimmed one she wears on holidays. She and Gran quickly covered the long oaken table with an immaculate homespun linen cloth and changed the candles in the pewter holders from tallow to beeswax. The trouble they felt obligated to go to for Dr. Lamb seemed to amuse Henry. He had never received such special considerations when he visited Tuttle Farm, but he was always treated like family. Dr. Lamb, on the other hand, was being treated like the exotic stranger he was. It is doubtful anyone had ever sat at Gran's kitchen table dressed in white silk tie and waistcoat before.

Dr. Lamb brushed aside all inquiries after himself beyond saying he had his medical practice up in Augusta.

"You mentioned you had been to Plumford before," Henry prodded.

"I believe I said I was familiar with this area of the country, and so I am. But I have not been back in a good long while." Ignoring the bowl of stew set in front of him, Dr. Lamb delicately picked up his glass of applejack and took a tiny sip.

"Well, I reckon it looks the same to you," Gran said. "Nothin' much changes round these here parts."

"Everything has!" His dark eyes flashed. "All the abundance that made our lives so rich has disappeared."

"Or will soon enough," Henry said, "if we do nothing to preserve what is left of the wilderness around us."

"It is already too late," Lamb insisted and turned to me. "I am most eager to ask you more questions regarding the article you published."

"You published somethin', Adam?" Gran said. "Concernin' what?"

"My experimentation with hypnotism."

"What in tarnation is that?"

"Inducing a person into nervous sleep."

Gran narrowed her eyes. "Sounds like the devil's own mischief."

Her reaction did not surprise me. Indeed, it was the reason I had never talked about my experiments, much less the article concerning them, to her. And I was not inclined to do so now. I went back to plying my spoon to my stew and said no more.

But Dr. Lamb had become most loquacious. "Your grandson wrote a most fascinating commentary regarding hypnotism in a highly respected medical journal, Mrs. Tuttle. One of his subjects recalled being an Indian going to battle against other Indians in this area long ago."

"Well, fancy that!" Gran said. "Accordin' to the local history I was taught in dame school, the Nipmucs was always fightin' with each other like the savages they were. Not an Injun from that tribe left around these parts."

"So it seems," Lamb said.

Gran peered at him. "Except for your paleness, you have the look of an Injun yerself, sir. If you have such blood in you, I did not mean to cause offence. And if I did, I do beg yer pardon."

Lamb shrugged off her apology. "At any rate, this *particular* Indian I speak of killed two noble warriors. He downed the first one with a pink quartz ax that has great magic because of a blaze of black stone running through it. He killed the other by snapping his neck."

Gran cackled with glee. "That's how to do it!"

Henry and I exchanged a glance across the table. His expression reflected the amazement I myself felt.

"Now tell me, Mrs. Tuttle," Lamb continued. "Would you be familiar with the man your grandson hypnotized? He would be a dark-haired, powerfully built fellow, of my height or even taller."

"Can't think of anyone tall as you right off," Gran said. "But give me a minute to cogitate upon it." She got up from the table to refill my bowl.

"Why assume the man Dr. Walker hypnotized looks as you described?" Henry asked Lamb.

Ignoring Henry, Lamb spoke to me. "Have I not assumed correctly, doctor?"

"I am not at liberty to relate any personal information about my subject," I said, making sure not to glance at Henry. "That is why he remained nameless in my article."

"Surely you can tell a fellow doctor his name," Lamb said.

I shook my head. "It would serve no purpose."

"Yes, it would," Lamb persisted. "It would satisfy my curiosity."

"Hardly a sufficient reason to break a trust."

"You are most stubborn, Dr. Walker."

"You took the very words I was about to address to you right out of my mouth, Dr. Lamb."

We two regarded each other with like intensity. Rather, I tried to match the blazing gaze Lamb directed at me, but doubt mine equaled his in heat. All I wished to do was stare him down, but it seemed he wanted to incinerate me into a pile of ashes with the fire emanating from the depths of his black eyes.

"I just recollected a feller taller than you, Dr. Lamb," Gran said, returning to the table and plunking down a steaming bowl in front of me. "Solomon Wiley! Now there's a dark-haired, strappin' rogue who could twist a man's neck easy as a chicken's."

Releasing me from his vise-like gaze, Lamb gave Gran a tight-lipped smile. "Solomon Wiley, you say? Does he reside in Plumford?" Gran nodded.

"He wasn't the man I hypnotized," I said.

Discounting my protest, Lamb rose from the table and bowed to Gran. "Thank you for a lovely evening, madam." And with that he was out the door. A moment later we heard the crack of a whip, sharp as lightning, and then the thunder of his stallions' hooves as they sped him away.

Henry, Gran, Harriet, and I regarded each other silently for a moment, but then Gran laughed and said, "Well, weren't he a strange one?"

"I am glad he is gone," Harriet said, clearing away his uneaten bowl of stew and still full glass of applejack.

"Why did you hesitate about inviting Dr. Lamb in?" I asked Gran.

"I don't rightly know. Just couldn't make myself do it. 'Twas not my intention to be rude to yer friend, my boy."

"Oh, Dr. Lamb is not my friend, Gran. Until a brief encounter with him in Boston the other day, I had never laid eyes on him before. Same goes for Henry."

"Methinks I encountered him one time before that," Henry said and gave me a look filled with meaning.

A chill ran up my back when I guessed his meaning. "We will talk later."

"You two can talk all you want here and now," Gran said. "Me and Harriet won't perturb you. We got wimmen's work to do." She swung the crane and peered into the cast-iron stewing pot. "Not so much as a dent made!"

"I did my part, Gran," I said.

"You always do, my boy. If there's one thing I raised you up to be, 'twas a good eater. I just wish yer chum here weren't so particular about his victuals." She gave Henry a withering look, piled all the glassware and crockery on a tray, and whisked them off to the well room to do the washing up with Harriet.

Henry and I removed ourselves to two rockers in front of the fireplace for a better view of the brilliant show the roaring backlog was putting on.

Henry began without preamble. "I remember Lamb now from my past life regression, Adam. If he were dressed in a breechcloth instead of formal dinner attire, he would be the spitting image of the brave whose neck I broke."

"You are saying they have similar features?"

"I am saying they are one and the same!"

"Well, for a man who is over two hundred and fifty years old, Dr. Lamb has aged well. He looks not a day over thirty," I quipped, for my rational mind could not accept such a possibility. "Besides, did you not recall *killing* that warrior in your regression?"

"Perhaps I only thought I did, Adam. How could Lamb have described in detail the ax I wielded if he had not been present to see it?"

That was what had so struck me as astonishing too, for I had deliberately left out the description in my article. "There must be a logical explanation."

"Pray give it to me then." Henry rocked in the chair and waited.

I rose and worried the backlog a bit with the poker and shovel. Sap dropped from its ends and sizzled. "What about this?" I finally said, resuming my seat. "Lamb too has had a past life regression, and he was taken back to the exact same place, at the exact same moment in time as you were."

"Such a coincidence as that," Henry said, "would be truly amazing."

"Not as amazing as a two-hundred-and-fifty-year-old man," I replied.

"Here is a more feasible possibility," Henry said. "Lamb heard the details of my past life regression from someone. And the only other person present when I was hypnotized was Julia. Might she have related the incident to Dr. Lamb or to someone who knows him?"

"It is hard for me to believe Julia would be so indiscreet," I said, "but it is far harder for me to believe Dr. Lamb is the selfsame warrior you fought with over two centuries ago, Henry."

"Ah, but what if he is? Think of the enlightenment he could bring to us!"

"Dr. Lamb did not impress me as being particularly enlightened," I said. "If he is indeed the Indian you fought, why couldn't he recognize you as you did him?"

"Because I do not look in my present life as I did in that past one," Henry said. "Only my soul returned, reborn in a new human body. That is the very essence of Reincarnation."

Gran came out of the pantry, a pie plate in her hands. "What in God's name are you two jawing about? We live once and only once and go up to heaven or down to hell as we so deserve! Now put your mouths to better use than spouting blasphemy and eat some of my pumpkin and chestnut pie."

Henry did not need to be asked twice. Nor did I. Whatever deep and intriguing mysteries our minds had been engrossed in were forgotten for the moment as our stomachs took precedence. Henry made up to Gran for his severe breach of etiquette in refusing her stew by devouring three pieces of her pie.

"I used the chestnuts you brung me in it," she told him and blessed him with one of her sweetest smiles. He had been forgiven completely, even for blasphemy.

Henry left soon after, laughing off Harriet's fears that he might come upon the Night Stalker as he tramped his way

back to Concord. I returned to my rocker, intent upon con-
templating all that we had discussed. However, my thoughts
centered mostly on Julia. A short time later two of Gran's
farmhands, father and son, came through the back door. They
each carried a blanket and pillow.

"We would like to take you up on yer kind invite to sleep
in yer kitchen tonight, ma'am," the father said.

"I figured the barn would be too cold," she said, "with no
snow as yet coverin' the roof to hold in warmth from the
cows. Make yerselves to home, boys, and I'll dish you out some
stew."

I stayed a while longer to talk with the men. I'd worked
the fields with them as a boy, and we go back a long way. But
when I saw they were far more interested in chewing than
chin-wagging, I left them to their food.

"I'm off," I announced as I grabbed my coat and hat from
the wall peg.

Gran and Harriet came rushing forward to inquire where I
could be off to in the middle of the night. It was not even nine
o'clock yet, and I told them I had decided to spend the night
in my office, sleeping on the cot. I had been feeling most un-
easy thinking of Julia all alone in the house with a killer possibly still roaming about town. That she was not entirely alone,
but had another woman and a young boy for company, did not
give me much comfort. What protection would they be? And
now that Gran and Harriet had two hearty men under the
roof, they did not need me around to make them feel safe.
Even so, Harriet put up quite a protest, covering her head with
her apron and wailing most dramatically over my departure.
But Gran just wished me Godspeed, for she knows when I
make up my mind to do something there is no changing it.
She knows too that there is no changing my stubborn heart's
abiding devotion to Julia.

Napoleon trotted back to town most happily. He likely

prefers to be barned there, his home all the years Doc Silas drove him. I went into the house through the office passageway and found the kitchen dark. Lit a lamp and went to the hall, listening for voices. Heard none and supposed the ladies and Noah had all retired for the night. But then I discerned a faint sobbing emanating from the studio and went to see what was wrong.

Found Julia holding a candle in front of the portrait she'd painted of Doc Silas. Called her name softly so as not to frighten her. She turned, cheeks shiny with tears, but then her countenance brimmed with happiness at the sight of me.

Hurried to her, blew out her candle, and swept her into my arms. "Why are you crying, Julia?"

"Everyone I have ever loved in this world I have lost." She pressed her cheek against my chest. "And I have loved you most of all." Her words were muffled as she spoke them into the area of my waistcoat that covered my pounding heart.

Guided her to an armchair and sat her down upon my knee. Did not forget that the last (and only other) time I'd pulled her onto my lap, we had kissed for the first time as adults and had experienced a carnal desire so strong we near consummated it right there and then. Did not intend to kiss her tonight. Just held her in my arms for as long as she cared to have me do so and took the liberty of breathing in the scent of her hair and her neck and her hands.

After a while, I know not how long, she lifted her head from my shoulder and said, "Why have you come here this evening?"

"To protect you."

She merely nodded in response, as if this were her due. Perhaps it is. I have felt inclined to protect Julia ever since she was eight years old and have always done everything in a boy's and then a man's power to do so. She lifted herself from my lap with the grace of a gazelle and asked if I wanted some tea.

Followed her into the kitchen, and as we waited for the kettle to boil I asked her if she had ever told anyone about Henry's hypnotic regression. She assured me she had not. Told her about Dr. Lamb's mentioning the ax, and then went ahead and told her how Henry and I had actually found it. This astonished her, as well it should have, but we could not pursue the subject further for Noah came in, wearing an old-fashioned night shirt far too large for him. It must have once belonged to Doc Silas.

"Reckoned I heard voices in here," Noah said, rubbing his eyes.

Julia offered to heat him up some milk. He said he'd do it for himself and did so with quick efficiency. He also prepared the pot of tea for us, far more at ease in a kitchen than Julia has ever shown herself to be. He even served us up some macaroons, arranging them on a plate most artistically.

"Did Mrs. Swann make these?" Julia asked him. "Or did you, Noah?" The boy shrugged his scrawny shoulders and turned away. "He is too shy to take credit for anything," Julia whispered to me. Addressing Noah again, she said, "Go fetch your drawings, dear. I want Dr. Adam to see them."

He did as he was bidden and returned with a tattered and smudged sketchbook. I leafed through it and regarded the unskilled drawings of mundane household objects with the mildest of interest. But Julia murmured words of admiration and encouragement over each page. The last drawing was of some large-eyed, long-lashed creature's countenance, its features all skewwhiff.

"Is that me, Noah?" Julia guessed, and he nodded. "Perhaps Dr. Adam will pose for you one day, although he has always refused to do so for me."

"Not always," I said. "Have you forgotten the time I allowed you to make a life mask of my countenance and what followed?"

She did not reply, nor would she even look at me. No matter. I knew she remembered our first kiss as vividly as I did by the blush that suffused her cheeks.

We all parted in the kitchen a short time later, she to her chamber and Noah to his upstairs, and I to my office, where I continue to write although it is nigh midnight. Enough! To bed.

JULIA'S NOTEBOOK

Thursday, 16 December

When Adam enfolded me in his arms last night, I felt I belonged with him in every sense—physically, spiritually, exclusively, eternally. Alas, as much as we belong together, we cannot *be* together as husband and wife in this lifetime. Perhaps we shall have a future life together in which we will be free to enjoy conjugal relations. Perhaps we have been intimate partners in a past life. I can almost believe these things possible after what Adam told me last night.

He said that in August of '46, shortly after I'd sailed for Europe, Henry had taken him to a place called Bartlett's Hill, not far from his cabin. Henry believed this location to be the one he'd recalled in his hypnotic regression. There two boulders stood cheek by jowl, and they matched the ones in Henry's remembrance, right down to the crevasse between them into which the unfortunate Indian had fallen after Henry sank an ax into his head. (Not Henry in his present incarnation, of course, but some past Indian self.) And Henry had then wanted Adam to hold him by the ankles whilst he went headfirst into the crevasse to see if he could find evidence that this memory from a time two hundred years ago had actually occurred. Adam had tried to talk him out of such an imprudent endeavor, but had ended up assisting him. And lo! Henry had come up with a skull with an ax embedded in it!

This ax exactly fit the description of the one Henry had recalled in his regression. It was made of pink quartz and had a jagged blaze of black stone running through it. They had decided to tell no one of their discovery, for neither of them wanted the notoriety such a claim would bring. So they had tossed the skull, ax and all, back into the crevasse and had gone about the business of living in the present.

But last evening a man they had recently met called Dr. Lamb had described just such an ax to them. How would he know of it? Although I was there when Adam regressed Henry, I certainly have told no one about it. So how Dr. Lamb knew details never made known to anyone is a mystery far too deep for me to comprehend. Adam insists there must be some logical explanation. But I prefer to think our souls do come back again and again. And if Adam and I are truly soul mates, surely we will have another lifetime together. How I hope that to be so!

Meanwhile, my present concern is Noah. He has not come home yet, and twilight is fast approaching. I shall have to go out and find him post haste.

ADAM'S JOURNAL

Thursday, December 16

Another patient lost. Will I ever become inured to it? Even though I knew Arabel Phyfe's demise to be inevitable, I am still astounded that she left this world so quickly. A painless exit, I am thankful to report. I could do nothing to save her, but I could at least ease her passing.

As is often the case with Consumption, this young woman became more beautiful as she wasted away. Her sisters remarked that Arabel looked an ethereal angel, so delicate and pale, with eyes as bright as stars. She remained conscious almost to the last, and whenever I came to her bedside her eyes would brighten even more. 'Twas not me personally she was so joyful to see, but the black bag I carried, for she knew it contained the laudanum she so craved.

Today, when I took her pulse, I found her feeble heart to bc laboring away at a hundred forty beats a minute. Auscultation with the stethoscope revealed ever greater congestion in the upper lobes of the lungs, for I could hear the bubbling and gurgling of tubercular matter in the bronchi. She was no longer ingesting any food and had lost near all her life force since I had first examined her in my office but three days past.

I administered a generous draught of laudanum, and she drank it down with the only energy left to her.

The drug had an immediate effect, and she lay her head back on her silk pillow with a sigh of relief. Her peace lasted only a moment before it was interrupted by a violent bout of coughing. I lifted her up and held a bowl beneath her chin. In it she expectorated clots of blood and bits of lung tissue. That took her last strength. She lay back again as I wiped her mouth, pale cheeks now flushed from exertion, and I knew that Death had tiptoed into the room, along with her father.

"Is she better today?" Justice Phyfe asked me.

Such a pitifully futile question! Poor Phyfe had yet to accept that his eldest child was dying and that there was no way all the doctors and treatments his money could buy could prevent it. Arabel's breath came more and more slowly, each intake labored, made with painful effort. Having witnessed this stage of the disease far too often, I knew what next to expect.

"She has come to her last moments of life," I replied as gently and kindly as I could. "It is time to bid her good-bye."

Phyfe and his daughters knelt by the bed and began caressing Arabel's thin arms, stroking her hair, and kissing her face in a flurry of demonstrative affection. But of a sudden they stopped, for Arabel's labored breathing had stopped.

Although I knew she was dead, I still followed my established procedure. Felt for a pulse at wrist and neck. Held a small mirror close to her nostrils to see if any trace of respiration left a touch of fog on the glass. Placed my stethoscope to her chest and listened long and carefully. "She is gone," I said.

"Look!" the youngest girl said, pointing upward. "Her soul is floating away."

Although I saw nothing, it might well have been so, for Arabel had slipped away smoothly, without the final hacking struggle or desperate, wild-eyed fear that is more typical of Consumption's final moments. Her spirit did indeed seem to float from its mooring, leaving behind only a shell of flesh and bone that was no longer her.

When I returned to the office I was relieved to see there were no patients waiting, for I felt heavy of heart and exhausted. Dropped off my bag and went down the passageway to the house, seeking out Julia. Found her at the back door, dressed in cape and gloves, about to go out.

"How sad you look!" she said to me. "Has Arabel passed?" When I nodded her eyes filled with tears, but she contained them. "I will go to the Phyfe house to offer my help and condolences as soon as I find Noah. I want him safe inside the house before nightfall."

"Where do you hope to find him?"

"I'll try the new cemetery first. He often goes there to pray at the graves of his parents, or so Mrs. Swann tells me. She too has gone off, I know not where."

"I'll accompany you," I said. "You should not go roaming alone in the dark any more than Noah should."

Off we went into the silvery twilight, walking briskly up the post road to the cemetery that had been established only a few years ago, when the one behind the Meetinghouse ran out of space. At this time of day no one was about but for a tall figure standing amongst the gravestones. He was a long-armed, bearded man and seemed to be shaking out a coat with a curious fury. And then, as we drew closer, I realized 'twas a boy, not a coat, that the man was so violently shaking. The boy was Noah! And the man was Solomon Wiley. When Solomon saw me charging toward him, he ceased shaking Noah, but still held him up by his collar so that his feet did not touch the ground.

"Put him down," I demanded.

Solomon complied, but kept a grip on the boy's neck. "I found him here communicating with the undead," he told me. "He is their minion. He was born to it. See how evil marks the little fiend's face." He must have tightened his grip, for the boy winced.

"Free him," I commanded Solomon as calmly as I could, fearing he would snap Noah's neck.

"Free the Night Stalker's spy? I do not think so," Solomon said in a most reasonable tone that belied the madness in his eyes. "I have heard how he sets fires to call up the devil. This town would be far better off with him dead." He gave Noah's neck another wince-inducing twist. "Would not this little monster's head look better on a spike?"

Out of nowhere, a slate footstone came flying past me and hit Solomon smack on the forehead. I could hear Julia breathing fast and furious behind me, but dared not turn to see her, for Solomon remained upright and dangerous. The blow she had delivered to him, however, had caught him so entirely off-guard that he'd loosened his grip on Noah's neck enough for the boy to break free and run into Julia's arms.

Solomon flicked away the blood gushing from his forehead and moved toward Julia. "Give me back the devil boy, woman, or I'll twist off your neck, too."

Before he could take another step, I hit him with a right fist driven from my shoulder and legs as I had learned at the Harvard boxing club, but with more anger and brute power strength than I had ever hit a man with in sport. Solomon did not buckle under from the blow as I'd expected him to do, however. He merely shook his head and hooked a swipe at me that would have knocked my head right out of the cemetery grounds if it had connected. Fortunately I dodged in time. As I half turned and yelled at Julia to run with Noah, Solomon saw his chance and shot his elbow into my face. I reeled back, and he ran forward after Julia and the boy. His long legs covered the short distance between them with no trouble. He snatched Noah up. And shoved Julia to the ground!

Infused with rage, I rushed at Solomon. He threw down

the boy, knocking the wind out of him, to deal with me. He looked eager to do me great harm, but I was just as eager to do the same to him and landed another blow that caught him on the side of his neck. That slowed him down only a little. He is far bigger and no doubt stronger than I, and if I'd had any tool or weapon at hand I would have used it against him gladly. But all I had were my bare hands. And my head. When he caught me in his powerful arms to crush me, I butted my crown sharply up against his jaw, causing his own head to snap back. I pulled away as he staggered backwards into a tall marble monument.

He shook his head and then launched himself at me with a roar. Noah, prone on the ground, grabbed at Solomon's ankle and caused him to stumble, which gave me the opportunity to land another punch into Solomon's face. He swerved and fell, ramming his head against the monument so hard that he was knocked senseless. So Providence had indeed provided me with weapons to defeat the ferocious Behemoth—a small boy's hand and a marble stone. I was most appreciative.

Rushed to Julia, who was sitting on the ground looking dazed. Helped her to her feet, and she assured me she was un-injured. Noah had managed to upright himself and wobbled to us, head dizzy but limbs unbroken. Julia and I each took one of his hands, and off we all hurried toward the cemetery gate. Once we reached the public road, I told them to head home without me and that I would join them there shortly. I felt an obliga-tion as a doctor to go back inside the cemetery to see if Solo-mon was in need of aid.

Found him sitting up, rubbing his head. It appeared that he would fully recover with no lasting injuries. He looked back at me with such a hateful expression that I turned away, wanting nothing more to do with him. And as I turned I caught a flash of movement behind a white oak in the distance. I marched to it and found Mrs. Swann, all aflutter and breathless, peeking round the tree trunk at me.

"Oh, Dr. Walker, 'tis you, thank God!" she said. "As you came toward me I feared you to be the Plumford Night Stalker."

"What are you doing here, Mrs. Swann?"

"I was just asking myself that very question. What sane woman would end up in a cemetery just as night is descending? But the thing of it is, I lost my way on my ramble, being unfamiliar with these parts, and hoped cutting through here would lead me back to the post road."

"I shall lead you back to the road," I told her and gallantly offered my arm. In truth, if she had not been a friend of Julia's, I would have readily left her to manage on her own. Not only is Mrs. Swann unattractive, vulgar, and useless, she has now proven herself to be obtuse.

Julia had not gone home as I had directed her to but was waiting with Noah at the gate for me. She greeted Mrs. Swann rather coolly, I thought, so perhaps the warmth of their friendship is subsiding. Mrs. Swann was aghast when we told her what had just occurred in the cemetery.

"I must have missed the battle between David and Goliath by mere minutes," she exclaimed.

"It was more like the Archangel Michael defeating Satan!" Julia said.

I laughed at that for in truth I am no hero and even less an angel. I am not inclined to rush out and fight against evil, but when it comes upon me as it did today, in the form of Solomon Wiley, I have no choice but to grapple with it. The man smells of the grave.

JULIA'S NOTEBOOK

Friday, 17 December

Noah and I spent the morning sketching together. He seemed calm and content, as if he had forgotten all about his violent encounter with Solomon Wiley. The poor dear has most likely become inured to the harsh treatment of bullies over the years, but does he appreciate that his very life was in danger yesterday? By the way he now gazes with awe at his rescuer Adam, I think he does.

Henry called this afternoon. When I opened the door to him he presented me with a blue box that contained three dozen Thoreau drawing pencils! I thanked him heartily and offered to do a pencil sketch of him gratis.

"Surely you have better things to draw than my plain countenance," he said.

"Indeed I do not," I assured him, for his dynamic features are most striking. His large nose alone is worthy of study at various angles. The last time I studied one so aquiline 'twas on a bust of Caesar. His prominent eyes, too, might be drawn again and again, for they are ever-changing, the color shifting from gray to blue, the focus sometimes contemplatively vague, sometimes keen and sharp as an eagle's. His mobile mouth would be hard to capture, being down-turned one moment and then suddenly transforming into a radiant smile. Oh, yes, I could sketch Henry over and over again, and each time he would look truly himself and yet different.

He refused my offer, however, with his usual brusqueness, claiming that if I had nothing better to draw, he certainly had better things to do than pose for a portrait. I persuaded him to come into my studio anyway, with the promise I would not so much as touch a pencil, and after he'd settled himself by the fire I recounted to him our terrifying confrontation with Solomon Wiley in the cemetery.

Henry, of course, was outraged. "Have the wretch arrested!"

"By whom? The doughty Plumford constable?" I said with disdain. "Beers has neither the backbone nor the muscle to take on Wiley. Nor the inclination, either. Beers near worships Wiley as the heroic slayer of vampyres. And more to the point, they are drinking companions."

"Where is Noah now?" Henry said, looking concerned.

"Safe with Adam in his office."

"He is a most fortunate boy to have Adam and you looking after him."

"God knows he needs protectors!" I said. "No one else in Plumford cares a whit about him. Perhaps, if Noah had been born here, folks might have gotten used to his deformity and accepted him. But the Robinsons came here as strangers only a short time ago and apparently kept very much to themselves. Why, you heard what the Shroves said, Henry. Noah's parents did not even send him to school. Hence, he is nigh a stranger hereabouts, and a very strange-looking stranger at that. How the poor dear is made to suffer for his disfigurement!"

"Why is there such intolerance for those who look or act different?" Thoreau said. "I know of a man named Joseph Palmer who is persecuted unmercifully for wearing a beard simply because it is not the fashion. He has been jeered at and even physically attacked. But he is a hale and hearty fellow and can stand up to his tormentors. Indeed, he could even shave off his beard if he so chose. Noah, unfortunately, is too small to fight off full-grown aggressors, nor can he change his outward appearance."

"I have high hopes Adam can do so with an operation," I said. "But in the meantime, I am greatly concerned about Noah's safety. Townspeople are so frightened by Kitty Lyttle's brutal murder that they are apt to believe anything, even that Noah is the Night Stalker's apprentice."

"Apt to do anything too." Henry nodded. "Nothing is so much to be feared as fear, for it instills anger and irrational behavior."

"I wish Noah had relatives elsewhere who could take him in until sanity returns to Plumford."

"For aught we know he does," Henry said.

"Alas, Noah has told me more than once that he has no living kin."

"Could he not be mistaken? Perhaps he has kin his parents never mentioned to him."

"But where to look for them?"

"Well, we were told by the Shroves that Noah's father once worked at the Howard Theater," Henry said. "And I happen to be acquainted with a most agreeable lady who is employed at that very theater."

Henry never fails to surprise me. "Pray write to this agreeable lady forthwith and inquire if she was acquainted with Mr. Robinson."

"Better yet, I shall ask her in person. I plan to go to the Howard first thing next week to inquire about Kitty Lyttle."

"Allow me to accompany you, Henry! Kitty was a friend of mine, and I might be of help in your inquiry."

"You might at that. But will Adam allow you to get involved in a murder case?"

"Allow me?" My hackles rose. "Adam Walker is not my keeper!"

Henry smiled at my indignation. "As far as I am concerned, you are welcome to come along. I shall be at the Concord station at ten o'clock Monday morning."

"And so shall I, Henry."

That settled, he departed. And the rest of the day has passed without incident but for a rather annoying conversation I had with Mrs. Swann. She knocked on my chamber door just a while ago and said we must have a talk "for my own good." Since childhood, I have never appreciated talks that began with such a preamble, and I did not appreciate this one, either.

"It has come to my attention," she commenced quite starchily, "that Dr. Walker has spent two nights in a row sleeping in his office. Will he continue to do so?"

"I don't really know. But why should it matter to you, Mrs. Swann?"

"It should matter to *you,* my dear! Have you no concern for your reputation? You know how people talk. Here you are, a married woman living apart from her husband, with an attractive young man sleeping under your roof."

I laughed. "Dr. Walker's office has its own roof. And he is my *cousin,* Mrs. Swann. I do not think people will talk. Nor do I care if they do."

"Well, I care," she said, folding her arms across her ample bosom. "I too have a reputation to consider. It is unseemly to have a single man residing with two husbandless women. Two very alluring women, I might add."

I could not believe my ears! Was I hearing such prudish drivel from the lips of the very woman who enjoyed reciting passages from *The Memoirs of a Woman of Pleasure?* "Are you skylarking with me, Mrs. Swann?"

"I am not!" she denied most indignantly. "Dr. Walker is always around, everywhere I look, all the time, and it is driving me to distraction!"

Could it be that she is falling in love with Adam? Is this why she too finds his presence as disquieting as I do?

"We should both be grateful to have a man around whilst a crazed killer roams Plumford," I told her. "But if you object to Dr. Walker's presence so strongly, you are free to remove yourself from my house."

As soon as I stated this, I realized how relieved I would be if she left. In fact, I was near to the point of insisting upon it. But then she covered her face with her hands and wept most piteously.

"But where would I go? Where would I go?" she lamented.

So the next thing I found myself doing was comforting her. "You need not go anywhere," I said, patting her heaving shoulder.

"Thank you!" she said and gave me a heartfelt hug. She smelled pleasantly of bergamot, but I also discerned a faint trace of tobacco smoke. She spends so much time jabbering with the cronies at Daggett's store that her clothes must soak up their cigar and pipe smoke.

I gently but firmly extracted myself from her strong embrace, and we parted without further mention of Adam's "unseemly" proximity. Of course I would like him closer still, in my very bed, night after night. But it is enough to know he is nearby. When he told me that he had come to protect me, my heart swelled so in my chest I could not breathe, much less speak.

ADAM'S JOURNAL

Saturday, December 18

Arabel Phyfe was buried today, and the funeral procession from the Meetinghouse to the new cemetery was far longer than most have been of late. Even townspeople who had barely known the girl marched behind the crepe-draped coffin carriage to show respect for their First Selectman, Justice Phyfe. That the Consumption could take the daughter of such a wealthy and influential man as he seemed to comfort some I spoke to who had also lost children to the disease. 'Twas not that they were gladdened by Phyfe's loss, only consoled that Death does not play favorites.

Returned to the office after the burial service, intent on putting to order my long-neglected account ledger, when Mr. Jackson burst through the door and said his son had swallowed rat poison. Grabbed my bag and handed Jackson the box of stomach-pump gear and off we ran to the house.

Hyram was on the floor of his chamber, writhing and wailing and foaming at the mouth. I could smell the garlic scent of arsenic before I even crouched down over him.

"Where's the container of poison?" I asked his father. He pointed to an empty jar by the bedstead. "Was it full?"

"I used up half last time I put it out for rats."

"How long ago did Hyram ingest it?" I said.

"Couldn't have been more than ten minutes ago. He went up to his chamber straight from the Phyfe funeral, and soon after that I heard him thrashing and moaning. Went to see what the commotion was, saw the empty jar of ratsbane, and ran to fetch you."

The fool boy had downed enough poison to kill off a horse, much less himself, but I had hopes that his body had not yet had time to absorb it. "Let's pump him out," I said.

Brought out the five-foot length of flexible, half-inch tube and began to rub fish oil along its length to facilitate passage down the throat.

"We're going to save you, Hyram," I said.

He spat foam away from his mouth. "No! Don't want to be saved."

"He is going to fight us," I said to Jackson. I expected as much, as this was no accident, and if someone tries to kill himself, he generally is not of a mind to lend a hand in being saved. I was glad the father had more than enough strength to do what would now be necessary. Asked Jackson to draw a bucket of water and find a block of wood to place in the boy's mouth to hold it open so he couldn't sever my fingers or the tube with his teeth.

Jackson was back in a minute with both. Asked him to raise Hyram up into a chair, and he did so, seating him down hard. Hyram thrashed about and shook his head from side to side, until Jackson wrapped his huge arm around his son's head to hold him still. This was no time to be gentle, and I pressed hard on the sides of the boy's jaws. When the pain of it made him open his mouth wide, I forced the block of wood between his teeth. He moaned most miserably all the while, eyes wide as saucers, in pain from the arsenic burning away at his belly.

Held his tongue down and began to slide the tube down his throat. Although time was of the essence, took care to go slow and be sure not to direct the tube into the trachea instead of the esophagus. That mistake would fill the lungs with water instead of the stomach, and I'd end up drowning instead of saving him. Knew I'd gotten safely past the trachea when I heard only moans of discomfort and not ragged, blocked breathing. Hyram retched against the tube instinctively, his body convulsing to try and get rid of the obstruction, but to no avail. When the tube end would go no farther, I knew it had reached the pit of his stomach. Inserted a funnel into the other end of the tube and, holding it high, poured water into it. As the water went down the tube to his stomach, Hyram thrashed about like a crazed animal, but I soon got his stomach full. Took the funnel out of the tube, pinched shut the end of it, and lowered the end of the tube into the bucket. Hence, when I released my pinch hold, the tube acted like a siphon and pulled out the contents of Hyram's stomach in a long, foul gush that lasted a good ten seconds. Poor Hyram choked and groaned most miserably during this procedure, but we ignored his misery and went through the procedure once again for good measure.

After the second stomach flush, I carefully pulled out the tube and poured a good dose of fish oil down the boy's throat. He coughed some of it up, but enough reached its destination to make him vomit all over again, which I thought best for him. Only then did Jackson pull out the block from between his son's teeth. The boy by this time was weak and limp, as the entire process is most exhausting and revolting for the patient to endure. Some doctors would have used harsh emetics instead, but they burn the patient's stomach lining. Besides, emetics cannot clean out the stomach as well or as fast as the tube flushing method.

Jackson pulled off his son's wet, stained clothes and tucked him into bed as gently as he must have when Hyram was a child. He fell asleep instantly.

"Do you know of any reason why he would do this?" I asked Mr. Jackson as we hovered over the boy. "I am concerned he might try again with greater efficacy."

Mr. Jackson slowly shook his head as he gazed at his son. "All I know is that he has been acting strange for months now. And stranger still these last few weeks. But I did not make too much of it, for if the truth be told, my son has always been a bit strange. I reckon losing his mother as a youngster made him so."

"Well, if that be the cause, I too might be strange," I said, "for I lost my own mother when I was but seven."

"You, doctor?" Mr. Jackson regarded me for a moment with eyes that expressed deep sadness. "You are the most regular, rational, reliable man in Plumford. And I thank you from the bottom of my heart for saving my son." He turned from me quickly, and I knew he did so to hide his tears.

"I will sit with Hyram for a while to make sure he is on the mend," I said. "Could I trouble you to make me a strong cup of coffee, Mr. Jackson?"

He nodded and quickly left the chamber to do so, and to regain his composure in privacy.

In his sleep Hyram moaned most plangently, but I concluded it was from a bad dream rather than physical pain. I adjusted his pillow to make him more comfortable, and as I smoothed the case I felt a lump beneath it. I extracted a ball of pink silken fabric that, once unfolded, became a woman's stocking. I stared at it with more surprise than if it had been a turtle. How did such an intimate article of female attire come to be nestled in Hyram's pillowcase? I replaced it and rearranged the pillow under his head.

Did not mention the stocking to Mr. Jackson when he returned with my coffee. But I did ask if Hyram was courting anyone and so might be disappointed in love. To that Mr. Jackson sighed and said his son was far too shy to even speak to a young woman, much less go a-courting. So the stocking remains a mystery. Perhaps the boy simply stole it off some lady's clothesline.

ADAM'S JOURNAL

Sunday, December 19

Hyram Jackson's attempt to end his own young life for no discernible reason was not the only bizarre occurrence to bewilder me yesterday. Far from it! The events that took place last evening were more flummoxing still. My mind throbs with disturbing images as much as my head aches from the blows it endured.

And to think how ordinarily the evening began. Went to the Sun for a small beer and some small talk. Received both from the amiable Ruggles. But as we discussed the likelihood of getting snow before Christmas, I began sniffing the air, wondering if I still retained the scent of arsenic in my nostrils. Then I noticed the garlands of garlic hanging above the bar.

Ruggles noted my glances and smiled. "Yes, doctor, they are to ward off the Night Stalker. The precaution eases the minds of my customers." He turned to the seemingly ever-present Beers. "Don't it, constable?"

"My mind has not been at ease for over a fortnight, since the body of that young man whose name escapes me was found in our township."

"Chauncey Bidwell," I said. "And if you cannot even recall

his name, it indicates to me that investigating his death is not topmost in your mind."

"Well, I have a more recent murder to deal with, do I not?" Beers said indignantly. "But what is the point of investigating who murdered either of 'em if we already know who done it?"

"You have arrested no one," I said.

"And pray how do I go about arresting a vampyre?"

I groaned. "Stop using that fabrication as an excuse to keep from doing your job."

"Fabrication!" Beers sputtered. "I have evidence. I have a witness. I have the council of a vampyre authority who has slain such—" He looked toward the door and stopped talking. "Who be that?"

I followed his gaze and at first did not recognize the new arrival, but when the tall fellow looked my way, I saw that it was Dr. Lamb. He was now clad in a shabby overcoat, rumpled worker trousers, and a black slouch hat, the broad brim shielding half his face. Not only had he changed his dress, but also the very set of his face. The hauteur had been replaced by a dull, rather stupid expression, and thick, metal-framed glasses covered his piercing eyes. But despite Lamb's obvious attempt to look inconspicuous, he still drew suspicious looks his way. The appearance of any stranger now causes alarm in our town.

"That man is a doctor I know," I told Beers and hastened to go greet Lamb. "What brings you to the Sun Tavern?"

"You, of course," he replied. "May we talk in more privacy?"

We went to a table in the back of the room. "So how did you find me this time?" I asked him when we were seated. "Sheer luck again?"

He gave me a shadow of a smile. "I shall always be able to find you, Dr. Walker."

"So it seems. And did you find Solomon Wiley after you left my grandmother's house so abruptly?"

"Oh, yes. I watched him from a distance and determined he was a mortal man of the lowest order. He is not the one I seek."

"Is that not what I told you?"

"You told me *nothing!*" His intense anger flared for only an instant. "And to be fair, I have told you nothing of myself."

"You are not a doctor who practices in Maine?"

"No. I would make a poor doctor indeed, especially if required to bleed patients. And once you hear more about me, you will understand why." But he said no more.

Contained my impatience and waited. Had to wait for some time before he spoke again. And when he did, he related the following to me, as near as I can remember.

I was born a Nipmuc and lived in this region before the white man came. You cannot imagine the sweetness of life and the plenty before your coming! So many silvery alewives and shad ran in the Assabet they could be scooped up with just our hands to fill our reed baskets to bursting. And when the salmon ran, there were more fish in the river than water itself, and some of them were longer and heavier than men. We burned the brush under the trees to keep the land open for grass and plants to grow so that herds of deer would come to graze. They gave us hides for clothes, antlers for tools, and meat all the winter through. The bears were so many every wigwam had robes for sleeping, and we smeared their fat on us to keep out the winter cold. And beaver, how we loved to eat their fatty tails! Babies and maidens wore their soft, warm fur next to the skin when it was cold.

And what beautiful men and women we were! Far taller and stronger than you English, with sounder limbs and far better teeth. The air was clear, without the stink of cows, oxen, pigs, and horses, and yes, the stink of you who were far less clean than we.

How I long to hear my language spoken and chanted again! How I long to awaken on a cold night such as this in a wigwam and smell the bark roof, see in the flickering embers of the fire my bow and lance

*and arrows, and feel the body of my good wife against me. Even in the
winter we were content. While blizzards raged I sat and knapped
arrowheads while my son laid turkey feathers on the arrow shafts, my
wife sewed garments of deerskin, and my girl wove and painted baskets
of reed or folded birch bark. What more in the world could any man
want? We made with our own hands everything we needed. I scorn
your clapboard houses filled with chattels, your fenced-in farms with
penned-in animals, your binding garments and shoes. You surrender
your freedom in order to possess such unnecessary things.*

*You have heard of us only as people with dead eyes and mouths
bent down in sorrow and hate. But you brought us that sorrow with
your diseases, and you caused us to hate you for your greed. I tell you,
how we all laughed before you came! No people so laughed, so saw the
sweetness of life, so amused themselves with pranks, so enjoyed prat-
falls, so frolicked at a feast, so jested, so threw themselves into games of
every kind. Life was a game.*

*Even war was a game for the battle was about bravery, showing
daring and courage and skill. Women and children were spared, even
taken into the victor's clan and tribe. Men fought eye to eye instead of
firing weapons at each other from a distance. We fought to test each
other. You fight to annihilate each other. But there is no point in my
going on about all that. Your world is here, and my world is gone.*

*And you are no doubt weary of hearing about a life you cannot
understand, Dr. Walker. What you want to know is how I could live
so long. Or perhaps you have already decided that I am completely
mad, and nothing I tell you will change your mind. Nevertheless, I
shall tell you anyway, for it is such a relief to speak the truth of my
past.*

*I was the leader of the Wolf clan, and we were at war with the
Bear clan across the river. On that hill above the pond you call
Walden, my brother Tisquantum and I pursued a Bear warrior up a
high rock formation. Tisquantum raised his club to smite him, but the
Bear had an ax of powerful medicine and struck my brother first. Tis-
quantum tumbled down into a crevasse between the rocks with the ax*

sunk in his head. I did not mourn my brother for there is no better way for an Indian brave to die than in battle. I did revenge him, however, by stabbing the Bear in his chest with my knife. But as I made to stab him again, he played some devil trick on me, got his arm around my neck, and snapped it. He threw me down and left me for dead.

But I was not quite dead when clansmen bore me back to the village. All through the night my father chanted over me, his only remaining son, hoping to call up Witiku to save me. My father was a most powerful medicine man, and Witiku answered his call. He told my father that he might be willing to restore me in exchange for another life, and my father immediately slit his own throat. After drinking the blood that poured from my father's throat, Witiku brought his mouth to mine and poured the blood into me, transforming me into an immortal creature like him. So 'twas the blood of my father that gave me my second life just as his seed had given me my first.

And then Witiku took on the role of my father. He taught me the ways of a vampyre Witiku like him, as my first father had taught me the ways of a Nipmuc warrior. We roamed the wild forests together for many companionable years. We took what we wanted, but we never took too much. We were not rapacious like the white men who take everything from this land. When my Witiku father saw enough of your ways to know what was to come, he said good-bye to me and burrowed down into the earth, leaving me to find my way alone as a Witiku.

My eternal life became one of eternal suffering as I watched the destruction of my people. Your diseases came first and ravaged us before we had a chance to even fight against you. My people perished so quickly from the white man's poxes that there was no one left to bury the dead. I would walk through village after village, their bones crunching under my feet as our fields became yours. When Metacomet, the one you call King Philip, declared a war against you, in your year of 1675, I fought with all my Witiku powers beside him and the few of my people left to defend the life we had loved.

I was a tireless slayer and helped exterminate twelve of your towns. But there were always more of you coming. And so few of us left. When Metacomet's head ended up on a pike at the entrance of one of your forts, I wandered about, aimlessly killing white settlers for a time, and legends grew about me, the terrible man-eater Witiku. Eventually I grew tired of that, and like my vampyre father I burrowed underground. I buried myself in my clan's burial ground near here, to sleep away my sorrow. I could not face what was on the earth anymore.

Then curiosity got the better of me. I awoke to see if any of my own race still lived. By then it was a new century, and I had to learn the white man's language and ways to avoid too much notice. I found not a trace of my people left in these parts and was ready to go back into my grave when by the merest chance I read your article on hypnosis, Dr. Walker. I was astonished! And so should you be, for the man who recalled killing my brother and fighting with me is a vampyre like myself.

Now do not give me such a disbelieving look, doctor. That can be the only answer to explain how he recalled what happened two hundred and fifty years ago. You must tell me how to find him. I hope you understand why it means everything to me. We are the last two Nipmucs left! That we were of different clans and at war means nothing now. I long to be with one who thinks as I do, for an Indian sees the world as differently from you as does a bear from a fish. We are of different worlds. And you have imposed your world onto mine.

I cannot bear to live in your world alone. I will bury myself away again deep into the peaceful earth, perhaps this time forever, if I cannot find one of my own blood and mind.

So that is why you must tell me who he is.

He fell silent, and I then spoke most reluctantly. "Doctor Lamb, pray believe me when I tell you that the man I regressed is not an Indian vampyre. He was born only thirty years ago, is neither tall nor dark, has living parents and sisters, is of French and English descent, walks about in the daylight, and forebears from eating meat of any kind, much less drinking blood. All the same, he *was* the Indian you fought in another life. He is not that same man anymore, however, although his very essence might be the same."

Lamb looked at me in an inhuman fashion, his pupils red as hot coals. "You speak in riddles to confuse me. Dare not trifle with me, doctor."

"I do not wish to confuse you, but all this confuses me as well. The only explanation I can give you is that my subject recalled a past life."

"He came back from the dead?"

"No. But his soul was reborn."

"What is a soul, doctor? I hear white men speak of it all the time and can never understand what they mean."

"Most of us most likely don't know what we mean, either," I said. His eyes flamed behind the shield of his glasses again, and I held up my palm to stay his anger. "Forgive me for speaking in riddles again. But is not life itself a riddle? There is no answer to what awaits us after death. I reckon even *you* do not know, after all these years on earth as a vampyre."

"Ah, so you believe I speak the truth."

"No more or less than you believe I speak the truth to you," I hedged.

"About your subject's being reborn?" Lamb gave out a hollow laugh and leaned so close to me I could smell the clove on his breath. "I could easily prove to you that I am a vampyre, but you would unfortunately have to die from the demonstration. But how can you possibly prove this theory you call Reincarnation?"

"We have! To our satisfaction at least." I went on to tell him, without referring to Henry by name, how we had found the ax-embedded skull in the crevasse of the rocks. "We thought it best to return it to its resting place," I concluded.

"It rests there no more," Lamb said. "I too went back on that hill and crawled down into the crevasse where Tisquantum fell so long ago. I took his head with the ax still wedged in it and buried it in my clan's graveyard. Indeed, in my own grave, so if I return to sleep my brother will be with me. That is how lonely I am!"

We regarded each other silently in the noise of the boisterous tavern.

"If you truly found that skull, you may well be who and what you claim you are," I finally said, my voice shaky.

"And I am ready to concede there is such a thing as Reincarnation," he told me.

The door flew open, and Solomon Wiley barged into the tavern like a wild beast, grunting out greetings to one and all as he brandished a human skull on a pole. Some regarded him with wonder, others with repulsion. Lamb showed no emotion at all upon his pale countenance. Such unnatural self-control made me almost believe he was what he said he was, for the skull Solomon was showing off so proudly had an ax implanted in it, and that ax was of pink quartz with a black blaze running through it.

"I have been hunting for Witiku!" Solomon cried out.

"You have been plundering a graveyard!" I shouted back at him and left the table to talk to Beers. "Arrest this man, constable. It is now against the law in Plumford to desecrate human corpses." Of course Beers made no move to vacate his stool.

Solomon laughed. "This skull did not come from a *Christian* burial place but from that old Nipmuc boneyard up by Herd's pasture. How can you desecrate what is already ungodly?"

"I have no jurisdiction, I am sure, over such a place as that," Beers murmured.

"And hark this, my fellow townsmen!" Solomon bellowed. "I believe I have found the vampyre Witiku's lair!" He paused as men left their bar stools and tables to gather round him. "I found this skull in a grave by a boulder. I swear as I stand here that grave was fresh dug," he continued. "When that fiend discovers how I defiled his sleeping place with my own urine, he will have nowhere else to go tonight."

"You pissed in it?" I said in a jeering tone. "Why, you are no better than a dog marking his territory, Wiley."

That got a few laughs, and the more respectable tavern-goers started backing away from Solomon. Oh, how he did glower at me. I smiled back.

"Walker is too stupid to understand my intent," Solomon told those still around him. "Vampyres lose all their powers in the light of day, and if Witiku has nowhere to hide, he will be at my mercy. I intend to spend the rest of the night at that unholy place awaiting him."

"But won't the stink of your piss keep him away?" I said, since my vulgarity had gone over so well the first time. And sure enough, it got laughs once again. Indeed, it does not take much to get men at a tavern laughing. Humor pertaining to body parts and their functions rarely fails.

Solomon turned red with rage, but held his ground. "I am trying to save this town for you and your loved ones," he told those still listening to him. "And to do so, all the vampyres that inhabit it must be destroyed or driven off. I have spent this long day searching for Witiku and his minions in the Indian boneyard, and although I labored hard and long digging up ancient graves and strewing about their contents, I expect no payment for it."

I glanced toward Lamb to see how he was taking all this, but much to my surprise, he was no longer seated at the table, nor could I spot him anywhere in the tavern. I looked back at Solomon.

"Of course you expect payment!" I shouted at him. "As you expected payment for desecrating the bodies of Consumption victims until that was deemed against the laws of sanity and decency. So now you resort to destroying Indian graves to incite fear and drum up business for yourself."

"Slaying vampyres is not my business, 'tis my mission in life!" he replied in his preacher voice, addressing the others. "I was but a boy when I saved my own dear mother, who was dying of the wasting disease. My stepfather was preying upon her from his grave, sucking the life out of her as she lay in her sickbed, until I unearthed his coffin and beheaded him. She got up from her bed restored to health that very day. Has that man"—he pointed to me—"ever cured anyone from Consumption? His patients die off like flies!"

"At least I am not a shameless fraud like you are, Solomon Wiley," I said. "You defaced Chauncey Bidwell's body with rat's blood at the ice house to make it look like the work of a vampyre. And you then tried to bully his poor mother into paying for your services. Enough of your tricks and scaremongering. Get the hell out of our town." Men began to stand alongside me, leaving Solomon to stand by himself.

"Very well, heed this useless doctor who cannot save his patients from dying, instead of heeding me, who can destroy the very cause of their deaths," he said, his voice now sad and weary. "We will see whom Witiku chooses to kill next." With a parting glare at me, he stalked out of the taproom and into the night.

I too soon left the Sun, for the likelihood of Lamb's returning seemed remote, and I had no desire to swallow down more alcohol. The one small beer I'd imbibed had left me lightheaded enough to make me realize how exhausted I was. As I walked past the smithy shop I heard from behind it a weak cry for help. Thinking someone was injured, I hurried toward the sound and in the moonlight saw what I took to be a supine figure on the ground. But as I crouched over it I discovered it to be only an empty coat and hat. I heard the cry again and turned to see Solomon Wiley behind me, grinning over his clever trick. He whacked me in the head with his pole.

Awoke to find myself laid out atop a fallen log, flat on my back, my hands and arms forced behind me and bound tight around the curve of the tree. I could scarcely make out where I was, for being so tightly tied I had difficulty turning my head. Could just discern in the moonlight the thick trunks of cedars that thrive only in marshy ground. Figured I was in a swamp and no doubt far from where my voice might be heard.

I heard a crunching of thin ice underfoot and saw Solomon glaring down at me. "Well, doctor, you are about to become Plumford's next murder victim," he declared.

"So it was you who murdered Bidwell and Kitty Lyttle."

"I did not! I had nothing against either one of them. *You,* however, I hate for good reason. Your meddling and scorn have lost me money and repute. But I have a plan to win back both." He pulled a knife from his belt. "I will make it look like the Night Stalker killed you, Dr. Walker. You will be found with your throat slashed and not a drop of blood left in you. Your death will cause everyone to panic, and the town officials will turn to me for help. I will become Plumford's savior."

All I had to defend myself with was my wits, and most had been knocked clear out of my head when Solomon had brained me. Gathered what was left of them to keep him talking. "Have you ever killed a living person before, Solomon? It cannot be an easy thing to do."

"It was easy enough for me to kill my stepfather. He had it coming for his mistreatment of my mother. And then I had to kill him all over again when he became one of the undead. That bastard was the first vampyre I slayed, and I was no more than a boy at the time. 'Twas then I knew my life's calling was to destroy every last vampyre that walks the earth." His eyes glittered in the light of the near full moon. They were the eyes of a madman. "You too have it coming to you, doctor, for calling me a fraud. And for your interference with my great mission. You may very well be one of Witiku's servants, just as that deformed boy that you harbor is. And who was that young woman who hit me with a stone? One of Witiku's wanton paramours? I will make sure to meet with her again and test her virtue to the limits."

Horrible thoughts of what he might do to Julia filled me with rage, and I yelled out with all my might as I struggled mightily to free myself. But I was trussed to the log so tightly that I could barely move my head from side to side, let alone my arms and legs, and my struggle and shouting were soon ended by a hard blow to the jaw from Solomon, stilling me into a state of semiconsciousness.

"I just did you a kindness, doctor," he said. "You will feel less pain when I plunge my knife into your throat."

Those were the last words I heard Solomon Wiley utter, for in the next moment he let out a gasp and was yanked away from me. I heard him still, but he was no longer talking, only screaming. I could not twist my head enough in either direction to see what was happening to him, but whatever it was must have been causing him excruciating pain. In all my experience amputating limbs, I have never heard the likes of Solomon's howls of torment. I could also hear what sounded to be bones being cracked. And I could smell blood and bowels and excrement, as if a human body had been ripped open. Feeling myself in the presence of savagery unimaginable, I lost consciousness.

When I opened my eyes again all was quiet but for the sound of lapping and gnawing, and I wondered if a pack of wild animals was feeding nearby. Wrenching my head to the side, I glimpsed the naked figure of a male of amazing muscularity, his back to me, crouched over a headless, limbless, eviscerated corpse. He must have sensed my stare, for he lifted his head from the corpse and turned to me, fangs bared and mouth dripping with blood, eyes burning red as coals. It was the head of a wolf! I shut my own eyes quickly, for I did not want to be mesmerized by Witiku's gaze. 'Twas the same gaze Dr. Lamb had transfixed me with more than once. Before I again lost consciousness, I heard Indian chanting.

Awoke in the cot in my office today, with Henry Thoreau's frowning visage looking down at me. "It is well past noon, my friend," he informed me.

I sat up, grasping my reeling head. I was dressed in the clothes I had worn to the tavern, and my boot-clad feet poked out of the covers.

Noting the boots, Henry shook his head disapprovingly. "Julia mentioned you had gone off to the tavern last night, and when she went up to her chamber at midnight, you had still not returned."

I lay back with a groan, and all the memories I have recorded herein came rushing back to me. Told Henry to pull up a chair and proceeded to recount the evening's bizarre events to him.

He did not once interrupt me or so much as smile at the absurdity of my tale. Indeed, he regarded me most solemnly the whole time and did not utter a word when I was done speaking.

"Well, what do you make of it?" I asked him. "I had but one small beer, so it could not have been a drunken hallucination."

"There is no doubt in my mind that Solomon Wiley clobbered you in that dark alley to pay you back for besting him once again," Henry said. "But all the rest of it that followed might well have been a nightmare brought on by that hit on the head."

"How did I get back to my office?"

"Solomon himself might have hauled you here and put you to bed, feeling regret over his nasty deed."

Since I keep the key to my office door in my waistcoat pocket, that could have been what happened. "Only one thing is for certain, Henry. Solomon did indeed march into the tavern last evening with a skull on a pole. And that skull had a quartz ax stuck in it. If you do not believe me, let us go to the Sun and ask Mr. Ruggles. He and plenty of witnesses can verify seeing it."

"Oh, I believe you," Henry said calmly.

"Are you not astonished? Does it not prove the story Lamb told me is true? He is the one who pulled the skull out of the crevasse and then buried it at the Nipmuc grave site!"

"Yes," Henry said. "So I believe he did. But that does not mean everything else he told you about himself is true."

"How then did he know where to find the skull?"

"I have a theory which I have been developing since we last talked," Henry said. "Indeed, I came by today to discuss it with you. I think Dr. Lamb truly does have Nipmuc blood in his veins. That would account for his appearance. And he must have heard stories passed down by generations of his ancestors, just as you and I have heard stories concerning our own forefathers. That would account for his knowing about the ax. In my regression I saw but three Indians, myself and two others, both of whom I slayed. But what if another Nipmuc had been watching us fight? He would have described what had happened to other tribe members, and because they believed the ax had magical powers, the story might have become part of the Nipmuc lore."

"Yes, that would explain how Lamb was able to describe the ax. But I ask you again, Henry. How could he know where to *find* it?"

"Well, we found it, didn't we? It is simply a matter of putting all the geographic clews together. Lamb said himself he knows this area."

"Then you discount the possibility that Lamb is in fact Witiku?"

"I discount nothing." Henry stood up and stretched his wiry frame. "Let us go see the destruction Solomon Wiley has done to the burial ground, Adam. That is, if you are up to it."

"Just barely," I said.

All it took was a pot of Julia's strong coffee to put me right. Even so, I yelped like a puppy when I tried to put on my hat over the egg-sized lump on my head. Julia gave me a look I reckon wives give their husbands when they stay out too late at taverns. Decided to let her assume I had overindulged rather than tell her I'd had another run-in with Wiley—or, even more terrifying, an encounter with the flesh-eating, blood-lapping Witiku.

Drove Henry out to the dry and rocky hillock known to be where the long-disappeared Nipmuc tribe buried their dead. Had not set my eyes on the forlorn and vaguely disquieting place since as a boy I had hurried past when out grouse-hunting. There had been little to see back then but a few crude burial stones and memorial heaps of small stones amid cedar trees, brambles, and tall tussocks of dried grass. Now, however, Henry and I saw that wherever there was a grave marker, no matter how humble, the sandy ground around it had been dug up. At least a dozen fresh mounds of sandy soil dotted the knob. A scattering of human bones lay in the cold sun, along with burial artifacts such as beads and bits of blue and white quahog shells.

A huge boulder a good fifteen feet high towered over one of the graves, which was dug much deeper than the others. "This must be the grave where Wiley said he found the skull buried," I told Henry.

He leaned against a tall, old juniper that stood nearby and peered down into the grave a moment. Then he looked up at the boulder. "According to Mr. Agassiz at Harvard, such rocks as this giant were left behind when the great glaciers that once covered this area melted away. Hard to believe, isn't it?"

"No harder to believe than Lamb's claim that he is a vampyre."

"Exactly my point," Henry said. "How are we to know the truth about this world when so much yet remains to be discovered in it?"

We then gathered the bones, returned them to the soil from whence they had come, and used our hands to push back the dug soil over their graves.

JULIA'S NOTEBOOK

Monday, 20 December

The "most agreeable lady" Henry knows at the Howard Theater turned out to be a dark-faced Moor in a purple turban. Or so she appeared to me when first I laid eyes on her today. She recognized Henry immediately and beckoned us into the dressing room. To his credit, Henry recognized her too after but a moment's hesitation.

"I wager you are experimenting with stage effects for a production of *Othello,* Mrs. Perry," he said.

"You win that wager," she replied. "Junius Booth will be playing the part next week and cannot spare the time to let me experiment on his own important person. He is far too busy getting drunk and making bastards with his mistress in Maryland." She laughed when she saw our surprised expressions. "You think me indiscreet, but it is public knowledge. Indeed, it has been made most public by Mr. Booth's legal wife, who removed to Maryland from England to plague the illicit duo."

She yanked off her turban, and her mane of black hair streaked with gray tumbled down about her shoulders. Now she looked like a witch, albeit a handsome one. Against her darkly stained face, her teeth looked very white when she smiled, which she frequently did when addressing Henry.

"So you have come back, Mr. Thoreau," she said. "This time without your friend the doctor."

"His duties keep him in Plumford," Henry said. "But as you see, I have come with another friend of mine."

Mrs. Perry gave me a cold appraisal and turned her gaze back to Henry. "Well, your sweetheart has looks enough for the stage, I suppose. But I hope you don't expect me to help get her hired as an actress. I have no influence whatsoever with the stage manager."

"That is not why we have come," Henry sputtered.

He appeared too flabbergasted to continue, so I spoke up. "Furthermore, Mr. Thoreau and I are not sweethearts, Mrs. Perry."

"My mistake, dearie." She regarded me with friendlier eyes. "Pray give me a moment to make myself presentable, and then you can tell me the purpose of your visit." She seated herself at a table strewn with bottles and jars and began wiping the stain from her face with a wet cloth. "Traditionally burnt cork is used to darken the Moor's complexion," she said, "but don't you think my concoction looks more realistic?"

"More realistic still," Henry said, "would be to have a real black man play Othello instead of a white man in blackface."

"I hear there is an American Negro actor residing in Europe who plays Othello to great acclaim," Mrs. Perry said. "But that is not how it is done in Boston." She tossed aside the cloth and turned her gaze from the looking glass to Henry. "How do I look to you now, Mr. Thoreau?"

If she expected a compliment from Henry, she didn't get one. "You look the same but for the face stain," he said. He took a key from his coat pocket and dangled it by its black cord. "This was found on Chauncey Bidwell's body. Does it perchance look familiar to you, Mrs. Perry?"

"Well, it is not the key to *my* chamber, if that's what you are suggesting," she said archly. "I confess I favor younger men, but Chauncey was not the sort that appealed to me. I prefer a man who does not care so much about his appearance. A natural man such as yourself, Mr. Thoreau. My guess is that you smell of pine forest instead of cologne."

A blush tinged Henry's cheeks. "I was not suggesting that this was your key, Mrs. Perry," he said. "Only asking if you might have seen it before. It has occurred to me that it might be to some door in this theater."

"I do not recognize it," she replied. "Nor do I think poor Chauncey's murder is connected with the Howard. We are a most peaceful, loving lot here."

"Yet there has been another murder in Plumford, and that victim too had associations with this theater," Henry said.

"Another backstage fop like Chauncey?"

"No, a lovely young woman," I said. "Her name was Kitty Lyttle."

Mrs. Perry's eyes widened. "Who would want to murder that sweet little seamstress?"

"A beast!" I said. "Her throat too was slashed open."

Mrs. Perry gasped, dramatically clutching her own throat. "Surely Kitty was mistaken for someone else."

"Not likely," Henry said, "for she was murdered in her own home."

"Did Kitty have another lover before or even after she married?" I said, for no matter how much I doubted it, the question needed to be asked.

"No, Kitty was as innocent as a dove," Mrs. Perry said. "And how she was teased for it, especially by the actors she costumed. That is really all I can recall about her. In truth, I have not given her a second thought since she left the Howard, but now, of course, I am overwhelmed with grief."

Henry and I fell silent to allow Mrs. Perry time to compose herself. Which she did in short order, turning her attention back to her reflection in the looking glass as she pinned up her parti-colored hair. "I could easily hide the gray streaks with India ink," she said. "If done correctly, it looks most natural. But I rather like the contrast. What do you think, Mr. Thoreau? Should I keep the gray or ink it away?"

Henry only shrugged in reply.

"So you like my appearance just as it is," Mrs. Perry said, interpreting his shrug as she so chose.

I refrained from rolling my eyes. "There is another person we should like to ask you about, Mrs. Perry," I said. "Did you by chance know a set builder who once worked at the Howard by the name of Robinson?"

"How now! Was Edgar Robinson murdered too?"

"He died in a fire. But you say you knew him?"

"Oh, I knew him all right. In fact, I allowed him to take more liberties with me than I own I should have. But Mr. Perry had passed on, and I was lonely." She caught Henry's eye in the looking glass. "Do you know what it is like to be lonely, young man? Especially during those long, dark hours before dawn breaks?"

"I am never lonely," he replied brusquely.

"Could you tell us more about Edgar Robinson?" I urged.

She shrugged. "What more is there to tell? He tossed me over to marry another. Mary was the music coach here. And hark this. She was blind! Can you credit it? Of course he was paid plenty."

"Paid to marry her?" I asked.

"Not just that, but never mind." Mrs. Perry went back to dressing her hair.

"We are looking for any family Mr. Robinson and his wife might have," I said. "You see, their boy has been left a destitute orphan."

"Destitute?" Mrs. Perry tutted. "So Edgar could not hold on to all that money they gave him. What a pity."

"You know of this child?" Henry said.

"A harelip, is he not?"

"Yes!" I cried. "Pray tell us what more you know, Mrs. Perry."

"Only that his mother lives in great luxury on Beacon Hill."

"But she is not alive," I said. "Mrs. Robinson died in the fire with her husband."

"Mary Robinson did not give birth to that boy any more than Edgar Robinson fathered him," Mrs. Perry said. "They were paid handsomely to take the babe away with them and raise him as their own."

"Who is the woman who bore the boy then? We will go to her directly," Henry said.

Mrs. Perry shook her head. "If I told you her name, it would be most indiscreet of me."

"But you *are* indiscreet!" Henry said impatiently.

I feared he had offended her and she would tell us no more, but instead she laughed. "So I am. And why should I keep her secret? She was never my friend. In fact, we were rivals back in the days when I treaded the boards with her. She was the envy of all the other actresses because she had captured the heart of one of the wealthiest men in Boston. When he got her with child he even married her. But when the child was born deformed, they wanted nothing to do with it. Well, it is high time that vain, spoiled woman claimed the son she so selfishly gave up." Mrs. Perry thumped her fist on the table, and all the pots and jars rattled. "Palmira Trescot is her name! She lives at the top of Mount Vernon Street in a fine, four-story brick house with an iron gate at the entrance. I have passed by it often enough, but have never once been invited inside."

Upon our parting with Mrs. Perry, she took Henry's hand in both hers and bid him come see her again. She did not extend such a warm invitation to me. *Quelle surprise!*

Henry and I walked briskly from the theater to Beacon Hill and in less than ten minutes reached Mrs. Trescot's house. Through the iron gate we went, and up the granite steps to the oak front door, which was impressively flanked by white Doric columns. The door knocker was of polished brass, in the form of a clenched fist, and Henry worked it with vigor. A maid promptly answered, and when we told her we had come to see Mrs. Trescot, she beckoned us into the high-domed entrance hall, pointed to a silver salver on a mahogany table, and instructed us to leave our calling cards.

"We have not come to dispense pieces of paste board for Mrs. Trescot's perusal," Henry told the maid, "but to meet with the lady herself."

"Madam is not receiving callers," the maid said.

"What day is she At Home then?" I said.

"Madam has not been At Home for years."

"Mrs. Trescot does not live here anymore?" Henry said.

"I think she means Mrs. Trescot has stopped entertaining guests," I told him.

"We are not guests," Henry told the maid. "We are messengers."

"Do you have a message from Madam's attorney?"

I was about to say yes, but before I could lie Henry said no. "Just tell Mrs. Trescot we bring her important tidings."

"Tidings?" a gruff female voice called from above. An Amazon of a woman slowly descended the curving stairway, her felt slippers making not a sound upon the marble stairs. Over her simple gray gown she wore a crisp white apron, and her neat chignon was topped with a starched white cap. She approached us with a most severe scowl creasing her low forehead. "I trust you have nothing disturbing to impart to Mrs. Trescot. She is most unwell."

"I am sorry to hear that," I said. "Are you her nurse?"

"Yes, I am Miss Dibble. And who might you be?"

I introduced Henry and myself. "But Mrs. Trescot does not know us."

"Then why have you come to bother her?" Miss Dibble said.

Her question was most impertinent, but I allowed that she had become protective toward her patient. "We will only impose ourselves upon her for a very short time," I said.

"But that is just it. The poor lady has but a short time left on earth, and it would not do for her to fritter it on strangers. She is having a difficult day and should not be disturbed. But if you would care to leave your cards, I shall be sure to give them to her."

"Better yet, I will leave her a note," I said. Henry tore a leaf from the notebook he always carries and handed me a pencil. I wrote but one short sentence: *Noah is in need of his mother.* I added my name and address and folded the paper four times before handing it over to the nurse. "It is of a most private nature," I told her.

She nodded, tucked the note in her apron, and slowly made her way back up the stairs from whence she'd come as the maid ushered us out the door. Despite the festive Yuletide spirit ringing through the streets, Henry and I had no desire to linger in the city and went directly to the station. The cars were crowded, but we managed to find two seats together, and as we rattled back to Concord, I could barely contain my joy that we had found Noah's mother.

Henry cautioned me to keep my hopes for a happy outcome in check. "Mrs. Trescot did not want Noah a dozen years ago and might not want him now," he said. "She may not even respond to your note."

"Then I shall write her another and another, until she does respond. Or if I have to, I shall camp out on her doorstep."

"And there you will be when they carry her out in a coffin," Henry said.

"Well, aren't you the cheery one."

"I am merely pointing out that time is of the essence. Miss Dibble made it clear Mrs. Trescot is not expected to live much longer."

"Noah's mother *will* answer my note, Henry, and all will end well for the dear boy."

Henry did not contradict me again. Indeed, he stopped talking altogether, and knowing how little he appreciates idle chit-chat, I did too. We each, in a most companionable way, ignored the other's company to find entertainment in our own private thoughts. But as I reviewed our interview with Mrs. Perry, an image kept disturbing my mind until I could not help but disturb Henry with it, too.

"That key you showed Mrs. Perry," I said to him. "Let me take a closer look at it, if you please. There is something about it that nags at my memory."

"I surmise a female gave it to Bidwell because of the black silk cord attached to its base," Henry said as he handed the key over to me.

"The cord is what caught my attention. I have recently observed the Phyfe sisters engage in such handiwork as this. Two favored bright colors, but one plaited black ribbons only."

"Is it a common sort of feminine craft to practice?" Henry said.

"Not all that common, for it takes a great deal of practice and dexterity. These young ladies I speak of seemed quite proud of their skill. The eldest, Arabel, died of the Consumption only a few days ago. She was the one who favored black. Even before she was taken ill, she seemed most despondent, as if she had recently lost someone near and dear to her. Her sisters told me she fainted upon hearing of Bidwell's murder."

"She knew him?"

"She never professed to, but she could not bear to hear his

name mentioned in her presence. And I have heard gossip that Bidwell had a lover in Plumford."

"Where did you hear this?" Henry said.

"In the very house you presently reside at, Henry."

He seemed to take offence. "Lidian Emerson does not gossip."

"Indeed she does not. But her housekeeper, Lisette, does. She told me Bidwell was having his way with a girl from Plumford."

"Did she name the girl?"

"No. Nor did she describe her. But I am sure she would be happy to supply you with more details if you asked her."

"That I cannot do," Henry said. "Lisette and her husband have gone back to Canada. Tell me more about this girl who braided black silk."

"She was no more than eighteen and very pretty. But she is gone now and so is Bidwell, so what does it matter if she was his lover?"

"What matters," Henry said, "is discovering who Bidwell's murderer was."

"Surely you do not think his Plumford paramour, whoever she might have been, killed him?"

"Anything is possible in this world," Henry said, "although it does not seem probable that a young woman committed such a brutal murder as that, no matter how badly Bidwell used her."

"He mistreated her?"

Henry nodded. "In every way a man can mistreat a naïve female."

"And how do you know this?"

"There is gossip in the male sphere too, Julia. Of a coarse, crude kind that would shock you."

Since my marriage to Jacques Pelletier, I doubt anything

can shock me, but I did not press Henry to repeat what he had heard. I could tell he found the topic most distasteful.

"I would just as soon never learn who the poor girl I heard so maligned was," Henry continued, "but I think she could be connected to Bidwell's murderer. And I also think that key you are holding is to the door of the place where they held their trysts. Where else might he have been going to or coming from the night he was murdered?"

I fingered the black cord. "The Phyfe sisters once mentioned an empty cottage the family owned at the base of Wolf Hill, about half a mile from the path where Bidwell's body was found. I am loath to show them or their father this key, though. They are in deep mourning for their sister, and implicating her in Bidwell's murder would only distress them more."

"Tell me more about the cottage then. Perhaps I can find it on my own," Henry said.

"All I know is that a spinster named Augusta Phyfe resided in it until her death last year, and it is located by a spring-fed pond."

"That is more than enough to go on," Henry said. "There is no need to trouble the girl's family, especially since there may be no connection between her and Bidwell. You may trust my discretion, Julia."

"I always have," I replied.

And that was how we left it.

When I returned home Mrs. Swann informed me that Noah was at Tuttle Farm, where Adam had taken him to spend the day with Granny. Mrs. Swann seemed most curious to know why I had gone to Boston. Tempted to tell her the great news that I had discovered Noah's birth mother, I thought better of it. Henry had been right to caution me about being overly optimistic. Mrs. Trescot did, after all, reject Noah once. But surely she will not do so again!

ADAM'S JOURNAL

Tuesday, December 21

Since becoming a doctor I have seen blood and gore aplenty, but never the horror of what I witnessed today. And all because I brought Henry to the pond where I used to capture frogs as a boy to hide in Julia's pinafore pocket. Henry wanted to find the cottage wherein Spinster Phyfe once resided, which was easy enough to do, for I recalled that it sat not too far from water's edge on the north bank of the pond.

Our mission was to see if the brass key we'd found on Bidwell's body fit the lock on the door of this cottage, and so it did. But the lock itself was of little use for it had been pulled from its securing screws when the door had been kicked open. By a passing tramp? Or someone far more dangerous?

We entered cautiously. No signs of occupancy in the two empty front rooms, but in the kitchen wood and kindling sat in a ready pile by the fireplace, and blankets lay in a heap in front of the ash-filled hearth. The pale winter light streamed through a large bare window, and a faint but discernible scent of poppy smoke infused the atmosphere.

Henry noticed that one of the kitchen floor boards had no nails securing it. He pried it open with his pocketknife and found, nestled between two joists, a canvas bag that contained a yard-long pipe and other opium paraphernalia—a small brazier, a few metal and clay pots, and several pans and brass needles.

"So this must be the love nest Orton so crassly made mention of at Chandoo Gate," I said. As I glanced down at the rumpled blankets, I could not help but recall his very words: *Just poppy smoking and rutting.* "It is hard for me to credit that the young lady I treated for Consumption was the same one described so scornfully by Orton. What is the truth of it? Is it not possible that Arabel was quite in love and here passed blissful hours with a man she adored? Why damn her actions as abhorrent degeneracy?"

"Those who cannot love are often the most scornful of it," Henry said. He picked up the blankets and subjected them to a vigorous shaking. Out floated a woman's lone pink silk stocking. "Where's its mate?" he said.

"I believe Hyram Jackson has it tucked in his pillowcase," I said and explained to Henry the circumstances that had led me to see the stocking there.

"That Hyram attempted to take his own life on the very day Arabel Phyfe was buried," Henry said, "makes me wonder if he too had been her lover."

"It does not seem likely that Arabel would find such a callow, awkward fellow a suitable swain," I said. "Hyram's father told me Hyram had no sweetheart and had been behaving strangely for weeks."

"He certainly behaved so over Bidwell's body," Henry said. "He claimed the dead man looked up and spoke to him. Was that a delusion of a guilt-ridden mind?"

"Are you suggesting that Hyram killed Bidwell?" I said.

"Yes, but admittedly on evidence so thin it is near transparent," Henry said, plucking up the silk stocking and tucking it into his pocket.

We found nothing more of note inside, but before we de-

parted Henry insisted on carefully examining the grounds surrounding the cabin. He paused at a sycamore tree standing not
twenty feet from the kitchen window. Long gouges sliced
through the bark and deeply into the wood. I ran my hand
along them.

"There was scoring similar to this on the tree near Bidwell's body," I said.

"I believe the same weapon was used to slash both trees,"
Henry said.

"And Bidwell's neck as well?"

Henry nodded. "His killer lurked in this very spot."

Looking through the window from the outside, I could
clearly see the blankets on the kitchen floor. "He must have
stood here to watch the lovers!"

"Let us go talk to Hyram," Henry said.

We proceeded to the mill. Have always found it a pleasant
place, filled with the fresh smell of sawn timber and the sound
of water rushing through the flume to drive the mill-wheel.
The walls and floor vibrated as the ponderous gears of the
wheel powered the heavy blade of the saw. A half-dozen burly
workers went about the arduous business of heaving and
jostling heavy wet logs up off the ramp from the mill pond and
onto the saw-carriage, then moving them along to the saw.
The teeth of the saw blade sliced through those massive logs as
easily as Gran slices a knife through a pumpkin pie, and a few
of the workers, like their boss, Mr. Jackson, had fingers missing,
the penalty paid for a moment's careless lack of attention in
such close vicinity to the sharp, spinning blade.

Mr. Jackson was nowhere to be seen at the moment, but
Hyram was working alongside the other men at the saw-
carriage. He swung a hand tool with a long hook and a sharp
point with practiced ease, embedding it into the end of a log
to lift it into position in front of the saw. His hair, eyebrows,
and shoulders were coated with a thin layer of sawdust thrown

up by the blade as it screamed through the wood. He never looked up from his concentrated labor.

And Henry never looked away from him. "See how Hyram's hook gouges the log as he positions it," he said to me. "Have we not seen such gashes in wood before?"

I nodded, for of course we had—on the trunk of the tree near Bidwell's body and on the tree behind the cottage.

"And could not the laceration in Bidwell's neck have been made by the same tool?" Henry said.

I nodded again. "We might well be looking at both the murderer and his weapon."

"Easier said than proven, however. You know Hyram better than I do, Adam. Best that you be the one to ask him if he will meet with us."

Went up to the saw-carriage and gently laid my hand upon Hyram's shoulder to get his attention. He turned and did not look surprised to see me. When I asked if he could spare a few minutes to talk to Henry and me, he shouted to one of the men to take his place and led us to his father's office at the far end of the mill. As we followed I noticed that he still kept hold of his lift hook. It dangled from his hand like a curving claw. We stepped inside the office, and Hyram shut the door to the noise, then just stood there and looked at us with a blank expression until Henry brought forth the silk stocking. Then Hyram's eyes blazed with anger. "You stole that from my bedchamber!"

"No, we found it at the cottage," Henry said. "Where did you find the stocking you have?"

Hyram shrugged. "Same place, I guess."

"Do you know who it belonged to?" Henry asked.

"No."

"Did it not belong to Arabel Phyfe?" Henry said.

Hyram turned livid. "Why think you it was hers?"

"She had trysts with Chauncey Bidwell at that cottage, did she not?"

"Lie! Lie! Lie! Arabel was an angel. No man was good enough to touch her."

"Even so, Bidwell did. You watched him do so through the window," Henry quietly said.

Hyram's rage dissipated, and he lowered his head. "Yes, I watched. I could not help myself. The first time I saw them was by accident one summer eve. I was just passing by the cottage on my way to the pond for a swim. After that I would go there every evening and wait for them. Sometimes they would come and sometimes they would not, but I was always there waiting." He began to sob. Tears spattered on his dusty boots like raindrops. "I watched that devil treat my angel like a whore. Even so, I still loved her. She never so much as looked my way, but I knew one day she would. But first I would have to free her from Bidwell's evil spell."

"By killing him," Henry said.

He stopped sobbing and looked at us. "No! I only meant to scare him away from her. That's why I brought this along." He raised the hook clutched in his hand. His eyes, still damp with tears, turned hard. "I waited for him a good ways up the path from where he and Arabel always parted, and in the stillness I could hear a wolf howling on the hilltop. I suppose it was just the wind. When Bidwell finally came along I stepped out of the shadows to halt him. He tried to get past me, but I grabbed his shoulder and twisted him around to face me like a man. And then, looking at that goddam handsome face of his, I could not help myself. I raised my other hand, the one that held this hook, and took a swipe at him. The tip went into his neck, and when I yanked it free blood shot out of the wound like a geyser. He fell down and started crawling away from me, and then he stopped moving. It began to rain, and I remember hoping Arabel had gotten home safe and dry before the down-pour. I left him lying there facedown in the dirt and went home, too. The next morning I thought maybe I had dreamed the whole thing, as I had dreamed of killing him before. But then I had to go with Pa to pick up his body. It was then I knew for sure he was a devil, for dead though he was, he spoke to me. 'See you in hell,' he said." The sobbing resumed. "Yes, I am doomed for hell. And I shall never see my angel, who is surely in heaven, again."

"You will have to pay for Bidwell's murder, Hyram," Henry said. "But a good lawyer might save you from hanging."

"Oh, I would not mind hanging for it," Hyram said wear-ily. "I would go straight to the gallows right now if I could. But I will not go to trial and hear Arabel's name dragged through the mud. I could not tolerate that."

"Come," I said. "We will go to the constable."

"No! If you had been merciful, doctor, you would have let the poison kill me." He swung the hook at us in a slow arc. We both ducked. And he used that second to bolt out the door.

He did not run out of the mill, however. Instead he raced toward the whirring saw, shoved his neck against it, and sud-denly the air was filled with blood instead of sawdust. In the next instant his severed head fell to one side of the saw-carriage, and his torso to the other, gouts of blood erupting from all the severed veins and arteries.

All of us stood dumbfounded. One of the workers pulled back the handle of the saw to disengage it, but the free-spinning blade continued to whirl round and round for some seconds. It sprayed out a mist of blood and bits of skin and bone from its flesh-clogged teeth until it slowed to a stop.

Mr. Jackson came into the mill at that moment and started hollering at his men for stopping the saw. I hurried to him, took his arm, and led him outside, for as used as he must be to seeing death in all forms, I did not think he could bear to see what his son had done to himself. Yet when I told him what had just happened he insisted on going back in to take care of Hyram properly.

When the Coroner's Jury convened over Hyram's body, the torso and head were back together and shrouded. No one asked to get a better look at the remains. The verdict, of course, was death by suicide.

Henry and I then went to see Justice Phyfe. All the windows of his elegant house were shuttered, all the mirrors draped in black crepe. A servant dressed in black ushered us into Phyfe's study, where he sat in dimness behind his massive desk. He could barely raise his head to regard us, much less stand up to greet us. Arabel's death had obviously been a severe blow to his heart. He already knew of Hyram Jackson's death, for Coroner Daggett always reports to him directly and immediately, but he was most surprised when we told him that Hyram had confessed to us that he had murdered Chauncey Bidwell.

"What was his motive?" Phyfe said.

Henry and I had agreed, on the way to Phyfe's house, that there was no need to mention Arabel. What good would that do anyone? Phyfe loved his daughter and cherished her memory. Bidwell had already paid with his life for his immorality. And Hyram had brought justice down on his own head. So I simply told Justice Phyfe that we did not know Hyram's motive for killing Bidwell.

He gave me and then Henry a long, hard look. "Then it shall forever remain a mystery, won't it?"

We did not refute him.

Phyfe requested that we return the following morning to officially testify before him and the other two town Selectmen, which we readily agreed to do. He then pulled a black handkerchief from his black waistcoat and covered his face. We left him to his mourning.

Our last task was to return to the cottage and retrieve the

incriminating bag of opium paraphernalia. We added rocks to
the canvas bag, walked out to the middle of the frozen pond,
and Henry pounded a hole through the ice with the fireplace
poker. We stuffed the bag through the hole and watched it sink
into oblivion as the wind blew through the trees on the hill. As
Hyram had said, it sounded like the howl of a wolf.

ADAM'S JOURNAL

Wednesday eve, December 22

Almost died today. If Henry had not been there, doubt I would be around to write this.

He came to Plumford this morning to meet with Justice Phyfe and the other two Selectmen. They seemed eager to put an end to the Bidwell murder investigation and asked few questions of us. They even went so far as to propose the possibility that Hyram had been crazed enough to have killed Kitty Lyttle too, a theory that Henry and I vehemently spoke against. Even so I shall not be surprised if such a rumor begins to circulate about town. Whilst meeting with the Selectmen, I took the opportunity to register complaints against Solomon Wiley for laying rough hands on Noah and Julia and for bashing me on the head with a pole. Did not mention the terrifying incident in the swamp, for the more distant that memory becomes, the more I believe it must have been a nightmare. But when Justice Phyfe said that Solomon's brother had reported him missing since Saturday, a chill did run down my spine. The three Selectmen all expressed the hope that Solomon had left town for good. Henry and I exchanged glances and remained silent.

We left Phyfe's and walked together in the bright morning sunlight, he on his way to the Concord road and I on my way to my office. We were about to part company when Julia came out of her house with Noah. Each had a pair of ice skates in hand.

"Noah found a box full of skates in the attic," she told us. "I'm taking him to Beaver Pond."

"What a perfect day to go skating!" Henry said with boyish enthusiasm. "May I come along?"

"Of course," Julia said. "Noah, go fetch a pair of skates that will fit under Mr. Thoreau's boots." She looked at me most invitingly. "And a pair for Dr. Adam, too?"

I nodded. Noah gave a whoop and ran into the house. A few minutes later he came out with the box of skates. Unfortunately, Mrs. Swann accompanied him. "I'm coming too!" she informed us.

We brought the skates to the smithy, who sharpened the blades in a jiffy, and off the five of us tramped to Beaver Pond. Nary a cloud appeared in the crystal blue sky to filter the brightness of the high winter sun, and a golden clarity brought the world into such distinct focus that distant Monadnock looked to be just beyond the next hill. Henry seemed as eager as Noah to get on the pond. He hurried ahead of us to go talk to the ice fishermen and evaluate the ice.

"We have a safe, crystal roof of three inches to skate upon!" he reported back. "But the fishermen told me that around that corner yonder is a cove where the stream that feeds the pond runs fast and hard, preventing the water around it from freezing. Let us all make sure to stay away from the area."

We strapped on our skates, and each in his or her own fashion pushed off onto the hard, glistening pond. The manner in which a person skates, as far as I am concerned, is a better indication of character and personality than any contained in the learned texts of physiognomy or phrenology.

Noah kept to short, cautious strokes with his feet, more like walking than skating, but that did not keep him from landing hard on his tail the first few feet from shore. He was up in an instant, however, ready to try again, and after another few steps, down again he did go. Up, down, up, down, the little jack-in-the-box never gave up.

Julia stayed poised on the shore for an instant, gathered herself, and then in one quick leap sprang out onto the ice and glided smoothly on one skate and then the other. She used her arms and legs with an elegant economy to confidently build speed and then, with a nonchalant ease, turned and glided backwards. She gave me a smile over her shoulder, the cold air brightening her cheeks, her teeth white as freshly cut ice shavings, her lips red as partridge berries. Was she recalling that it was I who taught her to skate so well? I could not get enough of the sport as a boy, and because I could not get enough of her company, either, I had insisted she skate with me. We would dash all the way down the frozen river to Concord and back again with the speed of shooting stars.

Mrs. Swann claimed she had little experience on skates, so she must have kept her balance by sheer power of will. Yet as awkwardly as she moved, she somehow managed to skate deftly backwards when Noah came barreling toward her, once again out of control. She made no attempt to break his fall and barked at him to watch where he was going. No one could accuse Mrs. Swann of being overly fond of children.

Henry skates, as he does all things physical, very well. Although short of stature, he is very strong, and his superb fitness gives him a refinement of movement any athlete would envy. Moreover, physicality brings him great joy, and every stroke of his blades was a bright gesture of this joy. He laughed and clapped his hands together, gamboled and whirled and made airy leaps, all to no purpose but the sheer pleasure of it.

"We have wings of steel!" he shouted. Then he noticed Noah struggling and glided up to him. "Come, let us go look into the parlor of the fishes, lad." He took Noah's hand and kept him upright as they sailed off.

I followed along, curious to see such a place myself. A group of fishermen were sitting on the shore, eating their luncheon, and we skated up to one of the holes they had cut in the ice.

"Look down through the opening and you will see this fish parlor I spoke of, Noah," Henry whispered as if sharing a great secret. "It is softly lit as through a window of ground glass and has a bright sanded floor. Do you espy it?" Noah nodded vigorously, perhaps more spellbound by Henry's description than by what he was actually observing. "There below a perennial waveless serenity reigns as it does in the sky," Henry continued. "So you see, Noah, heaven is under our feet as well as over our heads."

Noah nodded again, and, for aught I know, he understood Henry far better than I did. We went over to a well the fishermen had cut in the ice and looked at the fish they had caught. Ordinary pickerel they appeared to be to me, but Henry pronounced them fabulous creatures of dazzling and transcendent beauty.

"How I would like to capture such luminous colors on my canvas," Julia said, having silently skated up behind us.

She casually hooked arms with me and pressed close, as in days of yore, when we were innocent children. Not so innocent anymore, I yearned to press her closer still and kiss her breath away. Instead, I pretended to continue admiring the doomed pickerel.

We eventually moved away from the fishing holes, and Henry soon had Noah kicking a chunk of ice back and forth with him as they skated. The boy became better balanced the

less he thought about falling, and as Henry advanced the piece
of ice farther and farther ahead, Noah extended his stride and
began to skate faster.

Julia and I found ourselves falling into a practiced hold, her
right arm crossed over my left arm, our hands clasping. On the
same exact heartbeat, we both glided forth on the right foot
and skated off together, our long strides in perfect harmony.
And once again I felt her to be my soul mate, my other half,
my completion. We made a moving, physical heaven together
as we sailed past the dark, majestic pine trees lining the shore.
The ice was so clear that we could see the fishes swimming beneath our feet, dashing this way and that around us. We swept
around a sharp turn of the shore, our eyes locked for a second,
and thanks to our mooning nearly swept ourselves into a clear
patch of water and a dangerous dunking. We stopped short of
the danger in a spray of silvery shavings from our skates and
laughed at our foolishness and excitement.

We turned back, totally mystified as to whether we had
been alone for five minutes or an hour, such was our happy
bliss. Out on the ice we spied Henry doing various leaps and
dithyrambic steps from some aboriginal dance his instinct must
have called up. He very much skates to his own rhythms, but
his boundless energy lends his limbs, however they may gestic-
ulate, an original, if most unconventional, grace.

"Where is Noah?" Julia wondered, holding her gloved
hand to her eyes as she scanned the shimmering ice surface.

"There," I said, pointing across the pond to the far shore.
Mrs. Swann and Noah, hand in hand, were skating into the
cove.

Henry joined us and followed our gaze until the woman
and boy disappeared from view. "I cautioned them to stay away
from there. It's dangerous to skate near a running stream," he
said. "We'd best go after them."

We three raced across the ice, pumping our limbs for greater speed. We curved round the corner of the cove and saw disaster before us. Noah had fallen into the tongue of water the gushing stream prevented from freezing and was clinging to the edge of solid ice that rimmed it. If he let go the inlet current would surely sweep him under. Mrs. Swann had fared better. Although she too had fallen into the water, she had managed to drag herself onto the shore, where she lay in a sodden heap. When she saw us approach she sat up and began shouting and waving and pointing to Noah.

"Halt!" Henry commanded when we were about a rod from the boy. "The ice ahead is too thin to hold us!"

We all three slid to a stop and regarded poor Noah. His eyes were the size of saucers, and he made a mewing sound that cut to my heart.

"I am the lightest by far," Julia said, "and so the least likely to break through the ice. I will get a hold on him." Without waiting to hear any opinions on that course of action, she skated back ten feet, took three full strides, and threw herself down forward on the ice, arms and legs spread, and slid like an otter to Noah. As she extended her hands to Noah, he grabbed and hung on. In the next instant the ice beneath her gave way, and she was down in the freezing water with him.

Henry immediately began heading for shore. "I'll come back with a branch to pull them to safety," he shouted over his shoulder.

But I could not wait for a branch! The ice was thicker at the new break point because it was farther from the rushing stream, and praying it would hold me, I slid myself toward Julia and the boy, arms extended. Julia grabbed hold of one hand and Noah took the other. His grip was very feeble as the current tugged at his body, and he looked to be only a few seconds away from losing consciousness.

"Try and push Noah up and over the edge so I can pull him out," I told Julia. "But keep hold of my hand!"

She nodded. Her lips were already blue with cold. She let go of the ice edge and tried to raise the boy up with one hand, but could not do it. She wrenched her hand from mine, grasped the boy beneath his arms, and as she pushed him upward, she went under. I pulled with all my might and slid Noah to me. Pushed him onto thicker ice and turned back to Julia. She had disappeared! I looked through the ice directly beneath me and saw her staring up at me from a world away, her hands pressed upward against her icy tomb. Then she turned and attempted to swim back to open water. But the current was too strong, and she was carried farther along under the ice. I tried to break through it, jumping up and down as hard as I could on my skates.

I screamed in frustration and then got my brains to working. Tore off my skates, shoes, and coat and slipped and slid again toward the open water. My only hope was to swim to Julia and haul her back against the current to the safety of shore.

Plunged into the water, the shock of the cold taking precious air from my lungs. Went under the ice and saw her but fifteen feet away, drifting not just farther away but downward too as her heavy, soaked clothes weighed her down. The current pushed me forward, and I was quickly at her side. Seized her arm and turned back toward shore, but swimming against the current turned out to be far more difficult than I'd surmised. Indeed, I was exhausting myself yet making no progress whatsoever. It began to seem a hopeless struggle until I heard a sharp clicking above our heads. Looked up and saw Henry jumping on the ice and pointing with a long branch. He was motioning toward a faint light that indicated to me a hole in the ice. Began to swim toward it, pulling Julia along with me.

My lungs burned in earnest now, and my movements were

growing uncoordinated from the cold, but at least now I was swimming crosscurrent rather than against it. Glanced at Julia. She was no longer moving her limbs, and her eyes were closed. Gripped her arm tighter and struggled toward the light.

But the light began to dim, and I realized that I too was losing consciousness from lack of air. Began to fade into a black torpor when, most strange to recount now, I somehow experienced slipping from my body as smoothly and easily as a snake slipping out of its old skin. I rose through the imprisoning roof of ice, free of my body, and observed my corporeal self from above, still trapped under the ice with Julia. As my spirit hovered over the frozen pond, I heard Julia's spirit calling to me from the water. *Do not leave me!* Suddenly I was reeled back into my body like a fish on a line, struggling for survival once again.

Held Julia close, determined to save us both, even as I felt the boney hand of Death brush against my face. Ignored it. It then poked me in the chest. Hard. Opened my eyes and saw that it was not a skeletal hand at all but a long tree branch. Twenty feet or so away I could dimly discern the lower portion of a man standing in waist-deep water and holding on to the branch. Realized Henry had jumped into the ice hole. Wrapped my arm around Julia's waist and grabbed the branch. Henry pulled us hand over hand to him and, taking hold of my hair, yanked my head out of the water. In the next instant I had Julia's head up as well. Rejoiced as cold air filled my lungs, but then my pounding heart nearly froze when I saw that Julia was not breathing with me.

Henry and I got her out of the water. I laid her head to one side on the ice and pushed down hard against her chest, repeating the motion, up and down like a bellows, to free the water from her lungs. After the longest wait of my life, she suddenly spat out water in a most unladylike burst, gasped, coughed out more water, and began sucking in whistling gasps of air, one after another. What music!

Minutes later the ice fishermen came running to us with sleds equipped with blankets and brandy for just such mishaps as this. They had already attended to Noah and to Mrs. Swann on the shore, and, after wrapping us up too, they drove us all back to Plumford in their wagons.

The first thing I had everyone do, including myself, was change into dry clothes. I gave Henry some of Doc Silas's clothes to wear, which fit him far better than mine would have. Henry fired up the kitchen stove, and we huddled around it, but Julia and Noah could not stop shivering so I prescribed hot baths for both. We filled the wash tub in the kitchen alcove with hot water for Noah and carted up gallon cans of hot water for the hip bath in Julia's chamber. Mrs. Swann offered to assist her in bathing, but Julia insisted she could manage on her own.

After the bath had warmed Noah up I put him to bed and layered quilts over him. No longer shivering, he fell asleep immediately, and I stayed by his side for a bit to listen to his respiration. He is a fine-looking boy except for his cleft lip, and my recent research has led me to believe I can rectify this deformity. As I studied Noah asleep I imagined him lying on the operating table in the MGH amphitheater as I performed the corrective surgery; he would be just as peaceful thanks to this new practice of inducing deep sleep with ether. I intend to do the operation gratis, but even so, the hospital costs will be steep. How fortuitous it will be if the woman on Beacon Hill that Julia and Henry heard about turns out to be Noah's mother. Apparently she is near death, and time is of the essence if Noah is to be acknowledged as the rightful heir to her fortune. But she has not as of yet responded to Julia's note.

Left Noah breathing soundly and returned to the kitchen where I found Mrs. Swann still apologizing profusely to Henry for her reckless behavior on the pond. Henry hardly deigned to look at her, and when he did it was with disdain. I avoided looking at her too, for she was most unattractive to behold in a voluminous robe of stiff bombazine, her head swaddled in a fringed shawl, and her face covered with a thick layer of cream she claimed would save her complexion from reddening after such a prolonged exposure to cold and wind.

"What a foolish woman I am," she said for the fiftieth time, "racing about and frolicking with that child as if I were a child myself. But you see, it was so exhilarating to be skating so free and easy. As you said, Mr. Thoreau, it was like having wings of steel!"

"I also said to stay away from the stream," he replied with cold, quiet anger.

"I know, but we were having so much fun, little Noah and I, that I did not heed where we were going. I am sorry! So sorry! Oh, how very sorry I am!"

And oh how very tired I was of hearing her grating voice. When I recommended that she go rest in her chamber after such an ordeal, I was greatly relieved that she followed my suggestion.

"There is something out of kelter with that woman," Henry said when she'd left.

Did not ask him to elucidate. Had no interest in discussing her further. We talked of Noah instead. Henry agreed that another attempt should be made to talk to Mrs. Trescot, and the sooner the better. He said the only day he would be free to go to Boston before Christmas was tomorrow, and so it was settled we would meet at the Concord station at four, after I'd made my rounds.

By now it was dusk, and Henry had a three-mile walk back to Concord ahead of him. His own coat was soaking wet, and I insisted he take Doc Silas's overcoat, an old-fashioned caped Garrick. When I told Henry he looked quite dashing in it, he almost took it off. Also gave him Doc's rabbit skin hat. We'd all lost our hats at the pond, but at least Henry had not lost his head. Thanked him again for pulling Julia and me to safety.

"The moment I took hold of that tree branch, I knew we would be all right," I said. "It was like gripping your very hand, Henry."

He smiled. "Am I not partly leaves and vegetable mould myself?"

Henry is a wonderful friend to have. Indeed, he is a man truly full of wonder. Even so I was glad when he departed, for all I wanted to do was go up to Julia's chamber and be with her.

How pleasurable it is to see the woman you love in bed, propped up by pillows, with her golden hair down about her shoulders, and the glow of lamp light upon her lovely face. And how excruciating it is too, when every atom in your being desires her although she is wed to another.

I had brought her a warmed brick wrapped in a towel and offered to tuck it under her bedcovers. Rather than permit me this intimacy, she took the brick from my hand and placed it against her lower torso. "Oh, how good it feels!" she sighed.

"Would that I were that brick."

She laughed. "You are a brick, Adam. A brick of a fellow."

Sat on the edge of the bed and reached for her hand. She allowed me at least that familiarity. Played with her fingers. Stroked the beautiful blue vein of her wrist. The logs in the shallow fireplace crackled, and the little clock on the mantel ticked off the minutes. We had never minded sharing silence together, Julia and I.

But finally I spoke. "What I meant to say, Julia, is that we should be sharing a bed together as husband and wife."

She gently extracted her hand from mine. "But we cannot."

"Only because you already have a husband."

"He is not the only reason, cousin."

By calling me that, she seemed to be taunting me. But of

course she was not, for she remained ignorant of the facts concerning our relationship. And the time had come for her to know the truth.

"I am your cousin in name only, Julia. We have no ties of consanguinity. The man who sired me was not your uncle Owen Walker. As Gran Tuttle put it to me, I was born on the wrong side of the blanket."

"That cannot be! Your grandmother must be lying."

"Oh, Gran lied all right. For years and years. To protect her daughter's good name. And also out of kindness to Doc Silas, for he cherished the belief that I was the child of his beloved dead son. But I was no more kin to your grandfather, Julia, than to the man in the moon. So neither am I kin to you."

"No kin to me?" she repeated as the meaning of this registered in her mind. "Are you telling me, Adam, that we could have married and had normal children?"

"Yes! Gran told me the truth right after you sailed for France, and I went after you on the next ship. I might well have flown there on the wings of happiness, for I was sure you would marry me now that the only obstacle between us had dissolved. Imagine my mortification when I learned that another obstacle had suddenly appeared between us in the form of a husband. It is most difficult to propose marriage to a woman who is off on her honeymoon with another man."

"You must stop reproaching me for that, Adam. I became acquainted with an elderly gentleman named Jacques Pelletier on the very ship I took to get away from you. When I reached Paris I found Papa gravely ill and about to be carted off to debtor's prison. Jacques offered to pay off Papa's debts if I agreed to marry him. He seemed good and kind, and so I did. Why not? Since I could not marry you, I knew I would never marry for love."

"But we *could* have married!" I near shouted at her.

"So you tell me now. And I do not thank you for making

me realize that I have ruined my life for no good reason." Tears filled her eyes as she looked at me.

"You had to know the truth, Julia."

"Why?"

"So that you and I can be together as we are meant to be."

"How? Divorce has been abolished in France. I will never be free to marry you, Adam." She buried her face in her hands and rocked back and forth, moaning. Tried to take her into my arms to comfort her, but she pushed me away. "I have ruined my life for no good reason!" she said again, glaring at me through a shimmer of tears as if it were *my* fault. "My suffering has become meaningless, and I am left with nothing but regret."

"But don't you understand, my love?" I said. "We no longer have to avoid physical intimacy because we fear the consequences."

Her eyes grew hard as she regarded me. "Ah, now I do understand. You are proposing I become your mistress."

In truth I was. As much as I hoped to marry her someday, I certainly did not want to wait until we found a legal way to make this possible. That might take years. Yet hearing her state my desire so frankly made me ashamed. And that in turn made me angry.

"How long do you expect me to wait for you, Julia?"

"I never expected you to wait for me at all! I expected you to forget about me and find a suitable wife for yourself. And I still expect you to do so. We have no future together, Adam."

"Then why did you call me back?"

"Call you back from where?"

"Death! As I near drowned today, your spirit cried out to mine not to leave you behind."

Her eyes softened. "I am glad you heeded it." She began to cry again. "Pray go away, Adam. I cannot bear to look at you now that I know I gave you up needlessly."

"Allow me to say one thing before I leave you, Julia. We are kindred spirits and belong together. Nothing else matters. And the sooner you realize this, the happier we both shall be."

Left her an hour ago. Hope she has ceased her weeping by now and found a modicum of solace in sleep. Doubt I will sleep a wink tonight. Do I hear footsteps coming down the hall?

JULIA'S NOTEBOOK

Thursday, 23 December

If what I did last night was wrong, why do I feel so good about it? I do not repent in the least. Indeed, I cannot wait to repeat the experience again and again.

It took me a good while to collect myself after Adam left my chamber last night, for what he told me turned my world upside down and inside out. He and I have no blood relation! We could have married fifteen months ago and foregone all the wretchedness that ensued upon my leaving him. I would not have met Jacques Pelletier, much less married him. But what is done is done. There is no changing it, only dealing with it as best we can.

So rather than suffer further, or make Adam suffer for no better reason than propriety's sake, I dried my eyes and went to him. I would have walked barefoot in the cold night air all the way to Tuttle Farm to reach him, but all I had to do was go down the stairs and through the hall to his office, where he has been staying in order to keep watch over me whilst a killer roams our town.

When he looked up from his writing and saw me at his threshold, there was such joy upon his beloved countenance that I began crying all over again. He sprang to his feet, took me into his arms, and kissed me with such pent-up passion that I felt myself swept into a vortex stronger than the current that almost carried me to my death. We surrendered to each other, *drowned* in each other, a confluence of male and female energy united at last as one, our souls and bodies throbbing.

Flushed with the pleasure we had given each other, we floated together in bliss, naked limbs entwined as we lay upon the narrow cot. But when I opened my eyes I saw lurking in the shadows a most horrible, hollow-orbed figure regarding us. I cried out and Adam leaped up, fists raised to do battle. When I realized 'twas only his anatomical skeleton that had startled me, I could not stop laughing. My well-knit flesh and blood man did not seem to find this as amusing as I did, but I easily cajoled him to lie with me again, and we resumed silently drifting together in the pleasure of the present moment.

Alas, we did not stay silent, and conversation soon brought both the past and the future into bed with us, almost crowding out our newfound happiness.

"We must find a lawyer who knows the legalities involved in dissolving a marriage made in France," Adam said as he caressed the small of my back. "It will take time and patience and money, no doubt about it, but one day you shall be my wife in the eyes of the law as you already are in the eyes of God, my dear Julia."

"In the eyes of God I have committed the grievous sin of adultery," I bluntly stated. "Leastways that is how most religions created in His name would view my actions. As does society as well as the law."

"But do you?" Adam asked me. He sounded hurt.

I hugged him closer to me. "In my heart I do not believe I have sinned, Adam. It is my personal belief that there is no sin but one—to intentionally do harm to another being. My love for you does no harm to my husband for he has no love for me. And how can I break marriage vows when they have already been shattered beyond repair by him? He took up with his established mistress less than a month after we were wed."

"Is that why you left him?"

"No. I felt not the slightest jealousy toward her, only gratitude that she kept him away from me. I left my husband when I learned how he had made his fortune for I could not abide living off the profits of his trade. Jacques Pelletier was a slave trader, Adam. He shipped slaves from West Africa to Martinique."

"My God, Julia. What manner of man did you marry?"

"More monster than man, I sadly discovered. But I am far away from him now."

"Will he come after you?"

"Since he has not yet, I do not think so. He is an old man, with limited energy and many evil ways to expend it. He will not make the effort to get back a wife who has rejected him. His pride will not allow it."

I could not bear to tell Adam what depths of despair and depravity my marriage had cast me into, and to stop further questions from him, I pressed my mouth to his. In the next moment our blanket was thrown off in the heat of our renewed passion. I did not leave his office until daybreak.

We have been apart for only a few hours, but I miss him with every fiber of my being. I pray he will succeed in gaining a personal audience with Mrs. Trescot. I wish I could have accompanied Adam and Henry to Boston, but felt it best to stay at home and keep watch on Noah. As he sits here in my studio, drawing contentedly on his pad, I see no signs of illness after his dip into the icy waters. What a spunky lad he is! And I am feeling quite spunky myself this afternoon. How wonderful it is to be able to love Adam without reserve. I await his return with shameless anticipation.

ADAM'S JOURNAL

Thursday, December 23

When Julia brought Noah into her home three weeks ago, how could she have known what evil accompanied him? Henry and I learned of this lurking malevolence today, when we met the woman who bore the boy.

A maid answered Mrs. Trescot's front door and greeted Henry with a curt curtsy. "I have brought with me a doctor to see Mrs. Trescot," he told her.

Apparently that phrase had the magical power of Open Sesame, for the maid let us in without the least hesitation. "Yet another doctor," I heard her murmur as she led us up the staircase and right to Mrs. Trescot's chamber door. She rapped softly and peered into the room. "There's a new doctor to see you, madam," she said.

"Let us hope he is better than the last one," came a weak and weary reply. "Allow him in."

I entered whilst Henry discreetly waited in the doorway. Mrs. Trescot, reclining on a chaise longue, was draped in shawls and blankets, but I deduced from the appearance of her thin neck and sunken face that she was wasting away. Despite her wizened appearance, I guessed her age to be no more than thirty-five. She looked at me with half-closed eyes, as if in a stupor.

"Are you Dr. Blough's associate, come to bleed me?" she said.

Bleed her! Her emaciated body could not have contained an ounce of blood to spare. "No, Mrs. Trescot. Although I am a doctor, I have not come to treat you." I beckoned Henry into the room.

"The purpose of our visit is to reunite you with your son," he told her gently.

Mrs. Trescot's eyes shot wide open. "Thank God you have found him!"

"It is you we have been looking for, Mrs. Trescot," Henry said.

"You are not the detective my lawyer hired to find my son?"

"I have never met your lawyer, madam," Henry said. "Nor am I a detective."

A tall, broad-beamed nurse marched into the chamber and glared at Henry. "You again!"

"You recognize this man, Miss Dibble?"

"Indeed I do, madam. He came with the young woman who left you that bogus note. But I have not seen this other fellow before."

"He professes to be a doctor," Mrs. Trescot said.

"Ah, so that's how they managed to trick their way into your chamber." The nurse threw back her shoulders. "Leave immediately, the both of you!"

Henry paid her no heed and kept his eyes upon the invalid. "Hear us out or you shall forever regret it, Mrs. Trescot. And so will your son Noah."

"I have no son by that name. That is why the note I received claiming Noah needed a mother made no sense. So I turned it over to my lawyer rather than reply to it myself. My son, you see, was named David."

"Well, he is called Noah now, and he is residing in a town not far from Boston."

"You know not of what you speak. My son resides somewhere in New York City."

"Do not give these charlatans any more information, madam," the nurse cautioned.

"Charlatans! Don't be absurd," I protested.

Henry ignored the insult. "Please listen, Mrs. Trescot," he said most patiently. "The boy we have come to tell you about has a cleft lip."

She blinked a few times. "When was he born?"

"On December 25, twelve years ago come this Christmas."

"As was David," she said softly. "My husband told me he had given our child to a good Christian couple in New York. That is where my lawyer sent the detective."

"How long have you been searching for your son?" I asked.

"Since my husband died in May. When he was alive, he would not allow me to do so." Mrs. Trescot brought trembling hands to her temples. "I am in need of some medicine, Miss Dibble. I am becoming distraught."

"Calomel will only upset you more," I said, quite sure that was what was causing Mrs. Trescot's tremors and the loss of several fingernails.

Miss Dibble glanced my way. "Maybe you really are a doctor."

"Of course I am. And I do not prescribe mercury poison to my patients."

Miss Dibble nodded and heaved a sigh. "Alas, most doctors do, and Mrs. Trescot has come to rely on it so."

She went to a table laden with bottles and poured a dose of

a heavy, yellowish-white liquid into a wineglass, added water from a crystal pitcher, and stirred the mixture vigorously. Mrs. Trescot took the glass from the nurse and could barely drink from it, it shook so in her claw-like hand, but she managed to get down a few swallows.

"That's better," she said and returned her attention to us. "How I want to believe you! But how can I be sure the boy you speak of is *my* son?"

"When you see him you will know," I said. "The cleft in his lip has a most distinctive shape, and surely you remember what he looked like when he was born."

"How could I forget? I stared and stared at him in horror and disbelief. I confess that I could not bear to hold him. Yet as soon as he was taken from me, I longed to have him back. I begged my husband to return him to me, but he refused. He simply could not abide raising a child who looked like that. You see, he married me for my beauty and expected me to give him beautiful children. But we had no other children after David. That was our just punishment for giving him up."

"Your boy's adoptive parents died recently," Henry told her. "They worked at the Howard Theater, as we were told you once did."

"I did not *work* there." She lifted her chin. "I *played* there!" For a moment her eyes blazed as they must have on stage, then just as suddenly they dimmed. "I was so very vain in those days. So very foolish too. Who were these people who took in my child?"

"Edgar and Mary Robinson."

"I *knew* them! Edgar built sets at the Howard. And Mary taught me to sing light opera. She was patient and kind and most competent, despite her blindness. Yes, she would have been a good mother to my son, I think."

"He is a fine boy," I said. "He was raised up well."

"Is he in good health?"

"Yes. As strong and spirited as any boy his age. Intelligent too."

"What joyful news that is!" Tears streamed down Mrs. Trescot's face, and it seemed they magically washed away the ravages of illness. She could not stop talking, so infused was she with newfound energy. "I cannot wait to tell my brother when he returns to Boston! He is my only other living relative, and now he shall be an uncle."

"Did you tell your brother that you were searching for your lost son?" Henry asked her.

"I am sorry to say I did not tell him right off," Mrs. Trescot said, "for my lawyer advised me against it."

"And why would your lawyer give you such advice as that?"

"I suppose because I changed my will after my husband died, making my son, if he were ever found, my primary heir instead of Orlando."

"Perhaps your brother guessed that is what you would do if ever you became a widow," Henry said.

"Indeed he did! And when he asked me outright about it, I could not lie to him. He was most sympathetic and understanding. Why, he even offered to help find David himself! As vain and selfish as Orlando can be at times, he has always been a loving brother, and he knows I shall always take care of him."

"Is your brother, perchance, an actor?" Henry said. "I recently heard the name Orlando mentioned at the Howard Theater."

"Oh, I am sure he is much talked about there for he is one of the Howard's best actors. Orlando can play any part ever written."

Henry nodded. "Both male and female, according to Mrs. Perry."

"Mrs. Perry?" Mrs. Trescot turned her nose up. "Is that blowsy bit player still strutting the boards?"

"She paints the actors' faces now," Henry said. "She is the one who directed us to you."

"Then I am grateful to her. Tell me more about my son."

"You have the rest of your life to get to know him," Henry said. "Let us continue talking about your brother for a while longer, if you don't mind."

"Oh, I never mind talking about Orlando. He has so much charm! But so few scruples. I have found that to be so with most handsome men. And Orlando is very handsome. He is a perfect Adonis."

"Perfect but for his left eye?" Henry said.

"Well, yes. He lost sight in that eye as a boy when he caught the measles from me. I have always felt guilty about it. Perhaps that is why I indulge him so." Mrs. Trescot studied Henry a moment. "How did you know about Orlando's eye if you have never met him?"

"But I have."

"Then why did you not tell me so right off?"

"I was not sure that your brother and the person I met in Plumford were one and the same until now," Henry said and looked at me.

I stared back at him aghast. "Mrs. Swann?"

He nodded. "It all fits."

"Who is Mrs. Swann?" Mrs. Trescot asked.

"Someone who is residing in the same house as your son," Henry replied, maintaining a calm demeanor.

My own face flushed with rage at the realization that Swann was in actuality Mrs. Trescot's brother. All I wanted to do was race back to Plumford and expose the vile fraud. But rather than upset poor Mrs. Trescot, Henry and I took our leave most civilly, promising to bring her son to her very soon.

Nurse Dibble insisted upon showing us out and slowly led us down the stairs. She further detained us in the foyer by blocking the door with her large frame. Her blunt countenance appeared most kindly now that she regarded us with a smile instead of a scowl.

"Pray deliver the boy here as soon as you can manage it," she told us, hands clutched against her starched apron bib. "It will save dear Mrs. Trescot's life. And dear she truly is, as good and generous a soul as you could want, but pining for her son all these many years has made her heartsick."

"The calomel makes her sicker still," I said. "Will you help me wean her off it?"

"I will! And I assure you that her son will have the best of care from me and his mother." She gave my hand a strong, hard shake, and then shook Henry's. "Forgive me for my initial rudeness and distrust, gentlemen, but I feel it my duty to protect Mrs. Trescot. We go back many years, and I have seen her through many troubles and sorrows. Her selfish husband was the cause of most of them, and her worthless brother only made matters worse. All Orlando Revere has ever cared about was getting his greedy hands on the Trescot fortune."

"Revere is Orlando's surname?" Henry asked sharply. The nurse nodded. "Then there is no time to lose! Move aside, my good woman." Out the door he went, me right behind him. It was clear to us both that Swann was a murderer.

We ran all the way to the station only to see the train to Concord pull away from the platform. There was no other course of action but to leap on the tracks and race after it. I jumped down an instant before Henry did, so I ran afore him in the narrow space between the parallel tracks. A conductor stood in the open door of the end car and placidly watched us as we neared the train just as it began to pick up speed. I poured it on and managed to grasp the handrail of the car and twist myself onto the lowest step. Leaned back over the tracks as far as I could with my arm extended. Henry's first try at grasping my hand near ended in disaster as he stumbled and almost plunged down the side of the rail bed. He just managed to regain his balance by wildly wind-milling his arms, but that caused him to lose speed. He made a desperate lunge at me, and our hands forged an iron grip. I hauled him up beside me. We had made it just in time, for in the next few seconds the train attained a speed faster than any man could run.

"Tickets, gentlemen," the phlegmatic conductor intoned behind us.

I paid the man, and we found the last seats in the last car. The stove smoked and gave little heat, but we were mighty hot under the collar already.

"*Revere,* not *revenant,*" Henry said after we had caught our breaths. "That was what Mrs. Lyttle was writing on the wall. The last name of her killer."

"She must have known Orlando Revere from the Howard Theater," I said. "If he is capable of killing a woman so viciously, he is capable of anything."

"Such as killing a child to protect his inheritance," Henry said.

I recognized how true that was. "He has already attempted to do away with Noah at least twice. First fire, then ice."

"Pray we get back to Plumford in time to stop him before he tries again," Henry said.

My heart squeezed tight. "Or harms Julia."

We arrived in Concord, ran to the stable, harnessed Napoleon, and jumped into the gig. I lightly touched the horse's flank with the whip, and he surged away. Napoleon never needs more notice than that to bring out the best in him, and like all good doctors' horses, he senses when there is an emergency. He flew over the hard ground so fast I had to pull him in on a few bends in the road or we might have rolled right over. Never covered the distance between the two towns so fast.

'Twas not fast enough, however, to keep my beloved Julia and that poor boy out of harm's way. I shall never forgive myself for leaving them at the mercy of such a fiend as Revere/ Swann. And now Justice Phyfe and Constable Beers are pounding on the door, no doubt to question me about the fatal stabbing.

JULIA'S NOTEBOOK

Friday, 24 December

Here I am a professional artist, yet it took a child to draw the truth for me. Noah had been sketching so intently yesterday afternoon that I held back from instructing him, not wanting to interfere with the creative spirit that seemed to have seized him. Occasionally I would look up from my own work to observe the back of his spindly neck and little round head bent over his drawing pad, and so tender a picture this appeared to me that I began sketching Noah sketching.

At last he brought me his drawing, and I sensed that my reaction would be most important to him. Apprehension was evident in his expressive eyes, and I smiled to assuage his concern.

"I am sure I will like it," I told him before looking at his work.

I had not expected what I saw. Most of Noah's drawings have been of ordinary household objects or depictions of horses and dogs, and the only person he has ever attempted to portray is me. But this was a drawing of a naked man, unpolished in execution, yet painstaking in detail—the most obvious detail being a male organ. The man's face was too inexpertly drawn to attribute to a specific person, but again there was a telling detail—a cigar stuck in the mouth. Behind the figure were drawn, not in proper perspective but still recognizable, a hip bath and a highboy with a distinctive bonnet top.

Noah, most likely, had seen naked men on occasion, but I ventured to ask him if his drawing was of a real or an imaginary man.

"It is Mrs. Swann," he said softly but emphatically, looking at me with a worried frown.

I could not help but smile at his mistake. "Do you mean Mr. Shrove?"

He shook his head impatiently. "Mrs. Swann."

I had heard Mrs. Swann ready a bath this morning, employing Noah to aid her in bringing up the cans of hot water, and I thought perhaps this occurrence had become confused in his mind with another bath taken by another person of another sex. Surely the excessively modest Mrs. Swann would not have exhibited herself naked to the boy. I had never seen her otherwise but fully clothed.

"Now, Noah," I said, "how could you possibly have seen Mrs. Swann bathing?"

"The keyhole," he said.

His blush indicated he knew this intrusion into another's privacy was wrong, yet he had made a drawing proving his own guilt. For this reason I began to believe that he had drawn exactly what he had seen through that keyhole. The bonnet-top highboy, with eleven drawers carefully delineated, was certainly true to the one in Mrs. Swann's bedchamber. Was Mrs. Swann true to life too?

"You have drawn Mrs. Swann as a *man,* Noah. Do you know the difference between a man and a woman?"

Indeed he did, for with the tip of his pencil he pointed at the figure's male member. I sat back, stunned, and regarded Noah. It was obvious that he knew something was deeply wrong and wanted me to know too.

Had I not already felt that something was amiss with the way Mrs. Swann comported herself? I recollected all her touching and caressing and staring at me and the Phyfe sisters, and all her bawdy talk in a low, insinuating tone. But would a man go through all that trouble to pass himself off as a woman just to take such liberties with us? Was he a perverted peeper? A potential rapist? Or simply a male who enjoyed dressing up as a female? I had seen men such as that strutting the streets of Montmartre. But why would a man with such tendencies wish to reside in Plumford of all places, where his penchant would hardly be tolerated?

"Shall I make us some tea, my dears?" a cheery female voice asked, and I looked toward the doorway to see Mrs. Swann standing there.

My first reaction was to turn Noah's drawing facedown upon the desk. My second was to gape at Mrs. Swann most intently. She looked as she always did—a woman who was doing her utmost to make herself appear more attractive. The simplest explanation of Noah's drawing was that he had made a childish mistake. Yet how could he have made such a mistake as *that?* I had to find out for certain.

"May I beg a favor of you, Mrs. Swann?" I said. "I have just discovered that I've run out of linseed oil, and I need it to mix my paints. Would you mind going to Daggett's store right now, before it closes, and getting me some?"

"Why, I do not mind at all," she replied kindly. "A brisk walk in the cold evening air will do me good, I am sure. And whilst there I shall pick up a supply of whale oil, for we are running low."

The moment I heard the front door close I left Noah in the studio, ran up the stairs to Swann's chamber, and knelt down before her massive leather trunk. 'Twas padlocked, as I'd fully expected it to be, but I had disengaged locks before with the most common of womanly devices. I pulled two hairpins out of my chignon and slipped one in the bottom of the keyway for tension, whilst using the other to push up the tumblers. In a thrice the lock fell open.

I lifted the trunk lid and searched inside. I found several blond wigs and fake curls of the same brash shade attached to bonnets and caps, along with jars and bottles of face paint. That Swann wore false hair and painted her face came as no surprise to me, and I'd even suspected that she amplified her bosom with India rubber or some such padding. Many women use such artifices to make themselves more alluring. But how many women shave their faces with an eight-inch straight razor? I stared at the blade a moment, feeling an inexplicable revulsion, and then folded it back into its ivory handle. At the bottom of the trunk I found even more proof that Swann was indeed a man—a pair of trousers, a frock coat, a black cape, a compressed top hat, and a white linen shirt with blood on one sleeve.

"How now, Julia? What a naughty girl you are," a man's voice said.

I looked up and saw Swann, and it was as though blinders had been removed from my eyes. Although still dressed as a woman, he had lowered his mask of deception and was clearly a man. He held Noah to him, a pistol pointed at the boy's head.

"Scream and I will shoot him."

"I will not scream," I assured Swann in a quivering voice. I put the bloodstained shirt back in the trunk and at the same time slipped the razor up my sleeve.

"Put the razor back, my dear, or I will use it on you as I used it on poor little Kitty. I do not care to get myself all bloody again, for I must be leaving soon. And if you give me no trouble, I will trouble you no more."

Hearing him so callously admit to killing my friend filled me with fury, and my first impulse was to leap up and attack him with the razor. I did not stand a chance of getting to him from my kneeling position, however, before he pulled the trigger and killed Noah. And I wanted to believe, with every atom of hope within me, that if I did what he said, he would go away and trouble us no more. I returned the razor to the trunk.

"May I get up?" I asked him.

"I rather like you on your knees," he replied in a suggestive tone, "but yes, do rise to the occasion, Julia, for the show must go on. And we are in the last act."

I stood and my legs almost buckled, my horror of him was so great. How macabre he looked to me now in his paint and his wig. "What do you want of us?" I asked him.

"At the moment I want nothing of you but your obedience, Julia dear."

"Why did you come to Plumford?"

"Blame it on the boy." Swann smiled down at him. "Such a handsome fellow, isn't he?" He tapped the pistol against Noah's temple.

"Let him go, Swann," I said. "He has caused you no harm."

"His very existence causes me harm! I should have killed him when his father handed him over to me the day he was born. Instead, I put him in the care of a couple who actually wanted the little beast. So he has me to thank for a good twelve years of life. But he can have no more than that if I am to have a good life myself."

"You will *never* have a good life," I told him, "if you murder this child."

"I will if I don't get caught at it. The trick is to make it look like an accident. And I would have already succeeded but for that meddlesome doctor you are so fond of, Julia dear. My first plan was to dose the brat with laudanum and leave him to die in the burning barn, but damn it if Dr. Walker didn't come along just in time to save him. I then tried to get that lunatic Solomon Wiley to do the killing for me by convincing him the boy was an evil entity. But once again Dr. Walker came along in time to save his life. My third attempt was my most bold and daring one. I tricked the little imbecile into skating onto thin ice, and he would have drowned for sure if you hadn't gone in after him." Swann shook a finger at me. "That was very foolhardy, Julia dear. You might have drowned along with the boy if not for Dr. Walker. I should have done away with him, but he would have been far more difficult to kill than a helpless little kitten like Kitty."

"Why did you murder that dear young woman?" I sobbed.

Swann sighed dramatically. "Alas, I had no choice. I feared the silly twit would have eventually recognized me from the theater. Fortunately she had not yet done so when I rapped on her back door and announced myself as Mrs. Swann come a-calling. Much to Kitty's surprise she opened her door to a vampyre instead. That was my disguise in case her neighbors spied me. I am such a versatile actor!"

Realizing that Noah's life and mine depended on my own ability to act, I stifled my tears and pretended acquiescence. "I will help you in any way I can to get away from here, Swann," I said. "Just tell me what to do."

"How kind of you, Julia. You may start by walking slowly down the stairs and into the kitchen. The boy and I shall follow, and you may be sure my Derringer will still be at his head."

How I wished his razor were still up my sleeve! It had become clear to me, through my fog of fear, that Swann could not allow us to live after confessing so much. Yet every moment I could forestall our deaths seemed utterly precious.

We entered the kitchen and all stood together for a moment. I saw Swann was puzzling through how best to deal with the two of us at one time. His solution was to suddenly punch me in the jaw.

I next awoke lying face downward on the floor, tightly

bound hand and foot with clothesline cord, my mouth stuffed with rags. I tried to rise, but could not. Swann had passed one of my arms round a leg of the kitchen stove before he had tied my wrists. Noah lay beside me, similarly bound and gagged. That he was still alive gave me hope we might survive our ordeal. Hope truly does spring eternal. It is all we humans have in the end.

"My Juliet awakens," Swann said, looking down at me. He was *smiling*. "I would have much preferred to put you to sleep more gently. Indeed, I had always planned to drug you with laudanum, as I have been drugging the boy all these weeks, and have my way with you. I regret there is no time for that now, but I assure you, my dear, that the drawing Noah made of me does not do my manliness justice by half." He began pouring the contents of all our whale oil lamps around the kitchen, concentrating most of it on the wood in the bin and then drenching our clothes. "I never did go to the store for more oil," he said. "Now I rather wish that I had. But this should suffice."

Realizing he intended for us to burn alive, I tried begging for mercy as best I could through the gag, in an anguished moaning.

Swann raised his brows and pulled down the corners of his mouth in a performance of sham regret. "Yes, it will be a miserable death, and I am most sorry for you, Julia. But you got yourself into this fine mess. If you had not bid on this little monster at the vendue auction, I would have done so myself and taken him away. Neither Mrs. Swann nor Noah Robinson would have been seen again, and Orlando Revere would remain his sister's only heir. Regrettably, now you must die with Noah. The whole town knows what a fire starter he is. Mrs. Swann made sure of that. You will be burned to a crisp, along with any evidence of your bindings. All that shall remain of lovely Julia is her charred bones. So sad!"

He bent down and placed a kiss on my forehead. And then

he struck a match with a steady hand, threw it on an oil-soaked towel in the wood bin, and headed for the back door. He turned back. I thought for a blessed moment he'd had a change of heart. But no, he was heartless still. He only came back to get the pistol he had left on the table. He tucked it into the amply stuffed bodice of his dress.

"Good Night, Good Night! Parting is such sweet sorrow," he declaimed in his best theatrical manner, giving us a bow before he exited.

The dark room filled with smoke as the flames from the wood bin rose and cast flickering shadows on the walls. My eyes smarted from the acrid smoke, and I gagged from the stink of so much spilt oil. I twisted and yanked my wrists and ankles to try and loosen my bonds, but I could not break free. I did, however, manage to get to my knees, and I tried to push over the stove with the weight of my upper body. Noah followed my example, but even together we could not budge the iron beast. I looked at the boy and saw such fear in his eyes that my heart went out to him. I too was afraid, of course, but at least I had lived on this good earth double the time span he had. How grateful I was that I had allowed myself to experience love and passion. My last thoughts, I promised myself, would be of Adam, even as the flames consumed me.

Keeping my eyes locked on Noah's, I attempted to silently communicate to him my belief that we could not truly die and would continue on in some form or other. The terror in his eyes did not diminish, however. So I began humming a lullaby, hoping that would assuage it. My tune came out a hoarse croak, barely audible through the rags stuffed in my mouth, yet Noah's expression changed immediately. The fear in his wide eyes was replaced by joy, as if he were staring at an angel coming toward us through the black smoke.

Perhaps he was. But I do not think Henry David Thoreau

would care to hear himself described as an angel. He certainly did seem heaven sent, however, as did Adam a moment later. They together tipped over the stove to free my arm and dragged Noah and me out the back door to the porch, our clothes smoking. Henry went back to smother the fire whilst Adam cut through our bonds with his pocketknife.

Once free of my gag, I tried to talk, but had a coughing fit instead. 'Twas Noah who spit out the name Swann.

"Where is he?" Adam said, making clear he knew Swann's secret.

"He left us but moments ago," I sputtered. "Garbed as a woman."

We heard an alarmed neigh from Napoleon, and Adam raced to the front of the house, where he had left his gig by the gate. I ran after him, my speed hampered by smoke-filled lungs, and as I rounded the corner of the house I saw Swann pull away in the gig and Adam sprint down the road in pursuit of him. He caught up to the gig and grasped the back of it. Swann turned around and lashed at Adam with the whip, but Adam would not let go even though he was being beaten and dragged.

His weight made Napoleon slow his pace, and Swann faced front again to whip the horse instead, repeatedly slashing his flanks. Not used to such treatment, Napoleon whinnied in pain and looked back to see a stranger in Adam's seat. He skidded to a halt in protest, rose up on his front legs, and kicked back with his rear hooves into the dash of the gig. The blow knocked the carriage right off its frame, and Swann jumped out, landing on his feet. He lifted his skirts and shot off across the Green.

Adam picked himself up, charged after Swann, and grabbed his shoulder. Swann whirled and kneed Adam most viciously in the groin. My poor dear buckled over in what must have been blinding pain, but continued to stagger after Swann as best he could. Which was not near fast enough. I caught up to Adam as Swann got farther away.

But this chase was not yet over for Henry now continued the pursuit. He ran past us in an amazing burst of speed and tackled Swann, wresting him to the ground and then throwing himself upon him. My heart rejoiced! The fiend was captured!

But then, most unexpectedly, Swann started screeching for help in a falsetto voice. People came out of the houses surrounding the Green to see what the matter was, and several men, including Mr. Daggett and Mr. Lyttle, ran toward us with lamps. They hauled Henry off Swann, shouting severe rebukes at him for treating a female so roughly, which drowned out his own words of explanation. Mr. Lyttle helped Swann up from the ground and offered a handkerchief from his tailor's apron.

Adam and I witnessed all this as we staggered toward the group, hollering to them that Swann was a man. In all the confusion no one paid us any mind until we got close enough for Adam to lurch toward Swann and rip off his wig. What followed was a moment of stunned silence as lamps were lifted to illuminate Swann's face, now set in a savage grimace.

"He tried to kill Noah and me!" I screamed, pointing my finger at Swann. "And he admitted to killing Kitty Lyttle!"

"You killed my wife?" Mr. Lyttle asked Swann in a stunned voice.

In one swift motion, Swann grabbed hold of the tailor, pulled out his pistol, and brought it to Lyttle's temple. "I will shoot this man as easily as I slit his wife's throat if I do not have a horse within two minutes," he demanded.

The first to react was Lyttle, and he did so with lightning speed. Roaring with rage, he drew the scissors from his apron and twisted around to bury them deep into Swann's throat as the pistol discharged in the air.

Clutching his throat, Swann fell to the ground. He had a look of utter astonishment upon his painted face. "Has the curtain come down for me?" he choked out as blood spewed from his mouth.

Indeed it had. He was dead a moment later.

"Clearly an act of self-defense on Mr. Lyttle's part," Coroner Daggett declared.

I walked back to the house with Adam and Henry, and we told Noah that he was now safe.

ADAM'S JOURNAL

Saturday, December 25

As I stood looking out at the Green this afternoon, blanketed in white and glowing with sunlight, I sent up a prayer of thanks with each breath that floated up into the icy atmosphere. All the myriad troubles we so suffered have been swept away in a gale of revelations and rescues that have left us peaceful and safe at last. And the Consumption epidemic that has so plagued our community seems to be abating.

Napoleon neighed at my back and gave me a shove with his nose. So much for contemplation. Time to be off! No wonder he was eager. I'd given him a Christmas feast this morn—an extra ladle of oats and sunflower seeds and an added, high forkful of timothy grass as well. Lord knows he deserved it. And I'd combed out his mane and long tail and brushed him till his coat shone bright. And he did so enjoy pulling a sleigh. He stamped with impatience to be off trotting through the drifts.

Called out that the Christmas express to Boston was ready to depart. Out the door pounced Noah with a shout, Julia right behind him, and we three climbed onto the red-cushioned seat of the sleigh, Julia thigh to thigh with me. I pulled the thick buffalo robe across our legs, and off we went! As we sped past the Green and over the bridge we seemed to be sliding along on a surface of cloud and cotton, the only sounds the hissing of the runners, the jingling of the sleigh bells, and the soft thud of hooves. Hill and dale all glinted and glistened pure white in the sun. Pointed to a dozen pine grosbeaks with their russet caps and breasts feeding on crimson dogwood berries. Noah spotted a fox that sat atop a snowdrift watching the world go by. Julia waved to a whirling flock of snow buntings. All the world seemed intent on entertaining us.

Napoleon in his turn expressed joy in every shake of his proud head and every stride as his hooves sliced deliciously into the packed snow. He snorted in the air that was so clear that each inhale to man and beast alike was like an energizing medicine.

Yesterday's blizzard had deeply stacked the snow against the windward side of farmhouses right up over porches and near up to the roofs. Shovels could just be seen above the drifts as farmers and their sons heaped the snow yet higher to get from house to barn. Everyone gave us a wave and a cheer when they heard our jingling bells.

On every high hill we saw children flying down the slope on sleds with wide runners of supple softwood that held the sleds atop the snow far better than the newfangled runners of iron. Adventurous and foolish boys on one precipitous slope careened downhill and flashed across the road ahead of us at breakneck speed to slam into a snowdrift and roll out all coated and caked in snow, sputtering with laughter. We laughed too.

We had the company of sleighs of every size and description on the road all the way to town. Despite Napoleon's proud heart and sturdy physique, he had to pull three of us in a heavy old sleigh, and so we were on occasion passed by young sparks and their girls in light-as-a-feather, new speeder sleighs, all lacquered and gold-gilded, pulled by purebred racing trotters.

Did not believe any man luckier than myself as I sat under that buffalo robe with Julia beside me. What a gem, what a treasure, what a strong, fine, sensible, imaginative, serious, happy, gay, thoughtful, passionate, bold, and wildly, touchingly, beautiful woman she is. A few flakes of wind-swirled snow had caught in her hair and on her long eyelashes, and when a few bold crystals dared to descend onto her full lips I could not resist and turned to kiss them away, tasting her and the sparkle together. That brought an extra flush to her rose-tinted cheeks, and her eyes flashed love.

On an even, flat stretch of road I handed the reins over to Noah. The boy swelled with happiness and pride as Napoleon, who sensed the lightest change in touch from the reins, glanced back and then surged ahead, I swear just to please the new young driver.

We glided past fields, pastures, woodlots, and farm after farm, most clad in chestnut shingles naturally weathered as of old, but more and more now painted white or yellow, the shutters black and the barns red. We saw mills springing up along the larger streams and shanties where the Irish immigrants are housed to work the new looms, presses, and forges.

We stopped at a farm by the road to water our horse, and the owner spoke around his clay pipe of current affairs, kept abreast of the world beyond his hundred acres by reading the new abolitionist newspaper published by Frederick Douglass. As we regained the sleigh I wondered aloud that soon there would be no quiet village left to its own peace in our entire country.

When we neared the city we decided to proceed to Beacon Hill by way of the Mill Dam, which is but a long extension of Beacon Street across the Back Bay all the way out to Brookline. There is talk of filling in all of the Back Bay to make land for building. Some call it a harebrained scheme, but I think it a grand idea. If Boston does not grow and progress it will surely become just a backwater for Brahmins and bankers.

Farther up Beacon Street we glided, alongside the Commons, where families were making fanciful snowmen and skaters swooped and swirled on the frozen Frog Pond. A group of rascally boys, standing beside the street as we passed, suddenly attacked us with a blizzard of snowballs that burst against the sides of the sleigh. I blocked one snowball with my hand, and the impact sent a shower of snow into all our faces and we laughed in surprise. I urged Napoleon on to pull us clear of the assault, which he did in a burst of speed.

Turned off Beacon and climbed slowly to the top of Vernon and the Trescots' high, brick townhouse. A servant appeared to lead Napoleon to the stable behind and assured me he would be unharnessed, wiped down properly, given a stall away from any drafts, and fed—but not too much grain, I insisted, as we would be going back home today. The same maid greeted us at the door, but this time with much cordiality, and escorted us right upstairs.

Miss Dibble threw open Mrs. Trescot's chamber door and beckoned us within. The sight of Mrs. Trescot gladdened my heart. She sat in the same posture on the chaise longue, but in just two days at least ten years had melted from her face. She was trembling far less, and her gaze had sharpened, and I did not see a bottle of calomel on the table. Her eyes were bright with anticipation.

Without ceremony, Julia stepped forward with Noah and introduced mother to son. These first seconds, I knew, meant everything. The boy walked to the chaise longue and looked at her with an open curiosity while she stared at him, studying his every feature, which of course included his deformity. When their eyes met I knew all was well. Mrs. Trescot slowly stood to embrace and kiss Noah.

"My son," she said, her voice breaking, "let me love you now. I promise to never let you go again."

He looked at her and nodded and buried his face against her shoulder, and I could see every muscle in his being relax as they held each other.

Well, that is all of true importance there is to record, although Julia and I remained for several hours, all of us happy and relieved. I detected a touch of sadness in Julia's joy for the boy, as she has grown most fond of him and had been ready, if necessary, to take him into her life for good.

There was much to discuss and explain and wonder over. We first spoke of Noah. Mrs. Trescot wanted the boy to stay from this moment forth in her home and grow to be a man under her care. I told her of my wish to mend his harelip. She was cautious, saying that she would much prefer him as he was to possibly losing him under the knife. That expressed a true, loving concern for the boy as he was, not how he might be. Noah did not hesitate to softly say he wanted the operation, and I noticed as he spoke she again looked at him with the uncritical love of a mother. She knew what she had already missed, and I could see she was determined to make up for those lost years. In the end, she agreed to the operation but not for a few weeks yet as she wanted Noah just as he was for now.

Mrs. Trescot told Noah the house was his now, and off he went exploring as we sadly related the unsuccessful attempts her brother had made on Noah's life. The man who had killed Orlando, we said, would not be charged with the crime for the Coroner's Jury had deemed it self-defense. Mrs. Trescot nodded in silent acceptance of this verdict, and after a moment of silence, she rapidly composed herself.

"My brother always had a titanic self-love, but that is common enough among actors," she said in a sad tone. "I was aware of his faults, but that is all I thought they were, a handsome, talented, self-absorbed man's personal flaws. I was blind to his rapacity, and I must say, his cold-bloodedness."

Noah came back from his first exploration of a house that no doubt far exceeded his wildest dreams of what a home could be. All he said, as he looked at us in wonder, was, "Ten fireplaces!"

"It's actually twelve, my son," Mrs. Trescot gently corrected him.

Noah then whispered something to Julia with a worried look on his face.

"No," Julia said, "I do not think you will be responsible for filling all the fireboxes with wood every morning."

We partook of small, finger-sized sandwiches and assorted sweet delicacies and sipped champagne for the remainder of the visit. Before we departed I insisted on a moment alone with Mrs. Trescot. I asked if I might give her a cursory physical examination to which she agreed, and my findings confirmed my suspicions. "I see no evidence of any bodily ailment in you whatsoever," I said. "If you will completely forego any further ingestion of calomel, I believe you will soon be well. Your symptoms have been brought on by your guilt and anxiety over losing your son and made immeasurably worse by this poison many of my counterparts in my profession call medicine."

She softly laughed in relief. "I have been bled and had disgusting leeches applied to my flesh as well. I believe your diagnosis may well be correct, but I will follow your advice only if you promise to visit me as your patient and bring Julia with you. I like her very much, and I do not want Noah to ever forget her kindness."

We shook hands to seal the agreement.

Mother and son, trusty nurse right behind them, stood out on the steps of their home and waved a fond farewell as we started away down the hill. Napoleon seemed to have enjoyed his city sojourn but was, as ever, eager to prance his way back to Plumford.

The ride home was a gliding heaven. Julia and I sat pressed together, ecstatic to be close for a few blissful hours under a sky so clear and dark the Milky Way seemed to ripple above us and every star winked at our love.

ADAM'S JOURNAL

Saturday, January 1, 1848

Henry and Lidian and her three children came by to wish us Happy New Year this afternoon. Such a pleasant family. And they do truly seem a family, with Henry acting as both papa and brother to the children whilst Mr. Emerson continues to tour Europe. Lidian looks exceptionally well, I am happy to report, for the last time I saw her I detected a mild case of jaundice. Today her complexion was peaches and cream. All three children are handsome and healthy and well behaved, but they soon grew restless nevertheless. They are very young and energetic, after all, the eldest only eight. Henry suggested we take them for a ride and leave the ladies to their talk of Art and their milk punch and biscuits. This seemed to suit Julia and Lidian as well as the children.

Off we rode in Henry's borrowed carryall. A three-day thaw had melted away most of the snow, the air was sharp and still, and the sun, low in a crystal clear sky, warmed our backs. Henry deemed it a glorious winter day because its elements were so simple. The children, sitting in the back of the wagon, sang "Auld Lang Syne" or rather their own version of it, laden with malapropisms, which delighted Henry no matter how many times they repeated it. Can't say I found it quite so amusing as he did, but I was in a fine mood nonetheless. Indeed, my heart was close to bursting with happiness whenever I thought that I would be spending yet another night with Julia. And another and another. For eternity, I hope.

Rather than ride around aimlessly, which is neither my way nor Henry's, we settled on going to the Indian burial ground to see if the bones and artifacts we had reinterred had not been disturbed. There has been no sign of Dr. Lamb or Solomon Wiley for two weeks, since my swamp nightmare, real or imagined.

At first sight all appeared to be well at the burial ground. The knoll was again a peaceful place. Until we let the children out of the carryall, that was, for Henry encouraged them to run and shout as much as they pleased. Meanwhile, he and I walked through the snow-matted brown grass, observing the humble stone markers on the ancient graves.

We went up to the enormous boulder that loomed over the grave in which Wiley had found the skull and ax. But there was no grave beside the boulder now. Henry studied the ground, then got down on one knee and studied it more closely.

"There looks to be disturbed earth *under* the boulder," he said. "I can just see the edge of it."

He stood and looked from the boulder to a juniper standing close to it, backed up a rod or so and regarded one and then the other again.

"When we were here last I remember there was a good yard's distance between the boulder and that juniper," he said. "And now there is only a foot."

Did not doubt him. His surveyor's eye measures everything and recalls each calculation. Even so, what he was saying seemed unreasonable. "The boulder moved?" I said.

"It does not seem likely that it moved itself. Someone moved it."

I smiled. "That does not seem likely either."

"Even so, it has been moved."

"Well, here is my theory," I said. "The tree moved."

Henry, usually inclined to return a jest for a jest, remained most serious. "Someone moved the boulder over the grave, Adam. How it was done I do not know. But I do know it *was* done. And now whoever or whatever is buried in the grave cannot be disturbed."

"But that is scientifically impossible."

"Science does not embody all that men know, Adam. The Universe is wider than our views of it."

Could not argue with him on that score. Began to walk around the boulder and stopped dead in my tracks. "Henry, come over here."

"What is it?" he asked, looking at my stunned countenance rather than at what I was pointing up at. But then he followed my eyes upward to near the top of the boulder. "The quartz ax! Can it be?"

"It sure looks like it."

"I would like a closer look," Henry said. "Let me stand on your shoulders, Adam." I clasped my palms together for his foothold, and up he went. "It is!" he called down to me. "It has a black blaze running through it!"

"Are you sure?"

He jumped down in front of me and formed a step with his hands. "Go look for yourself."

So up I went to stand on Henry's shoulders. It was the same ax all right, so deeply implanted in the boulder that I could not budge it. "But where's the skull?" I asked when back on the ground.

"In the grave beneath the boulder, I wager," Henry replied. "With Witiku. Or I could say with Dr. Lamb, for he and Witiku are one and the same creature. And when this creature was a mortal Indian centuries ago, he witnessed the ax now embedded in the boulder being smashed into his brother's skull. Methinks that same skull now comforts the vampyre known as Witiku as he lies in his cold sanctuary underground. There is nothing left for him in this world, and he cannot go on to the next one."

"It all seems so absurd, Henry!"

He smiled at me. "Yet so wonderful. Now let us leave all this behind us and spend the first day of the year with the people we most love."

He called to the children, and they came running to him. He picked up young Eddy and swung him up to sit on his shoulders, and we all strolled back to the carryall singing "Auld Lang Syne."